Warlord

BY ELIZABETH VAUGHAN

tor paranormal romance

A TOM DOHERTY ASSOCIATES BOOK
NEW YORK

This is a work of fiction. All of the characters, organizations, and events portrayed in this novel are either products of the author's imagination or are used fictitiously.

WARLORD

Copyright © 2007 by Elizabeth Vaughan

A Tor Book
Published by Tom Doherty Associates, LLC
175 Fifth Avenue
New York, NY 10010

www.tor.com

Tor® is a registered trademark of Tom Doherty Associates, LLC.

ISBN-13: 978-0-765-35266-8
ISBN-10: 0-765-35266-4

First Edition: March 2007

Printed in the United States of America

0 9 8 7 6 5 4 3 2 1

To Jean Rabe,
Writer, Mentor, Friend
who can't find her way back home
from the post office,
but who has never once steered me wrong.

ACKNOWLEDGMENTS

This book was written during a period of unprecedented upheaval in my personal and professional life. Without the aid of family, friends, and colleagues this book would not exist. To list everyone who helped me would be impossible. Please just know that I am grateful beyond what words can say.

I'd be remiss if I did not take the time to thank my writer's group: Spencer Luster, Helen Kourous, Robert Wenzlaff, Marc Tassin, and Keith Flick. They cheerfully read the raw material and helped me winnow the wheat from the chaff. Thank you!

Kurt Lindower was kind enough to sit with me and share his love of hunting. This city girl has only ever hunted the wild grocery, but Kurt answered all of my questions patiently. He also blew away all the stereotypes and showed me his abiding passion and respect for all aspects of the sport. Of course, he still hasn't shared his scrapple with me yet . . .

But for all the help that I've received, and all the research that I've done, any mistakes are my fault, and mine alone. I am perfectly capable of making horrible and embarrassing errors without any assistance.

Kandace Klumper, Patricia Merritt, and JoAnn Thompson were generous with their time and support, offering me constant reassurance. Tom Redding and Mary Fry read the final drafts, catching more mistakes than I care to mention. Phil Fry, Cathie Hansen, and Deb Spychalski are my long suffering coworkers, and I thank them again for their love, support and patience.

Anna Genoese, my editor, made this story stronger and richer with her deft touch. And my deep and abiding thanks go to Heather Brady, my copy editor.

But once again, most of all, credit must go to Jean Rabe, who pushed me into the pool, and to Meg Davis, who found me there.

1

I was terrified.

I shifted my sweaty grip on the handle of my sword, and watched my attacker's eyes. 'Watch their eyes,' they'd told me. 'The eyes will tell you their next move.'

I stared intently at him, but his eyes told me nothing. My left arm was trembling from the weight of my shield. 'Look over the rim,' they'd told me. 'Look over the rim, watch his eyes and react to hi—'

He came at me in an instant, rushing right for me. I managed to take his first blow on my shield and tried to stab at him with my blade, but my helmet shifted into my eyes and—

THWACK.

My arm went numb, and I cried out at the pain. My sword tumbled to the ground.

Rafe stood in front of me, horrified, staring at my arm.

"That's going to bruise," Prest commented dryly.

Rafe groaned, looking up at the skies as if for help.

"The Warlord will gut me where I stand." He glared at me. "Warprize, you were supposed to block the blow!"

"I tried!" I dropped my wooden shield, and rubbed my arm. "I watched your eyes and I kept the shield up, but—"

"Too slow. She doesn't have the speed," Ander offered.

"The shield is too heavy," Yveni added. "She doesn't have the strength she needs."

"Herself doesn't have the sense the elements gave a goose."

We all turned to see Marcus riding up to our group, glaring from under his cloak. "What's all this now?" he barked.

My guards all started talking at once. I sighed, took off my helmet and shook out my braid, letting the breeze reach my damp head. Trying to be a warrior-princess is uncomfortable, sweaty work.

Marcus and my four guards were arguing at the top of their lungs. Marcus, who was covered in his cloak lest the skies be offended by his scars. He'd been injured in a battle years ago, his left ear and eye burned away. Prest, with skin of light brown and long black braids, towered over Marcus. He stood silent, as usual, his arms crossed over his chest.

Rafe, his skin even paler than normal, was gesturing, trying to explain. His hair was dark against his fair skin, and his brown eyes were filled with frustration. He'd been the first in the prisoner tents to welcome my healing skills, and the first to learn my language.

Ander was gesturing as well, talking at the same time. The sun gleamed on his bald head, and his thick, bushy white eyebrows danced over his hazel eyes. Yveni stood as silently as Prest, tall and thin, her skin as black as any I'd seen among the Fire-landers. But she'd a smile hovering on her lips. She and Ander had replaced Epor and Isdra, who had died at Wellspring.

I heaved a sigh and looked off in the distance, back toward Water's Fall. The trees behind us had lost their color, and their leaves were falling fast.

It was hard to believe that it had been two months since I'd left my home to follow my Warlord. In many ways it felt like much more time had passed, what with all that had happened.

We'd left the village of Wellspring ten days ago, leaving behind our dead, both Xyian and Firelander. We'd resumed our trek to the land of the Firelanders, the Plains of Keir's people. Another few days' ride and I would get my first glimpse of that fabled place which lay beyond the border of the Kingdom of Xy. Another few days' ride, and the great valley of Xy would open up onto the wilds of the Plains.

Another few days' ride, and I'd be where I never dreamed of going.

I glanced over to where the army of the Firelanders moved past us, in their long slow march to their homeland. Keir had left half of his force to secure Water's Fall and Xy itself, under the watchful eye of Simus of the Hawk. He'd brought the other half with him, to return to the Plains. It was still an impressive sight as they wound past us, all on horseback, an army of fierce warriors, both men and women.

Or at least, what was left of Keir's army, after the ravages of the plague we'd suffered outside of Wellspring. We'd left our dead, to be certain, but there were still problems, still conflicts at the heart of the army. Conflicts as a result of an illness sweeping through the ranks of a people who see illness as a curse. Conflicts as a result of the presence of a Warprize in their midst and the changes that I represented to them. Conflicts that had been set aside for the rest of this journey, to be dealt with before the Council of Elders when we reached the Heart of the Plains.

We could have reached it sooner, but Keir had held the army to a snail's pace, claiming the need to regain strength in the warriors, to hunt and replenish food supplies.

In truth, we were dawdling.

I didn't object. Keir and I had spent the last ten days together, making love at night and dealing with problems during the day. How could I object to spending time with my beloved Warlord?

The silence behind me made me aware that I was the center of attention. I turned to face an angry Marcus, who had dismounted and was glaring at me with his one good eye. "Apparently this was your idea?"

I glared at my guards, but they all found other things to look at. I faced Marcus. "It was."

"Why?"

"Because I need to learn to protect myself." I looked at Marcus and lifted my chin. "I have to be able to protect Keir." Inside I winced even as I spoke.

"Protect Hisself?" Marcus gave me a steady look. "How so?"

I sighed, prepared for Marcus's scorn. "When we were in camp, when Iften was standing over Keir with his dagger, that scared me, Marcus." I gestured toward the others. "I can't be deadweight. You said yourself that the Plains are hard. I thought I could at least learn how to—" the words came hard. "How to fight."

Marcus considered me long enough that I blushed and looked away. "I know it must seem silly—"

"No, Warprize." Marcus looked off, down the valley, toward the Plains, and sighed. "Death comes in an instant, and you are learning that truth. A harsh truth, but a truth nonetheless." He shook his head. "But you are on the wrong path."

"She wants to learn," Rafe protested. "What's the harm?"

Marcus turned to face Rafe. "Let me show you." Even as the words left his mouth, he'd launched himself at Ander, with no warning or sign, so fast I never really saw him move.

What I did see was Ander ward off Marcus's dagger with his own blade, which he drew with unbelievable speed. It all happened so fast, and then they stood there, Ander at guard and Marcus making no further move.

Marcus stepped back, and bowed his head to Ander, who inclined his head in return. The weapons were sheathed, and Marcus turned back to me. "You see?"

I frowned, puzzled, and answered honestly. "No."

Marcus had a patient look on his face. "Ander had no need to think of the 'how'. He reacted. He knows the blade, knows the movements, knows in the depths of his body and blood. Has known since he cut his first teeth and his thea handed him his first blade."

I blinked. First tooth? But that was—

"You think, Warprize." Marcus continued his lecture. "You think, and then you tell your body and that delay is fatal. Never mind the weight of the shield, never mind that you—"

"You give babies weapons?"

Marcus fixed his eye on me. "What do you mean by 'babies'?"

The language again. Just when I think I know the language of the Firelanders, something new comes up. "Babies. Children that still crawl and soil their—" I bit my lip. "Like Meara, the babe we found in the village."

We'd found her crying, on the bed next to her dead mother. Meara had been the only survivor of the plague that had swept through the village of Wellspring. All of the Firelanders had tried their best to spoil the babe rotten once she'd recovered from her near-death from the illness.

Marcus shook his head. "No. First teeth." He opened his mouth and showed me his teeth. "All their first tooths."

I thought for a minute. He meant the first set of baby teeth—all of them. Which meant they gave weapons to children that were roughly two and a half, maybe three years old.

"Wooden blades, Warprize. The first weapon is wooden." Marcus looked at me closely. "The first true blade is at the first true tooth. You understand?"

I nodded slowly, taking that in. Firelanders wielded steel at roughly six or seven years old.

No wonder they were so fast. It occurred to me that I was very glad I'd sent Meara back to Anna at Water's Fall before we'd begun this march to the Plains.

"So." Marcus's voice called me back. "We will concentrate on what you can do. Not on what you can't."

I sighed, and let my shoulders slump. "But I can't do anything!"

"Pah." Marcus turned, and picked up the wooden sword and small shield that I had been using. "What did you do when that warrior-priest burst into your tent?"

I went and sat close to Prest, flopping down in the grass. "I screamed and ran."

"And?" Marcus asked as he seated himself, keeping his cloak tucked in. Rafe dropped down next to him, and pulled out a dagger and a sharpening stone. Ander and Yveni remained standing, on watch, standing close enough to hear.

"Hid behind Keir." I picked a stem of grass and started playing with it. "Bold warrior that I am."

Marcus snorted. "You, with your terrible memory. You have forgotten."

I looked up to see that Rafe and Prest were both grinning, as if at the memory. "What?"

Rafe answered promptly. "You threw that pot of muck at him. He was covered with it when he came out of the tent."

"Wish I'd seen that." Ander spoke, a smile on his face, his eyes still on the horizon.

"Heyla to that," Yveni added.

Prest chuckled. "The stink clung for days." He reached over and pulled his warclub close, preparing to re-wrap the handle with the leather strips. Of course, it wasn't just any warclub. I looked away from the weapon. It brought back too many painful memories. Of Epor and Isdra.

Of their deaths.

"So." Marcus continued. "What did you do? You alerted others that you were in trouble. You used what was at hand to distract the enemy. You fled to where there was help, and positioned yourself where your defenders could protect you."

I had forgotten. I'd whipped that jar of boiled skunk cabbage right at that warrior-priest's face before I'd fled. I sat up a little straighter. "I guess I did."

Marcus gave me a nod. "Teaching you to fight is enough to make a gurtle laugh. But teaching you to defend yourself, to respond under attack and get yourself to safety, that can be done."

I shook my head in despair. "Marcus, I froze when I found Iften hovering over Keir with that dagger. I didn't have the sense to scream."

"Fear." Prest spoke as he concentrated on his task.

Rafe nodded, even, as he honed the edge of his blade. "Fear holds you still when you need to move, and moves you when you need to be still."

"Fear makes you silent when you need to be loud and loud when you need silence," Ander said, almost reciting. I wasn't surprised; Prest had taunted Iften with a teaching rhyme back at Wellspring. It seemed Firelanders used rhymes a lot for teaching purposes. Which also didn't surprise me, since they had no written language. Everything was memorized, and their ability to do that was amazing.

"Fear closes your throat, makes it hard to breathe. Fear weakens your hand and blinds your eyes." Marcus took up the chant. "Fear is a danger. Know your fear. Face your fear."

I waited a breath, but when it was clear they were done I broke the silence. "But how do I do that?"

Prest turned his head, and smiled at me, his white teeth flashing against his dark skin. "Practice."

I should have kept silent. I'd only asked my guards to teach me to defend myself with a blade and a shield. I'd thought it would be easy; after all, they handled their weapons with grace and skill.

Marcus had other ideas.

We had been waiting to join the army at the very rear of the march. Keir had that little-boy smile on his face when he'd told me that I'd be moving to the rear of his forces. I was fairly sure that he wanted to make sure that he gave me my first glimpse of the Plains.

Marcus now demanded that we use the time to teach me what skills he thought I could really use. Easier said than done.

We spent the rest of the afternoon, as the army passed by, practicing. Each of my bodyguards would play the attacker, and then I had to work with the others to protect myself. Marcus stood back and watched while I got hot and sweaty.

Just when it looked like I knew how to handle the situation, Marcus called out for Prest to die, and Prest obligingly fell 'dead' at my feet.

So now I had to learn to move with my protectors, trying to stay out of their way, and be constantly aware of the threat I was under. Marcus was a strong believer in action as opposed to talking. When I got too tired, we'd stop and talk for a bit, get a drink of water, so that I could catch my breath.

The others never even broke a sweat.

Finally, as the sun was setting, Marcus 'killed' all my body guards, and I was facing my 'attacker' alone. Prest grinned at me as he lay dead at my feet. I looked over at Marcus, who stood there with two daggers, threatening me. "Now what?"

He tilted his head under that cloak, and glared at me. "What can you do?"

"I don't know!" Frustrated, I glared back at him.

Ander had managed to 'die' face down, and looked like he was taking a nap. "Look for a weakness," he whispered to me.

Weakness? Marcus had already proved he was deadly with those daggers, so what weakness did he have?

Marcus rolled his one eye at me.

Oh.

I darted over to his left, trying to get into his blind spot. But Marcus just pivoted to face me, keeping me in sight. I stopped, frustrated. "What good does that do?"

"Keeps him moving, keeps him from throwing his daggers," Yveni responded. She was laying on the ground, chewing a piece of grass, watching the perimeter. Rafe was seated a distance away, watching in the other direction.

"You could try rushing him, getting him to move away from you. Use our bodies to try to trip him up," Ander offered.

"Throw things," Prest added. I looked at my satchel on my hip, and nodded.

"You must take advantage of any weakness." Marcus

gestured at his face. "Mine is my blind side, Warprize. If you can blind a person with one of your mixtures, do it. It may be all that stands between you and death. Yes?"

"I will, Marcus."

"More important, if all your guards are down, where else can you look for help?" Marcus growled.

I eyed him nervously. I still remembered the 'lesson' he'd given me before, when he'd overborne me to the ground, and held a dagger to my throat. "The army?"

Marcus snorted.

Rafe caught my eye and jerked his thumb in the direction of our horses.

"The horses?" I looked to where our mounts were standing, waiting patiently. They were grazing, except of course for my Greatheart. I'd named my horse, which was not a tradition of the Plains. I had to smile, since Greatheart was fast asleep, his one hip cocked to the side, his head hanging down. As usual.

"The horses." Marcus drew my attention as he sheathed his daggers within the darkness of his cloak. The others stood, brushing themselves off. "Get to a horse, leap to its back, and it will take you out of danger."

"If she could ride," Prest said calmly.

I glared at him, but they were all smiling. It was an old joke now, but in their eyes it was true. I wasn't born in a saddle, like the people of the Plains, and to them my riding skills were horrible. But I could ride. Leaping into a saddle, however . . .

"But that lesson can wait," Marcus announced. "Hisself will be making camp soon, and the meal will not make itself." He headed toward the horses.

Thankful for the reprieve, I followed with my guards.

Since we'd resumed our march to the Plains, Keir had made some changes to my sleeping arrangements. My tent was a bit bigger now, enough that I could stand upright in it. He'd arranged extra padding for my bedding. It was saddle blankets folded and piled high, which made a very comfortable mattress. They were made from some kind of wool that I didn't recognize, but knew from its use in camp. But the biggest change, and the best change, was that I slept within his arms every night.

When we'd left Water's Fall, Keir had continued his practice of moving up and down the length of his army, in sight of his warriors and dealing with their morale. He'd left me in the center, where he'd thought I'd be better protected. But that had meant many nights of separation.

But now, with the events of Wellspring behind us, I traveled with him. Neither one of us wanted to be apart for any length of time. He continued to work with his warriors, of course, disappearing during the day to deal with any problems that arose. But every night he returned to our bed. To my arms. To me.

This night would be no different.

Marcus bustled about, keeping an eye on the warriors that set up our tent, and cooking over an open fire at the same time. I sat close to his fire, watching as he worked. Rafe and Prest had gone off to see to their own camps but Ander and Yveni remained, keeping watch over me. Once Keir arrived, they'd leave as well. Although Keir circled our tent with guards, Ander and Yveni stayed well back now, giving me an illusion of a bit of privacy.

Firelanders had a very different attitude toward privacy than my people. For Firelanders bathing together and strolling nude was the custom, with no regard for modesty, even between men and women. As Joden had pointed out to me, there was little privacy to be found in the tents of the Firelanders.

I sighed. Joden was something else I didn't want to think about.

In the overnight camps, no one wasted time cutting down trees for seats. Instead, we used the saddle blankets as pads. Dirt and moisture seemed to fall right off the odd wool. Seated by the fire, with a cloak over my shoulders, I was comfortably warm. Winter had moved into the mountains, and while we were moving down onto the Plains, frost still nipped at our heels. The sky was clear, it would be cold tonight.

Marcus was cutting meat and brewing kavage, and would tolerate no help from me. I was too tired to do much more than sit. So I pulled my satchel close and opened the flap. I'd been using it since—

Since Gils died.

My hands stilled on the scarred leather. Gils was the young Firelander who'd asked to be my apprentice, breaking the traditions of his people. The image of his freckled face and red curls flashed before me. He'd been so young, so eager, with dancing green eyes and that cheeky grin.

I closed my eyes, and fought my tears. *Goddess, hold him close.*

And hold the souls of Epor and Isdra. The warriors who'd entered the village with me, and were the first to face the plague. Well, Epor had. Isdra had joined her bonded on the night of the mourning ceremony. Their faces, too, flashed before me. Along with the hundreds that had died of a sickness that I couldn't prevent or cure.

If only . . .

"Here," Marcus's gruff voice interrupted my thoughts. A cup of kavage was held under my nose. "Drink. Stop thinking on the dead."

I took the cup, the dark and bitter brew steaming in the cool air. "Marcus—" I sighed, cradling the warm mug in my hands. "How did you know?"

"Who does not brood over loved ones?" Marcus's voice was gruff. "Those of our hearts, that we will not see again until the Longest Night?" Marcus's voice softened and I looked up at him through my tears. "We have mourned the dead, Lara. For now, it is enough."

"But, I miss them," I answered, wiping my eyes with my free hand. "And I regret—"

"Their spirits ride with us until the snows," Marcus responded. "Unseen and unknown, unless they wish it so. Yet knowing and seeing, in their own way. Send your thoughts to them, yes. But not always the sorrow. Remember the joy as well. Like when the young'un read Simus's letter to you. Yes?"

I smiled at the memory. "Yes."

Marcus grunted in satisfaction, then returned to his work. I blew on the surface of the kavage and took a sip. The heat spread through my body, and I continued to sip, remembering Gils's eagerness, and the time I caught Epor and Isdra kissing by the well.

But there was still an ache in my heart.

Still, not everyone had died. We'd saved so many, including Meara. The baby had finally fallen ill, so quickly we'd barely noticed until she'd been at the brink of death. But we'd saved her, by the grace of the Goddess. I smiled as I remembered her angry cry when we'd revived her in the cold water of the lake. She'd been so furious, her face scrunched up tight, her eyelashes thick and dark with tears. But her cries had been like music. We'd come so close to losing her.

As we'd lost Gils.

I looked down at the leather satchel at my side. It had been Gils's. He'd made it from an old saddlebag, adding a thick strap and lots of pockets for 'useful things'. I'd used it since he'd died, but hadn't really cleaned it out. Just kept stuffing things in and rummaging around without really thinking about the contents. I pulled it closer, intending to empty it out and repack it.

"Heyla!"

Keir was coming at a gallop. The sight brought a smile to my face, for he was quite a figure, dressed in his black leathers, on his big black warhorse, framed by the setting sun. I threw back the cloak and ran to greet him.

He pulled his horse to a stop and dismounted with one swift move. His black cloak swirled out around him as he caught me in his arms, and hugged me tight, claiming my lips in a kiss. He smelled of horse and leather and himself, and I returned the kiss with passion.

He broke off with a laugh, and swung me up into his arms, striding toward our tent. I wrapped my arms around his neck, and nuzzled his ear, certain of his intent and in complete agreement.

"And what of the food?" Marcus demanded, as Keir marched past the fire to our tent.

Keir spun on his heel, and faced him. "Marcus! Want to know the best part of being a Warlord?"

Marcus's eyebrow rose.

Keir's mouth curled up slowly into a smile. "Getting what I want."

I laughed as Keir turned back toward the tent.

A growl came from behind him. "The Warlord's dinner will be dumped in the dirt if Hisself does not eat it now."

Keir paused in mid-step. From his expression, he was torn with rare indecision.

"The meal is ready now," Marcus continued. "It will be eaten now."

Keir looked at me with such a sorrowful expression in his bright blue eyes. Just then his stomach rumbled, and I laughed right out loud.

* * *

We ate as the sky above us turned a vivid dark blue and deepened to black. The stars hung bright in the night sky, with the moon glowing through the trees. Marcus finished refilling our mugs with kavage, and was cleaning the remains of our meal away when he asked his question. "How goes it with the warriors?"

I was seated next to Keir, leaning against his shoulder, a cloak over both of us. But I leaned away enough to see his face as he replied.

Keir sighed. "Not as well as I could wish. Iften talks, and the warriors look at empty pack animals and empty saddle bags, and wonder if they have done the right thing in following me." He reached over to stroke my hair. "I tell my truths, but words weigh little."

I leaned over and brushed his lips with mine. There wasn't much that I could say to that. Keir's conquest of Xy was a break in tradition for the Firelanders. Their normal practice was to raid and plunder what they could, to return to the Plains laden with spoils. But Keir wanted to change their ways, to conquer and hold, for the benefit of both peoples.

"Fools," Marcus grumbled. "They can't see past the heads of their horses."

"But Keir, that's not quite true. They've pots of fever's foe, and that bloodmoss that we gathered." I yawned. "They know more than they did before about fevers." Goddess knew that was true. We'd pots and pots of fever's foe left from treating the plague, and everyone had aided in the treatment of the sick. I'd spread the extra out, making sure that everyone had some, and was watching for signs of the plague's return. If the Sweat reappeared in our ranks, I wanted to know. Every warrior had agreed to carry some, and keep watch, even those who rejected my healing.

Except Iften.

Keir gave me a thoughtful look. "That's a truth I had not considered, Lara."

I smiled at him, and then yawned again, so hard my eyes watered. My stomach was full, and I was warm and growing sleepy.

Keir leaned in, taking the cup of kavage from my hand. "You are tired tonight, beloved." He moved closer, and put his arm around me. The warmth felt good, and I leaned in, putting my head on his shoulder, and let my eyes drift closed.

"She asked for lessons," Marcus answered softly. "She wants to be able to protect you."

"Protect me?"

I nodded, even as I felt sleep overtake me. Their voices continued, as the fire crackled. Then we were moving, and I found myself under the blankets with Keir at my side. I roused just enough to murmur a question in his ear.

He chuckled softly. "Warlords also learn to wait for what they want. Sleep, Lara."

Content, I drifted off to sleep.

At some point I felt Keir slip out from under the furs. I lifted my head, my eyes half open, to see him standing there, talking to one of the guards. I must have made some sort of questioning sound, for Keir turned toward me, his eyes glittering in the faint light. He gestured for me to return to sleep.

I let my head sink down, grateful that I didn't have to emerge from my warm bed. I'd adopted the Firelander custom of sleeping naked. It made more sense to my way of thinking. Less clothing for Marcus to clean, for example. A sign of my respect for the Firelanders. Goddess knew, Keir seemed . . . appreciative.

But as convenient as the custom was, crawling naked from warm covers to dress in cold clothes left something to be desired. So I lay my head back down and let sleep take me.

Much later, I roused again when Keir slid back into bed. He made every effort to keep the cold air from me, but his arm brushed mine in the process.

His skin was cold.

He whispered an apology and pulled away. But I'd have none of that. Without really opening my eyes, I moved closer.

He was *cold*. Fool Warlord, standing outside to talk to the guards, naked. I shifted slowly, crawling over him to press my body as close as I could.

He drew a deep breath as I covered his body with mine. A shudder ran through him as I pressed my breasts to his chest, letting my warm skin come into full contact with his chilled flesh. I lifted one hand to cup his cheek, and used the other to stroke the muscles of his upper arm.

I moved my legs between his, and tried to place my feet so that they covered his toes. With my head on his shoulder my hair spread out like a blanket over him. I hummed in pleasure at the feel of his body. The soft skin of his stomach, the coarse hairs of his legs. The occasional scar. All of it Keir. My Keir.

He relaxed beneath me, whispering thanks. I just smiled, and let my thumb trace the soft skin of his lips. The blankets and furs held the heat of our bodies and the scent of his skin.

I'd learned much in the ways of pleasure from my Warlord since the day he'd claimed me. As a woman, I appreciated each and every moment. As a healer, I knew that our love-making would have consequences, and in fact my courses had not come since we'd left

Wellspring. While I had hopes, I had no certainty that I bore a child. I could do nothing but wait.

There were sounds of movement outside, probably a change of the guards. The wind was picking up, causing the tent to vibrate a little. We were coming down out of the mountains with winter at our heels. Yet within this small shelter we were warm, safe, and dry.

Gradually Keir's body warmed and I shifted off to his side, so that the poor man didn't have to bear my weight. I was careful to return to my side of the bed. Keir slept with his weapons next to him, and I'd no desire to bed cold steel. I nestled down next to him, content with his comfort and ready to return to sleep.

But I'd warmed Keir in more than one way . . .

2

Now it was Keir's turn, his hands moving over my skin, causing my heat to rise. His touch was gentle and I sighed at the pure pleasure of it.

Encouraged, Keir claimed my lips and we spent long slow moments exploring each other's mouths. Not that his hands stopped for a moment, teasing my skin with soft strokes of his fingertips. I squirmed as he caressed my thighs, wanting more. "Keir . . ."

He chuckled softly. "There is no hurry, Lara."

"Keir," I pleaded, but he just kissed me again.

Boldly, I reached for what I craved, but he captured my wrists in one hand, thwarting my efforts. I growled, he laughed, and we tussled for a moment until he pinned my wrists over my head.

The bedding had fallen away and the cold air danced over my heated skin, tightening my nipples and stealing my breath from my body.

Keir loomed over me. There was just enough light to

see his eyes glittering with desire, and a playfulness that I'd never seen before.

I lifted my head, trying to gain his mouth, but he would only allow my lips to brush against his. I lay back, and puffed out a breath in frustration. Satisfied, he lowered his mouth to my chest, licked the skin between my breasts, and blew over the moist area. I sucked in a deep breath, closed my eyes and lost myself in the sensation.

Keir didn't stop, exploring my breasts with his mouth, ignoring the tips to concentrate on the flesh around them. I'd never felt that my breasts were attractive, being on the small side.

Keir seemed content.

He slipped his free hand under my back, forcing me to arch up into his mouth. Lips, tongue, even the barest scrape of his teeth, all combined to make me shiver.

"Keir," I begged.

"Lara," he murmured.

The cold air only accented the heat between our bodies. His legs moved over mine, keeping them pressed to the bed. I moaned, trying to shift him, trying to give him access, but he ignored me, and continued to worship my breasts.

Finally, he moved his hand to cover my lower belly, letting his warm fingers splay out. I moved my hips, but he wouldn't let his fingers move any lower.

"You are so beautiful," he whispered.

My eyes opened wide to stare into his. "I'm not . . . not really. I'm—"

"Perfect." His lips hovered over mine. "Everything you are is beautiful, flame of my heart."

I sobbed.

He moved then, his fingers seeking out my depths and stroking gently. He released my wrists and I clung to him, crying out my joy and pleasure all at the same time. But it wasn't enough. I wanted more, wanted him, and with a swift move he entered me, and I had what I wanted, and more, so much more.

We both lay gasping, our over-heated bodies cooling in the night air. Reaching for the blankets and furs almost seemed like too much effort, but I stirred, knowing that we'd need their warmth. I pulled them up and over us. They still held our heat, and I settled back with a sigh, making sure we were both well covered.

Keir opened his eyes and gave me a sated smile as I settled in next to him. We held each other close, and were just starting to drift off to sleep when he spoke. "You were hurt."

His hand was on my upper arm. I nodded. "Just a bruise. I didn't block the blow."

"Marcus said you want to learn to fight." He rubbed my arm gently. "To protect me."

"It scared me, when Iften . . ." My voice trailed off as I remembered finding Iften standing over Keir, as he lay in the grips of the plague.

Keir wrapped his arms around me, and I lay my head on his chest. "It warms me that you want to do this, Lara." His voice was soft in the darkness. "And to some extent, Marcus is wrong. With enough practice, you could become a fighter, if you choose. Maybe not as fast as those of the Plains, but with training you could do it. You could do anything, if you minded to."

I smiled against his chest.

"But your time is better spent at what you do best, Master Healer," Keir suggested. "Learn how to react, and to work with your guards, to be sure. But think on the abilities that you have now, and not the ones you don't have."

I lifted my head. "Just as well. All that armor is hot and uncomfortable. It makes me sweat."

His eyes took on a gleam, and he rolled me to my back. "Is there something wrong with sweaty?"

"Nothing at all." I laughed as I hooked my arm over his neck and pulled his mouth down to mine. "Let me prove it to you again."

And again . . .

The next morning I woke, with a smile on my face, to an empty bed. Keir had probably left me before dawn, his usual practice.

I stretched under the warm covers and relaxed. That was when I noticed the silence. Where were the normal sounds of the morning, the sound of moving warriors?

How late had I slept?

I reached out for the pile of clothing I'd left close to the bed. I eased them into the warmth, and lay there for a moment, letting them lose some of their chill before dressing quickly. I slung my satchel over my head and settled it on my hip before emerging from the tent.

Marcus was sitting there, with my guards. When I came out, they sprang up, and started moving toward the tent. Marcus spoke, his voice cutting through my morning fog. "Finally."

"Marcus?" I stepped out, pulling my cloak on behind me. As I left the tent, I heard it collapse behind me, and saw that Rafe, Prest and Ander were disassembling it even as I drank.

"Hisself said to let you sleep, and so I did," Marcus explained, as he thrust out a piece of bread with cold meat wrapped in it, and a cup of kavage. "We must ride to catch him."

I stuffed the food in my mouth, nodding even as I chewed. Marcus kicked the fire out and poured the last of the kavage into my cup, before packing the rest of his gear. I drank the bitter brew and looked around. The sky was a bright blue, with not a cloud anywhere to be seen. But snow lurked beyond the mountains. I could smell it in the brisk air.

The army had already packed up and started moving. I could see the last of the warriors and horses moving off into the trees. How I'd slept through that I'd nev—

Then I remembered what Keir and I had done last night, and smiled into my kavage.

Marcus moved off to aid Rafe and Prest in the packing. Ander and Yveni went for one of the pack horses that stood nearby. Greatheart was with the other horses. He was asleep, of course. I was fairly certain that was why he'd been picked for me, given my so-called riding skills. I gulped more kavage as the activity caused the big brown horse to open his eyes. When he spotted me, he whickered, and started to walk my way. The other horses shook themselves as well, as if understanding that we were about to leave.

"Where is Keir?" I asked as I finished the kavage down to the dregs. I felt much more alert with each swallow.

"We ride to meet him," Rafe answered, securing the packs on the horses. He said nothing more, but he had a slight smirk on his face, which was mirrored on Prest's lips. Something was up.

Greatheart was smelling my hair, and I reached out to stroke the scar on his chest and to scratch his ears. He was a good-sized horse, and I had to chuckle at the idea that I might be able to leap onto his back.

"Hurry." Marcus gestured for me to mount. The guards waited until I was settled in the saddle before they mounted as well, and we took off at a trot.

It didn't take long, since the army was moving at a walking pace. Marcus kept up our pace as we passed the warriors, clearly intent on catching Keir as quickly as possible. A few of the warriors called greetings to me as we passed, but others scowled. I had to sigh at the clear evidence that Iften was still spreading dissent among the ranks.

After a while, Marcus raised his head and warbled out a cry, calling to Keir. There was a response up ahead, and Marcus urged the horses to a gallop. Rafe and Prest had the lead, with Ander and Yveni following, easily keeping up the pace.

Then we broke free from the trees to see Keir galloping toward us.

We came together, and brought the horses to a stop. "Herself slept long," Marcus explained.

"She had good reason." Keir's face was neutral, but there was a gleam in his eye. I blushed, which made the corners of his eyes crinkle up. He sidled his horse close to Greatheart and leaned over to stroke my cheek with his hand. "I would ask something of you."

"Yes?"

He cleared his throat. "I would give you your first glimpse of the Plains, if you would come. The scouts found it during their sweep. You can see the Plains from there, and I wish to be the one to show you."

"Of course."

He looked a bit embarrassed. "Would you . . . could I . . ."

I gave him a puzzled look, since it wasn't like him to be indecisive.

Keir puffed out a breath in frustration. "I would have you in my arms for this first sight of my land." He held out his arm in a pleading gesture.

Without a word, I leaned over so that he could wrap his arm around my waist and pull me into the saddle in front of him. "I'd like nothing more, my Warlord," I whispered as I settled in front of him.

He flushed with pleasure, and urged his horse on. Greatheart followed, as did the others.

We headed off into the trees, working our way at an angle down a small track. I nestled in closer to Keir and felt his arms tighten around me. We'd ridden this way the second time he'd claimed me. Or I had claimed him, depending on who was talking. It felt right that my first sight of the Plains would be in Keir's arms.

The trail took us past a stone wall, overgrown with vines and falling down in some places. I craned my neck to see through the gaps what seemed to be an old tower, fallen into disuse by the look of things. I wondered how it came to be here, along the border, but I had no idea—I'd studied healing, not history.

Keir urged his black along and it didn't take as long as I thought to reach the spot, or maybe the time just flew faster than I realized. But Keir spoke into my ear. "Close your eyes, Lara." I smiled, and closed them tight.

I felt the sun on my face, so we were out from under the trees. He pulled his horse to a stop, and I heard the others surround us. He adjusted our positions so that I was facing out, and then with a satisfied tone, spoke out loud. "Behold the Plains, Warprize."

I opened my eyes, and my stomach dropped.

We were on a ridge that dropped away at a steep angle. Beyond, we looked out to where the valley opened up, the trees ended, and the land rolled out like a great, wide carpet. The land shimmered with heat, red and yellow flames flickering in the distance.

"It's burning," I said with a hush.

Keir chuckled. "No, Lara. The grasses, they turn all colors of red before the seasons of the snows. The winds move the grasses. But I will admit that it looks like it is on fire."

Of course. The Firelands. That must be how they were named. I could just make out the front of the army starting to touch the foothills, the long line of warriors snaking back toward us, to be lost in the trees below. I glanced back for a moment at the old keep. What a view there must be from the top.

But my eyes were drawn back to the horizon, a long flat line that stretched out endlessly. The land spread out for as far as I could see. The sky was huge, bigger than I'd ever thought the sky could be. It spread from horizon to horizon, and I had no words to describe it, or how I felt. I'd lived my whole life in the shelter of the mountains, looking down the narrow valley from the Castle of Water's Fall. It did odd things to my stomach, to see the world open and exposed, so wild, so free, so . . . limitless.

Just as my life had opened when Keir had claimed me.

I swallowed hard, taking it all in, and shivered. I'd grown comfortable with Keir, with his people. The last few weeks, I'd been so busy dealing with so many problems that I'd forgotten to be afraid.

But here I was, standing on the border of a strange land, speaking a foreign language, dealing with a people whose ways were strange and new. Now that I actually stopped to think about it, a wave of fear and home-sickness washed over me.

Keir's arms tightened, and his hands took mine in their warmth. "Do not fear, Lara," he murmured in my ear.

"It's just so different," I whispered, unable to tear my eyes away, unwilling to show him the fear in my eyes.

I felt him nod. "As frightening as a land where one is constantly surrounded by huge mountains of stone that restrict your sight and block the sun."

I looked back over my shoulder into his blue eyes, and his gentle smile of understanding. It was awkward, but I pressed my lips to his in a gentle kiss, which he returned.

I turned back, drew a deep breath, and relaxed,

knowing that my land must have seemed as strange when he'd first seen it. I leaned against Keir, and felt him lean forward to support me. And while the fear didn't flee, it did fade to something I could face. That we could face.

Together.

"If we don't start, the army will reach the Plains without its Warlord," Marcus groused.

Keir laughed. "That will not happen." He moved closer to Greatheart, allowing me to transfer back to my horse. "We ride!"

The track continued down the ridge, a steep switchback that brought us out in the foothills, not far from where the army was gathered.

Keir led the way at a gallop, urging us on, smiling in delight. I hadn't thought it possible, but the land seemed to become larger as we rode, expanding before us. The colors changed now, the patterns of red and yellow growing distinct. I knew now why they worshiped the elements, the sky and the land, the wind and the rain. How could they not, when confronted with this? What would it be like, to see a storm move over the land, or to watch the sun set in the distance? I urged my horse on, suddenly eager to learn all I could about this new world.

Keir swerved off, following the outer edge of the troops, to a rise where the warleaders had gathered. He pulled his horse to a stop, greeting all with a smile. They greeted him in turn, with varied levels of enthusiasm. Iften had spread his discontent well, even among them.

Iften was there, of course, mounted on a big grey horse, with the warrior-priest to one side, and Wesren on the other. None of them appeared pleased to see me. Especially the warrior-priest, since he was the one I had doused with the boiled skunk cabbage. Warrior-priests don't share their names, so I had no way of addressing him. Not that he had anything to say to me. Or I to him, for that matter.

It seemed to me that Iften was making every effort to stay away from me. That was fine, except for one thing. When Isdra had challenged him for the insult to her bonded, I was certain that she had cracked or broken his arm in the fight. But Iften had rejected my healing skills, only allowing the warrior-priest to cast 'spells' on his arm. He seemed to use it without any pain, but he used a leather bracer on that arm, and I couldn't get more than a glimpse.

Yers was there, a warm smile on his face. He inclined his head to me in a respectful greeting.

That was something else that I had learned about these people. The way they nodded or inclined their heads was an important indicator of status and consent. From the slight nod of a Warlord, to the showing of the back of the neck by one of very low status, it marked your position in their world. It was also a way of showing one's opinion about a situation. They did it without really thinking about it, and I'd only learned through watching carefully.

Because Simus had remained in Xy, and Iften was Second, Yers was now Third. A handsome man, with a rather large, crooked nose. He supported Keir, for which I was grateful.

Sal the quartermaster was there as well, and while she nodded in greeting, her position was almost completely neutral. So long as she could bargain for supplies for the army, she was content. Aret, who was responsible for the herds, was keeping an eye on both sides, and would support the winner. Tsor and Uzaina, the warleaders responsible for the warriors on the march, had also kept their distance, although they seemed to be leaning toward Iften.

Wesren, who had charge of the encampments, was clearly on Iften's side. But Ortis, the huge man who had helped care for tiny Meara, supported Keir. He also had charge of the scouts and the messengers that Keir relied on.

Joden was there as well, sitting on his horse, looking out over the Plains. I pulled to a stop next to Joden. "Good morning, Joden."

He turned his dark, broad face to me and gave me a nod. "Xylara."

I showed no sign, but the greeting hurt. Joden had been a staunch supporter of Keir and myself until the events at Wellspring. But since that time, he'd changed. Joden had lost some of his fire. Caring for the dead, singing for their souls, had put a burden of sorrow on him that words could not heal. He was honest in his opposition, and he'd told me directly, but it still stung. He'd been the first to call me Warprize, and he'd been the one to explain my position to me. But now he used my formal Xyian name, and no other.

Marcus shot him a glare, but Iften smirked. The tensions were there, under the surface and still brewing. But all were to speak before the Elders, and they would decide the truths. I felt a knot of tension start to build, right between my shoulder blades.

"Are we ready?" Keir asked of his warleaders.

I glanced over, unsure of his meaning. He was looking at his warleaders, watching them nod, all with a look of eagerness about them. What in the world—

"The scouts have ranged, and found no threats, Warlord," Ortis reported.

Yers nodded in agreement. "We are ready, Warlord."

Keir smiled in satisfaction. "Then we will celebrate our return home, and then camp for the night."

"We could still make time, a few hours of travel," Iften pointed out. "At the rate you have set, we will not reach the Heart of the Plains until the new grass has grown."

Keir gave him a long look. "After we dance, we will rest. Wesren," Keir continued, never taking his eyes off Iften. "Make plans for a camp tonight. We will move on in the morning."

I held my breath, for Iften had almost challenged Keir once before. But this time Iften faced a healthy Keir, fully capable of meeting him in combat. Iften looked away, and I let the breath ease from my body in relief. I was certain Keir could take him, but I didn't wish to see it brought to a test.

Keir seemed to reach the same conclusion, turning to look out over the warriors that stretched out before us. "Marcus, you'll stay?"

"I will." Marcus dismounted, and removed his saddle bags. He moved over to remove Keir's saddle bags as well.

"Keir?" I asked, concerned suddenly.

He flashed a grin at me, his face boyish and relaxed. "Off your horse, my Warprize."

I dismounted, a bit puzzled. Greatheart seemed to know that something was up. He danced a bit as Marcus took off his saddle bags as well. Once that was done, Marcus and I took positions off to the side, and I watched as Keir raised his face to the skies and warbled a long cry.

To a man, the warriors below turned and looked in our direction. I saw that their horses were stripped of saddle bags, even the pack horses were bare. There was a great, expectant hush that settled over all of them, man and beast.

"HEYLA!" Keir raised his arms high, palms facing out. "WE ARE HOME."

"HEYLA!" The response was loud and thunderous, and the entire army charged out onto the Plains.

The warleaders, even the warrior-priest, rushed to join them. Marcus's horse and Greatheart both surged forward. Keir slid from the black's back and it launched itself forward, belling with joy.

Keir moved to my side and took my hand and we watched the spectacle unfold before us. It wasn't the mad race out into the grasses that I had expected. It was a dance, the likes of which I had never seen. Eventually the swirling, interlocking patterns became clear, as horses and riders moved together.

The cries of joy, laughter, and the whinnies of horses came to us on the wind. Keir laughed too, a joyful sound. I looked over, and knew I was seeing a different Keir, without the weight of worries and responsibilities on his shoulders. For the moment, he was as light-hearted and happy as I'd ever seen him.

I looked back just in time to see the riders slip off their horses, as if on an unseen signal. The people started to run, forming their own patterns.

The horses danced alone now. Goddess, it was a pattern dance with the horses!

I squeezed Keir's hand. "You should be out there."

He looked over, his blue eyes alight with a smile. "I'd rather stand here and see it through your eyes."

I smiled back, then turned to Marcus, who stood with his arms folded tight to his chest, under his cloak. "Marcus, you should—"

He cut me off with a jerk of his head. "In that confusion with a blindspot? Are your wits gone?"

I turned back, and knew he was right.

The celebration continued for a few more moments, then to my wonder, the warriors began to re-mount. They would come together, horse and rider both at a run, then the warrior would reach out and pop into the saddle in an instant. In awe, I watched as more and more warriors returned to their seats, with no apparent effort or mishaps.

Three horses split off from the group and headed for us at a run. Keir's black, Marcus's mount, and Greatheart not far behind. They came pounding toward us at a full gallop.

Keir dropped my hand, and moved a step away. The black came charging up, Keir reached out his arm—

and was mounted and gone.

Marcus, too, was up and away.

I watched in horror as Greatheart plunged toward me at full speed. I took a step back and turned to watch as he ran by, brushing the edge of my cloak.

Greatheart pulled up short, snorting, as Keir's laughter rang out. The big brown gave me a disgruntled look, shook himself, then ambled over to bump his head against my chest. I'd clearly disappointed him. I reached up and scratched his ears as a consolation.

Keir rode up, still chuckling.

Keir re-established discipline over his tired but happy warriors. Packs and saddlebags were retrieved. The scouts were sent back out, and everyone set about making camp for the night.

I watched quietly, and noticed very quickly that camp on the Plains was different than camp in the Valley of Xy. There were no trees here, so the warriors searched for dried dung in the tall grasses to use for the fires. Fire pits were cut, wide swatches of grass sliced and pulled away to reveal the earth below. Marcus explained the dangers of grass fires, and the need for extra caution when the Plains started to dry.

To be honest, the openness of it all, the sheer weight of the sky on my head, was a bit overwhelming. Since Marcus wouldn't let me do any of the actual work of making camp, I distracted myself by looking at the various plants of the Plains. Who knew what healing properties there were to be discovered? I dug out one of my precious blank journals, sat in an undisturbed patch of grasses, and started in.

It wasn't just grasses. There were low bushes, and smaller plants, some of which held berries. I started picking, tasting, exploring with my senses to see if I could determine what they might do. If I picked and dried some leaves, I'd brew a few teas and drink them, being very careful to go slowly. This was more Eln's area of expertise than mine, so I'd make some observations, and then send him a few bundles with the next messenger.

I wasn't aware of the passage of time, until a voice cut through my studies. "Ah, my heart is filled with pain."

I looked up. The day had drawn on, and from the scent on the air Marcus was preparing our nooning for us. Keir was stretched out full length, the plants matted below him, looking at the sky. His hands were folded, resting on his chest. "Keir?"

"My love disregards me, neglects me, for another."

I smiled, tucking the last of the leaves into my journal and closing it firmly as he continued. "What is a Warlord to do, when another attracts the eye of his Warprize?" he asked of the open sky. "When she snubs and igno—"

I cut him off with a kiss, which only ended when we both needed air. He broke it off with a laugh.

"Fool of a Warlord." I smiled, and used a piece of grass to stroke his cheek.

He arched an eyebrow, with a gleam in his eyes. "I call your name, but you ignore me, your nose buried deep in dried grasses. What is a Warlord to think?"

"I'll show you." I leaned in closer to whisper in his ear. "In our tent. Tonight."

His smile widened, and he rolled over, slipping his arm around my waist. "Why delay, Warprize? The tent is set up, and is but a few steps away." His voice was low and rough and even through our clothing I could feel his heat. "We could—"

"WARLORD!!! EHATS!!!"

3

"Ehats?"

Keir bounced up immediately and I was right behind. I'd heard so much about these animals, I couldn't wait to see one. The closest I'd come was when the warriors had stomped around the living chess board, pretending to be ehats. I stuffed my journal in my satchel, took Keir's hand, and let him pull me through the grass.

Marcus was before our tent with a scout and Tant. Others were gathering, drawn by the news. The scout and Tant were both grinning like fools as Keir strode up. "Ehats?" Keir asked again.

The scout's smile grew broader. "Four ehats, Warlord."

Keir stopped, stunned. Then his face hardened. "You lie."

I sucked in a breath at the insult, since there'd been

no exchange of tokens. But the scout merely threw his head back and laughed. "I knew those would be your words, and can't fault you, Warlord. But may the skies and the earth witness that I speak true. Four ehats, young males, away from the herd, unmated and qualified for hunting."

Everyone stood there, stunned.

"Four ehats, Warlord." The scout patiently repeated himself. "As many as the elements themselves, and upwind of the camp." He paused for effect. "At least, for the moment."

"Four," breathed Keir. "A gift from the elements."

"Or a challenge." Joden spoke from behind us.

"Either way, it's one I will take." Keir looked back at the scout. "If this is true, I'll honor you with first meats. If false, I'll kill you with my own hands."

"Done," the scout responded, still grinning. "Know that you will gift the first meats to Lail of the Badger."

"Summon the warleaders, but use no cries," Keir ordered.

Warriors ran off, in every direction.

"We'll need musk teams and kill teams, ten members each," Keir snapped out. "Marcus, gather what we need for the musk teams, four in all." With a nod Marcus disappeared to do his bidding.

"You'll try for them all?" Joden demanded.

Keir gave him a defiant look. "The skies favor the bold, Joden." Keir turned to face me, then looked back over his shoulder. "Besides, you need something to sing of, yes?"

Only I saw the look of shock on Joden's face.

Keir faced me, his eyes alight. "An ehat hunt, Lara. It's rare enough to find two, but four is unheard of. We will try to take all of them, together."

"It's dangerous, isn't it?" I asked, stepping closer.

The warleaders were coming from all across the camp; I only had a moment to express my concern.

Keir drew me close, and lowered his voice. "Death comes in an instant, Lara. We both know that. But ehats are the finest meat on the Plains, and the leather, wool, everything down to the gut is valued for its use. Four ehats will fill the hands of all my warriors, and their hearts with the glory of the tale."

I kissed him gently. "Have a care, my Warlord, for you carry my heart with you."

I stepped back as Yers ran up, with Iften and Wesren right behind. The warleaders were gathered now, and Keir stepped forward. Yers smiled at him, with no hesitation. "Four ehats, Warlord? Simus will curse that he was not here."

"Is this wise, Warlord?" Ortis asked, his voice carefully neutral. "To risk for all, when we could easily take one?"

"Perhaps we should let them go, to appease the elements," Aret offered. She took one look at Keir's face and hastily added, "In case we have offended."

Sal snorted.

Iften stood, his arms crossed over his chest. "We are not worthy of this gift."

Keir's face was tight with anger, but he controlled it. "Our skill at the hunt will show our worth. Any who think they are unworthy," he glared at Iften, "or have offended," he moved his glare to Aret, "they are free to decline the hunt." His upper lip curled. "They can chant for their evening meal."

"I want fresh ehat, fresh from the fire." Yers smacked his lips.

Keir laughed, nodding in agreement. "As is traditional, I will take the first musk team. Iften, if you would hunt, you may have the second. Yers—"

Iften interrupted. "I'd rather first kill."

Keir raised an eyebrow in surprise. "You decline the honor?" At Iften's nod, Keir wasted no more time. "Yers, you may have the second musk team."

"An honor, Warlord." Yers reached for the buckles of his armor and started to remove it.

"Ortis and Aret, if you would hunt, you may have third and fourth musk." Ortis nodded, and handed his weapons to those around him. Aret paused, then shrugged, and started to remove her armor as well.

"Joden." Keir started to unlace his leather. "I offer you second kill."

This caused a bit of a stir, but Joden refused. "I must watch the hunt, Warlord, if I am to sing of it."

"Then Sal, Uzaina, and Tsor, you have the honors. Choose your warriors well."

They all nodded, and moved off, talking and sending runners off as well, apparently to summon warriors. Wesren stood silent for a moment, without an assignment. His face flushed, he turned toward Iften. That warrior-priest was there as well, handing something to Iften, who placed it in his mouth. I looked away before they could catch me staring.

Keir had dropped his leather armor in the grass, and started to pile his weapons on top. "Joden, would you keep watch over the Warprize during the hunt?"

"I will tend to Xylara," Joden answered. "See to your own hide, Keir. Ehat horns know no difference between warlord and warrior."

Keir nodded. "Rafe and Prest, would you ride with me?"

They both jerked in surprise, Prest's eyes going wide. Rafe responded, "YES!" They both began to strip.

"Marcus! Where is that oil?" Keir called, having stripped down to his trous.

"Here." Marcus led a pack horse close, and started handing out pots of a thick greenish paste. I grabbed one to look at. Keir took a handful from the pot I held and started rubbing it on his chest.

"What is this?" I asked, dipping my finger in and holding it to my nose. A faint sweet smell caught me by surprise, since it felt almost like lard. "I haven't seen this before."

"Sweetfat," Keir answered, stepping out of his trous, standing there naked. "Would you do my back?"

With a nod, I looked up to discover myself in a crowd of naked men and women, in the process of rubbing this stuff all over themselves and each other. I flushed, moved behind Keir, and focused on his back, and his back alone. Which was no real sacrifice, since his bronze skin looked well with the gleam of the oil. I tried to keep my mind on other things. "Sweetfat?"

Marcus came up beside me with another pot. "We use it for rough skin, or when the wind blows faces red and raw. Or to prevent the musk from sticking to skin."

"Musk?"

Keir was rubbing the oil into his face and hair. "Ehat musk is vile. We have to get the animal to empty its sac before we can kill it or the meat will be tainted."

I scooped up a handful and smeared more on his back. There was a very faint greenish tinge to the fat. "What kind of grasses do you use in this?"

Keir shrugged.

Marcus had gone to another pack horse, and was handing out cloths and garments that were torn and tattered. The warriors chosen for the musk teams were putting these on, tattered trous, or wrapping shirts and loose cloth about their loins. Old footwear as well was offered and everyone tried to find something that fit.

"The clothes will be burned when we are done. Water does no good to remove the stink. Instead we will strip and rub ourselves with dirt and grasses afterwards," Keir explained.

"It sounds unpleasant."

Yers laughed. "Which is why the 'honor' goes to the highest ranked warriors, Warprize."

I kept my eyes averted, but I pondered Yers's words. If that was the case, why had Iften refused a musk team?

The horses were being led up and I decided it was time to beat a hasty retreat out of the way. Joden followed, as did Ander and Yveni. By now most of the teams were covered, although they all shone from the fat they'd rubbed into their bodies. The decision made to hunt, the excitement and tension was starting to build.

"Ander, just how dangerous are ehats?" I asked as the teams started to wrap thin cloths over the horses' eyes. The horses had been stripped of their tack, except for their headgear. The riders were going bareback. Keir was searching for a cloth thin enough for his eyes as well.

"Very," Ander said.

"The teams will harass from a distance, Lara, trying to get the creature to spray them." Joden sounded reassuring. "They use the lances to kill from a distance, since arrows can't pierce the wool and hide."

Marcus had come up to us. "The scouts have found a place for us to watch this hunt. We need to leave now to be in position."

I mounted Greatheart, and looked back to catch Keir's eye. But Marcus got us moving, and my last glimpse was of Keir mounting his black and gathering his team.

No wonder they'd replaced the castles on the chess board with ehat figures. The animals were as big as castles.

Huge, in fact, with thick dark wool that dangled from their bodies in long shaggy strings. The horns were massive, wide and sharp, and stuck out from each side of the beast's forehead. One sweep would easily knock a horse from its feet and impale the rider. I swallowed hard from the image in my head.

"They're young." Marcus spoke softly. He was laying next to me on the rise, in the tall grass. We'd crawled here, he, Joden, and I, to watch the hunt. Ander and Yveni were down with the horses, keeping watch.

"How can you tell?" I asked softly. The animals had their heads down, eating the grasses. I couldn't make out their eyes, since the thick hair hung down over their snouts. The horns seemed to go on forever, and I couldn't take my eyes off the tips.

"If they were older, one would watch as the others grazed," Joden answered. "They'd also stay closer together."

"Why bother?" I asked. "What can harm them? Besides men?"

"Cats," Marcus replied. "A cat can pull one down."

A cat? I frowned, looking out at the hulking beasts, and opened my mouth to question Marcus, when a group of riders appeared, and charged the nearest animal.

I'm sure that the other groups charged as well, but whether by accident or plan, Keir was in the group closest to us. I had a clear view and I almost wished I didn't.

It was one thing to hear that Keir would be riding bareback and weaponless, with no armor, but it was another thing entirely to see it. He looked small and vulnerable, and I sucked in a breath as he and the other riders with him galloped toward the ehat.

They swept around the animal at a full gallop, yelling and waving their arms. Some threw stones, more to annoy than to hurt, since they seemed to bounce right off. I could see Rafe and Prest in the thick of things, trying to anger the beast.

The ehat raised its head from the grasses, its nostrils flaring as it took in their scent. It had a short, stubby tail that fluttered in annoyance at being disturbed. Even at this distance I could hear a deep growl, and then the animal snapped its head to the side, sweeping its horns at the nearest rider.

Dearest Goddess, it was *fast*.

Far quicker than I'd assumed it would be. I must have spoken out loud, because Marcus agreed. "They are, Warprize. It's tricky, it is. They need to be close enough to anger, but far enough to avoid the horns or being trampled." Joden nodded in agreement.

The other teams were also moving, but I watched only Keir as his team circled yet again. My heart stopped as Keir charged right into the ehat's face, and the black reared to paw at the sky, neighing a challenge.

The ehat's head came down with a terrific snort, and it stamped, as if preparing to charge. But Keir and the black had already moved off, to join the others circling back behind the animal, beyond the reach of those horns.

"That's done it," Joden said.

"How do you—"

"The tail." Marcus pointed.

I looked in time to see the stub of the tail stand straight up, and a thick stream of yellow ichor shoot out at the riders. Keir was missed, but others weren't so lucky. Prest seemed to be dripping in the stuff.

"Two left," Marcus commented.

"They can do it three times?"

Joden nodded, gesturing off to one of the other groups. "Looks like Prest took a full hit to the head."

I couldn't tear my eyes away from Keir. The ehat he faced was fully aroused now, stamping, and spraying out at anything that moved. I watched as everyone was sprayed, including Keir. As soon as it was certain that the animal had exhausted its supply, the riders moved off, away from camp.

"Normally, they'll not bring that stink to camp," Marcus replied to my questioning look. "They'd find a place to rub in the dirt and use crushed grasses on their skin and the horses. It takes the worst off."

"Oh, the poor horses."

"They're better off than the warriors. The stink doesn't seem to cling to horsehide as bad."

"What about water? Soap?"

Joden joined in. "Water seems to make it worse. After a few hours, the dirt and grasses absorb it, and then they'll bathe."

"But this is not a normal hunt." Marcus pointed off where Keir and the other musk teams had gathered. "They'd not miss this."

"Who would?" Joden agreed. "Simus will rage that he missed this."

"The kill teams are moving in." Marcus pointed, standing up, and waving to let Ander and Yveni know they could join us.

We'd crawled up the rise so as not to spook the prey, but that wasn't a worry now. I stood with Joden and watched as the next teams swooped in, full armored, and bearing lances. Two of the ehats seemed to realize the danger, and were trying to move closer to each other, but the teams were heading them off.

Their musk might be gone, but those horns were still wickedly sharp, and the ehats weren't afraid to use them.

"Any down yet?" Ander asked as he and Yveni joined us.

"Not yet," Joden responded. "But I think that far one is going down."

I looked to see the animal staggering, and the riders crying out as it fell.

"A quick kill," Marcus said. "Thanks to the skies."

Yveni came to stand behind me, looking out at the land behind us. She and Ander were taking turns, watching the hunt and our backs. Even here, even now, they didn't let down their guard. They shifted, so that she could see. "Good. The faster the kill, the less risk to one of ours."

Joden grunted, but never took his eyes off the scene before us. He was intent, tying to see it all. I knew he would remember it all, and wondered how he'd capture all of this in a song.

The air filled with the cries of warriors and the bellows of wounded ehats. Two more went down, leaving the last ehat, the one closest to us, still standing. "What is Iften playing at?" Marcus grumbled.

He was right, Iften was in the lead on this ehat. The animal was stamping, bellowing and using short charges to fend off the riders. I watched as Iften came around, a lance in his hand, aiming for the beast's head.

"He wants an eye shot," Joden noted absently.

"He cares more for his personal glory over the good of warriors," Marcus snapped.

I held my breath as Iften rose in the saddle, raising the lance, headed right for the head. He threw up his hand, brandishing the lance—

and dropped it.

There were gasps all around me as Iften fell back into the saddle, his arm cradled in front of him. But the ehat didn't hesitate. It swung its head hard, and its horn caught both Iften and his horse, throwing them both in a tangle far into the grass. The ehat bellowed its triumph, and swung again, trying to catch another rider.

"They'll lose it," predicted Joden, as the riders on the team changed their tactics, interposing to keep the ehat from trampling Iften. But that gave the ehat a way out, and it turned to flee. "If it runs, it will be miles before it stops."

I heard the cry first, a warbling that rang in the ears. It was Keir, racing in on the black, headed straight for the ehat. I held my breath in horror, he had no weapon or armor. What was he thinking?

But the cry had put new fire in the team, and they surged forward toward the animal, to try to cut if off. One warrior broke off and met Keir, tossing him a lance in mid-gallop.

"He'll try for it." Marcus spoke in satisfaction.

Goddess, he was going to do it. My mouth dried as he raced closer and closer to the beast, coming up from behind, under the horn. He seemed to rear up, the lance high, and then he threw.

The lance pierced the ehat's chest, just behind the leg.

"Lung hit," Ander announced with satisfaction. Marcus and Joden both grunted in agreement.

The ehat took a step, another, staggered, and then dropped in its tracks.

A great shout arose, the cheering of all the warriors.

Warriors were leaping in the air, shouting and dancing. They were giddy with their success. I shouted too, sharing their exhilaration and relief. But I was made even happier by the sight of Keir heading our way, riding his horse with graceful lopes toward us.

Until the wind shifted.

I am a healer, used to the sights and smells of corrupted and sick bodies. There wasn't any putrid substance that I hadn't dealt with before. Still, I didn't dare risk another breath. I'd empty my stomach for sure.

Yveni stood next to me, and leaned into my ear. "It

means much, when one greets a lover covered in ehat musk with a kiss," she said.

Mentally I rolled my eyes, and wondered if I could make this so called 'sacrifice'.

Everyone else drifted back as Keir came closer, even my guards. Not that I could blame them. The stench was horrific. As he got closer, I could see the yellow globs all over him, and his poor black horse. I frowned. It looked like the musk had thickened in the air. What was that stuff?

"Warprize!" Keir shouted, laughing and smiling. His poor eyes were streaming tears, as were mine. He pulled to a stop in front of me, and leaned down. Goddess help me, who could resist? I stood on tiptoe and kissed the man. His mouth was warm and salty and tasted of musk: I dropped down in haste, breaking the kiss.

Keir sat back up, breathing hard. His eyes sparkled with a deep, satisfied look. He laughed at Marcus and Joden and gestured out where the hunters danced around their kill and celebrated. "You must sing of this, Joden!"

"No one tells a Singer how to craft a song, Warlord," Joden chided him. "But this is a once in a lifetime sight."

Keir nodded, but his smile had dimmed slightly. "If not for me, Joden, then for them. They deserve to hear it sung."

"There is truth in that." Joden nodded his agreement.

"The truth that needs to be told is that you stink, Warlord." Marcus grimaced. "Be off with you!"

Keir laughed. He would have turned the horse away, but I spoke up first. "Wait." I fumbled in my satchel, looking for an empty pot. "I want some of that musk."

There was a collective groan from everyone around me.

* * *

We'd returned to camp, but Keir had been sent off to cleanse himself. I now had a small sample of the musk sealed in a pot and wrapped in leathers. If I couldn't figure out a use for it, I bet Eln could. Would that I could be there when he got his first whiff.

The camp was preparing for a party, with large fire pits for roasting and the grass in various places being trampled down for dancing. Drums and rattles were emerging from packs, and there was an air of happiness and excitement. Everyone was digging out streamers or scarves to add to their armor.

Marcus had laid out the infamous red dress for me to wear. Infamous at least in Xy, since that was the color worn by ladies of questionable morals. I'd worn it in the Throne room of the Castle of Water's Fall, and been insulted as a result. An insult that Keir had avenged with one swift stroke of his sword. But here, on the Plains, this red dress meant something different and I put it on with pleasure. It promised to be a night of celebration of both the return to the Plains and the four-ehat hunt.

There were even plans of a more permanent camp, which had surprised me until Marcus pointed out that it would take days to butcher the animals. Only something called the first meats would be taken tonight, with guards posted to drive off scavengers. Even with everyone working, it would take time to cut and preserve the meat and hide.

While Marcus and the others worked on preparations, I had a job to do as well. A few of the injured sought me out for healing. Nothing truly serious, thank the Goddess, mostly bruises and cuts. It pleased me that some of them trusted me to treat these ills, accepting my skills.

Not everyone felt that way. I knew full well that

there were others that would not come to me, and I made no effort to seek them out. There'd been no broken bones that I knew of, and I didn't bother to ask after Iften.

Let him consult the warrior-priest that cast the 'healing spells' on his arm.

I thought about that as I sat by the fire, putting away the last of my supplies. I was sure that he'd tried to use his injured arm to throw that lance, and from the looks of it, the pain had flared when he'd hefted the lance. It was only a matter of time before the swelling damaged the arm, numbing the muscles and curling the fingers into a useless claw. But he'd made his choice, and he'd have to live with the consequences.

The sound of horses brought me to my feet, and I watched as Keir, Prest, and Rafe rode in, covered in dirt and grass stains on what was left of that old clothing. I took a few tentative breaths, but Keir just laughed and swept me up by the hips, holding me high as he spun, laughing up at me. I clutched at his hair, breathless with my own laughter. Thankfully, the smell wasn't too bad, but it was still there.

Keir put me on my feet, and Marcus handed him saddle bags and his weapons. "Clothes and some soap. You have enough time to wash before the celebration begins."

My eyes widened as I took in Rafe and Prest. Rafe seemed fine, but Prest . . . "Prest, you shaved your head!" Those long black braids were gone. Prest's bald head gleamed in the light.

He shrugged and ran a hand over his baldness. "Easier to shave." He flashed me a smile. "It grows back."

"Eventually," Rafe added. "Until then, I will need to protect my eyes from the glare."

We laughed, then Keir took my hand. "I've something to show Lara down by the river. We will return."

Marcus put his hands on his hips. "None of that, now. There's a celebration to start, and no time for 'showing' her—"

Keir cut him off, as I blushed. "We'll be back in time."

Marcus gave him an evil smile. "I'll have the first meats waiting."

Keir grimaced, and grabbed my hand. "Come, Lara."

We walked out of the light of the fires, heading away from the camp, Rafe and Prest trailing behind. I knew there was a river nearby, since others had talked of getting water there, but hadn't ventured in that direction. It felt good to hold Keir's hand and walk as the sun set in the distance. He tugged me along, looking as if he was searching for just the right place.

Finally, he dropped the saddle bags, and took up his weapons. "Leave your satchel here. Walk behind me and stay very quiet. I want to show you something."

He gestured for my guards to stay behind. Then we walked slowly and carefully down a small path to the banks of the river. Keir urged me off to the side, under the shelter of some alders. We crouched below the branches, and Keir settled us down, draping my cloak over the both of us. "Watch the far shore."

We waited, sitting close together, silent.

I leaned closer, and put my lips to his ear. "What did Marcus mean? About the first meat?" I leaned back to look into his face.

Keir made a face, and put his lips to my ear. His breath tickled as he spoke. "A warlord is given the first meats, the heart, liver, and stomach, of the ehat as an honor, to keep or to share as he sees fit." I raised an eyebrow. He sighed. "I hate the taste of first meats. Always have."

I chuckled in spite of myself.

"So, I make a great show of sharing the meats with all my warriors. Out of my generous spirit and in honor of my warriors." Keir rolled his eyes. "I still have to eat some, but usually only a bite or two. With four ehats, my plate will overflow tonight."

I covered my mouth to stifle my laughter. "Marcus knows?"

"Marcus knows. And now you. My most shameful secret."

I opened my mouth to respond, but Keir placed a finger on my lips, and shook his head. His hand tightened on mine, and I looked over to see a creature making its way to the water.

It was big, its yellow eyes bright in the fading light. Its fur was striped like the grasses about us, black and orange. It padded to the water's edge and started to drink.

"What is that?" I whispered, barely breathing.

"A cat," Keir breathed back.

A cat? That was no cat, no cat like I'd ever seen in the mountains. I could easily see this creature pulling down an ehat by itself. I sucked in a breath as it lifted its head and looked straight at us. Then it shook its massive head, yawned, and started to drink again.

Goddess above, it had a lot of teeth.

"The scent of the kill pulled it close. The scouts told me it was lurking near here. I'd hoped to show you the symbol of my Tribe. Another gift of the elements." Keir sounded smug and very pleased with himself. "We are favored, you and I."

"Do you hunt those?" I asked quietly.

"No," Keir answered. "Unless they take to hunting among the people of the Tribes. Then there is no choice. But the body is buried with honor, and the spirit mourned."

The cat lifted its head, testing the breeze. Its mouth curled back in a silent snarl, and then it turned and padded off into the darkness, fading into the grasses in the blink of an eye.

"Come." Keir tugged my hand. "I'll bathe closer to people this night."

I readily agreed.

Keir bathed quickly, with the other men and women of the musk teams who had waited to give the dirt and grasses time to work. I stayed on the bank with his clothes and weapons and snuck glances of my naked, wet Keir. Rafe and Prest stayed close. There were others about, cavorting in the water, men and women warriors alike. I still flushed at some of their antics. But most knew my customs, and I noticed that an effort was made to stay out of my view.

Keir, however, made sure I could see him.

Once he was dry, he dressed. Marcus had given him some soft brown leather trous, a vest of black leather, and a tunic of soft white cotton. I could hardly wait to get him out of it, if I were to be honest with myself.

But that would have to wait.

We started back, laughing and talking. He was describing the celebration to me, how the ehat spirits would be thanked, the honors awarded, the first meats handed out, and the merriment that would follow well into the night.

I took his hand as we neared the camp. "I've yet to see you dance, Keir."

"I'll dance this night," he promised. "I'll dance this night for everyone to see, and then we'll dance together, you and I." He pulled me close. "In the privacy of our tent, beneath the blankets."

I blushed, and he laughed, keeping his arm around my waist. We walked right into their midst without a warning, not even aware they were there.

It was Marcus's stiffness that told us both something was wrong. Marcus jerked his head to the side, and we turned to see a horde of mounted warrior-priests, filling the intended dance grounds, their eyes glittering, their faces stiff and serious. The light of the fire pits made their multi-colored tattoos almost move over their bodies.

I gasped, without thinking, and Keir stepped forward, placing himself in front of me.

The warrior-priest in front urged his horse forward a pace. "We have come for the Warprize."

With a swift move, he plunged his spear into the ground at Keir's feet.

4

"No." Keir's voice was cold and hard as steel. Every warrior around us had his or her hand on a weapon, but who supported whom I couldn't say. I swallowed hard, and stayed as still as possible.

The warrior-priest looked down at Keir with disdain. "It is the order of the Council of Elders, Warlord, that we separate you from the Warprize, and take her to the Heart of the Plains. Would you defy them?"

"Yes," Keir snarled, a sound much like I imagined the cat at the river's edge would have made.

A strong female voice cut through the night. "Even if I am the Elder?" The horses of the warrior-priests moved aside, and a woman rode forward, pushing back her hood. Everyone around us dropped to one knee, which caught me by surprise. I'd never seen a Firelander bend knee to anyone before.

Keir remained standing, but he had relaxed. "Keekai. You honor us."

She tossed her head and gave him a sly smile. "I do, don't I?" She looked around. "Am I in council, or sitting in judgment? Up, up, all of you!"

The warriors rose, and Keekai dismounted and faced us. I was taken aback, for she looked enough like Keir to be his mother. She had his height and build, and wore armor with practiced ease of many years. Older, certainly, as Keir might look in another twenty years. But she had the same black hair and blue eyes; eyes that examined me closely. "So. This is the Warprize, Keir of the Cat?"

"She is, Elder. Xylara, Daughter of Xy, from the Kingdom of Xy." Keir smiled and gestured to our tent. "I would offer you the welcome of my tent. Would you hear my truths, Elder?"

"I accept the courtesy of your tent, and would hear your truths." Keekai tossed her reins to the warrior-priest nearest her.

The man caught the reins, but he was frowning, looking severe. "Keekai, we are to return to the Heart of the Plains with the woman, as soon as possible." His dark eyes flickered over me. "They are to be separated. As soon as possible."

Keir frowned and opened his mouth, but Keekai took control. "Pah. They have just returned to the Plains and there is a four ehat hunt to be celebrated. What is one more night, eh?"

The grim man opened his mouth, but Keekai forestalled him. "My old bones need food, heat, and sleep before I set forth. Make camp. We will wait for you, and then Keir can begin the ceremonies."

I looked at Keir, to see how he reacted to this assumption of his authority, but he seemed content to let Keekai deal with the warrior-priest.

The warrior-priest was anything but content. His

lips pressed firmly together as he contemplated us. "Your bones seem conveniently old, Keekai."

"A challenge, Still Waters?" Keekai gave the man a steady look.

Still Waters? Was that his name?

The warrior-priest's eyes narrowed, but he turned away, and he and the others melted into the darkness.

Keekai gave a grunt of satisfaction, and then brushed past us into the tent. Keir took my hand, and we followed her. Warm air swirled around us as we entered. Keir dropped the flap behind us, for the warmth and the privacy.

"Keir, you stupid warlord, what were you thinking?"

Keir's mouth tightened, but he remained silent as Keekai made herself at home on one of the pallets, and threw her cloak back and off her shoulders. A brazier burned in the center, and Keir and I sat opposite her. Marcus had been busy while we were gone. He'd enlarged our tent, giving us a meeting place and the back area for sleeping.

Keekai gave us a grim look. "We have much to discuss and little time."

Marcus entered with a tray of kavage and gurt. He'd removed the cloak, now that he was in the shelter of the tent. With a bow, he served Keekai first.

Keekai's blue eyes shifted to Marcus. She gave him a searching look. "Greetings, Marcus."

That was odd. Most warriors completely ignored the scarred, small man. But Keekai was looking at him steadily, ignoring his injuries.

Marcus hesitated, then offered her a cup of kavage. After a pause, she took it. Marcus then moved the tray toward Keir and me, serving us in our turn. As he was about to leave, Keekai's voice stopped him in his tracks. "Isn't there anything you'd ask me, Marcus?"

Silence. Marcus stood, still as a statue, his back toward us. Keir caught my eye, and gestured for me to remain silent.

Keekai clucked her tongue. "Stupid man."

Marcus turned then, his body stiff, his face filled with such pain.

Keekai arched an eyebrow, then shook her head. "I should let you suffer."

Marcus just looked at her.

"All is well, except for the pain you inflict on yourself, fool. No injuries from this season."

Marcus lowered his head, turned and was gone.

"That was cruel, Keekai," Keir said softly.

"Pah." Keekai took a long drink of kavage. "Who is the cruel one, I ask you?" She rolled her shoulders. "I have ridden hard in the company of humorless warrior-priests intent on making you suffer, Keir of the Cat." She leaned forward. "There is little time. Those fools will be back shortly, and I cannot be seen to have too much private talk with you. The Council of the Elders have sent us to escort the Warprize to the Heart of the Plains."

Keir snorted.

Keekai held up her hand. "They are not fools, Keir. They know that you delay in defiance of tradition, hoping that the seasons will force them to leave the Heart. They feel that you have had the Warprize long enough, and the separation must begin now."

"Keekai," Keir started but she slashed her hand through the air, and he closed his mouth with a snap.

"You have no choice, Keir. Those who would change our ways must first honor and obey them, yes? Have we not talked about this, time and time again?"

I looked at Keir, at the angry flush on his cheeks, and I reached for his hand. "Keekai, I am Keir's Warprize. And he is my Warlord."

"Xylara, Daughter of Xy, you are not." I pressed my lips together, trying to control my anger, but my eyes must have given me away. Keekai's lips quirked up. "There's fire in you, Xyian. I'll give you that. But." Keekai scowled at Keir, "with all respect, you are not his Warprize by our traditions and ways until the formal ceremonies are complete. The other warlords have the right to court you and—"

"Court me?"

Her eyes narrowed, and she focused on Keir. "Yes, Xylara. Court you." Her glare rivaled Marcus's. "I can see that Keir has not told you everything. What were you thinking?"

"Lara is—"

"Stop." She leaned back slightly to look into both our faces. "What is done is done, Keir. Only the skies know how this will end." She puffed out a breath. "Now, I feel an attack of the misery coming on, so our return to the Heart will not be as fast as they might wish. And I will use the journey to tell your Warprize some of the details you may have . . . forgotten." Without a token in her hand, that was an insult. I waited for Keir to draw a blade, but he just flushed again and squeezed my hand.

"You have four ehats to render, and an army to release." Keekai gave Keir a close look. "With luck, you will only be a day behind before we arrive at the Heart."

"Keekai, I have always listened and followed—"

Keekai snorted.

Keir glared right back at her, adding strength to his words. "And followed your advice. But now—"

"There is no choice. She must come out from under your protection and influence. The entire Council is agreed, Keir." Keekai gave him a long look. "Would you truly defy them, and destroy this chance?"

There were noises from outside, and Keekai drank more of her kavage. "In the morning, I will come to your tent and we will hold the separation ceremony. Xylara, you will answer my questions, and we will depart."

"Questions?"

Keekai rolled her eyes. "You haven't even told her that. What have you been doing with your time?"

Keir and I exchanged a glance, and I blushed.

Keekai snorted. "Well, make the most of tonight, for it is all I can give you. It will be days before you see him again." Keekai stood, and pulled her cloak on. "She will be under my protection until we reach the Heart, Keir. She will be safe. For now, tell her what she needs to know. Of the questions, the ceremony, the champion—enough to get her through tomorrow. I will tell her more on the journey."

"I will not be stopped, Keekai." Keir's voice was low and determined, and his grip on my hand tightened. "I will break their power over my people."

Keekai stopped and turned her head. She looked so much like Keir in the firelight. "That is why I fear for you, Keir of the Cat. They will kill you if they can."

Keir's nostrils flared. "Let them try," he grated.

With a shake of her head and a swirl of her cloak, Keekai left the tent.

In the silence that remained, the fire crackled and flared up.

"Skies," Keir growled. "This is the work of the winds." I leaned in close and he pressed a kiss to my temple. "Lara, I—"

I reached out and put my fingers over his lips. "The last few weeks, since the plague cleared, have been blissful."

Keir closed his eyes and nodded, his lips brushing against my fingers.

"We've both been avoiding this, haven't we?" I whispered softly, my eyes tearing. "Neither one of us wanted to face this. Both our faults."

Keir didn't open his eyes. "I didn't want it to end." He pulled in a deep breath, and reached up to take my hand and press a kiss to the palm. "I thought we had time, at least until we reached the Heart."

"And now, we have tonight." I took a shaky breath. "After the celebration, we will talk. All night, if we have to."

His bright blue eyes looked at me from beneath his black hair. "I am tempted to defy them. I would not have you go. Keekai is an Elder, and powerful, but you—"

I twisted my hand in his, until our palms were together. His large, callused fingers were a marked contrast to mine. I slowly curled mine until my fingers interlocked with his. "Two peoples into one, Keir. You and I, working together, for ourselves and our peoples."

He pulled me into his arms. "Tonight, after the celebration. We will talk."

I pulled back just enough to look up into those wonderful blue eyes, and gave him a smile. "Just remember, you promised to dance for me, Warlord."

The gleam was back. "I did, didn't I?"

Much of the celebration was a blur. It was as if I was two people, one watching from a distance and the other wrapped in worry and fear for the future. A platform had been built, so that we could see out over the firepits and the dancing grounds. Keir conceded the center seat to Keekai, and sat to her left, I was next to him, and the other warleaders were also scattered about the platform.

Although Keekai had joined us, the warrior-priests were seated together off to the side. They seemed intent on keeping themselves apart.

Marcus made himself busy, directing his helpers to offer water for washing and giving thanks. As he offered to pour the water for me, Keir leaned over, and murmured a question. "Iften?"

"In his tent. Being tended to by the warrior-priests. They use their powers to perform another healing," Marcus said. His tone expressed his opinion of that bit of news.

I snorted softly, which earned me swift smiles from Keir and Marcus, and a frown from Keekai. Keekai opened her mouth, but Keir held his hand up. "Marcus, see that Iften is taken a share of the meats. And enough for the warrior-priest as well."

Marcus scowled, but jerked his head in acknowledgment of the order.

Keir stood and held his hand up. The warriors quieted until all that could be heard were the crackles of the fires.

"We gather this night, to thank the elements. We thank them for the gift of the hunt, and for our return to the Plains. HEYLA!"

"HEYLA!" roared the warriors in return.

"Lail of the Badger, stand forward."

The scout that brought word of the ehats stepped in front of the platform.

"I doubted your words, Lail, and I take back those words before all. On the morrow, you will have a full backstrap, with my thanks."

With a wide smile, Lail bowed before Keir, and then returned to be congratulated by the warriors around him. Marcus was offering kavage, and must have seen the question in my eyes. "The choicest part of the meat, Warprize. A true honor."

I nodded my understanding, as Keir continued. "Tomorrow, we rend the bodies of our kill, and divide the spoils of the hunt. But tonight we celebrate their spirits." Keir gestured to the firepits. "By tradition the first meats are mine. But I would grow fat as a city dweller if I ate the first meats of four ehats!"

Laughter, and a few sly looks my way. But I joined in the laughter as well.

"I would share this honor with my warriors," Keir continued. "Let us eat and share in the ehat's honor and strength. Then we will dance to thank the earth and the skies, the wind and the rain for their gifts. For we are of the Plains and we are home!"

"HEYLA!" The warriors all started to gather about the pits. Talk and laughter rose around us as they were served. The warrior-priests may have held themselves apart, but I noticed that they took their share of the food.

Marcus had our portions, served with fried bread and gurt on the side. The other warleaders were served as well and we all started to eat. The meat was sliced thin. I rolled a piece up and popped it in my mouth. It was good, better than I expected. I hurriedly ate mine, and licked the juice from my fingers.

"You honor your warriors." Keekai spoke around a mouthful, obviously enjoying the taste.

"They are worthy of honor." Keir picked up a piece of the meat and ate it.

Keekai nodded, and turned to Marcus for kavage. I leaned over, and stole a piece of meat off of Keir's platter. He gave me a surprised look, but said nothing.

"So, has Joden survived the summer?" Keekai asked, scanning the crowd. "I would hear him sing if he will."

"He did." Something in Keir's tone told me that he wasn't comfortable with the idea of Joden singing. "Keekai . . ."

She turned, those blue eyes intent.

"Isdra and Epor have gone to the snows."

Keekai looked down at her meal. "Word of this has

reached the Heart, Keir. As has the manner of their deaths." She drew in a deep breath. "The Elders will not make this easy for you, Keir of the Cat."

Marcus moved closer, and Keekai held out her mug for more kavage. I got a clear look at her right wrist. It reminded me of the old cheesemaker in Water's Fall. Suddenly Keekai's talk of her 'misery' made perfect sense.

I leaned over and took another piece of meat from Keir. I popped it in my mouth, and spoke around it. "I want to see the dancing. We don't have anything like pattern dancing in Xy."

Keekai nodded her agreement, her mouth full. "This game called 'chess'. That is of Xy, yes?"

"Yes." I gave Keir a fond look. "I taught it to Keir, and some of the others."

"It is a form of battle, that requires quick wits and careful planning," Keir added, taking a bite of some of the fry bread.

Keekai's mouth quirked. "Ah. That must be why the warrior-priests have not yet learned it."

Keir threw his head back and I joined in their laughter. Then Tsor leaned forward, and asked Keekai of the news of the Heart, and they started to talk of people and places that I had yet to know. A shiver of fear ran down my spine suddenly. There was still so much I didn't know about these people, still so much that was strange and new. Could I really leave Keir in the morning?

I stared at my kavage. I'd first tasted it in the healing tents, with Rafe and Simus and Joden. I'd learned to enjoy its bitter flavor, especially in the morning when the day was dawning clear and cold.

I looked at the gurt on my platter. The little white pebbles looked innocent enough, but for some reason, I'd never get used to their dry, bitter taste.

I gathered up some of the gurt on my platter, and added it to Keir's as I took another piece of meat from his platter. He was talking to one of the warleaders, but shifted enough so that I could reach it easily.

I was afraid. That was the truth. But I'd been afraid when I'd walked the halls of the castle, to kneel at Keir's feet for the claiming ceremony.

I snagged the last of the heart meat from Keir's platter, and he gave me a grateful look.

I could do this.

"Who will dance?" Keir stood tall, at the front of the platform. The food had been eaten, and the warriors had settled around the dancing area.

To my surprise, Rafe stepped forward. "We would dance the elements, to thank them for their gifts. We have covered ourselves to honor the Warprize and her ways." Prest, Ander and Yveni came up to stand behind him.

I raised an eyebrow at their idea of 'cover'. They all had the barest of scraps for loincloths, and Yveni had tied a strip of leather over her breasts. Still, I smiled and nodded my head to them.

"Dance!" Keir commanded, and they bowed their heads and moved to stand an arm's length apart, forming a square and facing each other.

A warrior sat nearby, and placed a drum before him. The crowd grew silent as the drumbeat sounded, a slow steady beat.

"Earth!" Ander called out, and a warrior walked out of the crowd, bearing two bowls filled with dirt.

"Air!" Yveni cried out as well. She received two bowls as well, filled with something that gave off a steady stream of white smoke.

"Water!" Rafe called out, and was handed two bowls filled to the brim with water.

"Fire!" Prest was the last, and his bowls held flames that leaped and burned.

I leaned forward, eager to see what form this dance would take. I assumed it was another form of pattern dance. To my joy, it was and it wasn't.

Together they started to move, slowly, raising the bowls above their heads and stepping out a pattern together, moving as one. I held my breath, for what was easy with a bowl of dirt, was not easy to do with a bowl of water.

They lowered the bowls, now starting to move their bodies, bending and twisting down, only to work their way back up to a standing position. It was amazing to watch Prest, his body gleaming in the light, sweat glistening all over, as he moved. And while Ander and Yveni had the easier dance, with air and earth in their bowls, they still had to match the movements of Rafe and Prest. I could see the tremble in the muscles of Rafe's arms as he fought to make sure that not one drop of water spilled from his bowls.

After a few minutes, one stepped in the center, and the other three formed a triangle around the single dancer. I realized that they were mimicking their elements. Ander's movements were slow and steady, like the earth that he held in his hands. Yveni, when she took the center, moved as the wind moves, first one way and then the other, with no real set pattern. Rafe was as fluid as water. Prest was fire, first still and quiet and then bursting out in action as the flames in his bowls grew higher.

Finally, they stood there, facing each other, their bodies gleaming and their chests heaving from their efforts. With not one bowl spilled.

Ander held up his bowls. "Death of fire, birth of earth." He tipped one of his bowls into one of Prest's, dousing the flame.

Prest held up his other bowl. "Death of air, birth of fire." He tipped the burning coals into Yveni's bowl, and placed the bowl on top, smothering the smoke.

Yveni turned with her other bowl. "Death of water, birth of air." She tipped her other bowl's contents into Rafe's, sending up a burst of steam from his bowl.

Rafe held his other bowl high. "Death of earth, birth of water." With that, he turned to Ander, and poured out the water onto his remaining bowl.

Keir jumped up, and the crowd rose with him, screaming their appreciation. I was up too, amazed that my bodyguards could dance so well.

Rafe, Prest, Ander, and Yveni turned in their places, and bowed to each of the four directions. Then they were running, their smiling faces proof enough of their joy. They disappeared into the crowd.

We all settled back, except Keekai, who stood and called out, "Where is Joden?"

There were many cries, and people's heads turned, until finally Joden stood before us. "I am here, Keekai of the Cat."

Keekai laughed. "Well and true but why are you not singing, Singer-to-be? Why not sing of the hunt?"

There were many calls to this, as people shifted so that they could see Joden clearly. He was seated next to a warrior-priest. I was fairly certain it was the one that had claimed to heal Iften.

Joden shook his head, his broad face gleaming in the light. "The song of this hunt will take time to make, Keekai. But I would sing, if you wish."

"I wish it so!" Keekai laughed out loud. "A song of your choosing, Singer."

Joden shrugged off her compliment, looking around at his fellow Firelanders. His gaze drifted over to where I was sitting with Keir, and I felt Keir tense beside me. I turned my head slightly and raised an eyebrow.

Keir looked at me ruefully, then leaned forward just enough to whisper in my ear. "He who can praise can also mock."

I turned back to see Joden glance at us. It seemed to me that he knew Keir's concern. The warrior-priest next to him leaned over and made some comment for Joden's ear alone. I bit my lip. Would he . . . ?

Joden drew a deep breath, and walked forward. He turned in a circle raising his right hand, palm to the sky. "May the skies hear my voice. May the people remember."

The response rose from the crowd. "We will remember."

Joden lowered his hand, took a deep breath, and then he laughed, a deep strong laugh, and spread his arms wide. "The sun is rising and I have slept well. The day calls to me—but my belly rumbles. What shall I have for breakfast?"

Everyone laughed, delighted, and started to shift their positions, sitting with their legs crossed, and patting the ground next to them. Keir relaxed, and got into position as well, his smile catching my eye. "You will see."

With that Joden started the first verse, about a root found growing by streams. The verse told us what to look for, and how to peel the bark back and scrape out the soft white insides. I laughed, for this was clearly a teaching song, but the tune was infectious and everyone joined in on the chorus. Keir started clapping, slapping his hands on his thighs, and then on the ground beside him.

Everyone started following that pattern as well, slapping their thighs and lifting their hands to sway to the music. It was like dancing except no one got to their feet—instead everyone swayed to and fro, laughing and chanting. It didn't take me long to follow along.

Joden started the next verse and sung about berries, red berries that were sweet, green ones that had to be boiled first. And a warning to avoid the white berries, for they would make the shit run down your leg!

Joden hunched over, wrapped his arms over his lower belly, and groaned. He swayed back and forth, groaning aloud, and repeated that verse.

The warriors laughed, and followed right along. I laughed and clapped as well, but stopped when Keir rose from his seat in the middle of the song.

"A dance, Warlord?" Keekai smiled at him.

"A dance, Elder." Keir looked at me with his eyes half closed. He reached out and stroked my cheek. "For my Warprize."

I smiled at him, but Keekai grunted. "Afterwards, you will teach me chess."

Keir turned his head so only I could see, and rolled his eyes. But then he looked at me with eyes that burned, even as he answered her. "After I dance, Elder."

I blushed, and looked away, biting my lip. He chuckled, low and deep, and I watched as he left the platform and disappeared into the crowd.

5

The warriors stamped their feet and raised their voices, demanding more from Joden. So he sang two more songs after the breakfast song. One was a rousing song about a trouble-maker named Uppor, and how he stole something from each element to create horses for the Plains. The crowd loved it, especially the part where they all joined in the chorus.

The last was about traveling at night, under a full moon and a sky full of stars. Joden's voice soared above us, making my eyes travel up to see the stars that were spread out over our heads. The song seemed to hold us all spellbound. It took my breath away.

I wasn't the only one. There was a profound silence when Joden's last note quivered in the air. He bowed and walked back into the crowd, with Keekai's grateful thanks. Neither song had been about Keir, so I'd relaxed, grateful to my friend for staying neutral. Whatever his doubts about Keir's plans to unite our peoples, I couldn't see Joden being unfair or cruel.

"Ah! The battle dance!" Keekai gestured and I followed her arm to see a group of warriors taking the field, with wooden swords and shields in hand.

Keekai turned slightly. "Your pattern, Marcus?"

Marcus said nothing, but he came to stand behind me, cloaked as always, his arms crossed over his chest. I looked at him, and he gave me a slight smile from the depths of his cloak. With a nod, he turned my attention back to the dancing field.

Two groups of warriors faced each other, lined up on either side. Keir stood before the one group, dressed in his black leathers, but without his cloak. Yers faced him from across the field. Both held a wooden sword and shield, as did each of the warriors behind them.

Keir raised his arms. Yers raised his in response, and silence covered the crowd. Then they dropped their arms together.

At the signal, both groups leaped forward, charging, swords high, yelling blood-curdling war cries.

They came together with a clash, and I would have jumped to my feet had Marcus not put his hand on my shoulder. "Watch."

There was a wild burst of drumming and only then could I see a pattern to the confusion. Each warrior faced another, exchanging blows with their swords, defending themselves with their shields. It was a fight that also a dance. I relaxed slightly, but I couldn't tear my eyes away from the sight of Keir and Yers trading blows.

For all that it was a dance, it was clear that the warriors were giving it everything they had, from the sounds of grunts and the crack of wooden swords against shields. For all that it was a pattern, it held a fierce wildness that I'd not seen before. Each pair moved about the other, striking wherever they could, the cracks of wood on wood adding to the beat of the drums. Keir was intent on his dance, his body moving with all the power and grace he was capable of.

My mouth went dry at the sight.

A weapon cracked and splintered, and a warrior threw herself down on the ground to lie 'dead'. I feared an injury for a brief moment, until it was clear that she'd been taken out of the dance by the loss of her weapon. Her opponent turned to engage another, even as another warrior dropped.

My heart pounded with the drums as warriors dropped 'dead' on the field, the dancers now forced to avoid their bodies even as they continued their fight. Keir felled Yers, and then moved to another warrior with the barest of pauses. As I watched him move, I realized that he'd been holding back with me, holding back the wildness within, probably to protect me. A flash of physical heat went through my body as my heart beat faster still. I wanted that wildness, wanted to provoke that power within him.

At last, with a final blow, Keir was left standing among the 'dead'.

The drums beat once more, then cheers rose, as did the 'dead', to congratulate the dancers. They laughed and embraced each other in celebration of the dance. One woman warrior hugged Keir, and an ugly flash of jealousy pierced my soul. These people knew nothing of marriage, and while we'd pledged ourselves to each other, that woman was strong and had breasts the size of—

Keir gave her the briefest of embraces, and then turned to look at the platform, searching for me. His eyes found mine, and he grinned, his teeth flashing. He

strode through the crowd of dancers, headed for me.
Keir seemed to glow, the black of the leathers con-
trasted by the bronze of his skin. But as much as he
glowed, his eyes gleamed even brighter. They were
like sparks, flaring with joy and love.

I couldn't help myself. I left the platform and ran to
meet him. His smile lit his face, and he swept me up,
lifting me high by the hips, and spinning us in a circle.

I laughed, all my fears washed away by the look in
his eyes.

He set me on my feet, and kissed me hard, his hands
slipping down my back to press my hips against his. I
wrapped my arms around his neck and returned the
kiss, greedy for his mouth. It was only a lack of air that
forced us apart. Well, that and Keekai calling out to
us, "Keir, you promised to teach me chess."

Keir's eyes never left mine. "With all due respect,
Elder, ask Marcus." Keir called over his shoulder,
sweeping me up into his arms, "I've promised this
night to my Warprize."

Laughter rose around us, and I laughed as well, even
as I blushed. Keir strode toward our tent. Keekai called
something out, but we ignored her, focused only on
each other.

Once in the privacy of the tent, Keir gentled, setting
me softly on my feet. But I'd have none of that, attacking his leathers, trying to wrest them from his warm,
sweaty body. But the material clung, and I had to tug to
peel the leather off his arms. Keir chuckled, letting me
have my way, but offering no help. I growled, and finally stepped back in frustration, and huffed out a
breath.

Keir arched an eyebrow, but said nothing, although
his laughter was there in his eyes. He made no move to
disrobe.

Two could play that game.

I moved closer, close enough that my breath tickled the skin of his throat. A pulse worked there, throbbing under the skin.

He didn't move.

I pressed my hand over Keir's groin, and leaned forward to lick the pulse point. Holding still, I counted his breaths. One . . .

Two . . .

Leathers went flying. My clothes were not far behind.

Keir's arm was around my waist as he nuzzled my throat, but I pulled him to the bed. I was willing and wet, and I pushed him down, and impaled myself on his length. I cried out as he filled me.

He froze. "Lara, did I—"

I braced my hands by his head, and leaned down to scrape my teeth on his jaw. My hair fell about us, a curtain against the world. "You didn't hurt me," I panted. "But if you don't move, they will find your lifeless body outside this tent in the morning."

He surged up, and I cried out again, and our bodies moved together as one. But now I knew enough to lay claim to the body beneath me. Keir gripped my hips, trying to control my movements, but I had my own needs, and I would not be denied.

My Warlord met all of my demands, and made some of his own. His eyes glowed, fierce and commanding as he rolled us over, and pinned me to the bed. It was his turn to take control, and I knew all of his power and strength, but it was tempered even then.

For when the moment came, that infinite breath of hot, white light, he cried out my name even as I cried out his.

The night air cooled our bodies as we lay there gasping for breath.

"We should talk," I managed to whisper, even though my body craved sleep.

Keir sighed. "Talk?" He drew me close and nuzzled my neck. "With my wits gone with the winds, never to be seen again?"

I laughed, and kissed him, but moved out of his arms. If I knew Marcus, he'd have left something for us . . . and sure enough, he had. A pitcher of cool water, and gurt. I took up the pitcher and mugs he'd left behind and ignored the other. I got back into bed, where Keir was waiting to wrap me in the warm bedding.

We drank the cool water, and got comfortable together. I pulled my hair back and up, letting the air get to my neck, still damp with sweat. Keir gave me a hooded look, but I waggled a finger in front of his face. "None of that, now. Talk."

He sighed again, nodded, and drained his cup.

"Why do you have to release your army?" I asked. "Won't that leave you vulnerable?"

Keir smiled. "Once a Warlord arrives at the Plains after a season of raiding, he disbands his army, allowing his warriors to return to their tribal groups as they choose. The bounty is distributed and any that have shown valor are honored. The Warlord returns to the Heart of the Plains, to report to the Council of Elders, but only with a few warriors."

"But—"

Keir shook his head. "You are thinking like a city-dweller. The Plains are hard, Lara. Especially during the season of snows. If the army stays together, it drains the land of animals and water, you see? Spread out, with the tribes constantly moving, that is how we survive on the Plains. In the spring, we come together again for the next raiding season."

"There is more than one Warlord?"

Keir nodded as he put his cup to the side, and lay back, flat on the bed. "I must release my warriors soon. There will be ehat in their saddle bags, but not much more. It is important that I am here, to remind them of my plans, that the rewards we seek will come in time."

"Even as Iften reminds them of their lack."

"Even so." Keir smiled evilly. "It will not help his cause that he dropped his lance in the hunt." His smile faded. "Still, the warriors will listen. I cannot leave. And you must go with Keekai."

I placed my empty mug on the floor, and moved to lay next to him, propping myself up on my elbows so I could see his face. "The ceremony?"

"Normally, a Warlord brings a Warprize directly to the Heart of the Plains as soon as possible. There, they are separated, because the Warprize must come freely to the Warlord, without force or threat. They protect you from me, to allow you to tell them your truths."

"I know my truth, Keir." He smiled as I asked my next question. "Courting?"

"The other Warlords are given a chance to court the Warprize, to show that they are more skillful in battle and in leadership." Keir reached out to twist one of my curls around his finger. "So they each will court you, to try to get you to pick them."

I snorted softly, and he smiled.

"So, in the morning . . ." I prompted.

"Keekai will come for you. You will be removed from my protection, and taken under hers. She will ask if I have provided for you, and brought you to the Plains safely. She will ask if you wish to return to Xy, or go the Heart to face the Council. She will offer to allow you a Guardian, someone that you trust to go with you. It is not required, and no, you cannot ask for me."

I closed my mouth with a snap.

Keir tugged the curl. "Either Rafe or Prest would be

rewarded that way, for it is an honor to conduct the Warprize to the Heart." He growled slightly. "Normally, it is less than a day's journey, from the Warlord's camp to the Council tent."

"You trust Keekai." It was a question and a reminder.

"I do." Keir nodded. "She has great status and authority, and she will watch over you like a cat for its kits." He sighed again. "But I do not like this. I am trying to bring change to my people, Lara, and change is rarely bloodless."

I shivered at his words, then crawled into his arms, and placed my head on his chest. "I have to tell you the truth, Keir. I'm afraid." His arms tightened around me, and I shivered in his arms. "Marcus said that I have to—"

"Face your fear." Keir's voice was a soft whisper in my ear. "Easy to say, eh?"

I nodded, and hugged him closer. His breathing hitched slightly, and I lifted my head. "Keir? Am I too heavy?"

"No." He carded his fingers through my hair. "It's a comfort, to feel you next to me, skin to skin."

I smiled, and lowered my head to his chest and closed my eyes. I took a deep breath, taking in the scents of our tent, and the spicy smell of his skin. The warmth we shared beneath the blankets was one of those quiet pleasures that I didn't really appreciate until it was to be taken from me.

"I will tell you a truth, Lara." Keir's voice was soft. "I felt fear for the second time in my life as I lay ill. To have my body weaken that way, unable to move or aid myself." He shuddered beneath me. "I hope to never face that again. Now I know what I asked Marcus to deal with when he was injured, and I wonder that he didn't find a weapon and kill us both."

"Second time?" I lifted my head to look into his eyes. "When was the first? Your first battle?"

"Oh no." His voice was the barest of whispers. "I am trained for combat, my heart's fire." He shifted, moving us to our sides under the furs. "I have been angry and frustrated in battle, but not afraid. No, I swear to you that sitting beside you, terrified that every breath you drew would be your last, not knowing if you would live or die, and helpless to aid you—"

His words broke off, his pain so clear in his voice and eyes. I kissed him then, pressed soft kisses against his lips, his eyes, and his mouth. "I'm here, Keir. Alive and well."

"Never have the skies been so dark, never have I been so afraid." Keir pressed his forehead to mine. "And now I must watch you ride away with Keekai, to face the Council alone."

I lifted my head away, and stroked his cheek. "It will help that she looks so much like you. Could she be your mother?"

"The one who bore me?" Keir shrugged, and I knew he didn't see how that could be important. In Water's Fall, Atira had told me that the women of the Plains did not raise the children they bore.

Keir continued. "She is of my tribe, and a strong mentor and supporter, both as thea and as tribal elder and council member. You can trust her, Lara, as you trust me."

Bittersweet words. Keir and I had learned a hard lesson in Wellspring, about trusting in each other. Keir had said that trust could only be mended with time and deeds on both our parts. We'd sworn ourselves to each other, forever, with a new understanding of what that really meant.

I lifted my hands to press them to his cheek. "Keekai said that we would travel slowly. You will come as fast as you can. A few days, Keir. That's all." I smiled at him, through my tears. "I will tell them my truths and they will know that I claim you and only you as my Warlord."

"Lara." Keir kissed me then, with a hunger that I felt through my whole body. I surrendered to him, letting him ease his body over mine until he pressed me to the bed. My breath shuddered through my body as our passion rose between us.

Keir broke the kiss, hovering over me, his eyes glittering. I spread my hands over his chest, and brushed his nipples with the tips of my fingers. "Make me believe that the sun will not rise, my Warlord."

Keir crushed his lips to mine.

And in his arms, throughout the night, he almost convinced me.

Despite our efforts, morning dawned clear and cold.

A crowd had gathered before our tent, since word of my departure had spread during the night. I stood in the cleared area, with my bodyguards around me. Keir was off to the side, with Yers and the other warleaders. Iften was there, standing slightly apart, a smirk on his face, two of the warrior-priests at his side. I still couldn't tell them apart, except that both of them were male.

Keekai entered the cleared area, dressed in armor and looking so much like Keir that it took my breath away.

"Xylara, Daughter of Xy, from the Kingdom of Xy, you have been claimed as Warprize by Keir of the Cat, Warlord of the Plains." Keekai's voice carried to the crowd that had gathered around the dance area. I could tell that she was concentrating on her words, changing them to fit the setting. "He has brought you to the Plains, so that you may go the Heart of these lands and be confirmed as the Warprize. Have you taken anything from the hands of another on this journey?"

"I have not." I had to swallow to get the words out.

"Has he provided for you?"

"He has." My voice sounded stronger than I felt, which was good, since my stomach was filled with fluttering moths.

"I am Keekai of the Cat, Council Elder. I've been sent by the Council to escort you to the Heart of the Plains." Keekai held out her hand. "Step out from the protection of the Warlord, Xylara."

I walked forward, passing between Prest and Rafe, to stand alone before Keekai. I almost felt naked, I was so used to having my guards at my side.

"You are now under my protection, Xylara." Keekai placed a hand on the pommel of her sword. "Keir of the Cat cannot command your obedience or your actions. Do you understand?"

"I do," I said.

"A true Warprize is a rare thing. A Warprize represents chaos and upheaval. New thoughts, new ideas, and change. If confirmed by the Council of Elders, you will hold equal status with the warlords, and a place on the Council itself." Keekai looked out over the people gathered around us. "But to be an instrument of change is not an easy thing. Dangerous, even." She looked back at me and tilted her head to the side. "As the Plains themselves are a dangerous place."

I swallowed, but I held her stare.

"Do you understand, Xylara?" Keekai asked.

She wasn't telling me anything that I hadn't already heard. Still, it took me a moment to answer. "I do, Keekai."

"So." She paused, then continued. "I would ask you—do you wish to go to the Heart of the Plains to be confirmed by the Council as Warprize? Or do you wish to return to your land, to the arms of your people, to your home?" Keekai paused again to consider me closely. "None can force your decision. Speak, and it will be as you wish."

That was it, the offer of freedom. If I asked, I would be escorted back to Water's Fall, back to the arms of my loved ones.

Keekai's eyes were grim. "Understand what you do, Xylara, Daughter of Xy. You step into our world now, into our ways. A land unknown to you. Do you truly wish to leave what you have always known, for the unknown?"

She had sensed my fear. But the Plains were open and wide and something called to me to answer this challenge, and it wasn't just the love I felt for Keir. This was a chance to help my people and his. I turned my head to look at him, standing in the sun, wearing his chainmail, his arms crossed over his chest, a grim look on his face. But his eyes, they held the promise of all our tomorrows.

I turned back to face Keekai. I could feel the eyes of all the warriors on me, but I had no doubts as to my answer. "I wish to go to the Heart of the Plains, there to claim my Warlord."

Keekai's eyes were warm as the crowd parted to reveal Marcus leading Greatheart and a pack animal with supplies. Marcus came to stand just behind Keekai, hidden in his cloak.

Keekai spoke. "The Warlord has provided for your journey, Xylara."

"And did he provide that on her hip?" It was Still Waters, I think, or at least one of the warrior-priests standing by Iften. He was pointing at my satchel.

"Bought and paid for by my hand, in the city of Water's Fall." Keir voice was a low snarl, just this side of polite.

Still Waters sniffed, but said nothing more.

Keekai turned back to me. "Xylara, you have the right to a Guardian on this journey, one warrior familiar to you, to stand at your back, to see you safely to the Heart of the Plains. Would you have a Guardian?"

"I would." That caused a bit of a stir. Prest and Rafe exchanged glances and I could tell that they were pleased that one of them would be chosen. I was sorry to have to disappoint them.

"Who would you choose as Guardian?" Keekai asked.

I took a deep breath. "I choose Marcus."

The crowd around us exploded in anger.

6

I'd known, of course, that Marcus was considered to be less than whole because of his injuries. Never mind that he still held his knowledge or skills. But Keir accepted him, and the others that I'd seen interact with Marcus did as well. I'd thought that Marcus was accepted by the majority of the warriors.

I was wrong.

From the crowd's glittering eyes and angry faces, it was clear that his disfigurement condemned him. To their way of thinking, he wasn't even a person.

I gritted my teeth in the face of their anger and repeated my words. "I choose Marcus of the—" I paused, unable to remember his tribe. "Marcus. I choose Marcus as my Guardian."

"She honors a cripple!" Iften exclaimed, and everyone started talking at once.

Marcus stood silent amidst the uproar, his eyes

down. Only the white of his knuckles where he held Greatheart's reins gave away his feelings.

Keekai's voice cut through the rumble. Her face was neutral, but her eyes were sharp and hard. "Xylara. You are of a different land, and your ways are not ours." She gave Marcus a quick glance, then her gaze returned to me. "Your words are strange, you speak in a different tongue and this may cause confusion. The one you refer to is not—" She paused, as if looking for a word. "He is not eligible for this position. This honor."

"She mocks the elements and our ways," Iften snarled, looking around at the warriors. Heads nodded in agreement.

"Marcus saved my life twice with his weapons and his care," I snapped, letting my voice rise with my temper. "Without him, I would not stand here. How can he not be worthy?"

Voices arose, as angry warriors expressed their fury. And fury it was. I'd gone too far. Keekai called for silence not once, but three times, with no success.

As she tried to get control of the situation, Keir caught my eye. He was standing there, silent, his arms crossed over his chest. His expression was sympathetic, but he gave me a slight shake of his head. If Keir didn't think I should push this issue . . .

Marcus moved, dropping Greatheart's reins, and knelt at my feet.

The voices all cut off as his cloak settled down around him. In the silence he reached out and took my hand. "You honor me, Warprize, and I thank you. But choose another."

"Marcus." My shoulders slumped as I whispered to him. "I want you with me."

He looked up then, his eye glittering in the shadow of his hood, and whispered back. "I wish to go with you. To see you safe. But do not deny the truth of what is, for what you wish to be." His voice rose. "Any warrior you choose is honor bound to see you safe to the Heart of the Plains, Warprize. Do not fear."

I didn't want to choose another, Goddess knew, and I pressed my lips together to try to control my anger. It wasn't right. It wasn't fair.

But the look in Marcus's eye told me that I had to accept it. At least, for now. I nodded and released his hand. "I withdraw my choice."

Marcus rose, and pulled his cloak in to make sure that it covered him completely. He stepped back to his position by Greatheart. The warriors around us were settling down, the warrior-priests all grim and daunting. But Iften, Iften had that smug look on his face, as if all was going well in his world. I narrowed my eyes at that moment, and the obvious choice leaped to mind.

Keekai had her silence, and she turned back to me. "You may choose another, if you wish."

"I wish." I smiled sweetly. My voice must have given my intentions away because both Keir and Marcus stiffened. Keekai noted their reaction, and gave me a searching look. "Who do you choose?"

I stood there, staring over her head for just a moment, letting the tension build. Then I smiled at Keekai. "I choose Iften of the Boar."

That wiped the smirk off his face. Iften gaped like a fish, his face turning red. Everyone else looked at me with the same expression of astonishment.

I stood, outwardly calm, even though my heart raced in my chest. Afraid that I would burst out laughing, I held my breath and waited for an outcry.

But the only sound was the wind in the grass, and Greatheart's soft snores. Everyone around me stood in stunned silence, then all eyes shifted to Iften's face. Voices rose around us, but I turned my gaze to Keir.

He was furious, with that vein throbbing in his forehead, and those vibrant blue eyes pierced through me with their fury. I just looked at him, unable to go to his side and explain. '*Think about it, beloved.*'

Then his eyes grew thoughtful, and I knew that he was seeing some of the advantages that I saw. His eyes flicked to Iften, still struggling with the idea, and his mouth quirked slightly. When his gaze shifted back to me, the look he gave me was one of exasperation. '*I trust you, but you might have warned me.*'

I shrugged, and smiled at him. I'd have warned him if I'd thought of it before this moment.

"So. Iften of the Boar." Keekai's voice held a very formal and rather satisfied tone. "What say you?"

Iften's eyes darted around, from me to Keekai, to Keir, and then to the warrior-priests. I'd never seen him at a loss before.

It felt good.

"Iften." Keekai's voice was now impatient. "You have been offered the honor of Guardian to the Warprize. How say you?"

Iften's face was dark, his gaze coming to rest hard on mine. The hate was almost a physical blow. "I accept."

"Do you pledge to keep the Warprize safe and see her unharmed to the Council of the Elders at the Heart of the Plains?" Keekai pressed the point, more for Keir's benefit than mine.

Iften put his shoulders back. He'd recovered a bit, and the accustomed sneer was back in his voice when he spoke "I do."

Keekai nodded. "Then gather your gear. We depart when you are read—"

"Elder." Keir spoke, interrupting her.

"What now?" Keekai snapped.

"I'd ask that Joden of the Hawk go with you to the Heart. He should return quickly, so that he may be tested as a Singer." Keir's voice was bland, as if it meant nothing to him either way, but I knew he wanted someone he trusted with me on the journey.

Keekai gave him a considering look, and turned to speak to Joden, but once again, she was interrupted.

"No." One of the warrior-priests spoke. It might have been Still Waters, but it was hard to tell. "That one denied mercy and must answer for it."

Joden had kept his face neutral, but his eyes narrowed at that point. But Keekai was already shaking her head. "My goal is the Warprize, and no other. Joden must make his own way, in his own time."

"But—" Keir pressed his point, but Keekai would have none of it.

"No, Warlord." She cut him off with a simple gesture of her hand. She turned a bit, to look at the warriors that had gathered around us. She scowled. "And don't you all have four ehats to render? Off with you!"

The crowd broke up, warriors scattering off to their tasks. Iften headed to his tent with a warrior-priest, both deep in conversation. Keir moved over to talk to Marcus, and they spoke in low tones. Joden and Yers had stayed behind, along with my four guards. Rafe had a faintly offended look. I caught his eyes and shrugged an apology. He looked at me for a moment, and then his smile lit his face and he shrugged back. I was forgiven.

Marcus came toward me, leaving Keir to stand alone. He pulled Greatheart along, with a snort of protest from the horse. Without hesitation, he stepped between my warrior-priest guards and handed me the reins. Keekai turned her head to look, but didn't object. My new warrior-priest guards didn't even bother to look at him.

Greatheart immediately started snuffing at my hair happily. I reached over to scratch him on his chest, just over his scar.

"Hisself says to say he is not certain this is wise. Do not leave Keekai's side," Marcus spoke softly as he adjusted Greatheart's harness.

"I won't."

"I say you do this so as to look at that one's injury, yes?" Marcus's one eye gleamed bright.

I choked back a laugh, and reached out to put my hand on his arm. "I wish—"

Marcus shook his head. "It cannot be. But you have brightened my skies, Lara." He took my hand, and shoved the sleeve of my tunic up my arm. He was shielding our movements with his body and cloak.

"Marcus?"

With swift fingers, he strapped something to my arm. It took me a moment, but I recognized it. It was the knife that Heath had been given by Xymund—the knife he had been told to kill me with.

"You release it so, and it is in your hand." Marcus demonstrated quickly, then reset the blade and pulled my sleeve down. "Tell no one. Practice when you can."

I nodded, unable to speak. The noises around us told me that Iften was returning. "Keep him safe for me, Marcus," I begged.

"See to yourself, Lara," came the gruff answer, and Marcus turned to go. Iften was coming up, leading a horse with saddle and packs, his cloak over his arm. Marcus stepped in close and deliberately walked into Iften, knocking into his shoulder. "Be sure that you keep her safe, *cripple*," Marcus hissed.

Iften snarled, fumbling for his sword, but Marcus had already moved past.

In the midst of all of this, I looked through the bodies and the horses to see Keir, standing tall and silent, watching me. I looked over to where Keekai was about to mount. "Keekai?"

She turned and looked at me.

"May I say goodbye to Keir?"

"No." That from a warrior-priest mounted nearby. "It is forbidden."

"Pah," Keekai mocked. "As if her mind can be changed with a simple farewell." She jerked her head in Keir's direction, which I took as permission. My warrior-priest guards moved with me, as I walked the short distance to his side.

Keir stepped forward and I went into his arms willingly, wrapped in their warmth and security. I rested my head on his chest above his heart, and drew a deep breath. For one long, wonderful moment, I was safe in his arms, and the world around us vanished.

I felt Keir draw in a breath as well, and knew he felt the same. I hugged him close, trying to commit the moment to memory, waiting for his arms to fall away. But they didn't. They tightened instead, as if he'd hold me forever.

He couldn't let me go.

I lifted my head, to see the doubt, worry, and fear in his bright blue eyes. I hesitated, and Keir's eyes changed, as if he'd made a decision of his own. His arms released me, and I knew in another moment, he'd pull his swords and refuse to let me go.

I couldn't let him do that. It had to be my decision, my choice.

I shook my head slightly, and he paused. Silently, he stood and waited.

I went up on my toes, and pressed a kiss to the side of his mouth. Then I stepped back slightly, tucking myself under his shoulder, releasing him with my right hand.

Keir looked down as I took his left hand in mine, and lifted it, to entwine our fingers together, our hands at the level of our chests. I happened to catch Joden looking at us intently from the crowd, but I ignored him and everyone else.

Keir lowered his head to bury his face in my hair. "Are you certain, Lara?"

"For our people. For us," I whispered fiercely.

"For us," was his soft reply.

But still, he could not let me go. So I smiled gently, and slipped from beneath his arm, from the safety of his strength, turned and mounted Greatheart. I settled myself in the saddle, and faced the horizon.

"Keir, you should have said that she cannot ride." Keekai's voice rose behind me, and I stifled a laugh that was more of a sob. I didn't look back as I urged my sleepy brown horse into a gallop. With a snort, Greatheart launched himself forward.

It took but a moment, then Keekai and the warrior-priests were beside me, galloping alongside, steering me in the right direction. Which was just as well.

I couldn't see anything through my tears.

"So," Keekai drew the word out. I looked across the brazier to see her bright blue eyes alight with curiosity.

We'd traveled for most of the day, leaving Keir and the army behind, alternating our pace between a walk and a trot. As exposed as the Plains made me feel, they weren't truly flat. But at a distance, the gradual rises and hollows were hidden to the eye. Still, the lack of trees, of something between me and the horizon, was unsettling.

We'd covered a great deal of distance, but Keekai had called a halt well before the sun had neared the horizon, much to the dismay of the warrior-priests.

We were seated in her tent, a brazier glowing between us. Keekai had two warriors who took care of her tent, gear, and meals—Regular warriors, and I was thankful for that. I'd had my fair share of being glared at by tattooed warrior-priests all day.

"So. We've heat and kavage, and bells at the flap. You know what the bells mean?" Keekai asked.

"That we wish to be private." Keekai's tent was smaller than Keir's, but it was comfortable. Certainly it was warm enough. I was sweating under my tunic. Keekai wasn't though. She had a blanket over her lap, and another over her shoulders.

"So. Why Iften?" Her face was intent and curious.

I hesitated for a moment, but Keir had said that she could be trusted. So I smiled at her. "We have a saying in Xy. 'You can kill a cat with cream'."

Keekai laughed.

Iften had ridden next to me the entire day, apparently taking his duties seriously. He'd constantly scanned the horizon for trouble, but never once bothered to speak to me.

Which was fine with me. I used the time to get a good look at his arm and fingers.

Sure enough, they were swollen, and had a lifeless, curled look about them. The skin was too pale, stretched thin over the puffy flesh. He was handling the reins, but I knew what was happening. He was using those leather bracers to try to splint the arm, never mind that one needed to set the bone. He was going to lose the use of the arm. By his own choice. I'd offered aid, but he'd rejected my healing skills, publicly and privately.

Still . . .

"It got Iften away from the army," I continued. "And it allows Keir to talk to his warriors without Iften's subtle talk against him. Iften has his own sense of honor, one that will not permit him to do anything other than see me safely to the Heart of the Plains."

"It also gave him a chance to spread his truths in the Heart, Lara." Keekai shrugged. "Only the skies can say if it was wise or not. And that troublemaker Gathering Storm still remained with Keir."

"Who?" I asked.

"The warrior-priest that was with Iften when I arrived," Keekai answered. "He is called Gathering Storm, and well named, since storms arise wherever he goes." Keekai got a sly gin on her face. "But well worth it to see Iften's smirk wiped away, eh?"

I laughed, and nodded my head in agreement. But then I leaned forward, to ask the question that had bothered me all day. "Keekai, are you Keir's mother?"

"Mother?" Keekai asked with a frown. "One who bears a child?" At my nod, she shrugged, the blanket sliding down her shoulder. Her eyes dropped down to the fabric, but not before I saw pain in her eyes. "How would I know? My teats were always dry at the birthing, and the babes given to another to suckle as soon as they popped out. He is of my tribe, that is certain." She pulled the blanket up around her. "This is important to you? To your people?"

I gave her a nod, still caught up in the differences between our worlds.

"How different we are," echoing my own thoughts, Keekai continued. "Yet we share the same skies." She shook her head, and set her mug aside. "We will talk, you and I, as we go. I have so many questions that I wish to ask, I don't even know where to start. But there is time. We will sleep on it." Her grin flashed. "Besides, Still Waters will have us up at the break of dawn." She stood and reached for my mug. "Best that we sleep together, you and I. Iften has his own honor, but let's not test it too far, eh?" She headed for the tent flap. "I've been told you Xyians have privacy about your bodies. I'll leave so that you may prepare for sleep."

I thanked her, and took advantage of her courtesy to

strip down and climb into my bedding. I also stripped off the knife harness and tucked it deep into my satchel.

Keekai returned within moments, and set about laying out her weapons within reach and preparing her pallet for sleep. Safe under my bedding and fur, I listened as her breathing slowed. It was only then that I could really think about what had happened this day: the anger of the warriors at the attempt to honor Marcus; the look on Iften's face when I asked for him as Guardian; the feel of Keir's arms around me, and the look in his eyes as I'd slid from his grasp.

Something crackled in the brazier and I shifted under the bedding and sighed. Keir would be about his business and come after me as fast as he could.

But oh, how I missed him. I missed his being there, his soft breathing, his warmth. Somehow Keekai's soft snores just weren't the same. And not just his physical presence in my bed. There were a hundred things I wanted to tell him or talk over with him. To laugh with him over Iften's reaction. To debate my choice of Guardian.

I yawned, thankful for the tiredness that washed over me. My bedding had been packed by Marcus, and I snuggled down, trying to convince myself that Keir's scent was still in the blankets, and the fur that lay on top of me. I closed my eyes and allowed myself to drift off to sleep. *Goddess, keep watch over Keir and keep him safe, wherever he is.*

The next few days were filled with much the same routine. We'd break camp at the earliest that the horses could travel, and then journey until Keekai called a break at the nooning. Then we rode again until she called to make camp. With the riding that I'd done before with Keir, it was no trouble to stay in the saddle for so long. Iften stayed by my side, and Keekai never let me out of her sight. There was a definite lack of conversation, but I spent my time wondering at the land around us.

It seemed to spread out before us forever, with nothing but the flat grasslands and the never ending sky. The grass was still afire, extending out in a thick carpet of reds, oranges, and golds. The sheer immensity of it took my breath away, and I found myself looking down into the grass below me just to keep my sense of balance.

As we rode, Keekai would sometimes move close and we would talk. But we were very conscious of our listeners, and so our topics were of Xy, and how we lived. Keekai was fascinated by stone tents, and city life.

But at night, each of us on our pallet, the brazier burning between us, she'd focus those bright blue eyes on me and ask deeper questions. "All I know of you is what is whispered on the winds," she said, her eyes bright. "What makes a city-dweller leave her lands to venture onto the Plains?"

So I told her, about the war and the tents of healing and Simus's wound and Keir. She listened intently, occasionally asking a question or two, but mostly listening, her eyes sparkling with her interest. She didn't criticize, or condemn, just listened. I talked about Anna the cook, and the kitchens under her control, of my Master Eln, and how he'd taught me everything I know. I even described the old cheesemaker and her cart in the market back in Water's Fall.

"Which reminds me." I dug around in my satchel. "I have a jar of joint cream here. It might help your hands."

"Eh?" Keekai leaned forward and reached across for the jar, settling back into her blankets as she looked at it carefully. "Some of your magic?"

I shook my head. "I don't have any magic, Keekai. Just herbs and knowledge of their uses."

Keekai sniffed at the contents, then looked at me with half-closed eyes. "So, you claim no magic?"

"None," I said firmly.

She grunted, dipped into the jar, and started to work the salve into her hands. We sat in silence for a moment, the flames in the brazier crackling. I looked up where there was a smoke hole cut in the tent, and saw the stars above us. It was late.

"I thank you." Keekai made as if to return the jar, but I gestured for her to keep it.

"I hope that it will help." I looked at her for a moment, then bit my lip.

She snorted, softly. "Do you wish for my token?"

"I might need it," I responded. "Keekai, why does Keir hate the warrior-priests so much?"

Keekai sighed. "That is a long tale, and not easily told." She yawned. "Still Waters will have us up at dawn yet again. But this time I will stop us at the nooning and tell him that a hunt is needed." She cackled. "They will hunt, and you and I will talk." She rose to give me privacy.

I shook my head at her. "What kind of name is that? And how can you tell them apart?"

She wrinkled her nose. 'When they become warrior-priests, they take on a new name, not the one that the elements gave them, but a name to signal that they are warrior-priests." She snorted again, reminding me of Marcus. "They take them from the plants and animals or the elements. Still Waters, Gentle Breeze, pah. Why not Dead Deer, or Rutting Ehat?"

I laughed out loud at that, and she grinned back at me. "As to telling them apart, look at the tattoos around their left eyes. There the pattern always differs." She raised the flap of the tent. "Get into your bedding and close those eyes, Lara. The sun will be up before we wish it."

Still Waters had us up even before the sun rose.

I stood, holding Greatheart's reins, sipping kavage as the camp was broken. Keekai was talking to one of the warrior-priests, announcing her craving for fresh red meat.

I ignored it, and watched the sun rise. Truly rise, on a horizon as wide as my eyes could see, seeming almost to leap up into the sky.

No wonder these people worshiped the elements, and swore by the skies. It was such an enormous part of their lives, affecting everything that they did, every moment of the day. Living in a castle, in a city, I was not attuned to it the way they were. I watched in awe, and wondered. What would a storm be like? What would winter be like?

My stomach tightened. It was all so new and frightening. I gazed out at the horizon, and wished for some nice, safe mountains to cut the openness. I felt so exposed. . . .

"As frightening as a land where one is constantly surrounded by huge mountains of stone that restrict your sight and block the sun." Keir's words came back to me, and I smiled. Was he watching the sunrise? Or hassling his warriors to work faster so that he could follow us?

I had to chuckle, since both Keir and Marcus were probably driving everyone around them to work as fast as possible. Goddess knew, Marcus would drive them hard.

I turned a bit, letting Greatheart shield me from the others, and tried the hidden blade. I'd used the privacy of Keekai's tent to strap it on. I jumped when it popped out and tried to clasp it tight in my hand. It would take practice to get it to work right. I pressed it back in as I heard someone come up behind me.

"Mount." It was Iften, leading his horse, his usual morning scowl on his face. I rolled my eyes, and then turned, but he must have seen my face. His lip curled, and he spit at my feet. A small piece of something brown hit my shoe.

I opened my mouth to protest, but he'd turned away, and my warrior-priest guards were moving into position. In the confusion, I reached down, scooped whatever it was, and tucked it into my satchel.

We'd see what the warrior-priests' 'magic' consisted of. We'd just see . . .

7

"Blind hatred is a weakness."

I said nothing, just watched as Keekai reached from her pallet to add fuel to the brazier. The flames rose and made the light flicker and dance over the walls of her tent.

She'd called a halt before the nooning and ordered a hunt for fresh meat. The camp was guarded, and Iften was roaming the perimeter, keeping watch over me from a distance. Keekai had us warm in her tent, bells in the flap, and a pot of kavage between us. Her warriors were without, with instructions to make sure that no one came near. We were as private as we could be on the Plains.

It was just as well she'd ordered that we make camp early. We'd ridden into a fine mist of rain, and the damp and the cold had seeped into my bones. I could imagine what it did to Keekai's body.

"I do not know the truth of all that has been, and can only speak the truth that I know." Keekai looked at me from her nest of blankets. "You understand?"

I nodded, unwilling to interrupt.

"I am no Singer, but you must know of the past before I can say more." Keekai rubbed her knees beneath the covers. "Long ago, a Warlord claimed the first Warprize. Together, they united all the tribes of the Plains. They created the Council of Elders as the wisdom of the Plains, the Singers as the knowledge, the Theas as the spirit. The Warrior-priests were supposed to be its strength."

Keekai sighed deeply and her shoulders slumped under the blankets. "It worked well, for a time. But something happened. The warrior-priests began to claim to speak for the elements, to have magic that they alone wielded."

Keekai paused, adjusting her blankets, and I poured us both more kavage. She pulled her hands out and held the mug in her blanket-covered lap.

"Now, Keir has always had the strength of a warrior. But he also has a heart, a caring for his people. It hurts him to see people suffer, and it infuriates him to see one in pain and another stand by and do nothing."

"Is that what the warrior-priests do?"

Keekai nodded. "They only use their magic on those they decide are worthy." She fixed me with an intent stare, as if trying to find the right words. "With Keir, the reason for his anger," she hesitated, "there was a woman—"

My heart froze in my throat. My face must have reflected my feelings, for Keekai stopped and frowned. "No, not a binding. A young woman raised beside him, eh? Of his tribe. Do you understand?"

"Like a sister?"

Keekai looked puzzled. "I do not know this word." I explained, and her face cleared. "Yes, yes. One does not lie down with a member of one's tribe. We track the blood of all, to insure strength in the children." Keekai pulled the blankets off her shoulder to show me her tattoos. "We do not mate or bond with the tribes of the ones that made us."

"Yes." I relaxed. "I understand."

"So." Keekai adjusted her blankets again, pulling them up and over her shoulders. "There was a woman of his tribe, who was bearing her first. It did not go well, and the woman died. I think, in the end, she was given mercy.

"Keir was enraged, for a warrior-priest refused to use his magic to aid her." Keekai looked over my shoulder, staring into the past. "Marcus had him dragged off and restrained, lest he challenge every warrior-priest and die in trying to kill them all. Keir saw reason. Eventually. But he vowed to destroy them." Keekai stopped, and took a drink of kavage, then set the mug down. "Destroy them all." She shook her head. "His hatred blinds him to his danger. And yours."

"And Marcus?" I asked. "What did the warrior-priests do when he was injured?"

She grimaced. "I was not there, but this truth I know, that it only added fuel to Keir's rage. Keir commanded Marcus to live, and Marcus obeyed."

"What is Marcus's tribe, Keekai?"

"Marcus has no tribe, Lara." Keekai's eyes were filled with sorrow.

I sucked in my breath.

She nodded. "I did not think you truly understood what you did, choosing him as Guardian. Marcus is no longer of a tribe, no longer of the Plains."

I chewed my lower lip, trying to remember. "When I first met Marcus, he said that he was 'token-bearer and aide to the Warlord'."

Keekai's face grew grim. "That is all he is. If not for Keir's protection . . ."

"Marcus would die," I finished.

Keekai nodded. "Just so. By his own hand, like as not."

I stared into my kavage. "That is not right."

"Life on the Plains is hard." Her voice sounded so much like Marcus's, I lifted my head, almost expecting his eye to be glaring at me. But instead, Keekai's blue eyes blazed at me, sending shivers down my spine. "Harder than you know," she continued. "For hear now the truth that the Elders know, and will not speak of. The People of the Plains are dying."

I sat upright, and sloshed my kavage in my lap. "Why?"

"We do not know why. Warriors in battle, that is to be expected. But there are more deaths during the snows, more women are dying in childbirth. Worse, our babes are dying without reason. Half the children born do not see the first true blades."

"Keekai, that's—" I swallowed hard. "Children do die, of fevers and accidents and the like, but not at that rate."

She nodded again, still grim. "None outside the Council know this, although I think that Keir has come to his own understanding of our plight. When he was named Warlord this spring, the lots awarded him Xy. He stood before all, the Elders and the Eldest, and announced that he would conquer Xy. With the intent of learning and absorbing their ways and knowledge." A grin flashed over her face, so much like Keir my heart skipped a beat. "So imagine their faces when word comes on the wind that

Keir of the Cat had claimed a Warprize, one who holds a healing magic of her own. The news rolled like a storm over the Plains." Keekai's arm emerged from the blankets to sweep the air before her.

I smiled back in answer to her grin, but then I remembered something that Keir had said. "Keekai, what is a 'Warking'?"

Her eyes narrowed. "Now, where would you have heard that word?"

I licked my lips, my mouth suddenly dry. Keir had said to trust her, but had I said too much? Regardless, the goats were out the gate now, and eating corn. "From Keir. He was ill and raving when he spoke the word." Even now I could see him, in my mind's eye, fighting the restraints and howling. *'Fear the day Keir of the Cat is named Warking!'*

"Raving?" Keekai asked.

"Like the battle madness," I responded, not wanting to have to give a lengthy explanation.

"Ah." She tilted her head to the side, and studied me. "Not a word to use lightly. Nor would I say it outside the bells. I am not surprised to hear that Keir's thoughts move in that direction now."

I waited, nervous.

"A Warking is a warrior that stands above all, even the Council." Keekai rubbed a finger over her eye. "There have been only two in the past, who rose when we of the Plains faced dire threats."

"You think Keir intends to become one?" I asked.

"I do not pretend to know that one's truths." Keekai was deadly serious, her eyes never leaving mine. "But speak of this only to him and to Marcus. You understand?"

"I do," I answered quietly.

Keekai shook her head again, as if in despair. "I have told that fool of a warlord that blind hatred of the warrior-priests is a dangerous thing. But that one, he is stubborn. Knows what he wants, and gets it."

I blushed and looked away, knowing that trait in Keir very well.

Very well indeed.

The hunters returned, with an odd looking deer that they soon had spitted and roasting. Keekai and I emerged to hear the tale of the hunt.

The warrior-priests seemed no different from the other warriors in their excitement over the hunt and the kill. I watched closely, trying to see the differences in the details of the tattoos.

Iften, grim and brooding, wasn't far away. He'd seated himself off with a group of older warrior-priests, and he was talking. From the glances that came my way, he was spilling his hatred into their ears.

I gritted my teeth, and tried not to think of going over and spitting on his shoes. I reminded myself that it would be mean-spirited. That it would bring me down to his level.

That it would feel really good.

"We spotted some warriors of the Plains when we returned from the hunt." One of the warrior-priests was talking to Keekai. "They kept their distance, followed us for a time, then disappeared over a ridge."

"They didn't identify themselves?" Keekai asked.

"No, Elder."

"Odd," Keekai said.

Still Waters was beside her. "Not so odd these days. The old ways of the plains, the courtesy of the land and of the tents, is gone."

Keekai shot him a look. "Or perhaps they thought warrior-priests would not welcome an intrusion. Still, it is unusual."

A grunt from Still Waters was the only response.

* * *

"A belly-full of meat, and kavage." Keekai sat on her pallet and patted her stomach. "Well worth the stop, eh?"

I nodded, drinking the last bit of kavage from my cup.

"And look." Keekai raised her hand into the air, and flexed her fingers for me to see. "The stiffness eases."

"Good." I smiled, pleased at the relief the salve gave her. Stiff joints and crooked fingers could be a source of terrible pain to the old. "Keekai, how old are you?"

"Eh?" she asked, tucking herself into the blankets.

"How many years do you have?"

"You count years?" Keekai looked at me as if I had grown horns.

I clenched my teeth. Honestly, how did these people manage? I thought for a moment. "How long did it take you to have your children?"

There was an odd look of remembered pain, but her voice was light when she answered. "Popped them out one after the other after my moon times came upon me."

"Were you late getting your courses?"

"Moon times?" She shrugged. "They came when they came."

"How many campaigns have you served in?"

Keekai's face lit with pleasure. "My first was under Rize of the Hawk. . . ." She proceeded to use that memory of hers to detail her military history. I counted out the campaigns, figuring that would come close to a year if the armies were disbanded before each winter.

"Then I became an Elder, and I have served to select the warlords seven times since then."

I blinked, rechecked my figuring, and then looked at her in shock. Keekai wasn't nearly as old as I thought she was.

She tilted her head to the side. "Your curiosity is satisfied?" She took my silence as such. "Then we must sleep. Still Waters will insist on an early start to-morrow, and I doubt he'll agree to a halt until the sun is down!"

I stretched out under the blankets, listened to Keekai's breathing, and thought about what I had learned.

Life on the Plains was hard. I knew that, or at least, I'd thought I'd known what that meant. But I didn't, not really. I'd had all the comforts of city life, plus the advantages of living in a castle. I didn't have a daily struggle for food and warmth, things I took for granted. But on the Plains, life itself was hard, harder on the body. Which meant that Keir wasn't as old as I'd thought. Perhaps we were closer in age than I'd realized?

I turned onto my side, and pulled the covers up over my shoulder. The brazier was not putting out as much heat now, and the air felt colder. A slight breeze moved the side of the tent, and if I turned my head and looked up, I could see the stars through the smoke hole. I shifted deeper into the warmth of my bed.

Did they live in tents in the snow? How did they find food in the winter? Even with raiding, how could they have enough?

What did bearing five children do to a woman's body?

Suddenly, I understood the depths of Keir's desire to bring change to the Plains. And just how valuable he thought my skills were. But even more than that, how pleased he'd been that I'd treat any that came to me. Tend the wound of an enemy. Set the broken leg of another.

A snort from the other side told me that Keekai was finally asleep. I reached out my hand and pulled my satchel closer. Quietly, so as not to awaken Keekai, I dug in a side pocket and took out the damp piece of something that Iften had spit on my shoe. There was just enough light for me to study it. A mushroom, that

I was certain. I smelled it carefully, but it didn't have a strong odor. I rubbed it on my skin and waited, but there was no effect. I shrugged. Only one way to know for sure. I put it in my mouth and bit down.

An odd sweetish taste filled my mouth, and I swallowed. My heartbeat seemed louder, and the tent began to spin . . .

I spat it out into my hand. A medicine, akin to lotus leaf, but far more powerful and fast acting then any I knew. If it had this effect after Iften had chewed it for a time, what would it be like fresh? What uses could I put it to?

I studied the damp bit in my hand, then placed it back in my satchel. Maybe the light of day would let me determine which mushroom.

I settled back down, lost in thought. Was that the power of the warrior-priests? Using herbs to mask the pain, instead of treating it? No wonder Iften could still use his hand. No wonder they refused to help, probably where pain drugs offered no help.

Even in the warmth of my blankets, I shivered. How would the warrior-priests react to true, skilled healing? What would they do to Keir?

I slept, eventually. But my sleep was uneasy and filled with vague, fretful dreams.

Keekai and I were finishing our morning kavage when Still Waters asked to enter the tent.

"Would you have kavage?" Keekai offered. "Would you sit by my fire?"

"Thank you, but no," Still Waters declined with a shake of his head, setting his long, matted braids to swaying. He remained standing just inside, stooped a bit so that his head didn't touch the tent. "During the night, the guards spotted a group of riders watching the camp. Two went out to offer the warmth of our fires, but the strangers rode off as they were approached."

Keekai frowned. "The courtesy of the Plains is not that dead."

Still Waters grunted his agreement. His face remained neutral, but his voice was condescending. "Had we traveled faster—"

"Ready the horses," Keekai cut him off. "Make sure that this day the scouts stay within sight."

She turned to me as he left the tent. "Keep close to me and to Iften."

"I will." I rose, and reached for my satchel. "Do you think there will be a problem? I thought those of the Plains did not attack each other?"

"Would that we were of one mind, one thought, always in agreement." Keekai strapped her sword to her waist. "But there are always those few who think with their sword. I doubt that there will be trouble. But—"

"Death comes in an instant."

Keekai stopped and looked at me with sympathy. "I can hear Marcus's voice in that. He taught you that lesson, did he?" I nodded. She grimaced and continued. "A harsh lesson, but that doesn't change the truth of the words. Come. This day, we will ride hard."

Before the plague had struck, Keir and I had feared that one of the villages of Xy had rebelled against us. Keir's concern had been that I was a target, and so I'd been hastily dressed in ill-fitting armor, helmet, and given a shield to hide behind.

Afterwards, Marcus had made it a point to outfit me with something protective that actually fit. He'd located a metal helmet, and a vest of hardened leather that laced up the front and fit over my tunic. I had a hard time managing the shield, because of the weight. Marcus and Keir had been satisfied that the armor and helmet were enough to guard me. I'd gotten a blistering earful from Marcus when I said it still wasn't very comfortable.

Apparently, that wasn't a concern.

So Keekai had those items brought, and I donned them without a protest. The laces took a bit of work, and I braided my hair to tuck up under the helmet. That made it easier to deal with. And this helmet came with a chin strap, so it didn't tip to the side, or fall on my nose like the last one.

That was a definite improvement.

Iften came up as I was adjusting the helmet and handed me my reins. His face was serious. "Mount."

I nodded, and tried to mount with some grace. Iften frowned at me from the ground, took my satchel, and secured it to my saddlebags. He walked around Great-heart, checking the various straps that made up the tack. When he was satisfied, he mounted as well.

The camp was abuzz around us, as the last tents were taken down and packed. I looked around to find Keekai not far, mounting her own horse.

"Xyian."

I turned, and lifted an eyebrow at Iften in surprise.

"If we are attacked by archers, do this." He lay down the length of his horse, his body pressed tight along the horse's spine, his face almost buried in the horse's mane.

I tried it, laying down on Greatheart's back, trying to mimic his actions. Greatheart stirred beneath me, turning his head to look at what I was doing.

Iften rose in his saddle and reached over to press at the base of my spine. "Lower still."

I grunted, trying to press myself further down.

"You must be low, less of a target." Iften removed his hand. "The horse is trained to run, if we are at-tacked and you lay flat like this. Do not try to guide the horse. He is smarter than you are. Your job is to stay on." He sniffed. "If you can."

I sat back up, adjusting my armor, and gave him a withering look. He ignored me.

"Your Guardian is right." Keekai moved her horse close on my other side. "It is a good move for you."

"One thing more." Iften dismounted, and called out to one of the younger warrior-priests. "Dark Clouds, do you still have that spare shield?" Iften turned back to me. "Off."

I got off my horse, but I was in no mood to deal with his rudeness. "The shield is too heavy for me. I just end up dropping it."

The warrior-priest approached, as Iften dug in his saddlebags, and waited to hand the shield to Iften. The tattooed man waited patiently until Iften was ready for the item.

"My thanks," Iften said. "Do you require—"

"No. As I said last night, it is an extra. You are welcome to it, warrior."

Iften gave him a nod, and turned to me. "Turn around."

"Why?"

He gave me an impatient look. "I will strap this to your back. The weight will not be a problem, and it will provide more protection."

"Oh." I turned and stood as Iften arranged the straps. I stood in silence as he worked, tugging at my armor. If he was going to act decently, so could I. "You get along well with the warrior-priests, better than anyone else."

"Why not, since I was almost one of them." Iften spoke absently as he tightened the strap.

"You were?" I turned, surprised at that bit of information.

Iften frowned at me, not pleased at his little disclosure. "Does it fit? Can you move?" I rolled my shoulders and moved my arms in a circle. "Fine," he said. "Mount."

Apparently Iften the Boar had a limit of polite conversation, and it had been reached. I turned and got back on my horse without saying another word.

We rode hard, Keekai setting a swift pace. She was no longer dawdling on an ordinary trip, now she was in deadly earnest. Everyone was on alert. The tension was enough to make my heart race and my stomach knot. I scanned the horizon like everyone else, looking for any sign of a threat.

Nevertheless, the horses still took priority. We stopped to water them, posting guards all around us. Each horse was quickly checked for problems as it drank. Everyone switched mounts at that point, quickly changing saddle and tack. I didn't want to leave Greatheart, but I knew he needed a rest from bearing my weight. Still, I was afraid that I would lose him, since they didn't string the horses together.

I need not have worried. Whether it was training or herd instincts, the riderless horses stayed with us. Keekai pressed us on, unwilling to stop even for a nooning. Everyone dug into saddlebags and pulled out food that was shared. Cold kavage, gurt, and some type of dried meat. It was very tough and hard to chew, but it took the edge off my hunger.

The warriors remained on alert, but after a while, when nothing happened, I fell into a kind of numbness, watching the never-ending grasslands pass with nothing to mark the land. Other than the streams and ponds that came out of nowhere, it was unending rolling red and yellow grasses.

Finally, as the sun neared the horizon, we stopped at

a small pond, watering the horses yet again. Greatheart trotted up to me, snuffling my hair, and butting my chest. Keekai walked over and smiled at his actions. "I'll have him saddled for you."

I puffed out a breath. "We're not stopping?"

"Another hour or two, and we will stop for the night." She looked me over carefully. "Can you do that?"

I was tired, but I wasn't going to admit to it, especially surrounded by warrior-priests and Iften. "I'm good for a few more hours. But don't expect much from me in the way of talk tonight."

"Aye to that," she agreed wryly.

Our attackers rose out of the grass like specters and swooped around us, screaming and yelling. Startled out of a daze, I twisted in the saddle, confused and uncertain.

But not Iften. He was beside me, glaring. "Ride! Ride!"

Greatheart needed no further urging. He leapt forward at a gallop, hooves tearing at the sod. The warrior-priests surged around me, drawing in close to protect us. Keekai appeared next to me, her horse easily keeping pace with us.

I caught a glimpse of the enemy as one galloped past, aiming a bow in our direction. It was a warrior of the Plains, and I had a moment to wonder that it wasn't a warrior-priest when Iften hissed, "Down."

I almost fell forward, crushing my breasts down under the armor. My hands tangled with the reins and the coarse hair of Greatheart's mane. His muscles bunched and moved beneath me. The thud of his hooves vibrated the length of my body. Gasping, I took deep breaths, trying to pull air into my body and quell my terror.

I was grateful for Greatheart's long legs and strength that pushed us forward at such speed. But I knew my poor horse was tired after a day's travel, as were the others.

We plunged on, surrounded on all sides. Greatheart's hooves beat out a rhythm as fast as the beating of my heart. I pressed myself low to his back, my face pressed into his mane. Iften's voice rang in my ears. '. . . *if we are attacked, you lay flat. Do not try to guide the horse. Your job is to stay on.*'

I was trying desperately to do just that. I wanted to look, but fear clawed at my throat and kept my eyes jammed shut. I could hear the sounds of horses, arrows, and war cries all around me.

Greatheart ran on.

I darted a look to the side, to see Keekai next to me. She appeared almost serene as she rode, as if she was a gentle lady out for a ride on a pleasant day. That image shattered when she nocked an arrow and drew, aiming at the enemy. Controlling her horse with her knees, concentrating on her target, she was a perfect portrait of a warrior.

She calmly released her arrow, only to draw another one. I couldn't see if she'd hit, but she'd a slight satisfied look on her face as she aimed at another.

Could Iften use a bow?

I tightened my grip as Greatheart ran, and lifted my head just enough so that I could look at him.

Iften was there, riding hard beside me, his attention on the foe around us. He didn't have a bow, but I could see a lance in his good hand.

His gaze flicked over me, and he frowned before he looked away. I got the message and focused on staying on Greatheart.

And still we ran.

Movement caught my eye and I saw Iften throw his lance and strike a warrior in the side. The warrior fell, and Iften pulled another lance. So sharp, so deadly. I remembered the damage they did when Keir was attacking Water's Fall and shuddered at the memory of sharp stone shards in deep wounds.

A cry, then a clash of steel. But we never stopped, even as the swords clashed. Our attackers' horses were fresher. I could feel a difference in Greatheart. His breathing was labored, and there was a tremble in his muscles that hadn't been there before. He was tiring. So were the others.

But something changed. Iften moved up and turned Greatheart, forcing him to change direction. Keekai wasn't alongside anymore, and I realized that the others in our party had somehow managed to drive the attackers away from me.

Greatheart slowed, and I looked back to see that the attackers were now only four, and surrounded. Even as I looked, two dropped from their saddles. Still Waters took another, and the last, realizing his plight, charged and broke through, intent on escaping.

With a cry, Iften launched his horse forward, chasing the lone warrior. I thought he'd try to capture him, but at the last minute, Iften rose in the saddle, and with his good arm, his off-arm, he threw his lance.

It took the warrior full in the back, and with a cry, the man tumbled out of the saddle, pierced through the chest, dead.

"Why did you do that?" Keekai was furious. We were all walking our horses, cooling them before bedding them for the night, watching as the warrior-priests saw to the dead. There were guards all around us, but the grasslands appeared to be empty of any threat.

"We could have learned his truths and discovered who was behind this attack!" Keekai snapped. "Dead, he is only silent."

Iften smiled, a sickly false smile. "The heat of my fury was so great, that any would dare to attack the Warprize."

"Don't mock me, warrior," Keekai spat, her face contorted in anger. She took a step toward Iften. For a moment, I thought he would offer a challenge, but he stepped back, and inclined his head in submission.

Keekai huffed, apparently satisfied.

Still Waters came up to us. "The dead are gathered, and stripped. We have their gear and horses. None recognize their faces or the fletchings on the lances."

"They wanted her alive," Iften stated flatly.

Keekai nodded in agreement.

"How do you know?" I asked.

"The way they attacked," Keekai answered. "We will camp, and rest the horses. But before first light we will be up and on our way."

Still Waters and Iften nodded their consent, and moved off to give the orders.

My body felt like my soul had been sucked out, I was so tired. I leaned against Greatheart's shoulder and looked at Keekai.

She shook her head. "There is no help for it, Lara. I will send a message back for Keir, but we must ride hard and fast to the Heart of the Plains. Your safe arrival in the Heart is all that matters now."

We rode then, from daybreak to sunset. I lost track of the days in the endless land. All I knew was the unending hours in the saddle, or asleep, with barely time to eat between.

So it took me a long moment when we topped yet another gentle rise, to understand what was spread out before me. It was sunset, and I'd thought we'd be making yet another short camp, until Keekai turned to me and pointed. "Behold, the Heart of the Plains."

The sun was fiery red in the distance, starting to slip from the sky. There was just enough daylight to see the Heart, and I had to smile at myself. I'd expected a city, with some sort of structures.

But the Heart of the Plains was a city of tents.

It was huge, to rival Water's Fall. But instead of marble or stone, there were tents of all shapes and sizes and colors. As the dusk rushed over us, lights began to appear, both inside and outside the tents, making everything glow.

Beyond the tents, I could see an enormous tent, far larger than any that I'd seen before. And beyond that, there was a shimmer, and I realized that it was water, a lake bigger than I'd ever seen.

I stared in amazement. Was there anything small on the Plains?

Before I could take it all in, Keekai was leading the way down off the ridge, and within moments we were within the city. The horses were exhausted, but they trotted with a lighter step, probably aware that their journey was over. We stayed together, and from all over, people turned to look and point at us. It was dizzying, the sights, the smells of cooking, the endless colors and noise. It was so very strange, and yet not that different from the sounds of the market back in Water's Fall.

Exhausted, I clung to Greatheart, and tried to absorb it all. It seemed to take forever to pass through it all, but we finally came to a stop before the enormous tent that I'd seen in the distance. It was really more like a huge covered pavilion.

Keekai was at my knee, urging me to dismount. "Come, Lara." She took my elbow, and I tried not to lean on her as I staggered forward, legs not used to walking after so many days in the saddle. We walked together into the huge tent and I stumbled a bit over some steps. The floor of this area was solid stone.

The pavilion was lit brightly with braziers. I blinked at the sight of men and women seated on stools on a three-tiered platform, widest at the top, and narrowing toward the bottom. Three figures were seated at the base, and the one in the middle rose as we approached. He was an older man, dressed in robes of bright red over leather armor, with a multi-colored sash at his waist that held a sword and two daggers. His face was brown as a nut, and deeply wrinkled. There was no welcome there, no smile at all.

We stopped, and the man gestured Keekai away from me. I thought for a moment that she would protest, but instead she inclined her head, and went to an empty stool on the second tier, off to the side. I swayed slightly as she moved away, feeling naked and alone.

Iften appeared next to me. Even he showed signs of exhaustion, but he stood tall and proud. "I was chosen as Guardian by Xylara, Daughter of Xy. I have brought her here, safe and sound, to stand before the Council of Elders at the Heart of the Plains."

The man nodded his head, and spoke. "You have served well, Iften of the Boar, and the Daughter of Xy is now under our protection. You are released from your duties, with our thanks."

Iften spun on his heel, and glared at me with eyes filled with hate. He paused as he stepped past me. "You and your poisons made it to the Heart. But we of the Plains can learn to use poison, too. Remember that, Xyian."

I leaned away, conscious of the threat he posed, but he brushed past and left.

"Outlander." The Elder in the middle faced me, his voice ringing out to everyone's ears. "You stand before the Council of the Elders of the Plains, to answer the charges that have been brought against you."

Charges? I wanted to look at Keekai, but couldn't tear my eyes from the figure in front of me.

"Outlander. You have lied to a warrior of the Plains. You have brought death and affliction to hundreds of our warriors. You have caused the death of a bonded pair, and caused them to die in shame. You have brought the filth of your cities to the Plains. You honor those afflicted by the elements." He glared, and pointed a wrinkled finger at me. "Worse still, you claim to be able to raise the dead."

Stunned, I stood there, my mouth hanging open.

"So tell us, Outlander, what do you bring to the Plains, other than lies, affliction and death?"

8

My fury rose at the Elder's words. I lashed out, lifting my chin in scorn. "This is not the Council of the Elders," I spat. "Am I offered cool water to ease my throat? Where is a seat for my weary body, or food for my belly? Not even water to bathe my hands and thank whatever power I choose for a safe journey?" I let my eyes rake over them, making my contempt clear. "Here I stand, in the Heart of the Plains, supposedly before the Council of Elders, and yet where is the courtesy of the Plains that I have come to know and respect? Nowhere that I can see."

I was trembling, in exhaustion and anger, and knew that in a moment I'd collapse as weak as an hour-old colt. But not here. I turned on my heel and left the tent.

Our horses were gone, there was no one to stop me. Without really seeing, I plunged into a chaos of people and tents, striding as fast as I could, away from the hatred within that tent.

With new strength born of anger, I strode off.

Thankfully, there were wide ways between the various tents. I chose the widest, lost in my fury. Every word spoken by that Elder had been false, or an exaggeration. How dare he say that of me? Of Keir?

I drew a ragged breath, choking and laughing at the same time. Father had always despaired of my temper. Fierce and hot, it would rise to the surface in an instant, unleashing my tongue with an angry retort, only to fade almost as quickly. He tried every way he could think to get me to control it. "Take a deep breath," he'd urge. "Mind that tongue of yours, and think before you speak."

Advice I'd never been able to follow.

My feet propelled me down the course at a fast pace, and it was only the laughter of children that brought me back to the world around me.

Off to the side, there was a large tent with a cooking fire in front of it. A few men and women were trying to get a group of small children to settle down before eating, with no success. The children, of all ages, were laughing and giggling in some game only they understood. A young man, no older than Gils had been, was trying to pour water over small grubby hands and getting nowhere for his efforts.

An older woman emerged from the tent and looked about. Suddenly, each child was settled, all with sweet smiles of absolute innocence and hands held out for the ritual.

I had to smile, and with that, some of my anger faded. Instead I was overcome with curiosity. So this was the Heart of the Plains! The home of the dreaded Firelanders.

I strolled now, looking about me, taking it all in. Clearly everyone was preparing for the evening meal, and tents glowed with light from within. There were some outside firepits, burning with coals and surrounded by people, talking and laughing and eating.

How like home it was. And yet, how different. Here there was color everywhere, and no one seemed conscious of rank or position. Men were cooking as well as women, and there were quite a few men taking care of small children.

But it was more than that. There was the tang in the air of grilling meat and spices I didn't recognize. There were no buildings, no mountains to block the vaulted sky filled with stars above us. The tents seemed to range from tiny shelters to large, sprawling structures cobbled together from many tents.

People were laughing and talking, and there was color everywhere, in the clothing, in the tents, in the banners that hung all over. The clothing ranged from full armor to scraps of cloth or complete lack thereof. All were at ease with their nakedness, from the smallest child to the tough, scrawny old warriors.

Naked or clothed, everyone carried weapons. Even the small children had wooden daggers at their belts.

But even as I looked about, I sensed that I was being watched as well. I knew from experience that to those of the Plains, my lack of weapons made me stand out like a sore thumb.

I sighed, suddenly very homesick: for Anna's big kitchen, and my old bedroom, with its small bed and a window that looked down on the city. My feet began to drag, as my newfound strength faded away.

"Keep walking," Keekai spoke softly from behind me. "I will guide you to my tent."

I stopped, and she stepped to my side, a serene look in her eyes. I flushed a bit, suddenly very aware that I'd insulted the entire Council of Elders just a few moments before. But there was no condemnation in Keekai's eyes.

With a sigh, I reached up and took my helmet off. My braid fell down my back, and the cool breeze touched my sweaty scalp. "Keekai . . ."

She gestured along the way. "Not far, Warprize."

With that, we walked in silence, as the shadows grew and the sky filled with stars. At the end of the way, the course branched, and there sat a tent that rivaled Keir's in size. Warriors appeared and opened the flaps for us to enter.

Keekai showed me to a small alcove off the main area. It was filled by a bed that was covered in blankets, furs and pillows, all in various patterns of reds and golds. On a small table by the bed, a tiny fat lamp sat, a small flame flickering in its depths.

"This night, you have the courtesy of my tent." Keekai gestured me within.

I sat on the edge of the bed, and didn't resist when Keekai took my helmet from my hands. She started on the leather jerkin then, helping me remove it. I heaved a sigh even as I toed off my boots. Keekai clapped her hands and a warrior came, with a pitcher of water and a bowl. I held out my hands for the ritual and murmured a soft prayer to the Goddess. Once that was done, a mug and a bowl of gurt were brought. I took the mug, to find it filled with a warm, sweet milk. It tasted wonderful and I drained the mug quickly.

"You did well, Warprize." Keekai smiled at me.

I grimaced. "By insulting the entire Council and stomping away like a child?"

Her eyes twinkled. "By demanding what is due you, under our ways. Antas had mud on his face when you turned and left."

I blinked at her. "What am I going to do, Keekai? They hate me."

"You will sleep. In the morning, you will eat and . . ." she shrugged, "we will see." She gestured, and the warriors drew closed curtains of thick cloth that blocked the alcove from view.

Keekai paused, just before she left. "But remember

this, Lara. They removed you from Keir's protection to show that you weren't under his influence or control. And your actions have proved you are capable of standing up for yourself. So do not be so quick to count this a defeat, eh?"

She turned to go, but paused again, and looked back at me over her shoulder. "I will tell you this truth, Daughter of Xy. I do not think I could do what you have done. To leave the Plains that I have known all my life would kill me." With that, she disappeared behind the cloth.

Oddly comforted, I yawned and stretched. Since my gear wasn't here yet, I stripped out of my tunic and trous. I was too tired to even ask to wash. I just pulled back the wonderful bedding, sank into the depths of the bed, and pulled the covers back up over me. Whatever happened, happened. I was too tired to think beyond the next moment.

My last sight was of the little lamp, sitting on the table, all fat and clever, with its tiny flame dancing a very satisfied little dance.

It was late when I woke, and later still when I stirred from the bed. The only thing that made me move was the demands of my body, and a raging thirst.

My saddlebags were just inside the 'walls' of my shelter, with my satchel right on top. I sat up, clutching the blankets to me, and pondered for a moment. A sudden, wild impulse came over me, and I clapped my hands.

There was movement outside, and a woman popped her head in with a questioning look. I grinned at her. I could get used to this kind of treatment very quickly. Maybe when I returned to Water's Fall? But the thought of Othur's and Anna's reaction to that idea made me reject it quickly.

Still . . .

Within a short time I'd water to bathe with and hot kavage to drink. I washed quickly, and yearned for Keir's tent with its clever drain of stones and buckets of hot water. I went to the saddlebags and dug for a clean tunic and trous. As I pulled on the cloth, I caught a gleam of red. I knew it in an instant.

The dress was bright red. Bright, bright red.

Marcus smiled at me. "There, now. That will do us proud."

Keir walked into the tent and stopped short. His eyes widened, and his face lit up. "Fire's blessing." He stood, looking at me with approval.

I smiled, remembering the moment and the heat of Keir's gaze. Curious, I pulled the heavy bundle out. The dress was as I remembered it, with a high neckline, long sleeves, and a flared split skirt. Once again I marveled as the fabric slid between my fingers like water glides over skin. It showed no sign that it had been wadded in the bottom of a saddle bag for days.

Marcus had even packed the slippers. And there, in the center of the bundle, were the two heavy silver bracelets.

I halted before the throne, and slowly sank onto the cushion. On either side, I could see two black boots broadly planted, and legs encased in black fabric. I was careful to keep my eyes down.

I took a deep breath, slowly lifted my hands, palms up, and silently submitted myself to what was to come.

The room seemed to stop breathing. I felt fingers at the base of my neck, gently unraveling my hair. Strong fingers ran through it, releasing and letting it fall free. I shivered, both at the touch and the implication that disobedience would not be tolerated.

Cold metal encircled my wrists. I heard a click as they locked into place. Surprisingly, they were heavy silver bracelets, with no chains. Weren't there supposed to be chains?

A deep male voice boomed above my head, in my language. "Thus do I claim the warprize."

I smiled as the picture flashed before me, of kneeling on that cushion and surrendering to the dreaded Warlord. Of looking up into Keir's blue eyes. I'd been so afraid, so terrified, yet I'd found love in Keir's arms. We'd come through so much since then.

We would come through this too.

"You slept well?" Keekai asked as she gestured for me to sit across the table from her. This was in another part of her tent, and a private area as far as I could tell. She clapped her hands, and for a few moments the area was filled with those bringing food and drink. But just as quickly the room cleared, and we were left alone.

"I slept well, thank you. The bed was very comfortable." I settled down, and reached for the kavage. "What time is it?"

"Well toward the nooning." Keekai shrugged. "I saw no reason to wake you. We both needed sleep." She flashed that grin of hers. "I suspect the Council will send us a message before the day is done."

I reached for flat bread and an odd looking meat dish that Keekai had already helped herself to. "I can imagine what the message will be," I said. The sauce smelled sweet, and had tiny flecks of red in it. I scooped some on my bread, and stuffed it in my mouth.

Fire exploded within my mouth and nose. My eyes went wide and filled with tears as I choked.

"Too spicy?" Keekai asked as I lunged for kavage. "It is my favorite."

I gasped for breath. "Keekai!"

"I'm sorry, Lara." She shook her head. "I forgot to warn you. I love my food spicy and strong. Try this instead." She pushed over a bowl filled with a creamy, thick paste.

Carefully, I dipped more bread in, hoping that it wasn't a soupy form of gurt. But I was pleasantly surprised to find that it had a sweet nutty taste to it. "That's more to my liking."

Keekai laughed. "Then eat and listen. We need to talk about the Council and its members."

I nodded, but kept chewing.

"Now, the stupid one that spoke out last night was Antas, Eldest Warrior. You saw how we were seated?"

I frowned, trying to remember. Keekai sighed, dipped her finger in her kavage, and drew on the wood of the table. "The four closest to the floor are the Eldest Singer, Warrior, and Warrior-Priest, and Eldest Thea."

I frowned, and swallowed my mouthful. "I thought you didn't count years," I pointed out. "How do you know who is Eldest?"

It was Keekai's turn to frown. "Elder is not because one is old. Elder is because one is best, or has the support of many others."

"So you are an Elder because of status?"

"Exactly so." She drew four damp circles in a row. "The Eldest sit here, closest to the earth and the flame."

She drew more circles behind the three. "Here sit the Elders whose rank is just behind. I sit among them. We are between the elements, earth and fire below, air and water above."

She dipped her finger again. "Behind us, on the highest tier, are the newest of the Elders. They are closest to the air and the water."

"So seating denotes status." I studied the damp spots as they soaked into the wood.

"Just so. The Eldest are always four. One Warrior, one Warrior-Priest, one Singer, One Thea. Antas is the Warrior, and Essa is the Singer. Wild Winds is the Warrior-Priest. The Eldest Thea rarely attends."

"I remember Antas," I said dryly.

"He is a fool," Keekai responded. "I told you that the winds had brought us word of you, but Antas listens only to the worst." She tapped the table with her finger. "Although it surprised me that he acted so. I'd have expected it from Wild Winds before Antas."

Once again, she dipped her finger in the kavage. "Those who would speak to the Council are placed between the fire pits." She drew the rest of the tent in for me. "Those who would observe, or wait their turn, stand on the other side of the pits, along the edges of the tent. Those who provide for the Council, they are behind the tiers."

I dipped some fresh bread into the meat dish with the red flakes, taking only a little with a large piece of bread. Warned this time, I nibbled at it carefully. It stung my mouth, but the taste wasn't bad, just different. Keekai chuckled as I ate. "You will become of the Plains before you realize it, Lara."

I took a deep breath as the spices filled my nose. "Has there been any word from Keir?"

Keekai shook her head. "It's too soon." She looked at me with sympathy. "I'm sure he'll be here as fast as he can, Lara. But even if he arrived today, they would keep you apart."

I nodded, staring down at the food. "I understand."

"Now, of the Elders present—" Keekai broke off, looking over my shoulder. "What is it?"

I turned on my stool to see a warrior at the tent flap. "A messenger from the Council, Elder." The woman smiled at me. "For the Warprize."

"Ah." Keekai arched an eyebrow. "Send them in."

I hastily chewed and swallowed my last bite, wiping my face with my hands.

A young girl walked into the area, obviously conscious of the importance of her mission. She faced us, tall, slim, and confident. "Greetings. I am Jilla of the

Bear. I carry a message for Xylara, Daughter of Xy, from the Council of Elders of the Plains."

Keekai deferred to me with a gesture. I cleared my throat. "I am Xylara."

Jilla gave me a nod. "Daughter of Xy, the Council bids me ask if you would be able to attend a Council senel this afternoon."

I glanced over at Keekai, but she deferred to me again. "As you will, Warprize."

"Please tell the Council that I will attend," I responded.

Jilla gave me another nod. "The Council wishes you to know that every courtesy will be offered to you. An escort will be sent, once the Council is met."

I nodded at that, and she slipped between the tent flaps and vanished.

"As close to an apology as we are likely to get," Keekai offered.

I turned back to the table, and reached for my kavage. Keekai continued on. "They may honor you with your own tent, Lara. And appoint new guards for you. This is an honor, but it also serves to separate us, something that will please Antas." She hesitated then. "We could delay them, if you wish. Claim that you are too tired to appear."

"No." I shook my head. "I want this over with. Now, please, help me remember Antas's accusations. And tell me more about the Council members."

"Welcome to the Heart of the Plains, Xylara, Daughter of Xy."

I nodded my head slightly, giving them no more, or less, than their due.

This time, Eldest Singer Essa greeted me as I walked into the tent. He was standing in the center, between Antas and Wild Winds.

Antas was in full armor, an impressive sight to be sure. Even more impressive was the expression on his face, dark and forbidding.

Wild Winds had a neutral look, as if I was no more than another warrior that appeared before them. He was seated, his arms folded over his tattooed chest. I took note of the tattoo over his left eye, determined that I would know him in the future.

I stood before them all, in the flame-red dress and matching slippers. I'd put on the bracelets, dotted a bit of my precious vanilla oil between my breasts, and braided my hair down my back. I also had my satchel slung on my hip, and while the strap may have marred the cut of the dress, I'd carried it anyway. In my own way, I was armed for combat, although they might not recognize the dress or satchel as such. Still, there had been a stir when I'd entered the pavilion, and it had given me a bit more confidence.

I would take every morsel I could find.

Essa continued. "We offer you the warmth of our fire, and a seat before us."

The tent we were under was huge, and it covered a stone floor that seemed perfectly circular. I was standing between two fire pits, where coals smoldered, providing heat. There were also other braziers scattered around, and a few torches as well, for light.

The three Eldest were before me on a low wooden platform, their stools behind them. Behind that rose three wooden tiers, also filled with Elders on their stools. The result was that the entire Council could sit and glare down at me.

A warrior strode out and placed a small bench between the two fire pits. I took my seat, placed my satchel by my feet, and adjusted my skirts.

"We offer you food and drink, Daughter of Xy."

Two warriors, one with a small table, another with a tray, approached. I was offered water to wash my hands, and then kavage and gurt were placed within my reach.

"I thank you for your courtesy." I poured a mug of kavage and took a sip. While the scent of the vanilla helped, there was still a tight knot between my shoulder blades. The Council had proved that it was willing to attack me at a weak moment. The person speaking may have changed, but I wasn't fooled. The claws were still there, merely sheathed for the time being.

Keekai and I had gone over the members of the Council, but everything was jumbled together in my head. Without being obvious, I drew a long, deep breath and tried to calm myself.

And I'd thought the Council of Xy had been hard to deal with.

"Xylara, Daughter of Xy, from the Kingdom of Xy, you have been claimed as Warprize by Keir of the Cat, Warlord of the Plains." Essa's words sounded familiar for some reason. "You have been brought to the Heart of the Plains, so that you may be confirmed as the Warprize."

He was repeating the ritual that Keekai had performed when she had taken me under her protection. I relaxed a bit, recognizing the questions.

Essa continued. "Have you taken anything from the hands of another on this journey?"

"No." My voice was clear, and as strong as I could wish. "My Warlord has provided for me."

There was a stir at that, and Essa lifted an eyebrow. "Keir of the Cat is not yet your Warlord, Daughter of Xy."

"Perhaps to your way of thinking," I responded quietly. "But not to mine."

Antas gave a great snort and stood, his armor rattling as he threw his arms in the air. "What cares she for our ways? She has brought nothing but death to—"

"Enough," Essa spoke, and Antas was instantly silenced. "We will continue the ritual, and then the questioning can begin."

Antas sat down heavily, scowling.

Essa waited for quiet before he began again. "Xylara, Daughter of Xy, do you wish to return to your land, to the arms of your people, to your home?" He paused, considering me closely. "The ties of one's own tribe are very strong. Speak, and it will be as you wish."

Again, it flashed before me. Home, a place of safety, with strong walls and all that was familiar and comfortable. Anna's cooking, Othur's warm hugs, Heath's teasing. Kalisa in the market, with her cheese and crackers. Remn's book shop.

But the cost of that comfort was too high, for it meant turning my back on the man I loved. I lifted my chin. "I am here to claim my place as Warprize, and my Warlord."

Antas leapt to his feet. "Yet all you bring with you is chaos and death. The army entrusted to Keir of the Cat has been decimated by your hand."

"We do not know that." Essa seated himself on his stool. "We have only words brought by the wind."

Antas turned to Wild Winds. "What say you, Warrior-Priest?"

"I would hear her truths." The man replied in a soft voice. It was my first chance to really look at him, when my eyes weren't blurred with exhaustion. He was fearsome looking, even in the light of day. A tall man, he wore only trous and a long cloak. But he had the multi-colored tattoos all over his chest, and a staff with three human skulls and feathers dangling from the end on leather strips. His hair was dark, and matted in thick ropes that hung down to his waist. His dark eyes studied me, in turn, but I didn't see any hostility there.

I didn't see friendship, either.

"What does she know of truth?" Antas growled. "A foul city-dweller?"

"City-dwellers tell the truth," I spoke up, indignant.

"HAH!" Antas shouted, making me jump. "You lied to a warrior of the Plains, we know of this. Do not deny that!"

"I didn't lie." My temper flared, and I snapped at him, not impressed with the weapons he carried. "I may not have told the entire truth, but I didn't—"

"You cannot deny it. She will appear before us, and then all will know," Antas fired back.

She? I sat there, my mouth open. She? He wasn't talking about Keir?

"Your so-called healing skill. You lied to a warrior of the Plains in order to work magic on her leg." Antas bared his teeth. "She will tell us her truths, and then we will see."

Was he talking about Atira? I'd set her leg when she'd broken it in a fall from her horse. But that had happened back in Xy, in Keir's camp. I frowned, puzzled. When had I lied to Atira? I opened my mouth to deny it, then snapped it shut. Atira would tell her truths? Did that mean what I thought it meant? "Is Atira here?"

"The Council has summoned those whose truths will be heard. Others have asked to speak before us." Essa spoke calmly. "But your truths come first, then our questions can begin." He gave Antas a hard look. "Without interruption."

Antas sat back down with a grunt.

"Begin, Daughter of Xy." Wild Winds spoke this time. "Tell us your truths, from the beginning."

I drew a deep breath, and started to speak.

* * *

The telling took hours. Facing those Elders, with their blank faces and unresponsive eyes, drained me of my strength. Even Antas stayed silent and still, boring a hole in me with his gaze. In the coldness of that tent, I struggled for the words that would explain my feelings for Keir.

But whenever I looked in her direction, Keekai's eyes were bright with support. And as I spoke, in my mind's eye I could see the love in Keir's eyes, the fierceness of Marcus's protection, the other Firelanders who had become so close to me so quickly. And while my truth may not have had the strength of a Singer's words, it was *my* truth. So I spoke, telling them everything, including the details of the ehat hunt.

When I stopped, Essa stood. "Courtesy demands that we see to all our needs, and the needs of the Daughter of Xy."

With that, the tent flooded with warriors, carrying kavage and hot food. I was offered water for my hands, and food and hot kavage. Everyone ate and drank, and then stretched, seeing to other needs.

The group began to settle back down when a warrior-priest entered and spoke to Wild Winds. He seemed familiar, and I stared at the tattoo over his eye, trying to place him. It took me a moment, but I recognized the warrior-priest that had come to our camp at Wellspring and befriended Iften. My heart beat a bit faster. He'd been with Keir at the camp the last I knew. Could it be? Could Keir be here?

Wild Winds inclined his head and listened for a moment, and then gestured for the younger man to leave. He did, but only after shooting a heated glance toward me.

Wild Winds then approached Essa, and Antas joined them. The room grew quiet, even as the three debated hotly. I seated myself and tried to prepare for the questioning that was to come. But my insides were shaking, even if my hands weren't. I smoothed down my skirt, and then folded my hands in my lap. I risked a glance at Keekai. She caught it, and gave me a slight shrug.

Finally, they seemed to resolve the difference. Or at least, Wild Winds and Essa seemed to agree. Antas had a permanent scowl.

Essa turned to face the Elders. "Those who have been summoned have arrived. We will hear those truths before questioning the Daughter of Xy."

This seemed to surprise a number of the Elders, but by the number of heads nodding, it seemed a popular decision.

Essa turned to me. "Xylara, Daughter of Xy. The Council has arranged a tent for your use, as well as a warrior to serve you." He glanced at Wild Winds. "You are now under the protection of the Council of Elders. You will have a guard at all times, to insure your safety."

Just as Keekai had predicted. I inclined my head. "Thank you, Eldest Singer."

"You may go where you will, Daughter of Xy. But you will not be permitted to see Keir of the Cat. Do you understand?"

"I understand, Eldest Singer." I stood, and from nowhere, four young warrior-priests appeared around me. My new guards.

"This senel is over," Essa announced.

The stars were out when we emerged from the senel, and I yawned as I followed my guards to the new tent. It was close, for which I was thankful, and appeared to be just a bit smaller than Keekai's. As long as it had a private sleeping area, it would be good enough for me.

The flap opened as we approached and a woman

stepped forth, her brown hair tied back in a braid. Her brown eyes seemed kind. "Greetings, Daughter of Xy." She held the flap open and I ducked inside.

I stepped into a meeting area, much like Simus's tent, back in the camp outside of Water's Fall. My saddlebags were there, laying off to the side.

"I am Amyu of the Boar." She nodded to me, and gestured for me to take a seat at the table. "I will serve you while the Council debates your status. May I provide kavage? Or something to eat?"

I heaved a sigh, and took off my satchel. "Amyu, if it would not offend, I think I just want a wash and to sleep."

She nodded and stepped off to the side to open another flap. "Your sleeping chamber is within."

I stepped forward to look inside. The bed looked familiar, with red and gold pillows. But what gave it away was the fat, happy lamp on the table. The flame danced a welcome.

"Is this bed from Keekai's tent?" I asked.

Amyu nodded. "She offered, and the Elders agreed. All these items have been donated for your use, Daughter of Xy."

"Amyu, please call me 'Lara'." I held up a hand to silence her protest. "At least within the confines of the tent." I stepped within and put my satchel on the bed.

"As you wish." Amyu looked at the brazier that burned in the corner. "The lake is not far, if you wish to bathe."

I sighed. "No, I don't think so. Maybe just a bucket of warm water and a few cloths?"

She looked at me, puzzled. "As you wish." She bowed and left before I could explain, which was fine with me. I knew from experience that the people of the Plains had no understanding of basic Xyian modesty.

I tucked my satchel in by the bed, and removed my

slippers to rub my feet. I was still feeling the effects of our wild ride, and yawned again. But while my body was tired, my mind was still whirling. Was Keir here? In camp?

Oh, I hoped so. I wanted this over, so that I could be in his arms again. I drew a deep breath, but the scent of this tent was different from Keir's. Only the faint aroma of vanilla was present, and that came from my own body.

A noise from outside brought me out of my thoughts.

"Out of my way! My healer is within, and I must see her!"

Voices rose in protest, and I lifted the flap just in time to see a large, black man force his way into the main tent. My smile had already started when his eyes met mine, and his white teeth flashed against his coal black skin.

"LITTLE HEALER!"

9

"Simus!" I ran over and he swept me up in a bear hug, laughing loudly. The sound made my heart dance, and I laughed with him as he twirled me around and then set me gently on my feet.

We were surrounded by my four guards and Amyu and everyone was talking at once, but that never dimmed the gleam in Simus's eyes. He put his hands on my shoulders and looked down into my eyes. "Are you well?"

"As well as I can be." I smiled at him. "I am so glad to see you."

His eyebrows danced and he turned to face our foes. "SILENCE!"

Everyone obeyed.

"The Warprize is my healer," he said, using the Xyian word. "She must see the wound that she tended. Out, all of you! This is done under the bells!"

They all looked at one another, and one of the

youngest looking warrior-priests shifted his weight from foot to foot. Amyu spoke first. "Our orders are that she not have contact with Keir of the Cat, or his supporters."

"Pah." Simus walked over to one of the stools and sat. "You may listen, if you wish. I will not use the bells. But outside. NOW!"

They scattered.

Simus looked at me and grinned. I couldn't help grinning back at him, even as I shook my head. "That was rude, Simus of the Hawk."

"They should not have sent girls to do woman's work." He replied in perfect Xyian. "They don't know how to deal with me. But they will have sent word to someone who does. So let us speak, eh?" He stood, and started to unbuckle his belt. "Let me show you the scar, Warprize. It is a wonder." He spoke in the language of the Plains, loud enough that anyone could hear.

"Should I get my satchel?" I tried not to laugh.

"Yes, by all means, please get your wondrous herbs and potions," Simus bellowed, yanked down his trous and sat back down. "Eln said to tell you that he thought it was doing very well."

I went and got my satchel, and returned to admire the scar along his thigh. It had healed well. "Did it give you any trouble on the way here?"

"None," Simus replied, then switched to Xyian. "And we rode hard. The Council sent word that they required the truths of Atira. I knew that you and your beloved would need my help. So, we are here."

"We?" I pulled out the scar ointment from the depths of my satchel, and started to open it. How odd it was to hear my native tongue again. I almost had to think before I spoke.

"We," Simus replied. "Atira, Keir, Marcus, and Joden. And one of your land, the son of the cook."

"How is her leg?" I asked, absently. But then my head snapped up in surprise. "Heath? Heath is here?"

"He is," Simus replied in Xyian. He paused for a moment, then spoke again loudly, switching languages. "The friend of your youth, Heath of Xy, he is here with messages of your people. I will send him to speak to you, if these fools will permit." Simus gave me a grin, switching back to Xyian. "I will send him with messages." He stretched his leg out, to give me access. "Keir is raging like a wounded ehat, furious that he cannot see you. But Marcus and I, with Keekai's help, are talking sense into that thick head of his."

I smiled. "I know what an ehat looks like now."

Simus laughed, and switched to his language. "You must tell me of the hunt. All the details, now!"

I laughed, but Simus grew serious, and switched back to Xyian. "There are dangers here, Lara. Make no mistake."

"There was an attack—"

"Keir and I know of it." Simus sighed. "What we do not know is who was behind it. You are safe enough here."

"Am I?" I asked softly, in Xyian. "Amyu is of the Boar and the guards are all warrior-priests."

"The honor of the entire Council depends on your safety." Simus looked grim. "Amyu is a child and will obey her elders. Your guards will protect you. But they will report if you try to see Keir, you understand?"

I nodded.

"Watch for Iften, and Gathering Storm. There is a warrior-priest not to be trusted."

"Gathering Storm? Which one is that?" I asked.

Simus grinned. "The one you doused with that stink, remember?" He turned his face slightly and spoke loudly for the listeners, switching languages easily. "You worked a marvel, Warprize. My leg is as new."

"Is there any pain when you walk?" I asked, following his example. I smeared the ointment on the scar, to soften the tissue.

"None." Simus gave me a genuine smile. "You saved my leg and my life as a warrior, Little Healer. May the elements allow me to return the favor some day."

I smiled at him, but looked away, and spoke in Xyian. "If you have spoken with Joden, then you know how he feels about me now. After the plague, he no longer supports us."

"Pah." Simus gave a snort. "The man is merely confused. I will set him straight." He leaned in closer. "The telling of truths begins tomorrow. It is not likely that you will be allowed to listen. But do not fear, Lara. All will be—"

Wild Winds strode into the tent, with my guards and Amyu just behind.

Simus looked over casually. "Ah, Warrior-Priest. Come to see the work of the Warprize? A Master Healer."

Wild Winds arched an eyebrow, then took another step to stare down at Simus's leg. He looked closely. "A deep wound."

"To the bone," Simus replied proudly. He stretched out his leg for everyone to see. Everyone stared at it, even Amyu, with particular fascination.

"What is the purpose of that?" Wild Winds gestured to the jar in my hands.

I stood and offered it to him. "An ointment that aids the healing. It will help the scar to fade."

"What?" Simus protested. "Why fade an honorable wound, honorably earned?"

Wild Winds raised an eyebrow. "Regardless, the

Daughter of Xy is not to have contact with Keir of the Cat, or those—"

"We spoke of healing matters." Simus stood, and pulled on his trous with great dignity.

"They spoke in the tongue of city-dwellers," one of the guards piped up.

Simus let his eyebrows raise. "You do not know the tongue? I didn't realize that." He turned then, and gave me a bow, reaching for my hand to kiss it. "My thanks again, Xylara, Daughter of Xy."

I gave him a curtsey, and he smiled, and turned back to face Wild Winds. "After you, Warrior-priest."

He herded them out, all but Amyu, who gave me an odd look as she tied the tent flap closed. I ignored her, and returned to the sleeping area and sat on the bed. I opened my hand and stared at the small bar of vanilla soap that Simus had pressed into my hand. I could hear him arguing with the warrior-priest, his voice fading in the distance.

I smiled at the little square, even as my eyes filled with tears. Keir was here, and close. Where else could Simus have gotten it? Keir had bought up every bar that the herb merchant in Water's Fall had for sale. I held it up to my nose and drew in the scent. It made me feel better, knowing that he was close. I just wished that he was here, with me, and could share my tent and my bed this night.

Atira was here. They'd summoned her, to hear her truths. But when had I lied to her? I sat there, trying to remember, but I couldn't. Of course, the first time I'd met her, I'd kicked her awake. I flushed at the memory.

But what was Heath doing here? Were Anna and Othur alright? I bit my lower lip, and worried it with my teeth. Heath wasn't really a supporter of Keir. Maybe they would let me see him, to get news of home. I flushed a bit, with a guilty sense that I hadn't given home much thought since leaving Xy. There was more at stake here than just Keir and me. My people would benefit as much as if not more than the Plains would if I was confirmed.

There was a slight cough, and I shoved the bar under my skirt. "Enter."

Amyu appeared, and inclined her head. "The hot water, as you requested."

"Thank you." I watched as she placed the bucket off to the side, along with some clean cloths. I'd have to be careful not to make too much of a mess. I yawned, as once again my tiredness swept over me.

"Is it true? That your people bathe under the bells?" Amyu asked, giving me an odd look under her lashes as she fussed with the placement of the cloths.

"Yes." I arched an eyebrow at her. "My Warlord was able to arrange for me to bathe under the bells at all times, when I was with him. Xyians are very private about their bodies."

She frowned. "But Simus of the Hawk was naked."

"Healers have to see their patients' bodies in order to heal them. It is an exception to the rule."

"I will see what can be done, about the bathing." I could see that she was still puzzled, but she gave me another glance. "It is said that you will 'heal' any that ask."

I nodded. "I will."

She looked at me intently, then abruptly left.

I narrowed my eyes, and almost went after her, to push the issue. But I didn't. I couldn't force people to accept my healing ways. I'd learned that lesson with Iften. Sooner or later, I'd learn Amyu's problem.

For now, I had hot water and soap. After that, sleep in a comfortable bed. The morning would be here, soon enough.

And, maybe, a glimpse of Keir.

* * *

I awoke at some point close to dawn. My eyes were heavy, the bed warm and soft beneath my body. I reached out for him, half-awake as my hand moved, fingers searching for the familiar skin.

Keir wasn't there.

That brought me awake, and I blinked in the darkness. I'd blown out my fat little lamp earlier, and all that was left was the glow from the braziers that heated the tent. That was the light I was used to, in Keir's tent.

The loneliness caught me by surprise. The deep longing had settled in my chest before I even really knew what was happening, and I had to stifle a sob. I didn't want Amyu and the guards to know of my weakness.

I sat up in the bed, tucking the soft blankets under my arms. The noises that I had grown used to, the sounds of an army around me, were gone as well. There were still noises, but it was mostly of pennants flying in the breeze, and the occasional footstep outside.

I ran my fingers through my hair and sighed. There was little chance that I'd sleep now. I could hear the accusations of Antas in my head, his shouts loud and clear.

Iften would testify, Joden would testify. How did Keir think that I'd be confirmed, with that kind of opposition? Especially when Antas clearly agreed with Iften? Would our truths be enough to sway the Council?

All the fear and tension of the last few days swept through me. What was I doing here, alone in the tents of the Firelanders? Who could be trusted? What was going to happen?

My head hurt. I rubbed my temples, and tried not to weep. But the weight of my thoughts bore down on me, alone, in the darkness.

Amyu had left some kavage by the braziers. I slid out of bed, into the cool of the darkness. I shivered, and padded over for a drink. I also found some tapers there, and put one against the coals of the brazier. A lick of flame popped up. I carefully carried it over, and re-lit my little lamp. The flame seemed to leap and chortle within its depths, as if happy to be there.

I slid back into the warmth of the bed, covering myself with the blankets. I pulled one of the pillows close. The fabric was smooth against my cheek as I hugged it, staring at the little flame. The light danced on the tent walls.

I closed my eyes and thought of Keir.

The way he'd looked on the practice grounds when I'd first realized that he'd claimed me in honor, not in shame. That afternoon meal by the pool, when we'd loved under the alders. Gently, the memories soothed me.

I opened my eyes to watch the light from the lamp as it sputtered slightly. A soft smile curved over my lips, and my body relaxed.

It had been my choice to allow Keekai to bring me here. I wouldn't let the fear stop me. Stop us. I'd trust Keir, as he trusted me. As we'd learned to trust each other.

I shifted slightly on the bed, and let my hand linger over my stomach. Still no sign of my courses. I'd no indications either way, but it was possible that I was carrying our child. Another memory flashed over my eyes, of Keir playing with Meara, making her giggle.

My child would be my heir, and would take the throne upon my death. How could I make these people understand that? Would they understand? Or would they insist that my babe be raised in the tradition of the Plains?

But from everything I'd seen of the Plains, their children were treasured and loved. They might not follow the traditions of Xy, but even the toughest warriors played and cared for their children.

I yawned. What would our child look like? My curls? Keir's eyes?

My eyelids grew heavy and I drifted off to sleep.

I was eating breakfast when Amyu announced Essa the Singer's arrival.

I'd just enough time to swallow my last mouthful and stand before he swept inside. He was a tall man, and very broad of shoulder. His robes were all different colors of green this morning, and his armor was hardened brown leather. He carried a sword and two daggers. But what really caught my attention was the tattoo around his right eye, of a bird's wing.

"Good morning, Eldest Singer Essa." I gestured to my small table, and the other stool. "May I offer you kavage? Have you eaten?"

He cocked an eyebrow, clearly aware of the irony, but he sat, carefully arranging his robes. "I would welcome kavage."

Amyu served us both. Essa nodded his head as he took the full mug. "My thanks, child." We sat for a moment in silence as we drank our kavage and Amyu began to clear the dishes.

"Daughter of Xy, the Council meets today to hear the truths of the Warriors that have been summoned. Your presence is not required."

"What if I want to be there?" I asked. "To hear what is said of me?"

"That would not be permitted," Essa stated firmly. "Each warrior will be heard separately."

"Who? Who will speak?"

He paused considering. "Simus, Atira, Yers, Iften. Some others, perhaps."

"Joden?"

Essa frowned at his kavage. I had the strong impression that he was upset about something other than my confirmation. "That has not yet been decided."

"Why wouldn't you hear from him?"

"It is not so much whether we hear, as to what weight his words are given."

I fussed with my mug for a moment, covering my thoughts. "Is that because he is not yet a Singer?"

Essa paused again, taking a long sip of kavage. He was stalling, probably trying to decide how much to tell me. I was fairly certain he wouldn't tell me anything, but he lowered the mug, and began to speak. "The words of a singer carry great weight. Iften of the Boar has asked that the Council treat Joden's truths as those of a Singer. He argues that this should be done because no full Singer was present." Essa shook his head. "But Joden of the Hawk has broken with our ways and there is debate as to whether this should be done."

Now it was my turn to delay, and I took a sip of kavage, uncertain how to reply. Joden was a friend, but he had made it clear that he would speak against Keir and me before the Council. "What is your position in all of this?"

Essa snorted softly. "You know that Singers hold words given to them in confidence close to their hearts?"

I nodded.

"They also keep their thoughts to themselves, as well."

I blushed at the reprimand.

Essa sat his mug down, and waved Amyu off when she would have offered more. I decided to change the topic. "If I can't listen to the truths, can I go out and walk around? I've never seen anything like the Heart of the Plains."

While his face didn't change, I could tell that he was pleased. "Of course. You may come and go as you wish. But your guards will accompany you. They have instructions as to who you may have contact with. I would ask that you obey those restrictions."

"I will follow your ways," I answered. "But may I see Heath?"

"I do not know the name. Of what tribe?"

"Of Xy." I smiled. "One of my lands, who came here with Simus of the Hawk."

Essa's blank look was replaced with one of humor. "I see no harm." He gave me an intent look. "We keep you from Keir so that—"

"So that I am free to make my own choice," I cut in. "Essa, if I was going to change my mind, I'd have done it when Antas was yelling at me that first night."

"As to that," he replied, "you must know that the Council has decided that while you are not yet confirmed, the courting should begin now. The snows approach, Daughter of Xy, and there is no time to waste."

My throat went dry. This had been explained to me, but I'd managed not to think about it. "Now?"

"The other warlords will be given a chance to court you. Each will send word, and Amyu will escort you to their tents. Each will try to convince you of their strength and skills." Essa smiled at me. "You control the courting, Xylara. If you wish it to end, you have but to say so. If you wish it to continue, indicate that as well."

I nodded, but didn't speak.

Essa looked over at Amyu, and then back at me. "Have your needs been seen to, Xylara? You have but to ask for something and it will be provided."

"A bath." I found my voice quickly enough. "With hot water."

Essa gave me a puzzled look.

"Xyians bathe under the bells," Amyu offered.

"Really?" Essa didn't seem impressed with the idea. "If that is what you wish, I will see what can be done." He rose and adjusted his robes and weapons, about to depart. "Is there anything else?"

I looked at him, tall and straight, really looked at him. He waited patiently, allowing me to study him, and that bird's wing around his eye.

"Would you sing something for me?" I blurted out.

Essa's eyebrows went all the way up. Amyu looked shocked.

I fidgeted slightly, and looked away. "I'm sorry. I heard Joden sing a few times, and he has a wonderful voice. You are a full Singer and I wanted to . . ." My voice trailed off.

"I am honored." Essa tilted his head. "What songs have you heard?"

I grimaced. "Mostly sad songs." I sighed. "Although Joden sang a funny breakfast song for us when we celebrated the ehat hunt."

"Perhaps something more fitting your mood, yes?" He took a deep breath, and began to sing. His wonderful voice filled the tent. It wasn't as deep as Joden's but it held the same kind of power.

I listened, spellbound, as he sang. The first verse spoke of the sun rising, and lovers laying in the cool grass, their bodies bathed in the light of the dawn. As the star disappeared from the morning sky, they appeared in his lover's eyes.

Essa took a breath, and the second verse talked of the sun at the nooning, with the lovers riding their horses side by side. Their shadows danced over the grasses and their skin was slick with warmth and sweat. The Plains shone gold in the daylight, but the stars were still in his lover's eyes.

Another breath on Essa's part, and the sun sank

down, to set on the Plains. Now the lovers danced in the light of the fire, their bodies yearning for one another. The stars were still hidden in the light of the sunset, but he turned to his beloved to see their gleam in her eyes.

The last notes of the song died away. Essa closed his mouth, and looked at me.

I swallowed hard. "That was beautiful, Eldest Singer Essa. But," I felt myself tearing up as I spoke, "there is another verse, isn't there?"

"There is." Essa tilted his head to look at me. "Would you hear it?"

"Yes. Please."

In the song, the sun was gone. The moon was high in the endless darkness, and his beloved had gone to the snows. His body ached for her scent and touch. The words explained that the darkness covered his sorrow, and his blade would end it. For even the stars cannot compare to the warmth of her eyes.

I dropped my eyes, remembering Isdra, and her pain.

As the last notes faded away, I looked up. Essa nodded his head to me, and left the tent.

Amyu wasn't going to go with me on my walk, claiming the press of chores. But I convinced her to come with me, since I knew that the warrior-priest guards wouldn't talk to me, or answer my questions. In point of fact, I noticed that the guards that appeared when I left the tent were older, and more experienced. I suspected that the younger ones had been replaced after the incident with Simus, but I didn't say anything.

Besides, I was proud of myself, that I could start to tell them apart. Once Keekai had told me of the one distinctive tattoo, it was much easier.

I exited the tent, putting on my cloak, and stopped dead in my tracks.

"Xylara?" Amyu was behind me, her cloak over her shoulders.

"I thought there was a wide walkway here. Last night, I am almost positive . . ." I looked around, puzzled. There was a wide open area in front of the tent now, with other tents surrounding it.

"There was." Amyu stepped forward, and my guards moved into position. "But the Tribe of the Snake wishes to dance tonight, for a new babe, born into the tribe."

"So they moved their tents." I took a few steps forward. "Does that happen often?"

"Of course." Amyu looked at me oddly. "They're just tents."

"Of course," I echoed. We started walking, skirting the open area to a walkway off to the side. "But if everything moves, how do you know where anything is?"

She took my question seriously. "Some things do not move. Waste areas, fire pits. And the herds are always beyond." She flashed me a look. "We have a saying. 'The Heart of the Plains is always beating.' "

I nodded in response, too busy looking around to talk.

There were people everywhere. Talking, laughing arguing. In front of tents, repairing tents, knocking tents down. Even as I watched, a section of tents collapsed, and warriors were loading them onto pack beasts.

"Are they moving?" I asked.

Amyu shrugged. "Moving or leaving. The snows come, and many are setting out."

"Does anyone stay here during the snows?"

Amyu shrugged. "A few. The lodges here are small."

The sun was warm on my face, but there was enough of a chill to the breeze that I was glad for my cloak as we walked.

But the people had caught my attention again. A group of small children ran past, laughing and chasing each other. They all had a wooden dagger in their belt, and a wooden sword at their side or strapped to their back. The children swirled around us, and then ran off between the tents. I laughed, enjoying their innocent mirth.

Then a man stepped between the tents, and blocked my view.

I looked up, right at Prest.

He stood there, tall and strong, with Epor's warclub strapped to his back. He'd shaved his head when he'd been sprayed with ehat musk, so his hair was still very short. I sucked in a breath in surprise at seeing him.

He waited until he knew I had seen him, winked at me, and walked off.

I stumbled a bit, but Amyu was walking ahead of me, so I focused on following her. None of my guards had noticed anything.

I stifled my grin. "So, do the Tribes stay together when they camp here?"

Amyu shrugged. "Most warriors like to be close to the theas and the little ones. So Tribes do camp together. But there are no formal lines that are drawn. All are free to camp where they please."

A fight broke out to our left, two female warriors taking blades to one another. My warrior-priest guards moved to avoid the clash when it spilled onto our path. I allowed myself to be steered off to the side. A flash of red caught my eye, and I looked behind us for a moment.

There stood Ander and Yveni, just behind us. Ander was grinning like a fool, and Yveni was smirking. They stepped off the path before anyone noticed them standing there.

I didn't bother to suppress my grin this time.

We rounded a corner, and I spotted a crowd gathered around something on the ground. Two warriors were sitting there, studying something on the ground between them. Others stood over them, watching intently.

As I drew closer I realized they were playing chess.

"I want to see this," I told Amyu, and moved closer, not waiting for her approval. I craned my head around to see the board that lay before them. Sure enough, it was chess, with pieces carved of wood. I chuckled when I saw the castles had been replaced with ehats.

One of the players looked up. "Warprize!" He scrambled to his feet. The crowd eased back so that I could get closer.

"Warrior." I gave him a nod. "How goes the game?"

He laughed. "I am showing them all my prowess, Warprize."

"Where did you learn it? Were you with Keir's army?"

He nodded. "I was, Warprize. Didn't last long in the tourney, either. Keir of the Cat is too good at the game."

The mention of Keir's name made my guards restless. I gestured for him to return to his game. "Good luck, Warrior."

"My thanks, Warprize." His voice followed me as he settled back to his game, and I returned to my guards.

Amyu was frowning. "I thought they planned a pattern dance."

I shook my head. "It is a game of Xy, called 'chess'. I taught it to Keir and some others. It is very popular with the warriors of his army."

We kept walking, and I soaked it all in, the sights and sounds of Keir's people. It was only when Amyu suggested that she needed to prepare the meal for the nooning that I agreed to return to my tent.

It was as we were strolling back that I spotted him. It

wasn't easy to do, but a movement in the shadows of a tent caught my eye.

It was Marcus. Fully cloaked, and hidden between two tents.

I almost felt like crying, but I kept moving, not wanting to put him at risk. How hard was it for him to move about, in a city of people who thought him afflicted?

They were here, all here, and that meant that Keir was close as well. I drew a deep breath of satisfaction, and kept walking.

We were almost to the tent, when a warrior came towards us, at a run. "Warprize! Warprize!"

"Here!" I called out, and the warrior ran over. My guards reacted, drawing their weapons as if to ward him off. The warrior stopped just outside their reach.

"Warprize." He sucked in air in order to speak. "Warprize, there is one that is ill. You must come."

"No." One of the guards spoke.

The warrior ignored him. "Warprize, I fear it is the plague."

10

For a brief instant, my heart filled with joy. It was a ploy. Keir would be waiting in a tent, pretending to be ill—

But then I saw the fear in Tant's eyes, and knew it was no gambit of Keir's. Tant was terrified. No one who had lived through the horror of the plague would ever take it lightly.

Goddess, no.

Deep within, a part of me started to wail in fear. The image of this city of tents burning, of these warm and vibrant people dead, flashed before my eyes.

But the other part, the Master Healer, awoke with anger and determination. Not here. Not if I had anything to say about it. I clutched the strap of my satchel. "Where?"

Relief flooding his face, Tant turned to lead the way, and we both ran into two of my guards, who had moved to block our path. "No. This is not—"

"*Bracnect*," I snarled. "Follow if you wish, but get out

of my way." I pushed past them, pulling Tant with me.

"Xylara," Amyu called, but I ignored her. I knew well enough that they wouldn't hurt me. As if to confirm my thought, two guards ran off, no doubt to report my transgressions.

"Keep moving," I whispered, and Tant obliged, moving off at a trot. I followed close behind, my thoughts racing with my feet.

Could it be the plague? We'd waited the required forty days after Gils died. A flash of sorrow cut me as I remembered the boy. His had been the last death caused by the illness. We'd waited the forty days, and dawdled as we'd traveled. Tradition said that was time enough for the plague to fade away.

But the sweat had been like no other, killing quickly and striking fast. Maybe we hadn't waited long enough. Maybe we'd carried it with us, an unseen enemy, into the Heart of the Plains.

My mouth went dry, but my eyes started to tear. *Oh, Goddess, please, no.* All these people. All these children. In my mind's eye I saw again the blackened village, used as a pyre for the dead.

We were at a tent and in before I could take another breath. The tent wasn't large, and held a pallet with a child on it, surrounded by three women, a small brazier off to the side. I focused instantly on the child, a boy, hair plastered to his forehead, damp with sweat. He turned wide, frightened eyes towards me.

"I found her," Tant started, but then Amyu and two of my guards burst into the tent.

"Outside," I barked.

They hesitated.

"Outside!" one of the women snapped, repeating my order with a glare as fierce as Marcus's.

That was too much for them, and they retreated out through the tent flap.

I knelt beside the pallet. "I am Lara, of—"

"Tant told us." The woman spoke. "I am Inde of the Bear, thea to Sako." She nodded her head toward the boy on the pallet. "Tant told us of the 'plague' and gave us this." She held out a jar of fever's foe. "We didn't know how to use it, and Tant said that you must be brought here, to treat the child."

The other woman protested. "She should not be here. Who is she, a city-dweller, to treat a child of the Plains? You offend the elements and the warrior-priests."

Inde's glance was a quelling one. "I will risk that, to protect the life of this boy."

The woman scowled, but closed her mouth in a tight frown.

"How long has he been ill?" I reached out to feel the boy's forehead, smiling at him. He stared at me unblinkingly. His wooden weapons were next to him, on his pallet, set out much the same way that Keir positioned his. That had to mean he was between three and four years old.

"A few hours." Inde took up a cloth, and bathed the child's forehead. "He complained of feeling tired earlier, and I put him to bed. I should have realized when he didn't protest that he wasn't well. I checked on him and found him sweating."

Tant was hovering over us. "I couldn't risk it, Warprize. Not after—"

"You were right, Tant." I gave him an approving glance, and he relaxed. "We can take no risks when it comes to the plague." I placed my hand against Sako's forehead. "But I doubt this is the sweat."

There was a noise outside. Before we could do more than look up, Wild Winds swept into the tent. "What is this?"

Tant and the women had lowered their heads, their eyes down. So I spoke up. "A sick child, Eldest

Warrior-Priest. They feared that it might be the plague, and asked me to see the child."

Wild Winds's eye narrowed, and he took a step closer. Tant pressed himself to the canvas to allow the man to pass. "Is it?" he demanded, the skulls hanging from his staff rattling against one another.

"No. It isn't." I answered firmly.

Tant sagged with relief, muttering a soft prayer to the earth.

"How so?" Wild Winds demanded.

"Do you hurt, Sako?" I asked softly. "Can you show me where?"

The boy nodded, and rubbed his throat and ears.

"Open your mouth," I asked, and sure enough, his throat was raw. "Does it hurt to swallow?"

He nodded again, his large brown eyes darting between myself and the warrior-priest.

"This is common for children among my people." I glanced at Inde and got a quick confirming nod. "It is not the plague."

Wild Winds turned, saying something soft to one of the guards outside. I heard running feet as Wild Winds turned back and folded his arms over his chest. "And how would you heal this, Xyian?"

Startled, I looked up into that tattooed face, but all I saw was honest curiosity.

"I would have the child rest and sleep. I would have his thea give him a dose of the fever's foe." I caught a flash of fear over Tant's face. "Out of the jar that I have given them." I reached for it, and scooped out some on my finger. "This much, every two hours." I showed it to Wild Winds, then turned back to Sako. "Open up. The taste is bad, but you are a warrior, eh?"

The boy bravely opened his mouth, and I scraped the fever's foe on his tongue. He made no protest to the

taste, warrior that he was. But that didn't stop him
from screwing up his face in disgust.

"How do you know this is not the plague?" Wild
Winds demanded.

"The plague strikes fast, and is very deadly. The
fever is hot and fierce. Any who take ill tend to lose
their wits, and sweat much more than this child." I
looked at the theas. "There is also an odor with the
plague, a very rank smell. Almost as bad as ehat
musk."

"So if the child had the plague, he would already be
dead," Wild Winds stated.

I nodded, even as the woman sucked in a breath in
horror. But Inde was made of sterner stuff. She'd followed our conversation intently, and now spoke.
"Warprize. I would ask for your token."

Caught off guard, it took me a moment to hand her
the jar of fever's foe. "You have my token, Inde."

Inde took the jar, and cradled it in her hands.
"Warprize, I would tell you a truth. The skills of the
Warprize are spoken of with praise, and you are known
to be a 'healer', with fabulous powers over life and
death." She kept her eyes averted, but turned her head
toward Wild Winds. "I would not offend, but I would
ask the warrior-priest to cast his spells of healing as
well." She shifted the jar in her hands. "The health of
the child is the most important thing."

Sako's eyes got even bigger, and he swallowed hard,
with obvious pain.

Magic. I might get to see magical healing. I kept my
face calm but my heart jumped at the chance. But
when I cast a look up at Wild Winds's face, he returned
my look with a neutral glance. I shifted my eyes away,
but the silence continued to grow. Was he really going
to refuse to heal a child?

I reached for my satchel, and shifted away from the boy's side. The theas were startled by my movement, but I ignored them. I tried to make my voice sound normal. "I am not offended, Inde. You are right. What matters is the boy's well-being."

I stood then, and stepped away, as if making room. As I brushed close to Wild Winds, I challenged him with a look, but said nothing.

Wild Winds arched an eyebrow in response, but also remained silent. I thought he would refuse, but then he let his cloak drop to the floor, and plunged his staff into the ground. With one step he moved to stand at the boy's side.

With wide eyes, the theas moved as well, Inde moving to Sako's head, the other woman to his feet. Tant was summoned with a flick of Wild Winds's finger, and placed opposite him.

Wild Winds took something from a belt pouch, and added it to the small brazier. Then he sank to his knees beside the boy. The others sank as well. Out of courtesy I sat down too, but with much less grace. The staff wasn't far from me, and those human skulls seemed to move on their own, dangling from the end of braided leather strips.

Wild Winds began to chant, calling the elements to him and asking for their aid. His voice was deep and strong. The others took up the chant as well, their heads down, their voices a soft undertone. Sako was perfectly still, his breathing deep and slow, his eyes closed.

Smoke puffed from the coals, and, to my surprise, spilled down over the sides of the brazier, a lovely, deep purple. It flowed down, covering the floor of the tent, and then started to rise slowly around us. It made me uneasy, but the others didn't seem to mind. I realized that their eyes were closed, and they were swaying slightly to the beat of the chant.

Wild Winds was an imposing figure, with those matted braids, and the tattoos that covered his body. The dim light made it seem as if they moved, intertwining, dancing over his skin to the sound of Wild Winds's voice. The skulls seemed to tremble with the sound, turning to grin at me.

I blinked a bit, sat up straighter, and tried not to breathe so deeply.

"We are of the elements," Wild Winds spoke as the others continued the chant. "Flesh, breath, soul, and blood." He reached and pressed his right hand down on Sako's left hand. "The soul is made of fire, and sits within the left hand."

The boy gasped at his touch, his whole body jerking, his eyes flying open. Wild Winds reached over and brushed his hand over them, and Sako closed them in obedience.

"The breath is made of air, and sits within the right hand." Wild Winds pressed on Sako's right hand. The boy's breathing was slowing again, as his body relaxed. I watched carefully, trying to see a change in his condition.

"The blood is made of water, and sits within the left foot." Wild Winds reached for the boy's foot and I remembered where I'd heard these words before. That night, in Keir's tent, after he'd attacked Lord Durst in the heat of anger. He'd used the same phrases. I tried to use them on Keir when he'd been ill, but I'd gotten it wrong.

Wild Winds pressed the boy's right foot. "The flesh is made of earth and sits within the right foot." He leaned back on his heels. "The elements will heal you, warrior of the Plains."

The brazier had stopped smoking, and the air was beginning to clear. Wild Winds reached out, and pulled the boy's blanket higher, over his shoulders. "Sleep now."

Sako stirred, opened his eyes and smiled into that fearsome face. "My thanks, Eldest Warrior-Priest." He yawned, and blinked sleepily. "You have honored me."

"Sleep." Wild Winds rose. The others were rousing as well, lifting their heads, and looking about as if confused. He looked down at them sternly. "Air the tent, but keep him warm."

"Our thanks, Eldest Warrior-Priest," Inde spoke, even as she and the other woman moved to obey, but Tant paused before me.

"I'm sorry, Warprize. I feared that the plague was here."

"You did the right thing, Tant." I stood as well, and gathered up my satchel. "We can't take any chances."

Tant nodded his head, and moved to help the others.

"I will escort you to your tent," Wild Winds said, retrieving his cloak and pulling his staff from the ground. He held the flap open and I emerged into the fresh, cool air. A breeze had sprung up, and I wrapped my cloak around me, even as Wild Winds brought his own over his shoulders.

Apparently, even warrior-priests could feel cold.

Amyu and the guards were waiting, and they stepped back as Wild Winds walked past them. I fell into step beside him, and Amyu and the others followed behind, silent.

After a moment, I risked a question. "What was in the smoke?"

"What was in the jar?" Wild Winds fired back.

"Fever's foe," I answered, using the Xyian words. "You make it by—"

"You'd share that?" He stopped and stared at me. "With me?"

I stood, and stared right back at him, ignoring the tattoos and focused on his eyes. "Yes."

We stood there in silence. I refused to look away as he studied me. One of my curls chose that moment to work its way loose, and float down to dance in the breeze.

Wild Winds spun on his heel, and strode off.

I had to run a few paces to catch up, determined to walk beside him, and not behind. The way before us was crowded with people and horses, but it cleared, as all who saw Wild Winds coming yielded the way.

The silence between us continued until I broke it again. "I thought you were in senel with the Council."

"I was, until word came that your affliction had appeared." He spared me a glance. "We are not stupid, Xyian. Whether it is an affliction or your 'illness', we fear your unseen enemy."

"I never said you were stupid," I answered hotly, and would have said more but for the obstacle in our path. A jumble of children and wooden swords came crashing out of a nearby tent. Absorbed in their game, they attacked each other in a flurry of blows, causing them to trip and fall over each other, and sprawl at our feet.

"What is this?" Wild Winds demanded, glaring down at them.

Three heads, covered in red curls, popped up. Pale faces, covered in freckles, went even paler, as three pairs of green eyes widened in horror at the sight of the warrior-priest.

I gasped. Gils . . .

A woman's voice rose from a tent, seeking the three troublemakers. That set the boys scrambling away through the tents, disappearing as quick as their legs could carry them.

Wild Winds snorted, and continued on his way.

I hesitated, but Amyu and my guards pressed me, and we followed behind.

Wild Winds didn't speak until we arrived at my tent. He turned to face me, folding his arms over his chest. His glare didn't bother me in the slightest. I just stood there, and crossed my arms too. And narrowed my eyes for good measure. "I do not understand your healing," I said.

"I do not understand yours," he replied.

"You use no herbs."

"You do not invoke the elements."

I dropped my arms, and sighed. "I've been known to pray to my Goddess."

Wild Winds hesitated, then gave me a quick nod. "I've been known to use certain plants."

We regarded each other. This time Wild Winds broke the silence. "Keir of the Cat despises warrior-priests and all of our ways. He would see us destroyed. This is no secret." He lowered his brows, and looked at me intently. "And you?"

I thought for a moment. "Keir is my Warlord," I said. "But there was a time when I feared all Fire-landers. I thought they were savage killers who breathed fire, and killed all living things."

Wild Winds's eyebrows shot up, but he simply nodded. "I will think on this."

I nodded as well. "So will I."

He turned and strode off without another word, and I watched him go, suddenly confused. Had I just made a friend? No, that was too strong a word. As was 'ally'. What did that mean?

"Wait," I called impulsively. Wild Winds paused and looked back at me over his shoulder. I took a few steps closer. "I want to know what is happening. What is going on before the Council?"

He scowled, the tattoos on his face moving to show his displeasure, but I took another step forward. "It's my life the Council is deciding and it's not right to keep me ignorant of—"

Wild Winds turned and walked away.

My mouth open, I watched as he strode off again.

"The warrior-priests keep their own counsel," Amyu spoke from behind me in condescending tones.

It was just as well that no one nearby understood Xyian. I vented my feelings with a few short, pithy comments about warrior-priests in general and stomped right into my tent.

A figure moved in the dimness, and I paused in the entrance, startled. "Who?"

A deep voice chuckled. "Pray to the Sun God my mother never hears you talk like that."

"Heath!"

I flung myself into my childhood friend's arms. Heath laughed, and leaned down to press our foreheads together, a ritual greeting just between the two of us. Then he lifted me up and twirled us around, holding me tight, and for a moment I was a child again, safe in the arms of my older 'brother'. I squeezed him again as he set me on my feet. "Heath, I am so glad to see you!"

"And I, you." Heath stepped back and spread his arms wide. "Look at you, Lara! A woman of the Plains."

Amyu paused inside the tent, frowning slightly. I smiled at her, taking Heath's arm to turn him toward her. "Amyu, this is Heath. He is of Xy."

Amyu's face cleared. "I was told of his coming. You may talk over the nooning, Daughter of Xy. But the Warlord Ultie has asked to court you after the meal." She removed her cloak. "I will bring kavage and food."

Heath laughed. "Well, I understood 'kavage' and my name. But not much else."

"This is Amyu of the Boar," I said. "A Warrior of the Plains."

Heath nodded his head. "Greetings, Warrior." He spoke the words slowly and carefully.

In a blink, Amyu's entire posture changed. Wooden-faced and stiff, she inclined her head and left the tent. I would have followed her, to ask how I offended, but Heath had all my attention. He pulled me toward the stools and table. "Lara, there isn't much time. We must talk."

I was so full of questions, I didn't know where to start. "Why are you here? What is happening in Water's Fall? How are Anna and Othur? And Eln?"

Heath shook his head, his own brown curls dancing. "Calm down, little bird! Let me get a word in edgewise!"

I laughed. We'd looked so alike as children, there'd been those that thought I was his sister, and daughter of Anna and Othur. But now his brown eyes regarded me seriously as he continued in Xyian. "But we'll speak this tongue." I gave him a questioning look, and he shrugged. "The Warlord thinks it wise."

Keir. He'd spoken to Keir! I sat up straight, and opened my mouth with a dozen more questions, but Amyu entered at that point, bearing kavage and a small bowl of gurt.

I accepted a mug, but Heath waved it away. "How can you drink that stuff, Lara?" Heath gave a mock shudder. "It's so bitter, and one mug sets my hands trembling."

"I've grown to enjoy it." I took a sip as Amyu left. Heath's gaze followed her as she left the tent.

"All was well when I left Water's Fall," Heath spoke softly. "There wasn't much time for farewells or letters, Lara. A messenger came, one of those fearsome looking warrior-priests, who walked in during a Council session in the throne room." Heath rolled his eyes. "The ladies of the Court fainted dead away at the sight.

"The warrior-priest brandished a spear and demanded that Atira go to the Heart of the Plains and appear before the Council to speak her truths." Heath's face grew grim. "Simus agreed, but once the messenger left, Simus told us that something was wrong. He swore Atira would not ride alone. We'd barely enough time to gather weapons and gear before we were on our way." He grimaced slightly. "I've never ridden that far, that fast before. We rode as if mountain demons were on our tails, changing horses every hour, or so it seemed. I suspect my body will feel it for days to come." He shifted a bit on the stool. "Mother and Father would have sent letters, but there wasn't time." He grinned. "Mother has taken the baby to her breast, and is cooing and clucking like a hen. It was a good idea to send Meara to her, Lara. The babe has filled her arms and her heart." Heath rolled his eyes. "But you should have heard her shriek when she saw the babe's tattoo."

I grinned, remembering my reaction. "Stain. They stain the babies."

"Stain," Heath corrected himself.

"Good." I was glad the babe from Wellspring was in Anna's hands. "But, Heath, I understand Simus's coming," I replied, "but why did you come?"

There was a touch of red on his cheeks. "I told Warren that we needed a representative of Xy with Simus. He wasn't happy, but had no time to argue."

I gave him a hard look, but he avoided my eyes. "When we reached the border, Simus and Atira started that weird warbling cry. It wasn't long before we found Keir and his men." Heath corrected himself. "His warriors. The Warlord was furious, having just received news of the attack on you." Heath reached out for a handful of gurt. "More horses and we were off again, riding hard. We arrived, exhausted and weary, only to have the Council summon Keir to appear before his feet even touched the ground."

"You were there?" I leaned forward.

"Oh, yes. I followed everyone into the tent. That huge tent was crowded, filled with people." Heath popped some gurt in his mouth and started to chew. "The Warlord, Simus as his Second." Heath grimaced. "Atira and Joden. And the one called Iften. They were all there." He popped another piece of gurt in his mouth.

"How can you eat that stuff? I've tried and I still can't stomach it," I said, more to distract myself than because I wanted to know. Was I the only one that was not at these sessions? What purpose did that serve?

Heath gave me a surprised look. "It's good!" I crinkled my nose, and he chuckled. "I guess I got used to it on the journey here."

"So, what happened in the senel?" I asked.

"Well, it was all in their tongue, Lara, so I understood only a word here and there. They were talking so fast, practically spitting their words at each other. I kept expecting them to come to blows more than once." He shook his head in admiration. "But the Warlord stood there before all of them, tall, strong, and defiant. He gave as good as he got, Lara, and never once released his temper or drew his sword. But Simus, oh, Lara, now there's a man for an argument. He'd pace back and forth, talking with his hands, smiling as if to charm the entire Council."

Heath grew serious for a moment. "After what seemed like hours, Keir sat, and that Iften spoke. Now there is one full of piss and wind. I'd not turn my back on him. Arrogant, he was, and strutting like a rooster."

Amyu came in, bearing bread, and meat with melted gurt. Her face was stony, and she didn't speak.

I knew something was wrong, but all my attention was focused on Heath. "And?" I demanded.

Heath picked up some bread, and waited for Amyu to leave the tent. "Iften ranted, Lara. I was sure at one point that Simus would pull his sword, but he didn't." Heath tore at the bread. "Lara, no one has told me the details, but I think Keir was punished by the Council. Their faces were grim as they spoke, and when Keir left the tent."

"Punished?" I asked. "How?"

Heath shook his head. "I do not know, Lara. They spoke so fast, and with such anger. Odd that such fierce warriors never once pulled their weapons during the council."

"Heath, you must take care." I put my hand on his arm to make my point, and felt the muscles there. "These people are fantastic warriors, and if they take offense, they attack without warning."

"I know about tokens, and their use," Heath tried to reassure me. He turned his head and smiled, and in that moment, I realized that my childhood friend had changed. He was thinner, harder, his muscles more defined. When he looked at me, his eyes seemed filled with pain, and a determination that I'd never seen before. "It helps that I still don't know the language that well. I'm careful what I say and who I say it to, that's all."

"Heath . . ." I cleared my throat. "What aren't you telling me?"

There was a long pause as he slowly chewed the gurt. I kept silent, and waited, knowing full well that eventually he'd speak. After a long moment, he raised his head and spoke. "You are not the only Xyian who lost their heart to one of the Plains."

11

When he and I were very, very young, Heath lost an argument with a porcupine in the castle gardens. Eln, who was the castle healer at that time, took control of the situation. He soothed Heath's tears, directed the castle staff, and dealt with Heath's pain calmly and carefully. It made a big impression on me as I watched him heal my friend, my own tears drying on my cheeks.

But now I looked into Heath's face and saw pain that I knew was beyond my abilities as a healer.

Would that the pains of the heart could be healed like the pains of the body.

I knew, of course, who it had to be. "Atira."

"Atira." Heath closed his eyes and sighed. "We started sparring when she was up and moving, at Eln's suggestion. She was so lovely, and so strong, determined to heal, to learn to read and speak Xyian. She learned our language so fast, and laughed at my attempt to learn hers. I helped her learn to read, she taught me some fighting moves, and, well . . ." He gave me a sheepish look. "One thing led to another, and . . ."

I gave him a gentle smile. "You don't have to explain to me, Heath."

He chuckled. "I guess not." He sighed deeply then, and looked off over my shoulder, lost in thought. The boy I'd known all my life was gone. In his place was a man.

"Your parents?" I asked softly.

"Mother and Father are less than pleased. I think they had plans for a placid Xyian wife and grandbabies." He used his free hand to run his fingers through his hair. "But Atira holds my heart."

I smiled.

Heath rolled his eyes. "Of course, Atira is not happy either. She wants nothing to do with 'bonding' and is displeased that I followed her. But I could do nothing else." He gave me that wry smile again. "I am of stubborn Xyian stock, and will not take 'no' for an answer."

"Heath—"

"Enough of my troubles, Lara." Heath drew himself up briskly, and helped himself to food. "The Warlord wants you to know that the truths are almost finished, and that the Council of Elders only have two things to do before the final debate and decision. First, they must determine what weight to give Joden's words. Then, they will hear your answers to their questions and accusations. The Warlord expects this to all come together within the next day or two."

I nodded, intent on his words.

"You are guarded now by warrior-priests, but he has others watching over you as well."

"I've seen them."

Heath nodded. "They did that on purpose, Lara. The

Warlord says that the warrior-priests are not to be trusted. If you are in need, cry out and help will come."

I relaxed a bit at that knowledge, but Keekai's words about blind hatred came back to me as well.

Heath flashed a smile at me. "Keir made me repeat this next part over and over. He does not trust my Xyian memory!"

He put down his bread on the table, and deepened his voice, as if imitating Keir. "All will be well, fire of my heart." Heath knit the fingers of both hands together. "Know that I love you, and that we will be together again soon."

My eyes filled with tears, and I looked up into Heath's understanding eyes. "Heath—"

"There is one thing more." His eyes twinkled. " 'But please, beloved, keep that temper of yours!' "

My mouth dropped open. "Why, that man . . ." I sputtered.

Heath laughed. "Oh, I think he knows you well, little bird!"

Amyu appeared in the entrance, clearly checking on our progress. Heath gave me a sly grin. "Eat up, Xylara, Daughter of Xy."

I watched as he reached for the meat dish with the red flakes in it, and didn't say a word.

"This courting is over!" I jerked open the tent flap. The entire structure shuddered under the force of my pull, but I just kept moving, not caring in the slightest if the entire tent collapsed on the Warlord Ultie. The arrogant, loud-mouth, overbearing, obnoxious, bad-breathed Warlord Ultie.

It would serve him right.

Amyu and my warrior-priest guards had made themselves comfortable nearby. Caught by surprise, they scrambled for their cloaks and gear. I didn't stop, just stormed off down the walkway, biting my tongue to keep from speaking my thoughts out loud. That self-centered, boorish cretin. How dare he talk about Xy that way? About Keir that way? To my face? I gritted my teeth as my anger grew with every step away from that—

"I would guess that this courting did not go well?" Amyu moved up to walk next to me.

I glanced at her, surprised to see the first very faint hint of approval on her face. I scowled. "That man is a—" I resorted to Xyian for the rest of the sentence.

"They are not all Keir of the Cat," came her very soft response.

I didn't say anything more, ever conscious of the listening ears of my warrior-priest guards. But I did slow a bit, as we headed toward my tent. It was mid-afternoon, and the Heart was beating with the pulse of its people.

Life on the Plains had a certain rhythm to it. The mornings were for chores, all the necessary things that needed to be done for life to be sustained. Afternoons seemed focused more on play and gathering, or maybe teaching was a better way to put it. Children were playing all around us, mock fighting with wooden swords and daggers. They ran and yelled, warbling cries just like their elders. I smiled to see them, but I knew there was a more serious tone here than just children playing. They were developing the skills that would keep them alive in this world.

I tried hard to let go of my anger and frustration. I was worried about what was happening. But there was no one I could ask who would answer. So I gritted my teeth and tried to be patient. But I feared for Keir.

Two women were playing chess between some tents, their board set on a stump between them. They hunched over, intent on the game. Four children had gathered close, watching the play. I could hear them asking questions, hanging on the older women.

A few steps more, and I was surprised to see a group of horses standing in the walkway, seemingly unattended, watching as two warriors examined the hoof of one of the mares. They had the leg up, and were checking it over, as the horse craned its neck to look too.

"They allow horses in the Heart?" I asked.

"Of course," Amyu responded. "If they wish. They are free to come and go."

"Don't they soil the area?"

"Do you?" Amyu answered, with a puzzled look on her face.

Honestly. I mentally rolled my eyes at that. For the love of the Goddess, they were just *horses*.

I spoke too soon. There, in front of my tent, stood Greatheart.

He neighed and trotted over when he spotted me. I smiled as he butted his head against my chest. "Hello, Greatheart."

Which earned me a few confused looks from my escort. I ignored them as I reached up to scratch between Greatheart's ears, and then along the scar that ran over his chest.

"Greatheart?" Amyu asked. "What is that?"

"It's his name."

"You name horses?" one of the warrior-priests asked, in an insulting tone.

I turned slightly, and glared at all of them. "Yes. Xyians name their horses." I arched an eyebrow. "It's also a Xyian custom to exchange names when you meet someone." I glanced at each warrior-priest in turn, making my point as clear as I could.

They returned my look with stony faces. Amyu shifted her weight, and spoke after she gave them an uneasy glance. "It is the custom of the warrior-priests not to give their names, Daughter of Xy."

"And not to speak, except to insult someone or their ways." I turned away, and buried my face in Greatheart's mane. He smelled of horse and grass and freedom. "Are you recovered from our ride, my friend?" I whispered, and watched as his ears flicked in response to the sound of my voice.

Greatheart snorted, and buried his wet nose in my hair, drawing in deep breaths as he took in my scent.

"The Warlord Osa wishes to pay court to you, Xylara." Amyu's voice came from behind me. "When you are ready."

I sighed for a moment, letting my fingers still. "Just how many warlords are there?"

"Four for each of the four elements," Amyu answered. She continued hastily when she saw my face. "But only eight wish to court you, Xylara."

I bowed my head, hid my face with my hair and rolled my eyes. It was all so frustrating and tiresome. Keir was *my* warlord, he would remain *my* warlord; they could parade all the stupid arrogant lummoxes they wanted before me, and he'd still be *my* warlord.

Greatheart snuffed and stamped his foot, and I resumed the scratching. I thought for a moment, and then spoke. "Amyu, is there any chance that this Warlord would want to go for a ride?"

It felt so good, to be on Greatheart's back and feel him move under me. We were galloping through the grasses, the wind in my hair. The sun was bright, even if the air was cool, and I smiled, taking deep breaths. It made my spirits rise, to be out and riding.

The blue sky was glorious, but it seemed to me that the reds of the grasses were muted, duller than when

I'd first seen the Plains. Just like the trees of Xy lost their vibrant red and yellow leaves before the snows. Winter was coming to the Plains.

Amyu gestured off to the side, and I saw a rise ahead where we could wait for the Warlord Osa. I pulled Greatheart to a stop and turned him to face the city.

Below us sprawled the Heart of the Plains. The first time I'd seen it, I'd been exhausted, unable to appreciate what lay before me. But now I could look my fill, and marvel at it.

The lake lay glittering in the distance. The huge Council tent was pitched on the shore of the lake, and the city of tents formed around that in a half circle. There was so much color there, in the tents and the banners. It looked like one of the patched quilts I'd had on my bed in the castle. I narrowed my eyes, and studied it for a moment. The city seemed different too, from the first time that I'd seen it. I'd been tired, granted, but still . . .

"It looks smaller, somehow," I commented.

"Some have left, for the snows are coming," one of the warrior-priests responded gruffly.

"The Heart doesn't beat in the snows. It sleeps, to beat again when the Plains awaken," Amyu offered, her tone just a bit more friendly. I sighed, and kept my eyes on the Heart. I was getting very tired of the disapproving looks, whether it was due to my skill as a rider, or my evil Xyian ways.

Of course, just as we'd mounted, it occurred to me that going off with only my warrior-priest guard wasn't the wisest course of action. But I'd wanted air and exercise, and I'd asked impulsively, without really thinking.

I'd underestimated Keir's cleverness. There was a constant flow of warriors in and out of the Heart; it was almost as busy as Water's Fall. I'd spotted Prest and Rafe in the first moments of our ride and had relaxed. If Amyu or the others had noticed our shadows, they'd not commented on it. So I was free to admire the sights and await the coming of the Warlord Osa.

He'd better not be like the last one. Goddess, that man had been just plain rude from the moment I'd stepped into his tent. Proclaiming himself to be superior to Keir in every way, and offering to bed me to display his skills. I scowled at the memory. If this new Warlord was the same arrogant ass, I'd leave him here without a word.

The pounding of hooves drew my attention to a group of warriors headed our way. I tensed, thinking it was an attack, but Amyu spoke. "Osa."

At the head of the group was a woman warrior, with hair like flame. She rode a pure white stallion, with a lovely long mane and tail. As they drew closer, I could see that she was dressed in rich brown leathers from the tip of her toes to the top of her . . . breasts. I was taken aback a bit, but I knew that the leathers were not intended as armor, since her more than ample breasts were thrust up and apart in an astounding display.

Her skin was fair, and she had a whip tied to her belt, opposite her sword. A stunning woman. She reined up close by, and I could see that her eyes were brown, and flecked with gold. She was the loveliest woman I had ever seen.

"Xylara, Daughter of Xy." She inclined her head in a regal manner. "I thank you for this opportunity."

All the breath left my body. *Goddess above, she was the Warlord Osa.*

Just as well that she turned then to wave off our escorts, and reached to tie bells in the mane of that lovely white horse. It gave me a chance to snap my mouth shut and recover my wits. Even my warrior-priest guards obeyed without question, melting away in the heat of her confident authority. She took no note, as if she expected to be obeyed. Her attitude reminded me so very much of Keir. That alone was enough to tell me that her power was equal to Keir's. In every way.

She was a picture of perfection as she turned and smiled at me. "I am the Warlord Osa of the Fox."

"Women can be warlords?" I blurted out. "I know they can be warriors, but—"

One perfect brow rose, but Osa was polite in her answer. "Of course, Xylara." She tilted her head, and studied me with warm brown eyes. "I'd heard that your ways are far different from ours, but surely not that different."

I opened my mouth, but words failed me. How could I explain my culture to this woman? I settled for the simplest explanation. "Woman warriors are rare in my land. Woman warleaders are rarer still."

She nodded then, knotting her reins in front of her, and starting to pull off her brown gloves. I was suddenly very conscious of my tangled hair, and my clothes. A little brown bird next to a phoenix.

I had to know. "Have you ever slept with Keir?" I blurted out, my face flushed in embarrassment even as the words left my lips.

Honestly surprised, Osa gave me an elegant shrug. "No, Xylara. Once I met my obligations to the Tribe, my bedmates have all been women. Men are not to my taste." She gave me a sly glance. "Which is why I asked to court you. I'm told that you had no experience before Keir. You might find the ways of loving between women to be more to your liking."

Goddess above.

Just as well that I was seated on a horse. My entire body went cold, then flushed hot as the world tilted around me. And I wasn't sure if it was fear, embarrassment . . . or curiosity.

Goddess above.

Osa's gentle chuckle brought me back, a gentle sound for so fierce-looking a woman. "I've shocked you. Maybe your ways are so very different from ours, yes?"

I swallowed hard. "I—I'd not give offense."

"I take none. And it didn't occur to me to ask for your token, so I hope I have given none." Osa shook her head, and her red curls danced in the sun. "What does it matter who sleeps with whom, as long as it is by agreement?"

A thought occurred. "Osa, is there rape here?"

"Rape?" I'd used the Xyian word without thinking. I explained and she grimaced in understanding. "Rare, Xylara. There are too many blades among us, and all are skilled in their use."

"Even the theas?"

"The theas are some of the deadliest of us all, Xylara. They guard and guide the young." She gave me a smile. "I suppose Ultie offered to show you his body and skills?"

I rolled my eyes. "He dropped his trous to show me his 'weapon'!"

Osa laughed, a warm, rich sound, then crinkled her nose. The gold flecks in her eyes seemed to dance. "And you wonder that I would choose women over men? Or you over Ultie?"

I choked on my own laughter, and coughed to clear my throat. "I am promised to Keir."

"So?" Osa gave an elegant shrug. "What of that?"

"My people do not have sex outside of a bond," I tried to explain.

Osa moved her horse closer, and she leaned in toward me. "What of that, lovely lady? You are not yet bonded. You are free to taste the pleasures of many before you commit to one." I watched mesmerized as she leaned in, her breasts moving within the leather, close enough to touch. Close enough to . . . kiss.

I jerked my head back in surprise. Greatheart shifted under me, responding to my movements, putting a bit of distance between us. Her smile gone, Osa pulled back and watched me intently, like a phoenix might study its prey.

I licked my lips. "Osa, I—" I had to breathe. "I can't."

She shrugged again, and somehow I knew that her elegance was as natural as breathing to her. She probably killed with the same exquisite movement.

"I was told that you had honor, Lara." Osa's smile was back. "And that your ways are strange. I take no offense."

"Thank you," I replied, still feeling a bit unsettled.

"So. Since I cannot court you, perhaps you would come to my tent, and we can share a meal. I wish to know more of your healing skills. I can promise to be better company than Ultie."

I made a face. "That wouldn't be a challenge, Warlord."

She laughed, and gestured for our escorts to follow us.

After Osa, I went to the tents of the next five warlords with my escort, and made my position to each one very clear. Keir of the Cat was my chosen Warlord, and my decision was final.

I was gracious, and kind, and they were polite in their acceptance of my refusal.

Exhausted, I'd returned to my tent. The last of the warlords would have to wait for the next day. All I wanted was my bed.

Only to find that the Tribe of the Snake was holding a dance near my tent, with much joy and laughter. I was too tired to watch, so I went inside, complained about the lack of a real bath to Amyu, and crawled between the blankets with a grateful sigh.

Oddly enough, the drums were more soothing than anything else. I fell asleep with no trouble.

They were still beating when I awoke with a start. There was a cloaked figure crouched by my bed.

I gasped, startled half out of my wits. The figure moved, reaching out a hand. "Healer, will you come?"

It took me an instant to understand. "Amyu?"

She moved closer, pressing her fingers to my lips. "Yes. There is a need. Will you come?"

I threw off the bedding and quickly dressed in the clothes she pressed into my hands. I ran my fingers through my hair, thrust my feet into my shoes, and grabbed my satchel. Amyu threw a cloak over my shoulders, and took my hand.

It was dark in the depths of the tent. I could hear the drums of the dance, but their beat was slower, and more sensual. I yawned once, cracking my jaw as I did so, and tried to shake the sleep from my eyes.

Quietly, Amyu headed for the back area, where she worked and slept. I couldn't make out the details in the dim light, but she walked up to that tent wall, and knelt, pulling it up just enough so that we could squeeze under. I paused, suddenly uncertain.

Amyu sensed my hesitation. "Please. We need a healer."

I nodded and knelt, pushing my satchel before me, and squirmed outside. Amyu followed, and we got to our feet together. "Your guard watches the dance."

Mentally, I rolled my eyes. I could just imagine the kinds of 'dances' they were watching.

Amyu's voice was the barest of whispers as she took my arm. "Come."

We hadn't gotten five steps when a large man loomed up before us. "What's this?" he asked.

"Prest." I spoke as I sagged in relief. He took a step

closer, and I could make out Epor's warclub in its harness over his shoulder.

Another voice came from the shadows behind us. "Warprize. This is not safe." Amyu spun, hand on her dagger, but I wasn't surprised to hear Rafe's voice.

"Someone needs my skills," I responded.

Amyu recovered. "You are Keir's men." I could tell she was surprised that they'd caught us.

"We guard the Warprize," Prest said.

"And we do not watch dances," Rafe responded firmly. "Now why do you lure the Warprize away?"

"She is needed," Amyu whispered urgently. "For a healing."

Rafe gave her the once over. "Can she be trusted?" He spoke in Xyian.

"I don't know," I answered in the same language. "But I won't let that stop me from healing someone."

Rafe looked at Prest.

Prest shrugged.

Rafe rolled his eyes, and let out a soft, exaggerated sigh. "You are of no help." He turned back to Amyu. "Show us the way."

She gave a quick nod, and moved silently away in the darkness.

We followed, quietly, as she took us on a path between the tents, careful to disturb no one. While the Heart never stops beating, it does sleep, and there were very few people about, and most were focused on their own tasks.

As we walked, I moved close to Rafe. "How is Keir?" I asked, keeping my voice as soft as I could.

Rafe smiled, his eyes twinkling under his hood. "Frustrated. Furious. But determined, Warprize. He hasn't killed anyone."

"Yet," Prest added.

I sighed. "He's not the only one."

Rafe gave me a sympathetic look. "I'll tell him, Warprize. Provided he doesn't kill me for letting you do this."

"Look." Prest pointed.

Ahead of us lay a series of tents, alive with torches and movement. Amyu guided us to the largest one and threw open the flap. The tent was filled with light, heat, and people, both men and women. And the all too familiar smell of blood, sweat, and fear.

"Call out if you need us," Rafe's voice came from behind me, and I absently nodded in response. All of my attention was on the figure on a pallet in the middle of the tent.

It was a woman, a very naked, very pregnant woman, sprawled on the bedding. Her skin gleamed with sweat, and she was clearly exhausted. Her eyes were glazed, unseeing. Surrounded by the others, she was gasping, panting through her pains. Her distended belly shone in the light, looking tight enough to burst.

"How long?" I asked. It had to be hours, by the look of things.

All heads turned as I spoke, and Amyu pushed in from behind me.

"Why have you brought her here?" A woman who looked as old as Keekai stood before me, as if to bar my way. She was naked from the waist up, and sweating as well.

"She is a healer." Amyu stood her ground, even as her voice trembled. "If there is any chance to save Eace—"

"That is not your place, child," the woman snapped. For a moment I thought I'd be thrown out of the tent, but her features softened. "What is done is done." She turned away, then, towards the woman on the pallet. I followed, to look between the woman's legs. She was open, and I could see a tiny foot, trying to emerge.

"I am Reness, Eldest Thea." The one who'd barred my path was speaking. "This is Eace's first. I've tried to turn the babe, but it will not shift." She reached out, and a man handed her a knife, its blade bright in the light. The flames from the braziers flickered on its surface, and in her eyes as she looked at me. "I have heard of your skills, you who would be a warprize."

She held up the knife, and looked at me, her face a mask of pain. "I've cut babes out before, but the woman always dies." She took a deep breath. "I would ask that you use your skills to bring her back from the dead, once the baby is born." She turned away, and brought the knife to bear on the woman's stomach.

12

One quick step, and I had my hand on the clenched fist that held the dagger, preventing it from touching the skin. I looked at Reness's stark face, and gave her a serious grave look, even as my heart sang with happiness. "I've cut out babes before, and the women have lived."

Hope flared in eyes where there'd been none. Some of the faces about us mirror'd hers. Reness stilled her hand. "You have?"

"I have." I looked around at hopeful faces, including Amyu's. "It is difficult and dangerous. But let me try."

There was silence for a moment, as the theas around us considered each other.

"She is not of the Plains." One spoke softly.

"Do not trust in this woman, Eldest Thea," another urged. "The winds may rise up in anger."

The woman moaned and writhed in pain. I didn't look away from Reness, who stared at me.

Then Reness nodded her head and sheathed her dagger. "Do it."

"Get a table in here, and get her on it," I ordered. "I need water, cloths for the blood, and the sharpest, smallest blade you can find me. Quickly. This has gone on long enough."

There was a flurry about us as they acted as quickly as I could ask. I concentrated on digging out one of my precious needles from my satchel, and some of the dried gut that I always kept there, trying to keep my joy off my face. My heart swelled, filled with a sense of comfort, of pure satisfaction and delight. Here was a task I could do, and do well, in a situation I'd been in many times before. A wonderful sense of being needed filled me, a sense of being wanted.

Of being home.

I schooled my face, and braided my hair up to get it out of the way as I watched the preparations.

Amyu was kneeling by my patient's head, smoothing back her damp hair, and murmuring something in her ear. She stayed with her even as they lifted Eace onto the table. I caught the words 'warprize' and 'help'. Eace's eyes seemed more rational now, her head straining up so that she could see me over her belly.

A small knife, probably a skinning blade, was pressed into my hand. I recognized the black flint that was used in the tips of their throwing lances. Ironic that such an instrument of death could be used to save a life. Everyone else was stripping off their tunics, men and women, due to the heat. One of the men offered me a bowl and a pitcher of water, and I held out my hands for the ritual blessing, praying as the water poured over my hands and the knife. *Goddess, please guide my hands.*

I took my place, and watched as another contraction

wracked through my patient. "Scream, Eace," I offered. "It will help with the pain."

"I will not," Eace panted, laying flat, her face white as snow, sweat pouring off her. "I am a warrior of the Plains. I will not move, I will not flinch. I will chant battle cries."

I exchanged glances with some of the older women in the room, about to roll my eyes at that comment. But their faces were grim, and I realized that they expected the pain. They thought that was normal. I sighed, and shook my head. "I will not take a chance. Hold her down."

Many hands reached, and Eace started to chant. "Birth of air, death of—"

Warrior that she was, the poor thing didn't scream. She jerked under their hands at the touch of my blade, and then conveniently fainted away. I worked swiftly to take advantage of that, making my first cut carefully. Two men stood off to the side, and used cloths to keep the site as clean as possible.

Eln had developed a new technique with these births, pushing the muscles aside instead of slicing them, cutting only where absolutely necessary. I strained, working my hands in, trying to keep my cuts as small as possible.

Once through the womb, I handed the knife out, and reached in to sort out the babe, feeling for the cord, to make sure it wasn't wrapped around—

I laughed right out loud as my fingers told me what I needed to know.

The theas looked at me as if I'd lost my mind. I just shook my head, and eased forth the babe, who popped out screaming. One of the men stood close, with a clean cloth held open for the child. I placed the crying boy in the blanket, the cord still attached.

"Heyla!" The man laughed and grinned at me. "Hear a warrior's cries!"

The others broke out into smiles, but I just plunged my hands back inside. "Then here's double the joy!"

I carefully pulled forth another baby, a girl, red-faced and furious, screaming at this new world. She was even louder than her brother, and she had every right to be, since it was her foot that had blocked the canal.

"Twins!" The theas around us crowed in joy, crooning to the babes.

Reness moved closer, and I looked to her. "Can you tie off the cords, Reness? I must finish here."

Reness drew her dagger again, her face as bright as the blade. "I am honored, Warprize."

I turned my attention to Eace, and worked to make sure that I cleaned her out well, before I started to stitch her closed. I tried to be careful, with small stitches, but I was fighting time and her bleeding. Amyu remained by Eace's head, stroking her forehead, and stared at me with wide eyes.

The babes were off behind me, being cleaned and checked over. But theas remained with me, helping to keep the site clear of blood, dealing with the mess. No wonder she had such a problem, the babes were so large, and Eace a small thing. I concentrated on my work, mindful that my patient was a warrior, and would want to leap to her feet at the first moment of awareness.

Which gave me an idea. Once I had the birthsack closed off, I gestured to my satchel. "I've bloodmoss in there, wrapped in blue cloth. Could someone—"

"I know it." One of the theas reached within, and held it out for me. I gave him a surprised look. He shrugged. "I was given some by one of Keir's warriors."

I checked first, to see that the birthsack was properly positioned, that the muscles had eased back into position. Then I pulled the skin together and applied the bloodmoss.

Sure enough, it started to seal the cut, leaving an angry red line in its place. I had to be careful, I didn't want the herb to seal the layers together. But the bloodmoss did its work, turned color and then pulled clean away from the wound. I took a step back, and drew in a deep breath of relief. Eace was still unconscious, but her breathing had eased. I placed my hand on her chest to find her heart beating steadily.

"She's . . . ?" Amyu looked at me.

I smiled, tired and sweating and feeling so very good. "She's well, so far. Only time will tell."

The theas moved in then, with water and cloths, cleaning the unconscious girl, and removing the soiled bedding, making her more comfortable. One offered me a bucket of water, soap, and a scrubbing cloth. I plunged my hands in gratefully, and started scrubbing. I had to chuckle when I saw the state of my tunic. Anna the cook had often claimed that I didn't own a piece of clothing that didn't have blood on it at one time or another. She was right.

I glanced over at my patient, proud and satisfied. Two lives saved, by my skill and the will of the Goddess. One still hung in the balance, but only time would tell if Eace would survive. Tears of joy sprang to my eyes, and I focused back on my scrubbing, not sure that any around would understand my tears. *Thank you, Lady of the Moon and Stars. Thank you.*

I scrubbed harder, blinking my eyes clear. I'd have to send Eln word that I'd used bloodmoss for this procedure. Although, knowing my old master, he'd probably already tried it.

Reness approached, bearing a clean tunic. She offered it to me. I glanced around the tent, but everyone was focused on Eace, so I turned my back on her, and quickly changed.

I turned back, to see that she was looking at me oddly. "So it is true what they say, about those of Xy."

I laughed. "Yes. Which is why I haven't had a decent bath since I got here."

"Bath?" Reness asked, puzzled. "But the lake—"

Eace stirred at that moment, looking around, dazed and confused. Amyu was beside her, crying and smiling. Eace blinked up at her. "What happened? Where is my babe?"

I looked about expecting someone to bring forth her babes. But I realized that the babes were gone.

"Where is my baby?" Eace cried out plaintively, struggling weakly to sit up.

The theas, male and female, all gathered around the table, hands reaching out to soothe her. Reness stepped over, to place her hand on Eace's forehead. "There were two babes, Eace. Two tattoos for your arm. You have done well."

"Two? Two?" Eace struggled even as they pressed her to stay down. "Where are they?"

"In the arms of the Tribe," one of the others offered, in a soft voice.

"B-but I want—" Eace started weeping, and my own throat closed. Why didn't they bring the babes back to her?

Suddenly, all of the male theas bowed low to Eace, low enough to show the backs of their necks, and left the tent. Reness stood tall at her side, and placed her fingers over the crying woman's lips. "We are the life-givers. Life-bearers of the Plains."

"This is our burden. This is our pain." The others crowded around as they intoned the words, their voices soft and low. I doubted that they could be heard outside the tent. Reness looked over at me, and gestured me to step closer. I took a step, and arms reached out to pull me within the press of bodies. Eace was surrounded on all sides, being touched and stroked by every woman around the table.

"The Tribe has grown. The Tribe has flourished," Reness chanted. Eace was still weeping, her eyes closed, but she'd stopped crying out.

"This is our burden, this is our pain."

"Our babes are taken. Our arms are empty." Reness's voice was a whisper. Eace stared up into her eyes.

I bit my lip, wanting desperately to go get the babies and place them in her arms. But it was clear that this was part of their world and their tradition. Eace's sorrow was deep, and reflected in the eyes of every woman around us.

"This is our burden, this is our pain." The other women were hugging each other, arms on each other's shoulders, forming a circle around Eace. I was included, wrapped in the press of their bodies.

Eace was nodding her acceptance now, although her pain was still there, raw and ugly. She whispered along with Reness, "This is the price of our freedom."

The tent was silent, then Reness leaned forward, placing a kiss of Eace's forehead. "You have served the Tribe well, child. Bare your arm, and receive your tattoos." She stood, smiling. "Then we will dance, yes?"

The women around us cried out in joy. Some were bringing out new supplies, and calling the men back in to the tent.

Eace frowned then shifted on the table, putting her hand on her flaccid stomach. "I thought you were going to cut the babes free? How do I live?"

Amyu spoke. "I brought the Xyian healer."

Eace's eyes widened. "Did she bring me back from the snows?"

"No." I wasn't going to let that rumor start. "I used

my skills to cut the babes out, Eace. You will be well, although it will take time to heal. Sleep is the best thing."

Eace just looked at me in astonishment. The theas started moving then, and Reness pulled me back, out of their way as they prepared to tattoo Eace's arm. She gestured for Amyu, who moved over by us reluctantly.

"She will heal?" Reness asked me, and at my nod, pressed further. "Will she bear again?"

I shook my head. "I don't know. That is in the hands of the elements."

"Her milk will come?"

"It should." I bit my lip. "Will she feed her own babes?"

Reness shook her head in response, gathering up my satchel to put it in my hands. "No. She'll nurse others."

"And what happens if she can't bear more?" I asked, curious. "I know that you require five before—"

Reness's eyes flickered to Amyu for a moment, and I followed her look to see that Amyu was in the process of putting on her tunic. She froze under our gaze, but all I could see was her left arm. Her bare left arm. No tattoos.

No children. Amyu had no children. My eyes met hers, and I saw another kind of pain in their depths.

Reness frowned. "You must return to your tent, before your absence is discovered. Go now."

Startled, I protested. "Eace must be watched for signs of—"

"We will do that." Reness threw my cloak over my shoulders. Amyu was pulling on her tunic.

"But . . ." I didn't want to leave my patient without aid. "You could have a warrior-priest check—"

Reness barked a laugh. "What warrior-priest would trouble themselves over a birth?"

I stared at her, dumbfounded. Reness ignored my reaction, and hustled me out of the tent, Amyu following behind with my satchel. "We will watch her carefully, I swear it," Reness said. "Now go, and quickly."

Rafe and Prest were waiting, and we started back in silence, much to my frustration. Amyu avoided my eyes, and I didn't press her with questions. I huffed out a breath, and pulled my cloak close around me. My questions could wait, until I'd had more sleep.

But as I left that tent, I knew one thing for certain. When the time came, if the time came, no one was taking my babe from my arms.

Unless I was dead.

I broke Amyu's silence at breakfast. She served kavage and food, and then tried to bow herself from the room, but I spoke first. "Amyu."

She stopped, clearly not happy, her eyes down.

"Amyu—" Now that I'd started I wasn't sure what to say.

"I am barren." Amyu's voice was flat, her face void of any emotion. "I have not quickened since my moon times came on me." She didn't look up, didn't move, but her hands clenched into fists. "I have prayed to the elements and tried every remedy suggested by count-less theas and initiators. I even managed to convince a warrior-priest to treat me, but still my body will not bear." She remained unmoving, but her knuckles were white. "What once brought pleasure is now almost too painful to suffer."

"Amyu." I gestured to the stool opposite mine, but she did not move. "I don't—"

"I was chosen to serve you, because even if I was contaminated by your ways, it would not matter."

I stiffened. "Why doesn't it matter?"

She lifted her face, proud and detached. "Bearing no children, I remain a child myself, unable to serve the

Tribes as a warrior. I will perform this last task, then I will seek the snows."

That explained why Essa and Reness had called her a child, then. I had thought it a form of endearment, but it wasn't. It was her status.

"Amyu." I leaned forward, desperate that she understand. "I have ways to aid a woman to bear children, but I don't have them with me. There are herbs in the mountains, horse grass for example, that might—"

"So I turn to your ways to bear for the Tribe?" Amyu spat. "What does that make me? Of the Plains? Of Xy?" She grimaced and turned to go.

"You asked for my help for Eace. Can't you accept that help for yourself?"

She paused, back straight, then headed for the tent flap. "Eat, Daughter of Xy. They are seeing to a bath for you."

She left me sitting there, with food before me, and no real appetite. What a waste that would be. How many lives, like Amyu and Marcus, did the Plains lose because of their ways and traditions?

I took a drink of kavage, dark and bitter on my tongue. Maybe there was a good reason to take babes from their mothers, but I couldn't see it. And I'd die a hundred times before I'd allow a babe of mine to be taken from me.

Suddenly, it seemed so hopeless. The idea that I could change anything about these people, even with Keir's help . . . it seemed so ridiculous. So impossible. That we could combine our peoples, and benefit both, despite their differences.

Keir. My throat suddenly closed. I missed him so much. I wanted him close, to talk, to argue, to touch. I hated this separation, hated not knowing what was happening to him. Maybe I could get a message to him, somehow. Maybe Rafe, or Prest? I took up the flat bread, and started chewing.

I stopped in mid-bite. Did she say something about a bath?

"This wasn't quite what I had in mind." I tried not to laugh at them, since it wasn't their fault. But my hosts had very odd ideas of what 'bathing under the bells' meant.

They'd put up a tent over a stream that pooled deeply next to the bank. The tent stretched from bank to bank, and down into the water. There was no top. They'd carefully asked if I had to be private to the skies, and I'd solemnly told them that it wasn't a problem.

"It's private," I conceded. The warrior-priests were glaring at me rather fiercely. Apparently Reness carried a bit of weight and they'd been told in no uncertain terms to arrange a bath for me.

"Of course, my Warlord provided warm water," I added sweetly.

Amyu suppressed a slight smile as my offended guards filed out. "We will guard upstream and down, so that you are not disturbed." Amyu offered a basket full of drying cloths, and a clean tunic and trous on top. I dropped my satchel on the shore, and took them with a great deal of satisfaction. It was going to be chilly, but it was a bath, and I couldn't wait to wash my hair.

Amyu gave me a nod. "Call out if you need me."

I waited until the tent flap fell shut, then stripped off my clothes. The sun was high, almost to the nooning, so that would help keep me warm as I dried. I'd wash out my underthings as well. Naked, I sat on the grassy shore, and dug out my precious bar of vanilla soap. There was a bit of vanilla oil left too. I'd save that for my hair. I chortled in delight. A bath. Finally!

I set everything out where I could reach it, and then slipped into the water, gasping as the cold stole my breath.

The bottom was sandy under my toes, clear of sticks and rocks. I reached down and added some sand to my hands as I worked the soap for suds. I was determined to get as clean as possible. The sand added a bit of grit as I worked the soap over every inch of my skin.

It didn't take long for the water to feel warm and the air cool. I waded out into deeper water, holding my breath to submerge myself completely, and started in on my hair. It would take time to dry but it would be worth it. It felt so good to scrub my scalp.

Finally, after sudsing and rinsing twice, I stood up straight. My hair felt heavy with all the water and I wrung it out as best I could. Twirling it up in a long rope, I laid it over my shoulder, and moved toward the bank. I'd dry it out and comb it once I was—

Something grabbed my ankle.

I jumped, squeaked, and dropped the soap.

Keir rose from the depths, dripping wet and glorious. I gaped in amazement, drinking in his face.

"Lara," he whispered, reaching out to me. "We need to—"

I leaped into his arms, reaching out to pull his head down, and claimed his lips with mine.

Keir moaned into my mouth, and his arms came up to wrap me in their strength. I kissed him again and again, craving his touch, his taste, his hot breath on my chilled skin.

Keir broke the kiss, gasping for air. "We must talk."

I reclaimed his mouth, and raised my leg to rub his hip, trying to get him closer. His arm moved down, his hand under my buttocks, and then both hands, supporting me, lifting me.

I held on for dear life, grabbing his shoulders, refus-

ing to release his mouth. He groaned as he entered me,
and moved me with ease, his arms and shoulders flexing under my fingers. I broke the kiss, and wrapped
my arms around him, urging him on with soft demands
in his ear, letting my fingers play with his wet hair.

It had been so long.

We both shuddered in release at the same time,
holding each other tight, fearful of making a sound.
The air was chill, yet there was nothing but heat burning within. I listened to Keir try to catch his breath as I
stroked his damp shoulders. "The skies favor the
bold," I whispered softly.

He pulled back his head to smile at me, and kiss me
again. "I had to see you. To know that you were well.
To taste—"

I kissed him again, desperate for more. Part of me
trembled at the risk he was taking, at the thought that
we might be caught.

The rest of me trembled for other reasons.

Keir shifted me then, lifting me a bit higher, and
carried me over to the bank where my clothing lay. He
placed me on the grass, and stood before me, gently
stroking my cheek. "There's not much time, Lara.
We—"

I threw my arm over his neck, and fell back, forcing
him to cover my body with his. He groaned again, a
sound filled with longing, want and need. My soul
sang to hear it.

He braced himself over me, breathing hard. "Lara."

I looked up into those wonderful blue eyes. "Take
me, my Warlord."

That was enough to unleash my Cat. He growled
low, and moved between my legs, and the entire world
exploded. I was pressed hard into the grass, and met
each thrust with an answering movement. I wrapped
my arms around him, and buried my face in his neck,

muffling my cries against the damp skin of his neck. And just as I could feel my body reach the heights, I bit his neck, playing with the thin skin with my teeth. He arched his back and pressed deep within, convulsing in my arms.

"Xylara?" Amyu's voice cut though my daze.

Keir pulled me up and forward, and we fell into the water together, the cold shocking me with awareness of the danger. I exploded up out of the depths, to find Amyu standing on the bank, her dagger drawn. My hands jerked over my breasts. "Amyu!"

"I thought I heard something." She scanned the area closely.

"I dropped my soap." I turned my back. "Now, if you don't mind . . ."

I looked over my shoulder and made sure that she left the tent. I bent down, peering into the water that surrounded me—

But Keir was gone.

13

We should have talked.

We really should have talked.

After I'd dried off and dressed, I'd staggered back to my tent and announced my intent to take a nap. Amyu had assumed it was because of the birthing, but the excitement and . . . well . . . vigor of my adventure with Keir had worn me to the bone.

I'd woken to a feeling of contentment that I hadn't felt in a long time. I stretched under the covers, and then smiled, completely relaxed and comfortable. Until I realized how stupid I'd been. I lay in my bed, staring up at the tent over my head, and cursed myself for a fool. Keir and I had needed to talk. And what did I do? I'd thrown myself into his arms like a love-starved slip of a girl.

Still . . . a smile curled over my lips at the memory.

Maybe Keir would find another way to talk to me. I sat up in bed, quite pleased with myself.

"Xylara?"

"I'm awake, Amyu." I ran my fingers back through my hair, and gathered the blankets to hug them to my chest. "Is it the nooning?"

Amyu stuck her head in, frowning slightly. "It is well past the nooning, Xylara."

"Oh." I smiled brightly at her. "I was more tired than I realized, I guess."

She gave me a doubtful look.

I continued, refusing to allow her disapproval to spoil my sense of well-being. "Some kavage, please? I can wait until later for food."

"The Warlord Liam of the Deer has asked to court you over the evening meal," Amyu reminded me as she left.

I puffed out a breath of frustration and reached for my clothes. I lifted my voice as I dressed. "Is this another like Ultie? If so, I can save us all time and trouble and say 'no' now."

Amyu returned with a tray. "The Warlord Liam has a very good reputation, Xylara." She set the tray down on the bed.

I reached for a drink. "I don't like this, Amyu. The Council is hearing truths, and I'm not permitted to be there or know what is being said. That is not right."

She paused, and then spoke. "You are of Xy. It is a matter of the Plains, to decide if you will become one of us, with the status of a warprize. These debates that the Council holds are open and free, and you being there might affect the truths of those that speak." She shrugged slightly. "You may hold some truths against the speakers, even."

"I know what a token means."

"Even those of the Plains sometimes hold truths against the speaker, even after the token is returned," Amyu chided me. "We are not all perfect, Xylara."

I nodded ruefully. "Amyu, how is Eace? Can I see her?"

Amyu's face lit up. "She does very well. Reness is watching her closely, and has promised to summon you if need be." She drew herself up, and placed a hand on her dagger hilt. "I thank you, Xylara, for the life of my friend. Eace and I were raised together, and she is dear to me. I owe you a debt."

I suppressed any smile. This was no child, and she was very serious. "No." I shook my head. "No debt. I swore an oath to heal all that came to me, Amyu. Thank you for letting me help her."

Amyu inclined her head, and left me to my kavage.

"Welcome to my tent, Xylara, Daughter of Xy. I am Liam of the Deer. May I offer you kavage?"

I stepped further into his tent, taking a moment to let my eyes adjust before speaking. The tent was warmed with two braziers, their coals glowing softly in the darkness. "It seems only fair to warn you that Keir of the Cat is my chosen Warlord. You waste your time courting me."

A soft chuckle came from the shadows. "Well, that is fair enough. I should tell you that I've no real interest in courting you."

Out of the darkness stepped a tall man, with long blond hair, silver mixed with the gold. His eyes were hazel, his smile warm. But it was the piercings of his left ear that reassured me even more. Liam of the Deer was bonded. I sighed with relief as he continued to speak.

"But I am interested in Keir, and his people, and his ideas. If we talk, you and I, and exchange knowledge, how can that be a waste?" Liam gestured to a platform full of pillows, much like the arrangement I'd seen in Simus's tent. "Let us eat and talk in comfort."

I sat on one of the fattest pillows, and Liam reclined on some others. He clapped his hands, and warriors entered with kavage, and bowls of gurt.

"We had the good fortune to hunt ehat on our way to the Heart," Liam offered. "Oh, not four, as I have heard Keir did, but enough that I can offer you roast ehat for our meal." He leaned back with his mug. "Would you tell me of that hunt?"

Happily, I recounted the details and told him of what I'd seen. He grunted when I spoke of Iften missing his throw, but made no other comment. When I mentioned kissing Keir, even though he reeked of the musk, Liam laughed. "A strong bond, indeed, Xylara."

"Please call me 'Lara'," I asked. "Xylara is my formal name, but I prefer 'Lara'."

"You honor me." Liam put his kavage down. "Is it true, Lara, that you can raise the dead?"

"No." I shook my head and glared at him. "Is this because of what happened with the baby?"

"The word of the winds is that you brought the babe back from the snows," Liam explained. "That you did that because the babe was Xyian, while all the other dead were of the Plains."

The kavage in my stomach turned sour in an instant. I sat there horrified, and stared at him.

"I would not offend, Lara. But you need to know what is said."

"I would never—" My voice cracked as I choked on my words. "If I had the power, Liam, I'd use it for the good of both our peoples. The oaths that I have taken as a healer demand that. But I do not," my voice cracked at the very idea. *"I cannot raise the dead."*

Liam stared at me intently. "The babe—"

"That the babe revived was the blessing of the Goddess, or the elements." I put my mug down and ran my fingers through my hair. "I was tired, we were all exhausted, Liam. I'm not even sure that the babe had really stopped breathing." I shrugged. "But I make no claim to be so powerful."

"I believe you, Lara." Liam nodded. "So, among your people, healing is freely offered? To any?"

Grateful for the change of topic, I started to explain our ways. Liam listened intently, asking a few questions, but he clearly was having problems understanding some of the Xyian concepts. Money being one of the them.

"What would be the purpose?" he asked. "I cannot eat your 'coin', cannot wear it, or use it to hunt food. So why would I take 'coins' in exchange for anything? Far better to trade and barter, than to 'pay'."

I was trying to make an argument, when there was a cough outside. "Ah, the meat is ready." Liam sat up straighter on his pillow. "And all this talk has my stomach growling."

I laughed, as the warriors approached with meat and flat bread. There were grains, too, but I recognized the small red flakes in their midst, and took careful bites.

We talked as we ate, and I realized that I was enjoying myself. Liam had seen warriors playing chess, and started to pepper me with questions about the rules. As the dishes were removed, nothing would satisfy him but that we play a game. "I know your memory is not like ours," he spoke eagerly as he pulled a wooden box out from under the platform. "So I bartered for this."

He pulled out the first piece with a flourish and pressed it into my hand. I studied it as he set the rest out on the board. The carving was amazing. It was a fierce warrior of the Plains on a galloping horse, poised to fling a lance at his opponent. But it was plain wood, with no color distinction.

Then I glanced at the board and realized that it wouldn't be a problem telling the pieces apart. One side was the Firelanders, clearly, lean and fierce warriors of both sexes, armed to the teeth. The others were all chubby city-dwellers, unarmored, with no weapons, cowering in fear of their attackers. Even the castles looked afraid somehow.

I arched an eyebrow at Liam, and he had the grace to look embarrassed. "The set is well carved," he offered as if in apology.

I chuckled. "Well, let's just see how you fare against me, Warlord."

The first game went swiftly, with myself as the winner. Thankfully, Liam hadn't learned all the strategies as of yet. I checkmated him, and then settled back with my fresh kavage as he studied the board, trying to find his mistake.

The warrior serving us had entered with a plate of small buns. "Are those bread tarts?" I asked, reaching for one.

"They are, Warprize." The warrior gave me a quick smile, putting the plate next to me. "You should have moved your ehat sooner," he chided Liam in a soft voice. "She couldn't use her mounted warrior then."

Liam grunted, "Go away."

I bit into the bun, and there was a familiar explosion of spice in my mouth. Spicy, yet sweet. The taste took me back to the first time I'd seen a pattern dance, when Marcus had been so proud of his treat. "This is so good!"

Liam looked up, and reached for one. "They are one of my favorites."

The warrior smiled at me. "I was taught to cook them by a master."

Liam's face stilled as the warrior bowed and left us.

"He's right, you know." I nodded to the board. "You should have moved your ehat to block me."

The odd expression on Liam's face was still there.

He picked up the ehat, and ran his thumb over the de-tailed carving. He seemed distracted somehow.

"Another game?" I reached out to set the pieces in their positions.

Liam didn't look up. Instead he kept his gaze on the ehat and cleared his throat. "Lara? How does Marcus?"

His tone was offhand, as if it didn't really matter, but something gave me pause. "You know Marcus?"

He looked up then, those hazel eyes flooded with pain. I drew a breath, as he turned away, and I could clearly see the bonded piercings, the wire running along the outside of the ear, the beads and small trin-kets woven within.

I sat my mug down, dazed.

Isdra nodded, then took a deep breath. "Lara, Mar-cus was bonded."

"Really?" I jerked my head around, to spot Marcus behind us. His chin was on his chest, and he appeared to be sleeping in the saddle as his horse walked along. "But his ear—" I stopped myself. His left ear had been burned away in the accident that left him scarred.

Isdra nodded again. "Aye, his ear spiral melted away with his flesh. I do not know the details, Lara."

"Oh, Goddess. Was she killed, Isdra?"

Isdra shook her head. "I will say no more, Lara. For lack of knowledge, and for courtesy."

"Goddess," I breathed out. "You are Marcus's bonded."

Liam jerked his head in a nod, but didn't look at me.

I had to remind myself to breathe. And breathe again. Marcus was bonded. Marcus was bonded to a . . .

My world seemed to shift around me, as if all of my assumptions of the world were wrong. I breathed again, and remembered to speak. My voice sounded like it was coming from a long way away. "He is well, when last I saw him, when I asked that he be my Guardian."

"You did?" Liam smiled. "I had not heard that. I bet that caused a furor."

"It did." I frowned suddenly. "Is that why you rejected him? Because of his—"

The room went ice-cold in a moment, and those hazel eyes pierced right through me. This was a Warlord of the Plains that sat before me, and he was well and truly angry. "Were you of the Plains, I'd kill you for that insult."

I bit my lip, but didn't look away. "Then why?"

"By Marcus's choice," he snapped as he slammed the ehat piece down and rose to his feet. He started to pace, back and forth before the platform, a very angry Warlord of the Plains. But I felt no fear.

His anger was aimed at himself.

"'This worthless carcass is not your bonded,'" Liam snarled. "That is what the stubborn, stupid man told me." He talked with his hands, gesturing to the air. "I begged him to return to me until he threatened to go to the snows, regardless of his oath to Keir." Liam stopped and rubbed his face with his hands. "It's two campaigns now since I've seen him."

I caught my breath. "Two years?"

Liam let out a ragged breath. "He serves Keir. And never comes to the Heart." My face showed my thought, and Liam caught it in an instant. "He's here, isn't he?"

I nodded, picking up the poor abused ehat figure. "I've seen him."

"Do you know how hard that is for him?" Liam shook his head, and crossed his arms over his chest. "His loyalty to Keir is absolute." He examined me intently. "And to you as well, it seems."

Suddenly, Keekai's words to Marcus when she'd

seen him made perfect sense. "He worried about you. When Keekai arrived, she told him that you hadn't been hurt on campaign."

Liam sagged. "But he didn't actually ask, did he?"

I sighed, looking at the ehat carving. "No."

"When Keir brought Marcus back to me, and Marcus recovered enough to speak, the first thing he did was call me to his tent and announce that the bond had melted away in the fires, along with his ear." Liam struggled with the words.

"He pushed you away because of his scars, didn't he?" I asked, softly. I placed the ehat on the board. "It would affect your status, wouldn't it?"

"What of it?" Liam cried out. "Do you know how empty the days are? How empty my arms are at night?"

He turned to pace again, so he didn't see me blush. That was something I wasn't ready to think about. My people didn't . . . such a thing was not approved of. And it was one thing to know that Firelanders had those kinds of relationships. I'd known that. Certainly Osa had made it clear.

But now it was someone I knew, someone I cared for. I swallowed hard. Marcus, who had protected me with his blades and cared for me when I'd been so deathly ill.

Marcus, who I considered a friend, had bonded with a man.

I swallowed hard.

Liam still prowled, and I watched his hands clench into fists. I couldn't deny the longing in his voice. I'd heard it in my own, when I spoke of Keir.

"I will not give up," Liam vowed. "One day I will find a way across the plains that he has placed between us. I'll have him back, at my side, I swear it by—"

"Warlord."

Liam and I both jumped, and turned to see his warrior pull the flap aside. Liam frowned. "Yes, Rish, what is it?"

"Word from the Council."

Finally!

Finally, I'd see the Council. I fussed with my hair as I tried to match Liam's stride. Wiping imaginary crumbs from my tunic kept my nerves at bay for a moment.

What I really wanted was a moment to change, to put on that red dress, to arm myself against the foe. At least I had my satchel. I adjusted it on my hip, tugging the strap into place between my breasts.

We'd been told the summons was urgent, and Liam had offered to escort me, along with Amyu and my warrior-priest guards. I accepted gratefully, although I couldn't help but wonder if he didn't want to try to get a glimpse of Marcus.

The Council tent appeared, looking even larger and more imposing. I trotted to keep up with Liam. We entered the tent to find the area filled with people. Liam headed toward the main area between the fire pits and I followed close behind. He stopped, and I stepped to stand beside him.

Off to the left, I saw Iften and Wesren, standing with the warrior-priest Gathering Storm. Their faces were not welcoming, and I turned away, grateful that Liam and Amyu walked with me between the fire pits.

The Eldest were ahead of us, standing on the base, the tiers behind them filled with Elders. I looked around, and suddenly familiar faces filled my sight. Atira, with a wide smile, and Heath just behind her. Joden, his face still so filled with pain. I gave him a smile, and then behind him—

Keir!

Joy rang through my entire body, and I ran toward him without thinking. "Keir!"

My arm was grabbed by one of the warrior-priests, who jerked me to a stop. My satchel shifted, and I lost my balance, stumbling a bit, as one of the other guards grabbed my flailing arm.

"Take your hands off her!" Keir's voice cried out, and there was movement around me, but I was still trying to find my feet.

"Hold." Essa's voice boomed out. "HOLD."

Everyone around us stopped moving, and I managed to look up, to find a furious Keir being held back by Simus and Liam. I made eye contact, and smiled, trying to reassure him.

"Release her," Essa directed, and my guards obeyed. "Xylara, Daughter of Xy, are you hurt?"

"No," I answered, readjusting my satchel on my hip.

"There is to be no contact with Keir of the Cat," Essa chided.

"As if a hug would hurt. Or a word of greeting," Keekai said as she walked past, heading toward her seat. "Foolishness, if you ask me."

"Then it is well you were not asked." Wild Winds appeared, to take his seat beside Essa. "Still, the treatment of the Daughter of Xy was too rough. It will not happen again." He gestured, and my guards melted away.

"Lara, are you alright?" Keir asked, still seething.

"I'm fine, belov—"

"As if you really care!" Antas stood, and walked over to face Keir. "You, who have dallied with another, even as your so-called warprize attempts to claim you."

Dallied? Did that mean what I thought it meant? I flushed, and then went cold at the idea that Keir would turn to another while—

"Lower your hood, and show all how true you are to

the one you would bond with." Antas pointed at Keir. "Do it now, *warrior*."

There was absolute silence in the tent as Keir glared at Antas. But then his expression changed slightly, and his eyes crinkled in silent humor. Keir lifted his hands and lowered his hood to reveal a small purplish bruise on his neck. A love bite.

Oh Goddess above. I blushed bright red, heat flooding my face. *My love bite.*

Keir arched an eyebrow as the Elders reacted to the sight.

Antas, however, was nearly foaming at the mouth. "You see? You see? He has broken faith with this Xyian even before she—"

It took everything I had to say the words aloud before the entire Council of Elders. "I put that there."

"Eh?" Antas twisted to face me.

I drew a deep breath, and raised my voice. "That is my mark on his neck."

As the group reacted to that, my blush deepened, if that was possible. Then I made the mistake of looking at Keir, and had to cover my mouth to prevent myself from laughing. He looked so smug.

Simus was under no such handicap. He was howling with mirth.

Antas was scowling, as were Essa and Wild Winds. "How so?" Antas snapped. "You have been kept apart from—"

"Her bath." Amyu spoke. "It had to be during her bath."

I looked over my shoulder to see that she was none too happy either. I turned back to face the Elders. "It was in my bath," I admitted. "Keir snuck in to see me."

As one, the Eldest turned to glare at Keir.

Keir shrugged.

Simus laughed and slapped him on the back. "The skies favor the bold."

Antas paused as a ripple of laughter swept the room again. "So you talked to Keir, despite our rules, despite our—"

"We didn't waste time talking," I snapped right back, glaring at him. Then I realized what I'd announced to the room, and blushed bright red.

"HEYLA!" Simus shouted. "Truly, the attraction between Warlord and Warprize is as the heat of the summer!"

Joden's head jerked up at that, and the movement caught my eye. He gave Simus a startled look, and then looked at me, as if seeing me for the first time.

The Eldest were all talking among themselves. I saw Keekai up on the tier, and she gave me a bright look. I looked over at Keir again, and he gave me a warm smile, full of reassurance. I flushed a bit under his approval, and smiled back, content.

Essa stepped forward. "Daughter of Xy. You speak the truth when you say that you did not talk to Keir of the Cat?"

"I did not. We . . ." I kept my eyes on him, resisting the urge to look down. "We spoke only with our bodies, Eldest Singer."

"What does she know of truth?" Antas growled. "She lies at any time, as she sees fit."

"I do not!" I replied hotly, stepping forward to face the Eldest Warrior.

"You lied to Atira of the Bear." Antas folded his massive arms over his chest, and sneered at me.

"How so?" I demanded.

"Atira of the—" Antas bellowed, but Essa cut him off.

"Before you bawl out for a truth, we will call this senel to order." Essa turned to face the Elders, who began to settle down. He turned back, and gestured to someone behind me. Amyu appeared, with a folding stool, that she set up for me between the fire pits.

I adjusted my satchel and sat. Amyu remained at my shoulder, standing just behind me.

Essa stood before all, watching as everyone settled down. As far as I could see, the tiers were full, almost crowded. Those that stood on the edges were clearly warriors of stature. Keir had taken his position as close to me as he could, on the other side of the fire pit. Liam and Simus stood with him, with other familiar faces just behind. I drew a deep breath, tried to relax my shoulders, and turned back to face the Elders.

"I call this senel to order," Essa announced in a strong voice. Everyone quieted magically. Essa turned to me. "Daughter of Xy, welcome to our tent. May we offer you kavage?"

"No, thank you," I answered.

"Daughter of Xy, we have now heard the truths of those that we have called before us, all but Joden of the Hawk. We delayed his truths, because Iften of the Boar and Eldest Warrior Antas, also of the Boar, have asked that his words be given the weight of a Singer, although Joden cannot yet claim that status."

So Antas was a pig, too. I wasn't surprised.

Essa folded his arms over his chest. "We have kept you out of these meetings, for you are not of the Plains. But now, a decision must be made, and we have decided that you should be heard on this matter."

"First, she must prove that she knows what truth is!" Antas jumped to his feet. "I say that she has lied to a warrior of the Plains."

"I deny that," I responded calmly, as my heart beat in my chest.

"Atira of the Bear," Antas called out. Atira stepped forward to stand before them, moving well. She crossed her arms over her chest and glared at Antas as if she wished to slaughter him with the sharpest weapon she could find.

"Tell us again, how the Xyian lied to you," Antas demanded.

"You are the only one that calls it a 'lie', Eldest Warrior." Atira's words were polite, but her voice dripped with contempt. "I say that the Warprize saved my leg and my life."

"Tell it!" Antas thundered.

Atira scowled, then turned to face me. She gave me a full nod. "Warprize."

"Atira." I greeted her with a smile. "How does your leg?"

Essa cleared his throat.

Atira winked at me, but turned back to face him. I was pleased to see her standing so tall and proud, her blonde hair gleaming in the lights of the fire. "As I spoke my truth before, so now I speak the truth again. I was practicing mounting a running horse from a standing position when I fell and broke my leg . . ." Atira retold the story of her fall, and how I insisted that she let me heal her leg. I was amazed at the detail that she could recall, right down to the words that I'd spoken.

". . . she reached over and handed me a piece of willow bark to put between my teeth. 'All right, Atira. Ten deep breaths, then we begin.'" Atira shook her head. "I closed my eyes and took a deep breath. Then another. Then, as I drew the third breath, she grabbed my ankle and my world exploded into pain."

"Thus I am proven," Antas said with satisfaction. "She lied."

A murmur washed through the crowd.

14

There was an outburst from Keir's direction, but I just gaped at Antas, caught off guard. "You can't possibly be that stupid."

It was Antas's turn to gawk at me. I pressed the point, speaking loudly enough to be heard by all. "That is not a lie. That is a skill. A trick of the trade. If you wait until the tenth breath, the patient tenses up, and the muscles fight against the healer." I crossed my arms over my chest. "Is it a lie to hide in wait for an animal while hunting?"

Antas scowled. "A warrior is no animal, to be—"

"Enough." Wild Winds stood. "The snows come. Do not waste time on this. The Xyian knows what truth is."

"Agreed?" Essa turned to the Elders. They were all seated, and no one moved. But Essa turned back, as if the matter was resolved. He looked at Antas. Antas glared, but sat back down. Essa then turned his attention to me. "Then, we will proceed. Daughter of Xy, Joden of the Hawk has been in training to become a Singer of the Plains. You know this?"

"I do."

"All listen well to the words and truths of a Singer of the Plains. They hold our ways and our knowledge. You understand?"

"Yes, Eldest Singer."

"Now, there are those who would have Joden of the Hawk named Singer now, without the normal contests, ceremonies, and celebrations."

Contests? I glanced over at Joden but he was studying the floor. Essa continued. "This has been done in the past, but under dire circumstances." He glanced over at Joden. "There are those that oppose this, because Joden of the Hawk has not held to our ways."

"Because of Simus?" I looked over to where Simus stood next to Keir, tall, proud and healthy. "But if Joden hadn't stayed his hand—"

Essa raised an eyebrow at my interruption, but he nodded in agreement. "Yes. Because of his failure to grant Simus of the Hawk mercy."

"For which I am deeply grateful," Simus chimed in, a large smile on his face. There was a stir of amusement amidst the Elders.

"No doubt," Essa spoke dryly, but there was a hint of a smile on his lips. "If I may continue?"

Simus grinned then, and inclined his head, as if giving permission.

Essa gave him a telling look, then turned back to me. "But only the Singers can allow this, and the Singers will not. I have consulted my brethren and we will not rush to allow Joden of the Hawk within our ranks. That is the end of that, for that is not something within the authority of the Council of Elders."

"I don't understand, Eldest Singer." I shifted a bit on my stool. "If you will not let him become a Singer, what is to be discussed?"

"The weight that his truth will be given." Essa answered plainly. "Joden of the Hawk is well respected. He has witnessed many of these events. Antas argues that his words should be given the weight of a Singer's, even if he does not yet have that status. The Council is free to determine the value and weight of his truth." Essa sighed, glancing back at the tiers of Elders behind him. "There has been much talk about this." He faced forward and grimaced slightly. "Too much talk."

There was another stir of amusement at his words, and I took a chance and glanced over at Keir. His face told me nothing, gave me no hint as to what was going on. I licked my lips, and turned back to look at Essa as he spoke. "So, Daughter of Xy, what say you? How shall we treat the truths of Joden of the Hawk?"

I looked down at my hands, clasped tight in my lap, and considered his question. The tent fell silent around me, with only the crackle of the fire to be heard. "May I have some kavage now?"

"Of course." Essa's voice was full of amusement. "And a moment to collect your thoughts, if you wish. But kavage would be welcome for all, I think."

I kept my eyes down, thinking. I could hear the sounds of people moving, and the clatter as mugs were filled. Amyu held a mug out to me in silence. I took it with whispered thanks, but she said nothing. It was hot and black, just like I liked it.

The room settled back down. I placed my mug on the floor and stood before I spoke, lifting my eyes to the tiers, trying to look confident. "Joden of the Hawk was the first to call me 'warprize' after Keir of the Cat claimed me in Xy. He was the first to help me understand what 'warprize' truly meant." I glanced over at

Joden's solemn face, but his dark eyes gave nothing away. "He was also the first to come to me and explain his opposition to Keir, and to my ways."

I focused back on Essa. "I have seen what happens to a land when its leader surrounds himself with men who speak only the truth he wants to hear."

I looked pointedly at Iften, standing opposite Keir on the other side of the fire pits. "I've seen what problems it creates when opposition is not expressed openly or honorably."

Iften bridled, glaring at me and putting his hand on the hilt of his sword.

I turned back to face the Elders. "I value Joden as an honorable friend and warrior. His truths deserve to be given the highest value."

"Even if his truth is spoken against you?" Wild Winds prodded.

"Even so."

That created quite a stir. I couldn't resist looking at Joden. He was considering me gravely. I inclined my head to him, and after a brief hesitation, he did the same to me.

"Keir of the Cat has said much the same," Essa commented, drawing my attention back to him. "Thank you, Daughter of Xy."

I sat down.

"So." Essa turned, speaking to the tiers of Elders. "Enough has been said. Do we give the truths of Joden of the Hawk the weight of a Singer's?"

A few of the Elders stood up, but the majority remained seated on their stools. Was that how they indicated their position?

"Very well." Essa stretched a bit, flexing his back. "This decision made, it grows late. We have been at this since the dawn. Let us meet again in the morning, to hear the truths of Joden of the Hawk."

"No," Antas demanded, as he jumped to his feet. "Let us do this here and now. The snows come, Essa."

"I know that well, Antas," Essa snapped. He glared for a moment, then turned to Joden. "Joden of the Hawk. What say you?"

Joden shook his head. "Eldest Singer, I'd ask for the night to think on my words. The burden of this is heavy and I'd wish to—"

"NO." A shout came from Iften who stepped forward, gesturing toward Keir. "Do not allow this! Joden will be influenced by Keir, by Simus—"

"By what right do you challenge, Iften of the Boar?" Essa pulled a dagger, and advanced on Iften. "You, who hold no status within this Council?"

Iften's face was a strange mixture of rage and chagrin. He glanced at Antas, as if for support, but even Antas was offended. As Essa approached, Iften went to one knee, and bowed his head. "I beg forgiveness, Eldest Singer."

Essa placed the tip of his blade on Iften's neck. Iften flinched, but made no other move. Satisfied, Essa walked back toward his stool, sheathing his dagger.

"The warrior has a point," Antas spoke as Essa returned to his place. "Joden should speak now."

"I agree," Wild Winds said.

Essa turned. "What say the Elders? Should Joden speak now?"

Everyone remained seated.

"Very well." Essa returned to his stool. "Joden of the Hawk, you are summoned to speak your truths. Daughter of Xy, please leave the Council tent."

The last caught me off guard. I opened my mouth to protest, even as Joden spoke. "Elders and Eldest, I would ask that Xylara be permitted to stay. It is right that she hear my truth."

Essa shrugged, and nodded. I settled back down on

my stool. Joden stepped forward and placed himself at the corner of the fire pit, in front of the Eldest, but not so far as to block my view.

Suddenly I was back in the throne room of the Castle of Water's Fall, seated next to Keir, and watching Joden emerge from the crowd to sing at the mourning ceremony. There'd been a light in his eyes then, a kind of peace deep within. Now he stood, a man who would be haunted forever by the events at Wellspring, where he'd sung for all the dead.

So many dead.

"Speak, Joden of the Hawk," Essa urged.

"Not before I've had my say," came a voice from behind me.

I looked over my shoulder to see Reness march into the tent. She'd caused a stir, and knew it. She strode between the fire pits to stand at my side.

"Eldest Thea." Essa was displeased. "Welcome to these discussions. Your absence was noted."

"I've better things to do than sit, swill kavage, and cluck like gurtles," Reness replied. "Days you've been at this, and still no decision? Pah." She huffed out a breath. "I'll speak my truth and be gone."

"About Joden of the Hawk?" Wild Winds asked.

Reness snorted. "No. As to Xylara, Daughter of Xy, and Warprize."

Antas sprang up. "That is not yet—"

"Fool," Reness spat.

Antas closed his mouth in a hurry.

"You wish to stop change from coming to the Plains," Reness said. "Might as well tell the winds to stop blowing." She shook back her hair. "I've spent the last few days listening and learning. Of bloodmoss and fever's foe. Of joint cream, and a game played on a board. Of the tales told by warriors newly returned, of the healing power of the Xyian woman before you."

Reness set her hand on my shoulder. "We need her ways, her knowledge and her skills. We'd be stupid to ignore the benefits that she would bring to the People of the Plains. The theas have discussed this, and I speak for all when we say that she is truly a Warprize."

Her statement was greeted with silence.

She nodded, well satisfied. "I've work to be done. Summon me, if you need to see me sit on my stool in her favor."

She turned then, but paused long enough to drop a whisper. "Eace is well and healing." With that, she was gone, long strides carrying her out of the tent and away.

A murmur of voices rose as she left the tent, but Essa seemed to take it all in stride. He gave everyone a moment to settle, and then once again turned to Joden. "Speak your truths, Joden of the Hawk."

He was still standing by the fire pit, the oddest expression on his face, as if he'd seen something long hidden. He jumped slightly, startled when Essa spoke his name, and it took him a moment to acknowledge the summons.

"Elders and Eldest, I thank you for the honor of speaking my truths before you." Joden took a long breath, and seemed to steady himself. His voice was deep and loud enough to be heard by all. "When I left the Plains this spring with Keir of the Cat, my feet were light and eager. Keir's intention to change our world and our ways was known, and I welcomed the challenges it would bring. Welcomed, too, the chance to witness and craft songs of what would happen."

His voice filled with pain. "It is well we do not know what the winds will bring. Had I known . . ."

His voice trailed off, but the tent remained silent. Joden lifted his head to look at the Elders. "I will not speak of what has already been told. Of the deaths due

to affliction. Of the loss of Epor of the Badger and Isdra of the Fox. Of the pyres that burned day and night.
Of my laments as I sang the dead to the snows."

I bowed my head, and squeezed my eyes closed
against the tears that came.

"Did the dead raise a blade?" Joden's voice was a
growl, full of anger. "Did they die in battle, and go to
the snows as warriors? No. They lay in their beds and
shivered, no awareness in their eyes, crying out for
friends and loved ones, their wits scattered to the
winds." Joden stopped himself, and drew another deep
breath. "No, I will not speak of it. Someday, I may sing
it. But not today."

Joden rubbed his face with both hands, to gather
himself together. The tent remained silent. I wiped my
eyes, and then clasped my hands tight in my lap.

After what seemed like forever, Joden continued. "I
have prepared to become a Singer. And I have learned
that a true Singer sings the truth. A Singer must not be
swayed by friendship or loyalties or the opinions of
others. A Singer must sing the truth as he sees it, with
his own eyes." Joden drew a shuddering breath. "But as
a Singer must stand against pressures from others, he
must also stand from the pressure within. He must not
be swayed by his own fears or sorrows."

Essa gave Joden a half-smile and spoke. "That's a
truth that cuts both ways. And not the easiest to understand. Or recognize."

"It is." Joden's lips pressed to a thin line as he
pointed to Keir. "Keir dares much, and it is said that
the skies favor the bold. But I fear that he goes too far
too fast. The 'plague' has shown me that to combine
the Plains and the Xyians is madness.

"Yet," Joden looked at me now, his gaze steady. "How
can I speak against the woman who saved so many,

Simus included? Who gave herself over to what she thought would be degradation and abuse, to save her people?" He turned back to face the Elders. "My truth is this. I was torn by my own pain. Never again do I want to tend to so many dead."

"So how say you now, Joden of the Hawk?" Wild Winds pressed, his voice soft contrast to Joden's. "What is your truth?"

Joden lifted his head, to look at Iften, and then at Antas. Both men were tense, as if waiting for . . . something.

But Joden looked away from them and focused on Wild Winds. "I would say this truth. Xylara, daughter of Xy, is a true Warprize of the Plains."

I straightened in shock. I wasn't the only one. All around the tent, heads jerked in surprise. Even Keir looked stunned, and Simus . . . Simus just smiled.

Antas was on his feet, his hand on the hilt of his sword. "This is your truth, Joden of the Hawk?"

Joden faced him calmly. "We have forgotten our ways, in our reaction to the change she represents. Acceptance of Xyian ways has nothing to do with her confirmation as Warprize." He turned to Essa, and lifted a finger. "A Warprize must be discovered during the course of a battle, or on or near a battlefield. A Warprize must render aid to the Warlord or his men."

Essa pushed out his lips, considering Joden's words.

Joden continued, his voice ringing in the tent. "A Warprize must be attractive to a Warlord, must spark feelings of desire. The attraction between Warlord and Warprize is as the heat of the sun that shines in the height of summer."

I sat, my eyes wide, and listened to the very explanation he'd given me in my stilltent, months ago.

"Now, once a Warlord recognizes a potential

Warprize, he must negotiate for the Warprize, making the best deal that he can." Joden turned his head to look at Keir. "Once he has done that, a Warprize must submit willingly to the Warlord, before witnesses of both their peoples. Then a Warprize is displayed to the Warlord's army. Upon their return to our lands, the confirmation ceremony is held before the Council of Elders."

Joden looked at his feet. "A true Warprize brings change. Until just now, I'd forgotten, in our tradition there is no requirement that the Council accept those changes."

He looked back at me, chagrined. "Xylara is a true Warprize, and this Council should confirm her as such." He drew a deep breath. "I do not know what will come of this, but I must speak the truth. I've seen the look in her eyes when she looks at Keir, and I know that she loves him. While Xyians do not love in public view, still the heat of their desire can be felt when they are together."

"Even when they are kept apart!" Keekai added from her stool.

The laughter around us was nervous, but it eased the tensions slightly. I blushed again, and risked a glance over at Keir, who stood there, looking pleased.

But when I turned back, Antas was glaring at me, and his eyes were filled with hate. "Joden, you're a fool," he said. "This woman will kill us all. She will destroy our Plains with her ways! Think of what you are saying!"

Joden's face flared with a rare fury. "I am speaking the truth, Antas! Give me one example, one time in all our stories where the Warprize is confirmed based on *what* change they bring to the Plains, and I will retract my words." His lip curled in disgust. "You let blind hatred and fear cloud your truth, Eldest. As it almost clouded mine."

I glanced up to see Keekai nod her head in agreement.

"I act for the good of the Plains and our people," Antas roared. "The ways of the city-dwellers are an offense to the elements."

The Elders in the tiers were all talking, some nodding in agreement, some shaking their heads. I felt Amyu move up close behind me, her tunic brushing against mine. The contact was welcome. It was good to know I had someone at my back. I glanced quickly over at Keir, but he was staring at Antas. The vein in his jaw was throbbing. Even Simus looked grim as he scanned the tiers.

"Essa," Wild Winds demanded, turning all eyes on the Eldest Singer. "Is what Joden says true?"

The tent silenced. Essa was looking off, above our heads, clearly thinking hard. After a moment, he spoke. "Joden is right." He sat down slowly on his stool. "I do not know how we lost sight of that."

"What does that matter?" Antas demanded. "Are we to allow our traditions to expose us to affliction and weakness? Your wits have been taken by the winds—"

Wild Winds gestured toward me. "You see such danger from one who carries no weapons? And the affliction, this 'plague', happened while they were still in the lands of Xy. It is not here."

"Yet," Antas spat. "But everywhere I look, some warrior plays this 'chess', and she has already corrupted the theas."

"I'd like to see you say that to Reness's face," Essa replied. There was a brief chuckle at that, but the tension was still there.

Antas gestured toward his supporters. "We have heard the truths of Iften and Gathering Storm. We know that this woman is a danger to our people. She perverts our ways, luring a young warrior to give up his sword, convincing a warrior not to follow her bonded to the snows. I say—"

My spine snapped straight. "I didn't. Gils made the decision on his own, that surprised us all." I flushed up, embarrassed. "I did ask Isdra to stay, because we needed—"

"You perverted her," Gathering Storm announced. "She only went to the snows because I sent her there."

The outcry was tremendous. The entire tent was on its feet at that. But Gathering Storm faced them all. "I am a warrior-priest of the Plains. Isdra of the Fox would not do what had to be done. I did it for her."

Wild Winds's eyebrow went up. "Yet that had no place in the telling of your truth, Gathering Storm."

Iften stepped by his side. "This Xyian poisons everything, even as her 'brother' did. Gathering Storm did what Keir of the Cat should have encouraged, no, demanded Isdra of the Fox do."

"That's murder," I cried. "You killed Isdra."

Some of the Elders were rising from their stools. They seemed angered and upset.

"Be silent," Antas stood and roared. "Your truths have no place here."

"Have a care, Antas," Keir roared right back. He took a step forward, his hands opening and closing in his anger. "You insult my Warprize."

Essa stood, trying to re-claim control. "No, Keir of the Cat. That is what this senel must decide. We have heard the truths of Joden of the Hawk, and his words are to be given the weight of a Singer's—"

Antas glowered at Essa. "No."

Essa gave him an astonished look. "It was at your insistence that Joden's truths be—"

Antas pulled his sword. "There will be no decision from this Council of fools. I will make this easy." He turned and pointed at me with his sword. "Amyu! Kill the Xyian!"

15

"Amyu! Kill the Xyian!"

The words resounded in my head as I tried to draw a breath into my paralyzed body.

We'd talked about this, Marcus and I, when he'd trained me. We'd talked about how fear took your breath away. How it froze your muscles, how your heart would pound as your mind raced. We'd talked about what I should do, how to work with my guards, how to stay out of their way. About not doing anything stupid.

We hadn't talked about betrayal.

"Amyu! Kill the Xyian!"

"LARA!" Keir's scream filled my ears, even as I gathered my legs to spring off my stool. But it was too late. Amyu had the shoulder of my tunic wrapped in her fist. She yanked me down, and followed me to the floor, drawing her dagger with her free hand.

"Are we barbarians, to pull weapons in Council?" I heard Essa cry out, as the sounds of swords clashing filled the air.

"LARA!" Keir's voice sounded closer.

"Stay down," Amyu hissed. She covered me with her own body.

Relief flooded through me, at the same time that I realized what it must look like to the others. Keir's scream was now an incoherent roar. "Amyu, Keir will kill you!" I gasped.

"The least of my worries," she whispered. I watched as she raised her dagger and made it look like she'd plunged it into my body.

I heard Antas roar out in satisfaction.

The rage was palpable, as bodies launched over us. I had the briefest glimpse of Iften and Gathering Storm, but I couldn't tell what was happening. I twisted under Amyu, getting to where I could see—

In time to see Keir leap over the fire pit to land at my side.

He landed like a cat, sleek and deadly, intent on his target. The light reflected on his two blades, and in his eyes. Amyu sucked in a breath, and I couldn't blame her for her terror. She got to her knees, ready to use the dagger to fend one of the blows.

"Keir!" I cried, and his eyes flicked over to me, then flicked back to Amyu. He took a step, about to strike. But then his gaze returned to mine, and sanity flooded into their depths. "Lara." It sounded like a prayer, even as Keir sheathed one of his swords. He reached down to pull me to my feet. Amyu scrambled up as well.

I'd thought that would stop the fighting, but it didn't. Chaos was all around us. Warrior fought warrior, Elder fought Elder. It was hard for me to make sense of it all. Keekai was running from her stool, down the tiers toward us.

Rafe and Prest, Ander and Yveni were suddenly surrounding me. Rafe gave Amyu a grim look. "Couldn't do it, could you?"

Amyu grimaced.

"To the horses," Keir growled. "Get her out of here."

"No," I protested, but Keir had already turned, and I could see Simus guarding his back, fending off two warrior-priests. Antas had attacked Essa, and—

Wild Winds was fighting Gathering Storm.

Warrior-priest against warrior-priest? I blinked, trying to understand, but there was no time. Prest grabbed my collar, and brought me around to face him. "Remember your lessons."

I nodded. He released me and took the lead. Rafe was beside him, and Anders and Yveni were behind us. Amyu was next to me, dagger at the ready.

"The Xyian lives!" Iften's voice boomed through the tent, and I winced at the attention focused on us. We'd barely cleared the firepits when we were pressed from all sides. Prest and Rafe stopped, and turned to form a line with Ander and Yveni. Keir plunged past them, caught my elbow, and we ran for the tent entrance. Amyu followed.

Outside, warriors and horses milled about in confusion. Keir warbled, and four horses came running, his black and Greatheart among them.

Battle cries came from behind us, and I turned to see warriors charging toward us, Iften in the lead.

Amyu ran toward them, slashing with her dagger. The warriors stopped, preparing to cut her down. But Keekai came running out of the tent and attacked them behind, wielding two swords, and screaming in fury. Behind her were Ander and Yveni.

As that group clashed more warriors came out, with no friend of ours in sight.

I felt two hands at my waist and gasped as Keir

tossed me onto Greatheart's back. Struggling for balance, I buried my hands in his mane

"Go," Keir snapped, looking back toward the fray.

"Not without you," I snapped right back, angry and terrified in an instant.

Keir's head whipped around, and he looked up at me, his eyes so very blue. For a moment, time seemed to stop as he gave me a tight, wry smile. "Stay on, beloved."

"Keir—"

Keir reached out, and smacked Greatheart on the rump. "Flee!"

Greatheart lurched in surprise.

Caught by Greatheart's movement, all I could do was cling to his back. Keir had already turned, drawing his swords and running to aid Keekai and the others.

Greatheart's muscles bunched under me, preparing to run. "No, Greatheart—" I tugged on his mane. "No, don't—"

Greatheart leaped away, with several of the other horses who'd heard the command.

A horse neighed in rage. In my confusion, I looked over my shoulder, hair and tears in my eyes, to see Keir's black horse, riderless and rearing, pawing the air, trumpeting its anger. I blinked, tossing my head to try to clear my eyes. For one long heartbeat, I looked back.

The warriors were a mob now, a confusion of bodies and blades. Centered on one tall, dark-haired figure, fighting with two swords.

I looked just in time to see Keir die.

The first blade dug into his neck.

I screamed then, an echo to the black's.

A sword plunged into his chest then, buried to the hilt. Keir dropped, his swords falling from his hands.

I screamed again.

It had only taken a heartbeat. Greatheart had taken

no more than a stride. Now he tore the ground with his hooves, plunging through tents and people, obeying Keir's last command.

Crying, I looked forward as he ran, and tugged on his mane, but he ignored me.

I turned back, to see warriors running from the tent, mounting their horses, pointing at me. I cried out again, in fear and anguish, and turned back to bury my face in Greatheart's mane.

Weeping, I clung to his back, pressed low. *Stay on, stay on, stay on.* The words repeated over and over in my head, like a chant for the dead.

We cleared the tents, and still Greatheart ran, the other horses surrounding us, taking us deep within the herd. I could see other horses from the corner of my streaming eyes, running alongside, but I paid no attention. Still, Greatheart didn't slow.

The pain in my chest left me gasping for air. My eyes and nose were streaming, my hair was in my face. I didn't care. I gripped Greatheart tighter with my legs, and twisted my fingers in his mane. The sun had gone down, the stars were coming out, and still Greatheart ran.

Stay on, stay on, stay on.

A flicker drew my eye to my left. I glimpsed a rider, and fear coursed through me. They'd caught me. I turned to look, straining to see if it were friend or foe. The man seemed to glow in the light, as if he were stardust or moonbeams. I sucked in a breath.

It was Epor.

There was no mistaking his bearded face, grim in the moonlight as he rode, warclub on his back. His hair, his armor, his skin all glowed in the light, washed in silver.

I jerked my head forward. No, no it couldn't be. I was—

Isdra was two horses ahead of me, her long braid glowing silver. She looked over her shoulder, her face intent and serious. She wasn't looking at me, but over my shoulder, as if watching for my enemies. She turned back then facing the front and urging her horse to go faster.

"*We of the Plains believe that our dead travel with us, ride along beside us, unseen and unknown, but knowing and seeing.*"

Marcus's voice rang in my head. "*Until the longest night. On that night, we mourn our dead, who are released to journey to the stars.*"

I looked down at my hands, shivering, wanting to throw up. But curiosity forced me to glance to my right, to see if—

Gils was there.

Ah, Goddess, no. That had to mean that . . . I twisted as far as I could without risking my seat.

I caught a glimpse of Keir, three horses back, guarding the rear. Dark hair as he watched behind us, his two sword hilts jutting up behind his shoulders.

Pain flooded my heart. I cried out then, howling my grief and anguish to the sky. But the sky and the dead made no answer, and Greatheart never stopped. The sound tore from my chest, pouring out of me, but there was no comfort, no pity in the stars.

So I buried my face in Greatheart's mane, and let my sobs overwhelm me. The horse could take me where he willed. What did it matter?

Stay on, stay on, stay on.

I came back to myself when I realized that Greatheart had finally come to a halt. His head hung down as he drew in air and his sides were lathered.

I felt heavy, unable to do more than breathe. It took long moments before I understood what had happened, and longer still for me to lift my head and look around.

Nothing. Nothing around us but the plains and horses.

I turned my head to scan the area. It all had that eerie glow of silver, from the moon high above. I could hear water flowing nearby. A stream, perhaps. But for miles in all directions, all I could see was horses and grass.

A sob escaped my throat. It was all I had strength for.

Greatheart took a few steps, and lowered his head. I could hear him drinking, great gulps of water. Part of me worried that he'd make himself sick. But he was thirsty, and I was too weary to care.

Down. I needed to get down.

I looked at my hands, wrapped tight in the horsehair. I had to think to get them to loosen their grip. They'd cramped so tight in the rough hair that I sobbed as they slowly let go. I slid from Greatheart's back to fall in a heap at his feet.

Keir was dead. My beloved . . .

I curled into a ball and wept, until the blackness of despair and exhaustion claimed me.

I awoke, warm and safe, wrapped in blankets that smelled of Keir. I sighed, and smiled and reached out . . .

"Muwapp?"

I jerked up and awake, my heart pounding in terror.

An animal stared back at me, sitting by my feet, its long fur hanging down to cover my toes. It gave me a mild look, and started chewing its cud.

"Muwaaaapppp."

They were all around me, six of them, my blanket of the night. I shivered a bit in the cold morning air, and realized that they had kept me warm. I sat still, breathing hard, letting my heart slow, recovering from the shock.

The one closest burped, and I was awash in grass-sweet breath. I laughed in spite of myself. They looked like large shaggy goats, except they had longer necks and large, floppy ears.

I reached out and scratched one between the ears, and it burped again and almost seemed to purr.

"Muwapp. Muwapp." The one at my feet got up, and shook itself like a dog.

The others rose as well, cranky and objecting, but obeying anyway. They moved to the stream to drink. The last one looked at me like I was some sort of very odd creature, and then followed the others. It left a tuft of wool behind, caught on the matted grasses. I plucked it, and held it to my nose. It had that spicy scent of Keir's. I twirled it in my fingers, and smiled when I realized that Keir smelled like a goat.

Keir was dead.

It felt like I'd been struck in the chest, right between my breasts. I covered my heart with my hands, and bent over, moaning as the pain and memories washed over me, over and over. As the memories spilled out and re-played before my eyes.

Just when we'd sworn ourselves to each other. Just when we'd learned to trust and have faith . . .

My chest was so tight, I could barely breathe. I rocked back and forth, sobbing until exhaustion silenced my tears.

Something nudged me. I looked up to see Greatheart standing over me. He lowered his head, and sniffed my neck.

"Oh, Greatheart." I reached up, and hugged him. He waited patiently as I clung to him, trying to get my tears under control.

When I could, I let go and tried to struggle to my feet. As I shifted to stand, I realized that my satchel was still on my hip, the strap between my breasts. I eased the strap over my head and just sat for a moment, trying to get my bearings.

I was a mess. My tunic was stained and wrinkled. My head was pounding something fierce, and my stomach was empty and growling. My hands hurt, and I opened them to see they were swollen, hot and raw. There were sharp cuts where Greatheart's mane had sliced into my palms.

The goats were gathered at the bank of the stream, drinking and eating and chattering like old women on laundry day. Greatheart took a step and scattered them, so that he could drink, noisily sucking in water. The goats scolded with their odd sounds, but splashed through the water to the other side of the stream. I got to my feet and staggered over to kneel by the water, upstream of Greatheart.

I thrust my hands in first. The touch of the water made me hiss as it cooled my heated skin. I cleaned them as best I could, then cupped them and drank the cool sweet water. Only then did I splash my face, drying it on the sleeves of my tunic.

That done, I got to my feet, to look around in the light of day.

Grass and horses. No people. No tents. No enemies. No ghosts.

I was just as grateful for the last.

I didn't want to think, didn't want to feel. My hands still hurt, so I decided to think about that for now. I walked back to my satchel, sat next to it and opened it wide. There was a salve that would help, somewhere in the mess.

The first thing I pulled out was bloodmoss. Carefully, I used a bit to close the cuts. They were still raw, still swollen, but some of the pain was gone.

The next item was my vanilla soap, dried and wrapped in cloth. I held my breath, not wanting to inhale the scent. Not now. I couldn't think about that now. I set it in the grass, as far away as possible.

I rummaged further, surprised to see nothing broken, even the jar with the ehat musk. I wasn't really sure what all was in the satchel. Gils had made it from an old saddlebag and a wide leather strap. He'd told me that he was putting in pockets for 'useful things'. I could see him seated on the floor of my stilltent, looking up at—

I wiped my nose on my tunic, and tried to force myself to think about other things. But the images flooded into my head.

Gils convulsed, limbs jerking in spasms, his head thrown back, gasping for air.

Yers staggered, almost dropping the lad in horror. But Isdra stepped closer to Yers, taking more of Gils's weight. They both managed to hold steady as Gils stopped thrashing as quickly as he had started.

My head came up, my eyes popped open. I looked out over the grasses, but I didn't see them. Instead, I went over that horrible moment again and again, with the eye of a healer. A cold, unemotional eye.

Gils convulsed, limbs jerking in spasms, his head thrown back, gasping for air.

The patient had convulsions.

I moved then, my hand on his forehead. Gils was warm, but not extraordinarily so. "Gils?" I called his name, but there was no reaction, no indication that he was aware. I placed my fingers at his neck, feeling a slow, weak pulse.

The patient had not had a fever.

Quickly, I checked for any kind of head wound, or perhaps he was choking. But his head showed no sign of injury and his throat was clear. There was no sign of other injury, it had to be the plague, and yet there was no odor, no real sweat on his body. But the headaches could cause these kinds of problems, if they were severe enough. Gils's breath was rapid and labored, perhaps . . .

No head wound. No odor, no sweating. Breathing was rapid and labored.

Again, Gils jerked in spasms. His breathing was slowing, as was the beat of his heart. I looked around, finally focusing on Keir's face, a question in his eyes. I met his gaze, and let my tears fall, answering with a shake of my head.

His heart had slowed, his breathing had slowed. My throat was as dry as a bone, my heart was racing. Seen now, with a cold eye and distance, I knew—

I swallowed hard, and faced the truth. Gils had not died of the plague.

But the only thing that I could think of that might cause those symptoms was poison.

I stared at the satchel, numb.

Iften spun on his heel, and glared at me with eyes filled with hate. He paused as he stepped past me. "You and your poisons made it to the Heart. But we of the Plains can learn to use poison, too. Remember that, Xyian."

I remembered, all right. I also remembered that Iften had been alone with my brother at one point, when Keir had used him as a messenger. That attack in the market, they'd used a lance fletched with Iften's pattern. Keir had no proof, but . . ..

Monkshood caused convulsions. Monkshood, the poison my brother had offered me, to 'preserve my honor'. I'd left it behind in my room when I'd given myself to Keir.

Left it in my room for my brother to find.

Was it possible that Iften had poisoned Gils?

I sat staring for some time, before the stinging of my hands brought me back to my task. I forced myself to concentrate on the tasks at hand.

I dug deeper into the satchel's depths, pulling out all the contents for the first time. My medicines were there and I set them out by my feet. When I found the jar with the right salve, I stopped for a moment to rub some into my hands. I bit my lip as the medicine stung. That meant it was working.

At least, that's what I told my patients.

I stoppered the jar, and continued to empty out the satchel. Clean cloths for bandages. A small leather pouch with . . . could it be?

The gurt spilled out into my hand, the familiar white pebble cheese of the Firelanders. My stomach rumbled, but I winced at the idea. It was so dry . . . my stomach gurgled again, and I shrugged, popped one into my mouth, and chewed.

It tasted wonderful.

I crammed in another piece. Of course, it was only the hunger that made it taste good. Or maybe that my nose was so stuffed that I couldn't smell it. I kept eating as I continued my hunt.

More of my familiar medicines, and the scrap of leather that held the bit of mushroom that Iften had spit out. I set them all aside and kept digging.

An unfamiliar jar proved to be sweetfat. I recognized the smell. I wondered what kind of grasses they used to make it, even as I set it down.

A small wooden box, with flint, steel, and tinder. *Bless you, Gils*.

Another small pouch, with leather working tools. A battered tin pot. Another small pouch, with . . . kavage beans!

Dried meat, wrapped in a few folds of leather. A wooden comb. I started to cry over my riches when my fingers closed over a last item.

The spring knife that Marcus had given me.

I'd thought my tears had gone dry.

I'd been wrong.

* * *

I crushed the kavage beans between two river stones. They boiled in the small battered pot, over a tiny fire that I managed to get started on the third try with the flint and steel.

I drank the first bowlful before it really cooled, and set the crushed beans to boil again as I worked at the dried meat. Tough chewing, but my belly didn't care.

There were berries by the water, hanging fat from low bushes only as high as my ankle. I almost plucked some, but the words of Joden's song rang in my head. About what white berries did to your bowels.

I decided I wasn't that hungry.

After the second bowl of kavage, my headache was gone. I repacked the satchel, and put what was left of the meat and gurt back into one of the pockets. I boiled the kavage beans a third time, carefully feeding the fire twigs and dried grasses. They curled in the small flame. The third time made a very weak and bitter brew. I drank it anyway, with the crushed beans, and sucked on the bits that remained.

I took my tunic off, and strapped the knife to my arm, as Marcus had taught me.

Keir was dead. Marcus had probably joined him, if not by another's hand, then by his own.

"Death comes in an instant."

Oh, Marcus.

I closed my eyes for a moment, then put my tunic on, and sat back on the matted grass. The sun was higher now, and I was warm enough. My little fire was dying, but I had no further need. I stared at it as my hands took up the wooden comb, and worked on my hair. Greatheart grazed nearby. The goats had wandered off.

I didn't want to think. Didn't want to feel. I sat numbly, and combed my hair.

The comb hit a bad snarl and I yanked in frustration. Might as well take this trick knife and cut it all off.

Marcus spoke. "If the sweat is as bad as you say, maybe we should cut her hair. It will be hard to keep clean, and will tangle."

"No," Keir answered softly. He was beside me, running his fingers through my hair, pulling it off my face. "No need. I'll braid it for her. I'll not see it cut."

I closed my eyes at the memory, and the pain washed over me again. Keir . . .

I flushed with shame, knowing now what I'd asked of Isdra. She'd been prepared to follow Epor into death, and I tried to stop her, with the weakest of arguments. How hollow my words seemed now that I wanted to do exactly the same thing. There are no words, no medicine, to heal this wound. I was mortified that I had even thought I could.

My tears welled up again, the pain that I so desperately didn't want to feel rising within my chest. We all like to think we're strong, until we are faced with our own loss. I opened my eyes, and stared at the comb in my hands.

Goddess above, what was I to do?

My breathing slowed. Death held no fear for me, if I'd ride at Keir's side to the snows.

I dropped the comb, and twisted my wrist. The blade popped out, just like it was designed to do. Bright and sharp. Xymund had intended that it be used to end my life, back at Water's Fall.

It was sharp enough.

I looked at it for long moments, feeling a strange sense of peace. I knew the hows of the deed. I was a healer, after all.

"No." I gripped his arm with my good hand and tried to pull myself up. Keir helped me without even thinking about it. *"I want a bath now. I stink. I don't care what the water is like."*

Keir blinked and frowned. "Gils needs to check—"

"Gils can check it after I have bathed."

"Gils said—"

"Who is the healer here?" I took a step.

His lips quirked. "Master healer, if I remember right."

I smiled. "The Master wants a bath."

He smiled. "Then, Master, you shall have one."

I smiled even as I sobbed, placing the blade against my wrist. Better to die at my own hand than at Iften's.

Keir would be waiting.

Marcus would be waiting.

Papa would be waiting. . . .

16

"*The price of privilege is responsibility.*"

I stayed my hand. Papa, no. I want—

But I heard Papa's voice as he spoke those words, remembered the lessons at his knee. I saw the faces of the people of Xy, kneeling in the hallways as I'd walked through the castle. Remembered the babies' faces and their cries as I'd delivered them from their mother's body in the tents of the Plains.

Guilt washed over me. I was their queen. Even as I had pledged myself to Keir, I'd pledged myself to them as well. To lead them, protect them, to rule over them all.

I moaned, and started to sob all over again. I wanted to die. It would be so easy. I wanted Keir so badly, as Isdra had wanted Epor. I couldn't imagine life without him. I squeezed my eyes shut as the tears welled up and rolled down my cheeks. The blade was cold against the thin skin of my wrist.

Except Isdra hadn't made her choice, had she? Gathering Storm had forced one on her, hadn't he.

Arrogant bastard.

Anger cut through my pain and grief. The warrior-priests and that bastard Iften had done this. Killed my Warlord, destroyed his plans and dreams for his people. They'd tried to kill me, to make sure that my skills were lost. They'd isolate their people from new ways and new ideas to preserve their power and position, at the cost of their people's lives. They wouldn't truly lead. Not like my Keir has.

Had.

My pain welled up again as I corrected myself.

But Keir's dream wasn't dead, so long as I lived. I frowned at the blade pressed against my skin. Reness had supported him, Osa had expressed interest. Even Liam might be looked to for support.

And Xy needed me, needed Keir's dream, and a ruler who cared for her people.

I stared at the blade. It would be so easy.

And so selfish.

I closed my eyes, and rocked as my grief returned. It would be so hard without Keir with me. Long days of pain and loneliness. I couldn't do this. It was too overwhelming.

So easy just to go.

I tried to wipe my nose on my sleeve. Besides, maybe Keir wanted me to join him. I puffed out a breath. Except he'd helped save me, hadn't he? I shivered at the memory of my Keir, all silver in the moonlight, riding so far behind me.

The knife trembled in my hand.

If I did this, if I joined him in death, Keir's dream and hope for his people died with me.

I took a long, deep breath.

I took another.

If I killed myself, those miserable, rotten, tattooed bastards would win. Iften, that murderous bastard, would win.

If I killed myself, our unborn child would die too.

Oh, Goddess.

I pulled the blade away from my wrist, and started to work it back under my sleeve.

My heart was broken. It felt as if my life was broken as well, shattered with his loss. I'd grieved for my father's death, but this was beyond any sorrow I'd ever felt. Part of my soul was gone, shriveled and black, a physical wound that would never heal.

I'd seen people live with pain, adapting to their injuries, re-building their lives. But it was never the same.

I'd never be whole again.

I would see to our peoples, as best I could. I would see to our child, if indeed I was pregnant. Only then would I join Keir in the snows.

And beyond.

I sat and contemplated my satchel. The sun hung high over my head. Those goat-like creatures had moved further down the stream, chortling and chuckling among themselves.

What was I going to do?

It was all very well to decide to live, to carry out Keir's vision, but just how was I going to do that?

What did I want to do?

I pulled one of the long blades of grass, and played with it. What did I want?

I wanted Keir.

My tears threatened again, but I dashed them away. I needed to think, not weep.

I wanted to go back to Xy. It made no sense to stay on the Plains, especially if my status as Warprize was not going to be confirmed. With Keir gone, I wasn't sure that was even possible anymore.

I wanted Keir.

My head snapped up, and I knew what I wanted. What I needed to do.

I wanted to go home. And I wanted to take Keir with me.

It made no sense, of course. To go back to the Heart of the Plains and demand the body of my Warlord? Goddess alone knew who survived that fight, who was in control. But even Iften had a degree of honor. I was almost certain that an unarmed woman would not be killed outright.

Almost certain.

I was going to return to the Heart of the Plains and claim my Warlord.

I used my sleeve again, to dry my eyes. If they'd burned him, I'd demand the ashes. I'd let Reness know that I'd heal any that came to me, and teach healing to anyone who wanted to learn. That keep by the border, the one that overlooked the Plains. We could rebuild it into a school of healing. Those of the Plains who came in peace would be welcome.

Yes. That was what I would do. But first, I was going to claim my Warlord, and find out what had happened in the Heart. Who lived? Who was in charge? Perhaps Rafe or Prest survived? They hadn't been with the dead, but—

Marcus hadn't been either.

I worried my lower lip with my teeth. If Marcus were dead, he'd be at Keir's side; I'd no doubt of that. I tried to remember what I'd seen, if there'd been anyone with Keir. But he'd been so far back, and I'd been crying . . .

I wasn't sure.

But there was a chance that Marcus lived.

I glared at the hapless blade of grass in my hands. I'd claim Keir's body. I'd claim Marcus as well, dead or alive. I might just give what was left of the Council a piece of my mind, while I was at it.

I glanced over to see that Greatheart was napping, his head down, his hips cocked to the side. Poor old beast. He'd worn himself out carrying me to safety.

The more I thought about it, the more I knew this was what I had to do. I was going to go and find my Warlord and claim him for a final time. I'd take him back, to lie on the borders of our lands. I'd lie next to him, eventually. When the time came.

I started crying again, for what we'd lost. Our time together, the life we would have shared. The children we would have had, watching them grow, and having children of their own.

Goddess, Lady of Mercy and Light, please let me be pregnant.

My stomach rumbled again, and I reached back into the satchel for a few more pieces of gurt. I should conserve my supplies, but my stomach wanted gurt, and it wanted gurt now. I shrugged, and ate, following it with more of the water from the stream. That would have to hold me for a while.

I stood, slung my satchel over my shoulder, and brushed myself off. The sun was starting to move. If I was going to do this, I needed to set aside this pain for now. My grief could wait. I had to get moving.

I dug back into the satchel and took out some of those bandages to wrap around my hands. Greatheart woke with a snort as I tugged on his mane. It took me a while to get on, without a saddle, but he stood patiently as I pulled myself up.

Once mounted, I looked around and realized I didn't have a clue how to get back to the Heart. There were no landmarks, no roads. The herds were not moving in any particular pattern that I could make out.

"Greatheart, take me back," I asked.

His ears twitched, but he didn't move.

"Home," I tried.

Nothing.

"Back," I tried again. "Return?"

Greatheart shook his head, and looked like he was falling back asleep.

"What am I going to do?" I asked.

The goats' heads all popped up from the grasses around the stream, and they all looked off to the left. Greatheart looked in the same direction, and whinnied, as if in welcome.

A shiver went down my spine. Slowly, I turned my head.

There were four warriors on horseback, on the farthest ridge.

The hairs rose on the back of my neck. Even at this distance I could make out Epor's smile, and Isdra's braid. Gils's mop of hair, and Keir . . .

Oh beloved.

His armor gleamed, the hilts of his two swords jutting over his shoulder.

I shuddered, even as my eyes filled with tears. The riders were colorless, somehow, as if the sunlight was going right through them. But clearly, Marcus was not there. That gave me a shred of hope, and that was enough for now.

Epor and Isdra disappeared behind the ridge. Keir lifted his arm, and gestured for me to follow. He and Gils disappeared, following Epor and Isdra out of sight.

I took a deep breath, and pointed Greatheart in that direction, and urged him into a trot.

* * *

"STOP!"

Greatheart snorted, and pulled up short. We'd been traveling for some time, trotting along on the path set for us by the dead. I'd only caught a few glimpses of them since we'd started out, always at a distance, always when I'd lost my sense of direction. But it had been a good hour since we'd seen them last.

Startled by the command, I looked over to the left and blinked in surprise. There was a mounted warrior, scowling fiercely at me, weapon at the ready. Her mount looked angry as well, stomping its foot.

I'd have been terrified, except that the warrior wielded a wooden blade, and I had tunics that were older than the warrior. The girl was dressed in leathers, her hair pulled back in a braid. She looked fierce, and determined, but it was hard not to laugh right out loud at the child.

She was mounted on one of those furry goats.

I stifled my smile, for I'd no wish to offend. "Greetings, warrior."

The girl swelled with pride. "I am Pive of the Snake, Warrior of the Plains, and Guardian of the Gurtle Herds," she proclaimed in a ringing voice twice her size.

"Greetings, Pive of the Snake." I inclined my head toward her. "I am—"

"You are an intruder! And my captive!" Pive waved her sword. Greatheart shied a bit, uneasy. I had visions of my shins taking a beating from that blade. "You must come with me, to my camp, and surrender to my warleader."

"Who is your warleader?"

"Gilla of the Snake." Pive's face was screwed up with determination. "Surrender or die."

I shrugged. "As you wish, warrior."

Poor little Pive almost fell off her gurtle at the ease of her conquest. Her mouth gaped open, then she recovered and gave me a grin that ran from ear to ear. "Follow me!" She sheathed her sword, and tugged on the reins. "Hup! Hup!"

"MUWAPP!" the gurtle protested, but it turned and started off at a trot.

I could grin now. Pive's legs were lost in the fat, fluffy fur, but her toes hung down, almost scraping the ground.

I urged Greatheart to follow my captor.

It didn't take long. Over two rises and down along a ridge, I could see a tent close to a small pond, surrounded by gurtles.

Pive was overcome with her accomplishment. "Heyla!" she called, forcing her gurtle into a gallop.

The gurtle ran, but it complained the entire way. The gurtles of the herd all answered those complaints with their own, setting off a chorus that could probably be heard for miles.

The tent flap opened, and an older girl emerged, followed by a boy at least her age. Their weapons were metal, their faces grim.

"Pive! Stop this noise!" the girl called out, only to stop in her tracks at the sight of me on my horse. "Warprize!"

"No, Gilla! That's my prize," Pive said as she dismounted, and hopped up and down in her glee. Her mount shook itself all over, and then plopped down right where it was standing. Pive paid it no mind. "My prize! I captured her!"

"Warprize?" the boy asked, his hand on the hilt of his sword.

"I saw her, in the Heart," Gilla answered, moving toward me. "Our tents were near hers." She looked up at me, frowning with concern. "Warprize, I am Gilla of the Snake. Please let me offer you the courtesy of our camp."

Pive stamped her foot in frustration. "No, no. She can't be the Warprize. She's not stinky, she doesn't have sores like a city-dweller. And she doesn't breathe fire!"

"PIVE!" Gilla scolded. "Be silent!"

"Pive, come with me." The boy extended his hand. "We need to cry the others in for the night."

Pive's face lit up. "El, you'll let me warble?"

"I will." El smiled. "Bring your mount so we can get him a drink."

Pive took up the reins, and the gurtle stood. "Want to hear how I captured her?" Pive asked.

El gave us an amused look over his shoulder before turning to listen to Pive as they walked off.

Gilla gave me a wry smile. "I am sorry, Warprize. Pive meant no offense."

"I took none." I slid down from Greatheart's back.

Gilla gestured to the fire. "Please come and sit. Have you eaten?"

Greatheart ambled down to the edge of the pond for a drink. I kept an eye on him, not wanting to lose my mount. Gilla poured kavage, and offered me a mug.

"No, thank you, Gilla." I walked to the edge of her fire. A childish voice rose in a long warbling cry behind us.

"They call the other children in, for the evening meal," Gilla explained. "You are more than welcome to spend the night." She looked in the direction that I'd come from. "Do you travel alone?"

I had to admire her subtlety. "Yes."

She gave me an intent look. "Something has happened, hasn't it. In the Heart? We've had no news."

I nodded. "Can you tell me how to get back there?"

She raised an eyebrow. "Warprize, I'd offer to guide you myself, but I cannot leave. I have duties—"

"The children and the herds."

"Just so." Gilla may have been all of twelve or thirteen, but she acted like a woman my age. "I could guide you in the morning."

I shook my head. "No. I can't wait. And it might be dangerous to be seen with me."

She sighed. "Very well. You'll need to make good time, to get to the Heart before dark."

Greatheart walked back to my side, and stood next to me. I checked the wrappings on my hands and then mounted. She eyed me closely as I settled onto his back. "At least let me give you gloves, Warprize, to protect your hands."

I shook my head. "No. I take nothing except from my Warlord's hands. Just tell me how to get there."

"Follow that ridge, until it meets with a river." She pointed off to the left. "Then just follow the river downstream. You will mount a rise and see the Heart laid out before you, Warprize." She looked up into my eyes. "May the skies favor you."

"And you as well. Thank you for your courtesy, Gilla of the Snake."

She inclined her head, and I urged Greatheart into a trot. I'd demands to make, and a Warlord to claim.

The Heart looked different somehow.

Greatheart and I paused at the top of the rise, to get our bearings. And to give me a chance to work up my courage. It looked different, and this time, it wasn't the size, or the shifting of the tents. There, beyond the herds, it looked like the place was buzzing with activity. People moving everywhere.

There were pyres burning by the lake shore.

My heart started to race within my chest. I tucked my satchel up close to my body. Nervously, I checked the bandages that I'd wrapped around my hands. Then I took a deep breath and wrapped Greatheart's coarse hair between my fingers.

Greatheart was prancing slightly, my nervousness affecting him. I leaned in close, and whispered in his ear, "Easy, boy. Nothing is going to come between me and my Warlord."

Greatheart snorted, then shook his head as if in agreement, pawing at the ground.

I sat back up, and took a quick look behind me. The dead had not appeared since I'd left the children, but the way my skin crawled, I felt their eyes on me.

I turned back, taking a last long look at the tent city below me. It teemed with activity, warriors everywhere, tents being taken down. Best to do this before we were seen and stopped.

Or killed.

I took a deep breath, crouched down and then cried out, digging my feet into Greatheart's ribs. "Heyla!" I urged Greatheart on with my legs. "Run, Greatheart! Run!"

Greatheart leaped forward, down the rise. The grass flew under us, and within a few breaths we were down into the herds that were between us and the Heart.

Horses parted to let us through, some even running briefly alongside. Greatheart galloped, his hooves tearing at the ground, running full out. I leaned forward, staying low, trying to be less of a target. "Heyla! Go! Go!" I urged.

The horses's muscles bunched and flowed under me as he ran. I tried to remember to breathe, and tightened my grip on his mane.

That quickly, we were through the herd and in the tents, still running hard. I saw brief glimpses of gaping faces, astonishment frozen there for the instant before we passed. No brandished weapons.

Yet.

No matter. I wasn't stopping for anything or anyone.

Shouts rose behind us, but we were moving too fast for any to interfere. Greatheart seemed to know where we were going, since he headed straight for the large Council tent. He ran right up to the entrance, sliding and rearing to a stop. I slid from his back, and then hesitated. I didn't want to lose him now. I kept my hand on his mane, and started to walk. I needn't have worried. The wonderful horse followed me right into the tent.

I had to blink, to let my eyes adjust to the dimness. The tent seemed full of people, the Elders on their tiers, warriors milling about. I took a few more steps and my presence cut through the noise like a knife. There was complete silence as Greatheart and I walked between the two fire pits.

Essa was there, seated on a stool. Battered and bruised, but he appeared whole. He was gaping at me, the Eldest Singer at a loss for words. Wild Winds was next to him, also looking worse for wear. "Xylara, Daughter of Xy, we thought you—"

"Stop." My voice was hard, and only I knew how brittle it was. I was afraid I'd start sobbing, but my anger was white hot. "Your words are as nothing to me."

Essa blanched, and dropped his eyes. Wild Winds closed his mouth.

I glared at them all, letting my eyes roam the tiers. "Your words hold no truth, no meaning, and I will not hear them." I paused to take a breath. My knees were starting to tremble. Greatheart stood silently next to me, swishing his tail back and forth.

"I demand," my voice cracked, but I kept talking. "I demand that you give me the body of Keir of the Cat, my Warlord." Essa's head came up and his mouth opened, but I cut him off. "I will take his body, and return to the Kingdom of Xy, with any who wish to travel with me." I drew a shuddering breath. "I'll give him to the earth, where the Plains meet the borders of Xy, so that he will be of both lands, forever."

I straightened my back, and found the strength to continue. "I share Keir's dream. I will heal any who ask it, be they of Xy or of the Plains." My rage flared within me. "But I will not come before this Council again. Ever."

Wild Winds stood, a bit unsteady on his feet. "Xylara."

I focused my rage on him. "Give me my Warlord, you arrogant bastard."

There was a commotion from behind me, the sound of running feet. I tensed, sure that I was about to be attacked.

"Lara!" It was Simus. He caught me in a hug. "Lara, we thought you dead!"

That did it. The barriers I'd built about my pain started to crumble. I wrapped my arms around Simus's neck and clung for dear life. "Simus, I saw him die. I saw Keir die."

Simus pulled back a bit, head down to look into my eyes. He looked exhausted, as if he hadn't slept. "Lara? But—"

I didn't want to break down in front of the Council, but I couldn't stop my tears. "I was on Greatheart, and he was running, but I looked back and saw Keir die. Then he and Epor and Isdra were there, and they helped me escape."

"You saw the dead?" Essa's voice was hushed. The tent was so silent, I heard Wild Winds gasp. "They aided you?" Essa continued, his voice filled with wonder.

"Gils too. Keir rode with the dead, Simus." I ignored everything else except Simus's kind dark eyes. "My beloved is . . ." My voice cracked, and Simus drew me in close and wrapped his arms around me. "Simus, take me to him." I spoke into his leather armor. "Take me to Keir. Please?"

There was another commotion, the sound of warriors running into the tent. I didn't bother to look, just hugged Simus and waited for him to speak.

"Little Healer." Simus's voice rumbled in my ear. He pulled back, and put his hands on my shoulders. "You gave me back my life in Xy, when you healed my leg." His tired eyes sparkled and he gave me a gentle, knowing smile. "Let me give you back yours, eh?"

With that, he gently turned me around to face the entrance.

Keir stood there, out of breath, his mouth open, staring at me as if he'd seen a ghost.

17

It couldn't be.

Simus's hands were warm on my shoulders as I stood there, gazing at my beloved.

It wasn't him of course. It couldn't be. I pressed back against Simus. "Simus," I whispered in despair, trying to make him understand. "Keir rides with the dead."

"Look again, Little Healer." Simus's voice was soft, and seemed to tremble in my ear, whether from sorrow or laughter, I couldn't say. "He lives, Lara."

"Lara?" Keir took a step forward, his eyes wide and desperate. "Lara?" His voice was a hush, as if he couldn't believe. There was color in those blue eyes, blood on his . . .

I cried out then, and ran to him. His arms opened, taking me up and into their warmth, wrapping tight around me. He was warm and real and breathing . . .

Goddess and all the stars above, Keir was alive!

My arms wrapped around his neck as I covered his face in kisses. Keir's strength seemed to drain out of him, and he sank to his knees. My own body went boneless and I melted down with him. His cloak wrapped around us, cutting us off from the eyes of the Elders. We were sheltered in each other.

"I saw," I sobbed even as I stroked his face. His warm, living skin moved under my fingers. "I saw you . . ."

"Keekai. You saw Keekai, fire of my heart." Keir's voice was a rasp. "Keekai fell in combat, not I."

I clutched at him then, weeping. "It must have been her who rode with me into the herds."

Keir's face was stark, his eyes filled with pain.

"You're alive," I breathed, amazed. I moved my hands to his waist and then let them curve up around his back. The cold links of his mail couldn't disguise the feel of his hard body. I started sobbing, taking in great gulps of air.

Keir murmured in my ear, and rubbed his hands over my back. "I'm here, Lara."

It was almost too much to believe. Keir, alive, healthy, back in my arms, his breath tickling my ear. All our dreams, all of our future, all given back to me in an instant. I didn't dare believe.

And yet there was that spicy scent to his skin. I started to laugh, even as my tears fell. "Oh, beloved."

Keir wiped at my cheeks with his thumb, and then kissed me. The salt of my tears, the warm taste of his mouth, it was true, it was true . . .

Keir lived. And so did I.

I came to my senses, becoming aware of the people around us. I choked back my sobs, trying to get my emotions under control. I looked out from the shelter of Keir's arms, even as he looked up.

Prest stood before us, as did Rafe, looking out and

away. Ander and Yveni had our backs, facing toward the entrance. Each was battered and bloody, yet each had a weapon at the ready, and from their stance it was clear that no one was getting close to us. Prest was wielding a sword. Where was the warclub? But I had other worries.

Simus stood further in front of Prest and Rafe. He had his back to us, his arms crossed over his chest. The Eldest and Elders were focused on Keir and me, the entire tent silent.

I tucked my head back into the shelter of Keir's arms, but not before I saw Joden standing off to the side, his face stricken with pain.

"Keir," I asked softly, not wanting to be heard. "Who lives?"

Keir's head was down. He moved just enough so that his breath warmed my ear. "Those you see. And—"

Warriors entered the tent, apparently with a prisoner. Our guards tensed, and Simus pulled a sword as well. I lifted my head just enough to see a prisoner dragged within, around the outside of the fire pits, and then dumped at Essa's feet. The man's hands were bound behind him, and one of his guards grabbed his hair, and pulled his head up.

It was Iften.

He looked the worse for wear, stripped down to trous, and barefoot. He'd lost those bracers, and even at this distance, I could see that his arm was crooked, the fingers curled.

Another commotion. Everyone around me was already on guard, but this time it was Reness, striding past the fire pits. "She lives?" Reness asked of Essa. "You found her?"

"She found us." Essa gestured toward Keir and me.

Reness turned, her face lit up with a smile. "Warprize. Thank the skies you survived."

Iften jerked his head free, and turned to look over his shoulder at me. His face was full of hate, his lips in a snarl. I shifted a bit, fear washing through me.

Keir growled deep in his throat.

"Join us, Eldest Thea." Essa gestured to a stool set next to him. "This senel was called to determine the fate of this warrior."

Reness's lip curled. "What true warrior *surrenders?*"

Iften's head jerked back around. "I would speak!"

"Pah." Essa stood, unsteady on his feet, his face white. Either he was angered beyond belief, or in pain, or both. I narrowed my eyes, and studied him and Wild Winds carefully. "You'd speak now," Essa continued, "when you and the others failed to force your truths upon us."

"She is a threat to us all, a danger to our people," Iftan spat. "We had to try to make you—"

"Make us? Force us?" Wild Winds spoke from his stool. "Your truth had been heard and considered. All arguments had been made. But Antas would have used his blade rather than let this Council make its decision."

"I do not know how Antas convinced so many to betray this Council and the Plains," Essa spoke. "But all who lifted a blade in the Council senel died for it, or have fled the Heart."

"Except the coward that dropped his sword," Simus added.

All three of the Eldest glared at him. Wild Winds spoke first. "You have no rank to—"

Simus laughed. "You have no Eldest Warrior to sit on the tier. A warrior's voice should be heard, yes?" He spread his arms wide. "My truth is yours, Eldest of the Elders."

Keir snorted softly, but didn't say anything. I shifted so that I could see his face, thinking that he was looking at the tiers. But Keir was focused on Iften, and Iften alone.

Who chose that moment to cry out, "You will see." He came up on his knees, wincing as the bonds pulled at his arm. "She will bring disaster and death with her ways. Keir is a fool, to bring a city-dweller among us. Even her own people wished to be rid of her. Punish me if you will, but the truth will not be changed."

Essa took a step to glare at Iften. "I will explain this to you, Iften of the Boar, for it seems you have forgotten a truth of our People. You are not being punished for opposing the confirmation of the Warprize."

"No." Wild Winds stood, using his staff to pull himself up. The three skulls clattered against each other. "No, Iften of the Boar. Your crime was not to oppose Keir of the Cat and Xylara. It was to attempt to silence this Council's voices and impose your will."

Reness stood. "We are of the Plains and of the Tribes, our lives intertwined and dependent on each other. Yet you would use violence to force, not your voice or your wisdom to persuade. That is your offense, Iften of the Tribe of the Boar, Warrior of the Plains. And for it, I name you Outcast."

Essa nodded, folding his arms over his chest. "I, too, name you Outcast."

Wild Winds was grim. "I, too, name you Outcast."

Iften had paled, the bruises about his face in stark contrast to his skin. "No, I—" He swallowed hard. "You warrior-priests have much to lose if the Xyian's ways are brought to the Plains."

"Do we?" Wild Winds asked.

Essa turned to face the Elders on the tiers about him. "What say the Council? Shall Iften of the Boar, Warrior of the Plains, be cast out of his Tribe and out of the People?"

Reness and Wild Winds sat down. All of the Elders remained seated. Every single one.

Essa spoke again. "For this ceremony, an Eldest of the Warriors is required. Antas will answer to this Council for his actions. There is no time to select a new Eldest. I would ask that Nires of the Boar, Warrior of the Plains, Elder of the Tribe of the Boar, stand as Eldest for this senel. Do any oppose this?"

All of the Elders stood.

A figure moved on the lowest tier, walking down to stand next to Reness. "I thank you for the honor, Eldest Singer."

Essa inclined his head, then turned to face Iften. "Iften of the Boar, Warrior of the Plains. The Council of the Elders names you Outcast." He drew a deep breath. "May the very air deny you breath."

Iften's eyes were wild as he glanced at the condemning faces before him.

Wild Winds spoke. "Iften of the Boar. The Council of the Elders names you Outcast. May the very earth collapse beneath your feet."

Reness spoke. "Iften. The Council of the Elders names you Outcast. May the very fire scorch your skin."

Nires drew himself up. "The Council names you Outcast, without Tribe, without a name, no longer of the Plains. May the very water of the land refuse to quench your thirst."

Essa gestured to the guards. "Take this one out into the Plains, a half-day's ride, and leave him. Without weapons, without people, without a name. The elements will have him, to do with as they please."

His captors dragged Iften up, and dragged him off. He made no sound, said nothing, but stared at Keir and me as he was taken away. I shivered, and clung to Keir.

Somehow, Iften's silence was that much more frightening. I'd never know the truth of Gils's death. But in my heart I was sure that Iften had poisoned him.

Essa watched until Iften was removed. He heaved a deep breath. "That done, we must turn to the issue at hand. This Council must decide whether to confirm Xylara, Daughter of Xy, as Warprize."

"Can there be a doubt?" Simus asked.

Wild Winds scowled. "It is not your place to say, Warrior. And sheath those weapons. The violence is over."

Simus stiffened, then looked back over his shoulder at Keir. There was a long pause, long enough to make Wild Winds open his mouth as if to speak.

Something wasn't right. I looked into Keir's face. He hadn't relaxed now that Iften was gone, the arms around me were taut and his eyes were wary.

Keir gave a nod, and Simus turned back, sheathing his sword. But then Simus crossed his arms over his chest in a manner that let everyone know that he would not be moved.

Essa spoke then, his face strained and white. "The truth of Joden of the Hawk was interrupted by events. Joden of the Hawk, do you have any more to say?"

Joden stepped up. "I would add nothing. Whether the change Lara brings is for good or for ill, I believe her to be a true Warprize."

"Never before has the kind of change been an issue in the confirmation," Essa agreed.

"The dead rode with her," Joden continued. "And the herds protected her."

Reness's eyes widened. She turned to Wild Winds. "The dead aided her, and still you doubt?"

Wild Winds shook his head. "I do not know what to make of this." He swayed slightly.

"Sit down before you fall down," Reness snapped. "Or is your pride so fragile?"

Essa and Wild Winds both glared at her, but they each sought their stools. I lifted my head to whisper to Keir. "They're hurt."

His eyes flickered over them, and he grunted in agreement.

"I could—"

"Only if they beg," was his soft response. His arms tightened around me.

I relaxed against him, more than willing to be sheltered in their strength.

"Let it be done," Reness demanded. She stood, and faced the tiers. "Let us make this decision now. No more talk. No more debate. Enough is known. Is Xylara, Daughter of Xy, to be confirmed as Warprize?"

For a moment, no one moved. Then with a great rustle, the entire Council of Elders sat down. Essa and Wild Winds remained seated.

"It is done," Reness said with satisfaction. She turned to look at us, her face lighting up with a rare smile. "Only the ceremony remains to be held, and that will take a day to prepare."

"They should be separated until the ceremony," Wild Winds demanded. "She has not yet made her choice and he—"

I heard Keir's blade leave the sheath as I twisted my wrist. His sword was out, in front of both of us like a shield. My blade sprang forth, and I lifted my arm so that it could be seen.

"Never again," I spat. "You'll not separate us."

Keir snarled, "I'll kill any that try."

Silence filled the tent, to be broken by Simus's chuckle. "Separate them at your peril."

Essa frowned. "That is not—"

Wild Winds snorted. "Let them be. Why waste more time?" He stepped stiffly off the platform. "The ceremony will be tomorrow night, under the darkening skies. She will make her choice then." He looked over at Essa. "End this senel, Eldest Singer, and let us seek out our tents and our beds."

Simus cleared his throat. "I and Keir's warriors will guard the Warprize with the warrior-priests until the ceremony. I will protect the Warprize with my life."

Joden spoke then, causing all heads to turn. "I would guard her as well."

Keir stood, keeping me in the shelter of his arms. I rose with him, my legs trembling.

"You would be welcome, Joden of the Hawk," Keir spoke as he placed his hand at the small of my back and steadied me.

"This senel is at an end, for this session, and for the season. The issue of Antas will be dealt with in the spring," Essa said. "Word will be sent to you of the plans for the ceremony. You will be . . . ?"

"In the tent of the Warprize."

I looked up at Keir in surprise. His face was still taut and tense.

Essa inclined his head.

With one swift move Keir swept me up into his arms, and started toward the tent entrance. I sighed, and let my head fall onto his shoulder. My head hurt and my nose and eyes were raw from crying. The bandages that I'd wrapped around my hands were in tatters, my tunic was stained and filthy, and there had to be bits of grass and gurtle fur in my hair.

But under my ear, Keir's heart beat strong and steady. His arms cradled me close. His mail would no doubt leave a pattern on my cheek. I didn't care.

I'd never been happier.

We were out of the tent, and I shivered a bit as the

chill air touched my skin. The sun had set, and stars were starting to appear. With each step, I could feel Keir's body move, alive and well. I closed my eyes and breathed a silent prayer to the Goddess.

Oh, Lady of the Moon and Stars, thank you for Keir's life and health. Thank you for returning my beloved. Oh, Lady of the Moon and Stars, never let me take him for granted. Each day will be as a gift, each night will be a prayer of thanks.

"Her tent is a good choice," Simus spoke softly as we walked along. "The area around it is clear, and it will be easy to guard."

"Yveni, Ander, go fetch Marcus and the others, if they will come. Bring them to her tent," Keir ordered. "Go quickly, and be wary."

I opened my eyes at the sound of his voice, to see the others were surrounding us, weapons drawn. Yveni and Ander were running off through the tents, to carry Keir's message. I tensed, uneasy at the thought. "Do you think we'll be attacked?"

"Those that support Antas have fled," Joden answered.

"Perhaps. We take no chances." Keir's voice was grim. He kept walking, a steady pace.

"Essa seemed to think not." Simus looked back at me, and flashed a grin. "But who is to say?"

I worried my lower lip with my teeth. "Iften could—"

"There is no longer a warrior by that name, Warprize," Joden corrected me.

Keir's arm tightened around me. "How much farther?"

"Not far," Simus responded.

It wasn't. Rafe and Prest went in first, to check the tent. They emerged and indicated it was safe. Simus held the tent flap open as Keir tucked his head to enter. The tent was dark and cold, the sleeping area open to the main part. The fat little lamp was there by the bed, unlit and unhappy.

Prest and Rafe stayed by the entrance, on guard.

Keir sat me on one of the stools in the main area. He took off his cloak with a flourish and then wrapped it around me. The cloth held his warmth, and I pulled it in tight. Keir knelt for a moment, looking into my eyes with a look of wonder. "I'd thought I'd lost you."

I reached out and stroked his cheek. "I'm fine, Keir."

Joden stirred a brazier, as if looking for coals, but it appeared to be stone cold. "No one to tend to it."

That caught my attention. Was Amyu dead then as well? "What happened?" I asked Keir. "What happened after I left?"

"What happened to you?" Simus asked. He took a stool near to me. "That's what we want to know!"

The sound of running feet distracted us. Keir stood, and drew his sword. Joden and Simus stood as well. Then Rafe opened the flap, and in ran Marcus with Atira, Heath, and Amyu.

"Lara!" Marcus's face was a joy to see. I leaped up and we hugged, his wiry arms wrapped around me.

"Oh, Marcus, I've missed you so," I sobbed, pulling back a bit to look into his eye. "You are well?"

"Now that you are back where you belong." Marcus stepped back, and looked around. "What is this? A cold tent? This will not do!" he sputtered, covering the tears I was sure he was about to shed. "Not that you could take her to yours!"

I looked at Keir. "Why not?"

"He never had it put up," Simus said. "Too busy trying to gather support at first, talking and seeing people, sending us to guard you from a distance."

"I had other concerns," Keir growled.

"The Warlord would not let me return here," Amyu

explained. "Not after I disobeyed an Elder of my Tribe."

"Amyu." I hugged her hard. She stiffened for a moment, and then returned the gesture. "Amyu, thank you for sparing my life."

"For which I also thank you," Keir said.

Amyu inclined her head. "I am not so much a child that I cannot repay a debt, Warlord."

Rafe got a funny look on his face. "And such a debt. The Warprize actually reached into the body of the life-giver and pulled the babes forth." His voice was filled with admiration, but he looked a bit sick.

"I would hear that truth," Joden said.

"Atira! Heath!" I hugged Atira first, then threw myself into Heath's arms. But I pulled back quickly. "Heath! Your eye! What happened?"

His eye was black, with deep purple bruises and swelling all around. It was almost completely swollen shut.

Heath grimaced. "Nothing, Lara." He glanced over at Atira, who glared right back at him.

"Next time, you will not get between a warrior of the Plains and her enemy," Atira snapped, clearly unsympathetic.

"Oh, there's a truth that needs telling!" Simus crowed.

"First the braziers, then kavage and food." Marcus stirred himself. "The tent is small, it will warm quickly."

"But I want to hear her truths!" Simus protested.

"Pah," Marcus scolded. "When we're warm, inside and out. Move that lazy carcass of yours, and we can all hear, together."

"I'll fetch wood," Joden offered.

"Reness will have some stew," Amyu offered. "I can go and ask."

Simus grumbled, but he stood as well. "I'll start the fires."

"I have not the right to command—" Keir started.

I looked at him in astonishment, but Rafe cut him off. "You are our leader, Keir of the Cat. I will follow you, regardless of the Council's decision. That which has been lost can be regained."

Prest and the others nodded.

Simus smirked at Keir. "Told you."

Keir's face relaxed. "I thank you all." He straightened his shoulders. "Prest and Rafe, remain on watch," Keir demanded. "Yveni and Ander, take the back. We do not relax our guard." At their crestfallen faces, he amended his command. "Until the time for truth telling comes. Then we will sit together. Agreed?"

"My tentmates will aid us," Rafe offered. "If you wish, Warlord."

"I am no longer a Warlord, Rafe," Keir protested.

"You are," Prest said pointedly, "to us."

Keir considered him, then nodded in agreement. Everyone got to work.

I would have stood as well, but Keir's hand was on my shoulder. I looked up into worried blue eyes. "Is anyone seriously hurt?" I asked. I looked into his eyes and smiled. "I'm fine, Keir."

"Bruises only," Simus offered. "The blood belongs to others."

"I—" Keir drew my attention as he stopped, and cleared his throat. "It may be some time before I can let you out of my sight."

I leaned against him, and sighed, forgetting my concerns for the moment. "I feel the same, my Warlord."

Marcus was right, once the braziers were lit the tent warmed quickly. Amyu returned with a pot of stew and flat bread. The kavage was on the fire, and Marcus summoned my guards in to eat. We all crammed into the tent and settled close. Rafe and Prest remained by the tent entrance, their eyes constantly watching for trouble. The four women of Rafe's tent were posted all around, so that we were secure as we could be.

I managed to get Keir to sheath his sword and sit on a stool next to me. He was close enough that I could feel his breath on my cheek if I turned my head. Keir ignored the stew, but did take some kavage.

Amyu had lit the little lamp, and its flame flickered and danced in welcome.

"So, tell us." Simus leaned in, his face full of curiosity. "Tell us what happened."

So I did, between sips of kavage. When I finished, Simus shook his head, and turned to Joden. "Have you ever heard of such?"

"No." Joden shook his head. "There are stories of the dead appearing to the living, but never to one not of the Plains."

"I thought I'd sent you to your death," Keir said softly. "The horse should have fled to the herds. But it seems he took you much further."

"Just as well," Simus added. "Since those warriors got past us and into the herds."

Keir grunted. "Still. Out as far as where the Snake Tribe keeps its gurtles? Why so far?"

"The dead did it," I offered. "Greatheart ran, and they surrounded us and urged us on. Gils, and Isdra and Epor." I hesitated. "And Keekai."

We all went silent. A sob filled my throat. "She helped me so much." I looked over at Keir, the grief etched on his face.

"She believed in us," Keir offered. "And died to protect you."

I moved into the shelter of his arm and Keir hugged me a bit closer. "It took three warriors to take her down, Lara. And she still managed to take one with her. An honorable end."

"One to sing of," Joden said softly.

I nodded in sorrow, but then looked at everyone around me. "I am so glad you all survived. But, Prest, where is Epor's warclub?"

"Broke." Prest looked satisfied. "Gathering Storm answered to it."

"He fell like a stone when Prest hit him, and never got up again," Rafe added. "The club split clean down the center."

Joden was sitting next to him, and had an odd look on his face. Either he was playing chess in his head, or he was composing a song.

I leaned forward. "But what happened here? Keir threw me on Greatheart and . . . ?"

Amyu looked confused, but Marcus leaned over. "Herself names her horses."

Amyu's eyes widened. "All of them?"

Simus set his empty bowl down and belched. "Once you were away, and out of danger, we could focus on the fight. Before that we were hard pressed."

Joden frowned. "I knew that Iften and Antas were relying on my truths to support them. And I would have spoken against you, Lara. But it struck me, when you ran to Keir, that is when I remembered—"

" 'Like the heat of the summer sun,' " I quoted.

He nodded, embarrassed. "I didn't know that they'd use their swords to force the issue. When Antas called for your death, I was stunned."

"Not so stunned that you didn't leap to help us," Keir said.

Joden shrugged. "I may not support your ideas, Warlord, but I will not let them be silenced with death."

"Enough of the Elders felt the same way that their

swords aided us," Keir added. "Or the results may have been different."

Marcus passed the kavage. "So Antas fled?"

"Essa almost took him down, but it was a struggle." Simus seemed impressed. "I'd not thought Antas the better warrior."

"Gathering Storm went for Wild Winds, who was caught by surprise. If not for Keekai charging down, he might have killed the Eldest Warrior-Priest," Simus commented.

"Warrior-Priest against warrior-priest. What does that mean?" Yveni asked.

"I wish I knew," Joden responded.

"A trick, perhaps," Keir suggested. "To disguise his role, in case of failure."

Simus shook his head. "He had the true look of a man taken by surprise. And Keekai drove Gathering Storm off—"

"To face me," Prest added smugly.

"When Gathering Storm went down, Antas called for his warriors to flee," Joden explained.

"Wild Winds is hurt," I offered. "So is Essa. They try to hide it, but they both move with pain."

"Ah." Joden looked at me, questioningly.

I shrugged. "They know what I am willing to do, Joden. They know where I am."

Keir growled.

The talk continued as I blinked a bit, relaxing in the warmth. Others had been involved in the fight, names that I didn't know. But it was wonderful to be surrounded by my friends, warm and fed, with Keir by my side. I smiled, content, until I realized that Marcus had asked me a question. I blinked at him in confusion.

He gave me a wry smile. "Enough. Herself is exhausted, and we wear her out with this chatter."

Keir looked into my face, concerned. "Lara?"

Marcus stood. "Out, all of you. I've a Warprize and a Warlord to put to bed." Keir scowled and opened his mouth to protest, but Marcus snorted. "A Warlord who has not slept these last few days. Or eaten, for that matter."

Simus stood and stretched. "I'll sleep out here, in front of the entrance. Are you others able to take the night?"

"There's not that much left." Rafe stood as well. "Another mug of kavage and we'll do until dawn."

Prest nodded his agreement.

"Then we'll sleep and relieve you." Ander and Yveni rose and left.

"It seems we have no say," I chuckled, looking into Keir's face. His eyes flickered, and there was no amusement in those eyes. I stood, and stretched, reaching for Keir to steady myself. He reached for me as well.

"Some warm water, Warprize?" Marcus asked.

"That would be good." I nodded. "And another bowl of stew, Marcus." I tightened my grip on Keir's hand and took a step toward the sleeping area.

Keir swept me up in his arms and carried me over to the bed.

"Keir, it's just a few steps!"

He stopped and looked over his shoulder. Marcus took the hint, and closed off our portion of the tent. We were finally alone. Out from under the prying eyes of both friend and foe.

Keir eased me down to my feet. I placed my hands on his chest and looked up into his weary tired eyes, and smiled. "Keir . . ."

He took me in his arms, and claimed my mouth with his.

18

In the past day, I'd passed through curiosity, terror, fear, and despair, only to find myself in Keir's arms. I sighed, and melted against him. I was tired and dirty, but far more important, I was home.

I leaned in, letting him take control of the kiss, answering his passion with my own. His arms crushed me to his chest. But the rings of his mail pressed into my palms, and I broke the kiss, hissing at the pain.

Keir took my hands in his and gently started to work the bandages loose. He cursed when he saw the abused flesh underneath.

"It's not that bad," I whispered. "They're better than they were."

Apparently, that didn't impress him. "Marcus!" Keir called out, not bothering to lift his eyes from my hands.

"Warlord?" Marcus answered from the main area.

"Fetch Lara's satchel." Keir brushed his fingers over

my hands. I shivered at that slight touch. They did look better to my eyes, the swelling was down and the redness greatly eased.

But Keir remained unimpressed. He eased me over to sit on the edge of the bed.

Marcus coughed and entered with my satchel. He raised an eyebrow at the sight. "Next time, wear gloves."

I smiled, but Keir didn't see the humor. "As if she had a choice," he barked.

I jerked my head back in surprise at the tone in his voice. Keir still wasn't looking at me as he continued. "I throw her on a horse, no saddle, no reins, and expect—"

"And I'm taken to safety," I pointed out gently. "As you planned."

"Planned!" Keir grabbed my satchel and tore it open violently. His voice was filled with disgust. "I'd thought you safe and—"

"Find the green jar." I kept my voice mild, but I feared for my satchel and its contents, the way Keir was rooting around. If he broke the jar with the ehat musk in it, we'd all regret it. "Marcus, I could use more kavage. And more stew, if there is any left." Marcus gave me a nod and turned to go. "Oh, and gurt, if you've any."

Marcus turned, and raised his eyebrow.

I shrugged. "I'm hungry."

"At least you eat," he grumbled, with a sharp look at Keir. "I'll bring what I can." With that he vanished beyond the flap.

Keir had the jar now, the contents of my satchel strewn about the bed. He reached for my hands, but I pulled them away. "They'll bring water for washing, Keir. Once they're clean, we'll put on the salve." I gave him a smile as I toed off my shoes. "Why not take off your armor?"

"No. Better to be prepared in case of attack."

I raised an eyebrow. "You're not sleeping next to me in that. My hair will get caught, and then where will we be?"

His laugh burst out, catching him by surprise, and I knew that he'd remembered exactly when my hair had gotten caught in his mail. But he shook his head just the same.

My stubborn Warlord. I leaned in close. "Keir, I want you in my bed this night, and all the nights of our lives. Skin to skin, beloved."

His eyes blazed bright blue. He leaned down, and I lifted my mouth, and we kissed again. I reached up to pull him close when there was movement at the entrance.

The tent flap moved.

Keir snarled, pulled a dagger and lunged, placing himself between me and—

Amyu, holding two buckets of steaming water. She looked up, then dropped to her knees, the buckets sloshing over as they thumped down. Amyu lowered her head, showing the back of her neck.

"Keir," I cried out, afraid that he'd kill her. But Keir managed to stop, and stood over the poor girl.

A soft snort, and Marcus stepped in with a tray. He raised that eyebrow of his as he stepped past Amyu to set the tray on the bed. "Foolish child." Marcus carefully pushed the tray close to me. "You serve a warlord now, not a warrior. Never sneak up on a warlord. Always give warning, to let him know where you are and what you are doing."

"Forgive me, Warlord." Amyu spoke carefully. She remained on her knees, her head down.

Keir sheathed his dagger.

"Hisself is even more on edge than normal, given events," Marcus scolded Amyu as she rose to her feet. "You should know better. Fetch drying cloths now."

Amyu left as fast as she could.

"Marcus." I eyed the tray next to me, with two bowls of stew, a pile of bread, and two mugs of kavage. "There is enough here to feed an army."

Marcus snorted. "Eat what you can. You were wasting away on the slop the warrior-priests were feeding you, no doubt, if you ate at all."

There was a cough from outside, and Amyu's hands pushed through the flap, filled with cloths. Marcus accepted the bundle, and Amyu's hands disappeared. Marcus shook his head, and placed them at the foot of the bed. He then eyed Keir, who had not moved. "Simus has the watch. Rafe and Prest are outside. My daggers are sharp, as are Amyu's."

Keir drew in a deep breath, then gave a quick nod. He started to shrug out of the mail shirt, and Marcus moved to help him.

"I'll see to this," Marcus offered, as he placed the heavy mail over his arm. "You'll see to your own blades, before they are all over with rust?"

Keir nodded.

"I'll bring what you need, then. Call if you need anything else."

"Thank you, Marcus." I smiled at him.

He paused, then reached out to cup my cheek with his hand, a rare gesture from this man. "Sleep well, Lara."

I turned my attention to Keir as Marcus left. My Warlord was standing there, in his leather trous and thick quilted tunic he wore under the chainmail. His face was grim as he looked at me.

"Keir," I started, but he shook his head. He hefted a bucket and moved it close, then grabbed up one of the drying cloths. "Why did you say you could not command them?"

"Let me see to your hands." He knelt before me, and soaked one end of a cloth in the warm water. I held out my hands, palms up, and he lightly stroked the wet cloth over them.

I looked at his head, his black hair shining in the light from the brazier. But he was focused on his task, so I could drink in the sight of him. It seemed forever since I'd seen him last, although I knew it had been only days.

"What has happened?" I asked softly.

Keir sighed. "A warlord is responsible for the lives of the warriors that follow him, Lara." He kept his eyes on his work. "Those lives are dear, and are not to be wasted. Death in battle is honorable and expected. Death from affliction is a horror."

"The Council held you responsible for the plague?" I asked.

"For the deaths," Keir continued, his voice soft. "I am stripped of my title, Lara. No longer a warlord of the Plains. No army at my command."

I sucked in a quick breath.

Keir paused, and looked at me with tired eyes. "You may wish to claim another, Warprize."

I glared at him. "I did not come all this way, Keir of the Cat, to claim another. You are my chosen Warlord."

"Lara, this changes—"

"Nothing." I replied. Keir was worn, and tired. I could see it in the tautness of his jaw, in the depths of his eyes. "It changes nothing."

Keir shook his head, and focused back on my hand. "Oh, but it does. Antas made much of sending a messenger to Water's Fall, to the warriors I left there. What will they do, when they learn that I am no longer a warlord? What will your people do?"

"I am the Queen of Xy, Keir. That has not changed. You are still Overlord of Xy, and my chosen consort."

"There are those that will take advantage of this, Lara." Keir spoke softly, still focused on my hand as he cleaned it. "Durst will certainly see it as an opportunity to—"

I leaned in closer and whispered in his ear. "It changes nothing between us."

Keir's hands stilled, his head down.

"I thought you dead, lost to me forever," I choked out. "Yet here you are, warm and alive and next to me."

He lifted his head, his eyes brilliant with his own tears. Some of the light in their depths was dimmed. The Council's actions had been a blow to him, I could see that.

"Nothing else matters, Keir," I repeated. "Nothing except our love."

He drew a shuddering breath, and I leaned in and kissed him gently. His lips were soft and gentle, and the touch reassured us both. It might have led to more, except that my stomach chose to grumble at that moment. I broke the kiss, and Keir chuckled.

"Finish your work, my Warlord, so that I can eat." I held out my hands so that he could finish. "The warriors in Xy will probably do exactly what Rafe and the others have done. Continue to follow you. Besides, there is little chance that the messenger will get through the snows in the mountains."

Keir shrugged. "Only the elements can say."

"What did Rafe mean, when he said, 'That which has been lost can be regained'?"

"The Council agreed that I can enter the combats again, in the spring, and fight for warlord status," Keir said quietly. "A named warlord has only to defeat any that offer direct challenge. But I would have to fight my way through the tiers to win the status again." He flashed me a look. "Not an easy thing, Lara."

"You are a Warlord of the Plains, Keir of the Cat," I told him. "To me, to your warriors, to the People of Xy. What care I for the word of a Council of stupid bracnects?"

He gave my a wry look.

I made no further comment as he worked on my hands, getting them as clean as he could. I felt his need to care for me, as I needed to care for him.

Finally, when it was done to his satisfaction, he spread the salve over my hands, working it in carefully. I smiled at him when he stoppered the jar. "Another day or two, and they will be fine."

"So you say," Keir responded. He tore one of the drying cloths into strips, and wrapped my palms again.

"So I know." I sat back and flexed my fingers. Keir gathered up my things, and placed them back in the satchel, heedless of the order. There was a soft cough outside, and Marcus entered with a small wooden box. He said nothing, merely handed it to Keir, snatching up the used drying cloth on his way out.

"Keir." I patted the bed next to me.

He hesitated, then nodded and stood, to remove his swords and daggers, and placed them on the bed, well within reach. When that was done, he lowered himself to the edge of the bed, next to me.

I turned, settled myself so that I faced him. Carefully I pulled the tray around so I could reach it easily. "Keir, you did what had to be done. At Wellspring. At the Council. My hands are fine, and there's no sign that they'll sour."

"I never thought they'd draw blades in a senel. When Antas called for your death—" Keir shuddered. He opened the box in his hands, and I caught the faint scent of clove oil. Keir picked a cloth out of the box, reached for one of his swords, and started to clean it.

I took up a bowl of stew, dipped some of the bread in and started eating.

"They'd stop at nothing to prevent your confirmation." Keir scowled at his blade. "Honor and truth were abandoned in an instant when they thought they would lose."

I said nothing, merely ate, and listened.

"I should take you away from here. Back to Xy, where you would be safe and protected."

I reached for more bread. "Would I?" I dipped some bread in the rich broth and held it out to Keir. He opened his mouth, and I fed him the piece. "Would it really be safer, Keir?"

He chewed, looking at me though dark lashes. "We still don't know who attacked you on the journey to the Heart."

"I am safest here, within your protection, My Warlord." I took up another piece of the flat bread, scooped up some of the meat, and offered it to him. Keir obediently opened his mouth and took it. "You yourself told me that you were trying to bring change to your people, and change is rarely bloodless." I held out the bowl. "Hold this, would you?"

Keir swallowed and took the bowl from my hand, which let me reach for kavage. He reached for more bread as he spoke. "When word came that you and Keekai had been attacked, I feared the worst." He dug into the stew. "Simus arrived almost with Keekai's messenger. Atira and Heath were with him."

I handed him the mug of kavage, and he took a long drink. "What is the story behind Heath's eye?" I asked.

Keir handed me back the mug. The corners of his eyes crinkled, and his eyes danced. "Your Xyian friend has odd ideas. He leaped between Atira and her opponent, apparently to 'protect' her, or so he said." Keir shook his head. "As if that warrior needed protecting. He's lucky all she did was hit him for that insult."

I chuckled, taking his mug and pressing more bread into his hand. "Yet you leap to my defense fast enough."

Keir gave me a wry smile. "Your pardon, but you are not a warrior, Lara."

"True." I smiled as he started in on the stew. I picked up the other bowl of stew.

"Rafe and Prest told me what you did at the birthing." Keir looked at me oddly. "Is it true, you cut her open and pulled out the babes? And they all lived?"

"So far as I know, they live. Maybe now I can check on her openly." I smiled in quiet satisfaction as Keir mopped up the last of his stew. "I felt so much better that Rafe and Prest were there. I was reassured, knowing that they were watching over me, even from a distance."

Keir nodded, chewing. But then his head jerked up, and he swallowed and fixed me with his glare. "But there will be no more sneaking under tent walls to go healing!"

"I promise, Keir." I reached out, took the empty bowl and handed him the full one. "After what happened in the village, I promise that I will tell you where I go and why." I gave him a sly glance. "Not that I promise to obey, mind you."

"Might as well order the wind not to blow," Keir muttered. But the corners of his eyes were crinkled, and I knew he understood. I eyed him over the rim of my kavage mug, but said nothing. He smiled then, his shoulders easing down under his quilted tunic. He reached for more bread, and started eating again.

I reached for the gurt, and popped a few in my mouth. For some reason, it still tasted wonderful, and I chewed with enjoyment.

Keir reached the bottom of the bowl, and mopped up the last of the broth with the last of the bread. Marcus had been right. Not enough to feed an army, but enough to feed one empty warlord.

"I'll miss Keekai." I spoke softly, putting my empty kavage mug on the tray and reaching for a few more pieces of gurt. "She was a true friend to you."

"Even in death." Keir placed the empty bowl on the tray. "She kept you safe for me."

"She did." I caught my breath, remembering the pain. "I thought it was you, riding behind me, guarding me."

Keir lifted the tray and set it by our feet. "I could not find you." Keir's voice was just as soft. "I thought I'd sent you to your death."

I looked at him, my tears welling up. "Keir."

He reached out, and I went into his arms and hugged him tight, crying at what might have been. The gurt dropped from my hand, forgotten. No threat of chainmail, so I rested my head on his shoulder, and listened to the beat of his heart. "I'm sorry," I whispered. "I should be so happy, but I was so afraid. And now . . ."

"We're out of balance." Keir reached for my hand.

I smiled. "It takes the touch of another to bring us back, to center us, am I right?"

"That is so." Keir rubbed my knuckles, and then started to stroke the back of my hand. "The soul is made of fire, and sits within the left hand."

I watched as his fingers moved lightly over my skin. "Seems to me it's a convenient reason to touch another."

"Really?" Keir arched an eyebrow.

"Really," I whispered, reaching for his right hand, placing it in mine. "The breath is made of air, and sits within the right hand." I massaged his hand as best I could, rubbing it lightly with my fingers.

Keir made a sound of appreciation deep in his throat. "How clever we of the Plains are, to have a reason to touch."

His hands moved then to the bottom edge of my tunic. He worked them up and under, warm as they covered my back with soft strokes. I leaned back, and he eased my tunic over my head. My breastband was next, tossed in a corner. The air was warm, Keir's hands were warmer still. I shivered at the pleasure of his touch, but I couldn't resist. "I thought the feet were next?"

Keir smiled. He eased me down to sprawl on the bed. One hand covered my breast. The other worked through my hair, fanning it out over the bed. He chuckled softly, and then held up a piece of gurtle fur that he'd found there.

"The gurtles kept me warm." I smiled at the memory. "They slept close enough that their fur covered me."

Keir nodded. "They are trained so." He stretched out next to me, propping his head up with one hand. The other twirled the strand of gurtle fur, then reached to stroke it around one of my nipples.

I gasped at the sensation. The fur was so soft, yet felt rough against that delicate skin.

Keir chuckled, and continued his assault, moving the fur gently over my breasts in no particular pattern. My breath deepened, and I squirmed until I reached out and captured his hand.

Keir allowed me to wrest the bit of fur away from him. But now his free hand slipped down to my waist, and slid just under the band of my trous.

I shuddered as his hand spread out to cover my belly. "Oh Keir, I've missed this so."

Keir smiled then, that relaxed, sly smile that I knew so well. "I want to see you, Lara," he whispered.

I lifted my hips, and he tugged down my trous, removing my underthings all in one swift move. I would have curled up in modesty, but he placed his hands on my knees, his eyes hungry, his face filled with desire.

So I stretched out instead, my arms up over my head, and arched my back, feeling slightly embarrassed, but pleased at his reaction.

He rose then, to move up over me, but I lifted my hands to stop him. "Is this fair, my Warlord?" My voice was thick with my own passion. "I want to see you, my Keir."

He paused, then eased back to stand by the bed. His eyes on mine, he started unbuckling his belt.

I stood then, and started to work on the lacings of the quilted tunic. The garment parted, to show the base of his throat. I leaned in, and licked the pulse that throbbed there.

Keir closed his eyes and lifted his chin, granting me access. I continued, nuzzling the column of his throat, and then moved off to the side where my mark still marred his skin. I lapped at it with the tip of my tongue. "My mark, my warlord."

"Yours." Keir's voice crackled as he answered. "Yours, my warprize."

My fingers fumbled with the lacings, until his chest was exposed. I'd lost the bit of gurtle fur, so I settled for running my fingers over his skin, circling his nipples, scratching over them lightly with my nails.

Keir moaned, and grabbed my hips, pulling me close enough to feel his length. His mouth took mine for a moment, but I broke the kiss, and slipped from his arms. "Not fair! I've yet to see my prize."

Keir growled, but stood still, letting his arms hang by his sides.

I smiled, and reached up to ease the garment off his shoulders. His muscles flexed under my gentle touch, as the cloth fell to the floor. But I wasn't pleased to see deep bruises on his shoulder. He'd taken at least two rough blows there. It was a deep purple and black, but the skin wasn't broken.

The lover within me stepped back, the healer came forward. "Seems Essa and Wild Winds aren't the only ones to conceal their hurts." I stepped around Keir to get a full look. "Can you lift the arm?"

Keir sighed, then slowly raised the arm. He seemed to have full movement but with enough pain to make him wince.

I turned and reached for my satchel. "Strip, and I'll tend to this." I heard clothes rustling as I dug through the mess in my satchel. "Are you hurt anywhere else?"

"No. Those were the only blows that got through my guard," Keir grumbled. "Only because there were three of them."

I pulled out the thick paste I was looking for, and clean bandages besides. The water was still warm in the buckets, so I soaked one of the bandages, and wrung it out.

Keir was on the edge of the bed, naked. He had such a look of patient suffering on his face that I almost laughed out loud.

I stepped in close. "This will only take a moment, and it will aid the healing. You'll feel better in the morning." I smeared the paste over the bruising.

Keir placed his hands on my hips. "I know something that will make me feel better well before morning." He leaned forward, and kissed me between my breasts.

I placed the warm wet cloth over the paste, and pressed lightly with my fingertips. The familiar smell of bittergrass rose from the warming paste.

Keir wrinkled his nose.

"Just a bit longer." I stepped back to clean my hands. "The heat helps it go into the skin."

Keir heaved a false sigh of frustration, which turned into a yawn. He blinked as he gave his shoulder a glance. "Why does it smell so bad?'

I rolled my eyes, and reached to tug him up off the bed. "I'll remind you of those words when you can move with ease in the morning." I nodded toward the bed. "Pull back the bedding."

"I can move with ease now," Keir growled as he pulled back the blankets.

I put my supplies back in my satchel. Keir stood waiting as I peeled back the bandages. The paste had been absorbed into the skin, leaving a green tinge, and a faint odor. "I'll treat it again in the morning."

Keir's arm snaked behind me and pulled me close. He kissed me hard. I let the bandage flutter to the floor, and held on to him for dear life. His mouth was warm and he explored mine eagerly. I responded with enthusiasm.

We were on the bed then, a tangle of arms and legs. But I could feel a tremble in Keir's arms even as he moved us under the covers. I knew what I needed to do.

I wiggled around until he was flat on his back beside me, his mouth on my breast. I pressed in close, enjoying his touch, moaning as his hands explored my body. Finally, I kissed him, moving my hands to his chest, tweaking his nipples.

He murmured his pleasure as I slowly let my fingers trail down his chest, to circle his birth-hollow, and then continue on until my hand covered him. He was hot and hard beneath my palm. His hips flexed slightly, trying to increase the pressure.

I leaned in, and put my lips to his ear. "So do I claim my Warlord."

His eyes widened in surprise for an instant, just as I closed my fingers around him. But then he closed his eyes, lost in the pleasure of my touch. I taunted and teased, using my hand to take him to the brink, and then backed off, and watched as he writhed, powerless against me.

His eyes snapped open, clouded with his heat. "Lara," he croaked, gasping for breath. "Lara, I—"

"Surrender to me, my Warlord," was my command.

That was enough. Keir's eyes closed, his body convulsed, and his pleasure was mine. He melted down into the bed, a pool of boneless muscle.

I kissed his face as he relaxed into sleep, cleaned us both, then pulled the bedding up around us. I carefully put my head on his shoulder and nestled in close to his warmth, and breathed a prayer of gratitude to the Goddess.

I fell asleep, well pleased with my choice of Warlord.

Much, much later, I awoke to the feel of a hand stroking my hair.

I sighed in delight and opened my eyes to see Keir's face close to mine. He kissed me softly, his hands moving to cover my breasts.

I whispered encouragement as his hands explored my skin. Keir's touch trailed fire over my body, until his hand played wide over my lower belly. There he paused for a moment, and looked at me with a question on his face. "You've quickened?"

I smiled. "I'm not sure yet, but my courses are late."

He smiled, his eyes crinkling in the corners, proud and pleased. He kissed me again, a gentle brushing of lips over mine.

"Keir," I sighed into his mouth, and shifted to open myself to him. He needed no further encouragement, sliding into my depths slowly, filling me. We groaned together as our bodies merged. We paused for only long enough to kiss, then started a slow dance beneath the bedding.

Keir's hands continued to move over my body, and I explored his as well. Warm skin, soft from the heat of the bed, glided under my fingers.

Keir twisted then, moving so that I was on top. The move drove him deeper within me, and I arched my back at the feeling.

Then he stilled.

Dazed, I opened my eyes to look down at him. He looked back at me with those glittering blue eyes. My hair fell about us, creating our own private world.

"Claim me again, my Warprize," was all he said.

Challenged, I ground my hips down, and his eyes went wide for the second time that night. "Don't think I won't, my Warlord."

And so I did.

I awoke again, to the sounds of the Heart beating around us.

I was on my back, Keir's head on my chest. His arms were around me, his leg over both of mine. The covers were warm and I was so very comfortable I didn't want to move. But the tent smelled of breakfast, or the nooning, and I was hungry. If I didn't wake Keir, the noises in my stomach would.

I reached out to stroke his hair, thick and black. If I could get him to shift a bit, I could slide out of the bed without waking him.

Keir lifted his head, and smiled. "I was listening to your heart beat."

I smiled back at him. "Wasn't last night proof enough?"

He shifted then, and kissed me, his mouth firm and gently on mine. I lost myself in him, responding to his desire as the kiss grew warmer and wetter, making my own demands.

Breathless, we broke it off. Keir chuckled, and

leaned back against the pillows, smug. "Never enough, my Warprize."

I arched an eyebrow. "Are you so sure I'll choose you at the ceremony? Other warlords courted me, you know."

Keir gave a soft snort. "Ultie is a loud-mouth, over-bearing—"

"Arrogant, rude, stupid fool," I said serenely. "But Osa, on the other hand—"

Keir growled.

I laughed. "Not to mention Liam!"

"Liam?" Surprised, Keir sat up, letting the covers fall back. The cold air spilled over me. I shivered and grabbed for the blankets. "Liam courted you?"

"Not really," I assured him, tucking the blankets under my arms. Then I dropped my voice to a whisper. "He wanted to know about Marcus."

We both looked instinctively at the tent flap, and then at each other. I leaned in closer to Keir. "Why didn't you tell me about Marcus and Liam?"

Keir put a finger over my mouth and listened intently. Reassured, he pulled me closer. "What is there to say, Lara? It is his story, and out of privacy and respect, how could I tell it?" Keir cautioned me, "Say nothing to him, or we'll eat raw meat and weak kavage for months."

"But what happened?"

"I served under Liam as Second," Keir answered. "When we returned to the Heart after Marcus was injured—"

"Warlord," Marcus called.

We both gave a guilty start.

"Marcus?" Keir responded.

"A messenger, for the Warprize." From the sound of his voice, Marcus was at the main entrance to the tent. Thank the Goddess.

Keir frowned. "From?"

There were sounds then, some talk at a distance. The discussion ended, and I heard Marcus walk across the main area. The flap opened and he stuck his head in. "From the Eldest Singer Essa." Marcus's voice betrayed his surprise, and he spoke softly. "He asks the Warprize for a healing."

19

The Heart of the Plains was pulsing madly as we walked to Essa's tent. People everywhere were striking tents, and packing loads on horses. I looked around in astonishment at what appeared to be chaos. Prest and Rafe were ahead of us, clearing a path. Ander and Yveni brought up the rear. Keir walked at my side, glaring at any that dared to get close.

"What is going on?" I asked.

"Preparations for the ceremony," Keir explained. "The area around the Council tent must be cleared."

"Who attends the ceremony?" I asked.

"Everyone," Keir answered.

Everyone?

I wanted to know more, but we were at Essa's tent. Rafe and Prest remained outside, and two warriors opened the flap and welcomed us in.

I stepped in and blinked in surprise. The tent was filled with things, far more items than I'd ever seen in a Firelander tent before. It was a tent as large as Keir's but it was packed to the top. Weapons, armor, shields, fabrics, pillows, trunks that seemed to contain all kinds of trinkets and bowls. It reminded me of my Great Aunt Xydella, who could never throw anything away. There was barely room to move about, much less for company.

Essa was reclining on a platform, surrounded by pillows. On a stool close by, sat Wild Winds. They both stiffened when Keir entered behind me. "I asked for the Warprize," Essa snapped.

"You get both of us," Keir growled. "Or no one."

Wild Winds said nothing. I stepped forward, taking my satchel strap off over my head. "I am here, Eldest Singer. How can I help you?"

Essa and Wild Winds exchanged quick glances, then Essa licked his lips. "I would ask for a healing, Warprize. The use of your skills on an injury."

I nodded. "Of course. I'm more than willing to help you."

Essa cleared his throat. "I would ask for this healing under the bells."

I raised an eyebrow, and exchanged a glance with Keir. He was frowning, but said nothing, so I nodded. "That is the Xyian way."

"I would ask that Wild Winds watch your healing," Essa continued.

Before I could answer, Keir chimed in. "You die first."

"Keir," I broke in, trying to ease tensions, but Keir was having none of it.

"I'm not letting you out of my sight or reach." Keir crossed his arms over his chest.

Wild Winds stood, slowly. "I will protect the Warprize with my life." We both looked at him, shocked. He shook his staff so that the skulls tied there rattled. "I may not accept her ways, but she is a Warprize of the Plains, as confirmed by the Council of Elders." He leaned a bit, using the staff with both hands for support. "I will take the oaths during the ceremony, and I will see that no harm comes to her."

Essa spoke then. "This does not mean he supports you. You understand? But I told him that I intended to ask for aid, and he asked to watch. I agreed." Essa shifted on the pillows. "Will you allow this, Keir of the Cat?"

Keir's face was bland, but I could see the storm in his eyes. After a long moment, he turned to me. "Lara?"

"My oaths require that I treat any that ask it of me," I responded. "You are my Warlord, Keir of the Cat. I respect that you are concerned for my safety. Please respect my oaths in return. Besides," I smiled at him, "it's a tent. If I so much as breathe hard, you will slash your way to my side."

He gave me a look then, an unhappy look, to be sure. But I raised my eyebrows at him, and the corners of his eyes crinkled. "Very well. As my Warprize requests."

Essa struggled to his feet. "Please refrain from slashing your way through my tent, Warlord." He walked toward what must be his sleeping area. "This way, Warprize."

I picked up my satchel, and followed, with Wild Winds bringing up the rear. We went into a sleeping area that was as large as Keir's, if not larger. This area, too, was crammed with more items, odd looking drums, leather hangings, trunks with clothing spilling out. I wondered how he managed to have all these things and still wander the Plains?

Essa sank down on to the bed with a sigh. Wild Winds was tying bells into the flap. Essa looked at me, and gave me a weary smile. "I confess, I thought you would refuse."

"After all this?" I responded gently. "How could I?" I placed my satchel on the floor, almost afraid I'd lose it in the clutter. "Now, where are you hurt?"

Essa, proud Singer of the Plains, blushed. Flushed right up like a maiden. Surprised, I stood and waited, my eyes on Essa.

"It is not an honorable wound," Essa admitted. He stopped speaking.

I waited in silence for a moment, then cleared my throat. "A Healer treats a healing as a Singer holds words in his heart."

Essa looked at me closely. "Truth?"

I nodded. "I know that privacy is important to the one being treated. I will speak of it to no other."

Wild Winds spoke. "Even Keir?"

I looked at him, then back at Essa. "Do you tell all to your bed mates?"

"No," Essa confirmed. "I do not."

"Nor do I," I responded. "Unless it is something like a plague, where the illness can affect others."

We sat in silence for a moment, as they considered this. I thought I heard Keir's mail jingle in the other room. From the sound of it, my Warlord was pacing.

Essa cleared his throat again. "All the hours of sitting in Council has made it worse. And the itching . . ." Essa shifted on the bed. "It's enough to drive a man to the snows."

I arched an eyebrow, now knowing what the problem probably was, and started to dig into my satchel. "And your bowels? How do they move?"

With the relief of a confessed sinner, Essa started to give me all the details. I listened carefully, and pulled out one of the ointments that I always carry. "Call for warm water, please. And some cloths."

Essa didn't hesitate, nor did he pause when I asked him to drop his trous. I inspected the site carefully. "It's not so bad, yet. But you must take steps to avoid it getting worse."

So I gave him the cream, and we talked about his diet. I urged him to drink more water and kavage and avoid spicy foods for some time. I recommended that he sit in warm water at least twice a day. "If you do not take these precautions, they can get so bad that they hang out."

Essa blanched as I turned to wash my hands. "That is to be avoided, if possible."

"If possible," I agreed. "But I have ways of dealing with that as well. But let us try this first. The ointment will aid with the itching."

Essa sighed. "Council is over after tonight, for the season."

"That will help." I stood. "You might also consider using a cushion."

Wild Winds said nothing the entire time. He'd found a stool in amidst the clutter, and sat there, his arms crossed over his chest, and watched as I explained the treatments to Essa. Now Essa looked at him. "Well?"

Wild Winds's face was impassive.

"What?" I asked.

"He took a wound—"

Wild Winds cut Essa off with a gesture.

I looked down at my hands as I dried them off carefully. Essa spoke first. "She holds it as a Singer holds confidences. You're not a fool, Wild Winds." Essa crossed his arms over his chest. "Stubborn, but not a fool."

Wilds Winds stared at me.

I crossed my arms and stared right back at him.

"So," Keir said.

We were walking back to our tent, holding hands. I gave him a glance. "So?"

He looked at me questioningly.

"Ah." I looked forward, and leaned against him for just a moment as we walked. "You wish to know what was wrong with Essa."

"I didn't think he took a wound during combat," Keir mused. "Where was he hurt?"

I sighed. "Keir, healers treat a healing as a Singer of the Plains holds words in his heart."

Keir frowned "You promised to tell me—"

"Where I go to heal and why." I smiled at him. "I will tell you who I treat, but not the details. What's done under the bells is private, yes?"

Keir grunted. We walked a few steps more and he spoke again. "But Essa took a healing from you?"

"He did."

"And the Eldest Warrior-Priest watched?"

"He did."

"I am satisfied," Keir pronounced.

"I am glad." I gave him a smile. "I will show you how glad when we return to the tent."

Keir grinned.

We entered the tent together, Keir pretending to drag me within, saying something about claiming his Warprize. We were brought up short by the sight of Marcus and Amyu standing there, facing us. "It is time," Marcus said.

Keir stiffened. "The ceremony is not until sunset."

Marcus glared at both of us. "Herself needs to eat and bathe. You need to prepare as well." Marcus crossed his arms over his chest. Amyu copied him. "She will be well guarded, and protected, Warlord."

Keir scowled.

Marcus scowled right back.

Amyu looked nervous, her eyes darting between the two men. I waited for the inevitable.

Keir huffed at Marcus. "We can eat together."

Marcus inclined his head, and he and Amyu stepped aside to reveal a table loaded down with food. "Do so," Marcus ordered. "Quickly."

"So much food, Marcus." I smiled even as I moved toward a stool. "Why—"

"LITTLE HEALER!" Simus boomed from outside.

Marcus rolled his eye, and I laughed as Simus entered the tent. "Greetings, Simus of the Hawk. Welcome to my tent." I indicated the table with a sweep of my arm. "Join us for the nooning."

"Thank you, Warprize." Simus stepped aside. "There is another that seeks your company."

Joden stepped within the tent.

"Joden," I greeted him warmly. "Please join us."

"Thank you, Warprize." Joden inclined his head, and we sat together at the table. The first few moments might have been awkward, but Simus would not let that happen. He started in with pleasure, and started to tell tales of his adventures in Xy after we left. We were laughing helplessly soon enough, for his tales of sparring with Lord Warren over the tables at the High Court had me holding my sides and laughing until they ached.

Marcus hovered, and made it clear that time was wasting. Simus and Joden rose as the last of the dishes were cleared. "Come, Keir," Simus insisted. "Marcus has your gear in my tent. You will prepare there."

Keir opened his mouth, but Marcus would have none of that. "Go. I will see the Warprize started, and then help you."

Keir gave up, and we both rose together. I turned to him, and Keir took a step and took me in his arms. He kissed me hard, and I reached up to wrap my arms around his neck. It would only be for a few hours, but still. His mouth was warm and wonderful and I tried to kiss him back with the promise of tonight, our own private ceremony. He moaned and drew me closer and—

"Enough of that now," Marcus groused. "More than enough time for that later."

Laughter bubbled up within me, and we broke the kiss. Simus took the opportunity to grab Keir's arm. "Now, Warlord."

Joden grabbed the other arm. "Come, Warlord."

Together, they pulled Keir from the tent.

Amyu was clearing the last of the dishes, and Marcus took me into my sleeping area. "Come and see, Warprize."

I stepped within and gasped at the sight. There was a tub, a huge tub, easily large enough for me to bathe in. "Marcus! Where did you find it?"

Marcus looked smug. "Providing for you is a task well within my skills, Warprize."

I would have hugged him, but he held me off. "Wait. There is this as well."

There on the bed was a dress, a dress as blue as I had ever seen. My mouth hung open at the sight. It was cut as a traditional dress of Xy, one piece that flared at the hips. I reached a trembling hand to touch it, and found that it was the same silky stuff as the red dress that I'd worn in Xy. There were slippers to match, as well as a few ribbons of the same color.

"For your hair," Marcus explained. "The color matches your eyes."

I reached out, and held it up. The skirt was long, with enough fabric that riding would not be a problem. It had lacings that ran up the back from the base of what I hoped would be my spine. It would fit, but there'd be no wearing underthings with it. Still, it was beautiful. I held it in front of me and smoothed the fabric down. "Marcus," I whispered, my eyes brimming.

"None of that now," Marcus scolded. "Amyu will bring hot water, and help with whatever you need. You have your soap, yes?"

I nodded, unable to speak.

He frowned for just a moment. "You should have a belt, for a dagger. Or wear the spring knife. Death comes in an instant."

"No, Marcus." I shook my head, still holding the dress. "I come as a healer, not a warrior."

"As you say, Warprize. Very well, then. I will see to Hisself." Marcus moved to leave but I put out a hand. He paused, and looked back at me. Amyu entered the area with drying cloths in hand.

"Will you be there, Marcus?" I asked. "For the ceremony?"

Amyu's eyes went wide.

Marcus gave me a nod. "I will watch, Warprize. From the shadows."

I grimaced. "That is not right."

"But he is afflicted!" Amyu blurted out.

"Amyu!" I scolded. She looked at me in astonishment. "That is not—"

Marcus held up a hand. "Child, Herself holds a very different view of the world. Be careful, or she will open your eyes, eh?" He pointed at me. "Do not think to change everything overnight, Warprize."

I smiled, and inclined my head, placing the dress on the bed.

"So." Marcus smiled. "I will go see to the Warlord."

"He has to prepare?" I asked.

Marcus's mouth quirked. "Oh yes."

"How?"

Marcus barked out a laugh. "You will see." He turned away then, to go.

"Marcus?"

He turned back, his eyebrow up in a questioning look.

"Death comes in an instant, Marcus." I looked at him steadily. "But love lasts forever."

He rocked back, his face going pale, then his gaze dropped to the ground. "As you say, Warprize."

With that, he left the tent.

Amyu placed the drying cloths at the end of the bed. "I will bring more hot water for the tub."

She left, and I seated myself on the bed to remove my shoes, pondering what preparation Keir might need to make. Rafe's voice caught my attention. "Warprize?"

A few steps took me back into the main area. "Rafe?" I answered.

His head stuck in the tent. "Eldest Thea Reness wishes to speak to you."

"Of course," I answered.

Reness entered. "Thank you. This will take but a moment."

"May I offer you—"

Reness shook her head. "I will not even sit. We need to discuss—"

Amyu entered from the cooking area, buckets in her hands. She paled at the sight of Reness. Without a word she set the buckets down, kneeled, and pressed her forehead to the ground.

"Amyu?" I would have moved to her side, but Reness held out her hand to stop me.

"Amyu." Reness looked down at her with a stern face. "Warprize, we need to discuss this child."

"But," I looked at her sharply. "Amyu is no child."

"She is in our world." Reness frowned at me. "A child who disobeyed an Elder of her Tribe."

Amyu quivered, but didn't move.

"To save my life!" I protested.

Reness nodded in agreement. "Even so. But still she

disobeyed. Not something a child is permitted to do. Ordinarily, she would be punished. You see?"

I folded my arms over my chest. "No."

Reness pursed her lips. "This is the way of the Plains, Warprize." She glanced over at Amyu, still prostrated before us. "The theas of the Boar have discussed the matter with me. We have decided that Amyu is still of the Tribe of the Boar. That given the circumstances, she will not be punished. However, she is released from the control of the theas, and given to your charge."

"Me?" I blinked. "But—"

"No." Reness shook her head. "Amyu of the Boar, Child of the Plains is now your responsibility."

I looked over at Amyu. "Amyu, is this all right with you?"

Reness went stiff with disapproval. "It is done, Warprize. Her opinion matters not." She turned to leave.

"Reness, what of Eace?" I asked quickly.

"Sore of arm and belly, but well." Reness looked over her shoulder. "Come to see her tomorrow, when you wish. You may bring your child with you."

"There is one more thing," I said firmly.

Reness faced me now, clearly impatient. "What?"

I lifted my chin to look her right in the eye. "You are Eldest Thea of the Plains. Therefore, I say to you that if I should bear Keir children, those children will be raised by my hand and no other. Our firstborn will be heir to the Kingdom of Xy." I glared at her. "No one will take my child from my arms at birth."

Reness looked at me for a moment, and then bowed her head low. "I will inform the others, Warprize. None will challenge your word or your ways in this."

Before I could say another word, she was gone.

Amyu rose unsteadily to her feet. "I will pour these into the tub, Warprize."

"Amyu." I heaved a sigh.

Amyu looked at me then. "It is fine with me, Warprize. Better this than punishment." She hesitated. "Maybe you will open my eyes, yes?"

I smiled, and she turned to her task. Maybe I would, at that.

I bathed, taking full advantage to scrub myself clean with my vanilla soap. Amyu helped me braid my hair with the ribbons, so that they framed my face. The dress fit perfectly, as did the slippers. Marcus had seen to that, I was sure. Amyu helped me with the lacings in the back.

I'd toyed with taking my satchel, but decided against it. I didn't have the heart to mar the fit of the dress with its strap. I'd given it to Amyu, who promised to give it to Marcus. She looked at me, clearly pleased at the result. "Your eyes are as blue as the skies, Warprize."

I thanked her.

"Little Healer!" Simus's voice boomed from the entrance. "It is time!"

I emerged from the tent to see that the sun was setting, the sky a riot of reds and golds, to match the land beneath. Simus was waiting, with all of my guards, mounted on horseback. Everyone looked like they had spent the afternoon polishing their armor. Even the horses had ribbons in their manes and tails.

Simus's smile was as wide as the sky. "Finally! It is time to claim your Warlord, Warprize!"

I smiled right back. "Don't you all look wonderful!"

Rafe, Prest, Ander, and Yveni all smiled back at me, looking their best.

Simus laughed, his gold earrings gleaming in the light. He dismounted with a flourish. "We are your escort, Xylara, Daughter of Xy, Queen of Xy, and

Warprize of the Plains. We will ride to the Council Circle."

"Ride?" I looked over to where the Council tent was, only to find that it was gone. "Simus, where are we going?"

"You will see." Simus held out his hand. "Let me help you to your horse, Warprize."

I stepped forward. Simus wrapped his hands around my waist and lifted me easily to Greatheart's back. Sure enough, the fabric of the skirt floated down around my legs with no problem.

Simus mounted his horse, and we started to walk toward the lake. I looked around, astonished.

The Heart was gone. Well, the tents were gone, all but mine. The only thing left was grass, both tall and flattened, to mark where the city had been. Ahead of us were the People of the Plains, all seated on the ground, laughing and talking. There was one wide walkway through them, which Simus took us down, keeping to a slow pace. I recognized now that the firepits I thought so random through the tents were arranged in a pattern around which the crowds of people now sat.

As we reached the edge of the crowd, a cheer went up, and happy cries of 'Heyla' filled the air. Not all the faces reflected joy, but for the most part, my welcome was warm. Simus and my guards sat proudly as our horses walked down to where the Council tent had been.

The tiers were gone now, and only Essa, Wild Winds and Reness stood there, before their stools. I caught a quick glimpse of a cushion on the one behind Essa. Where the tent had been, only the odd stone floor remained, a large circle of grey.

Simus stopped his horse and roared out to the Council, "Eldest of the Elders of the Plains, I bring before you Xylara, Warprize!"

The roar went up as the entire crowd stood. The

ground seemed to shake as they all stomped their feet, and raised their voices. The hairs on my arms stood straight up, and my body shook. The excitement on the air was intoxicating, to say the least. Whatever the Elders might think, the People of the Plains were welcoming me with joy.

Simus dismounted, and helped me to dismount from my horse. Once my feet were on the ground, he offered me his arm, in the Xyian fashion. I smiled and took it, and we walked to stand before the Eldest. There, Simus bowed to them, and then to me, and walked off the circle and into the crowd.

Wild Winds held up his staff and the crowd went silent.

The sky had grown a bit darker now, and a breeze had blown up, teasing my hair. I lifted a hand to pat at it nervously, and waited.

"Xylara, Daughter of Xy," Reness spoke, her voice carrying over the crowd. I could hear her words repeated in the crowd behind me, creating an odd, echo-like effect. "You have been confirmed as Warprize of the Plains. We ask for the final time, do you wish to be released from this position?"

"No," I replied firmly.

"Xylara, Daughter of Xy." Essa's voice was high and clear. "You have been confirmed as Warprize of the Plains. We ask for the final time, do you wish to return to the lands of your people?"

"No," I answered again, only to hear my response echoing behind me as the crowd repeated it.

"Xylara, Daughter of Xy." Wild Winds spoke. "You have been confirmed as Warprize of the Plains. Do you wish to claim a Warlord?"

"Yes," I answered.

"Turn to the People, and claim your Warlord." Wild Winds gestured.

I took a deep breath, and turned to face the crowd.

The horses had been cleared away, all that remained were the people standing there, silent.

I drew another deep breath of cold, sweet air. "I claim Keir of the Cat as my Warlord!"

My words were repeated, over and over. I could almost see them move over the crowd like a wave over water.

"Warprize." Essa spoke, and his words were echoed by the crowd as well. "You choose a man stripped of his—"

"Were he naked and helpless, ill or injured, still would I claim Keir of the Cat as my Warlord." My voice rang out, defiant and clear.

The Eldest bowed their heads to me.

Essa lifted his head first, and raised his hands. "The Warprize has claimed her warrior."

He'd changed the wording, but I didn't care. As his words were repeated, everyone turned, looking down the wide walkway between them. The echos died and we waited in silence.

I'd thought he'd emerge from the crowd at some point, but no one moved. All heads were looking down that walkway, so I looked too, only to see a figure coming toward me in the distance, walking steadily. I squinted a bit, trying to make out who it was, until my eyes went wide with surprise.

It was Keir walking toward me, barefoot and wearing nothing but thin, white trous.

20

I sucked in a breath. He looked so vulnerable, without armor or weapons. Bare-chested, barefoot, he walked toward me, his face intent, his eyes blue as the skies.

I swallowed hard, recognizing the fabric of the trous. It was the same material as the shift I'd worn when I'd surrendered myself to him in Xy. As I had surrendered to him, he now surrendered to me, in full view of every Plains warrior here.

My heart swelled in an instant, with joy, with pride, with love for the fire of my heart.

My Warlord.

Keir advanced until he stood before me. His bronze skin shone as if oiled. I looked into those blue eyes, and would have reached for him, but he knelt, and lowered his head, so that I could see the back of his neck. The breeze blew again, and I caught the faint scent of vanilla.

"Your chosen Warlord comes before you, naked and

bearing no weapons." Reness spoke from behind me. Her choice of words made her support very clear.

Keir sank down further on his haunches, and bowed his head.

"Your chosen Warrior submits to you, Warprize," Essa added.

Keir lifted his hands, palms up, as I had done so long ago.

Wild Winds spoke now, with just a touch of sarcasm in his voice. "You are free to reject or claim him, Warprize. Speak, under open skies, and it will be as you desire."

The words Keir had spoken in the throne room echoed in my mind. I reached out, and placed my hands over his. "Thus do I claim my Warlord."

Wild cheering rose again. I tugged on Keir's hands and he rose to stand before me, blue eyes gleaming as he looked down into my eyes. I lifted his hands so that our palms came together, and slipped my fingers between his. "Kiss me, Keir."

"Lara." Keir leaned down, and the sounds of cheering melted away. His lips on mine, I leaned into him, conscious of the thin white material of his trous, and the scent of vanilla on his skin. It was passion, and heat, and love, with the promise of a lifetime behind it.

"The snows are upon us!" Essa declared. "The Council of Elders is closed, until the warmth and new grass appears. But for this night, let the celebration begin!"

Later, I found myself seated with Keir on the stone circle, as patterns were danced before us. Marcus was close, as was Amyu, and all of those who had supported us. Atira and Heath had just left, promising a special dance in my honor, something that Atira had designed herself.

I leaned against Keir's shoulder with a sigh. Simus

had produced Keir's weapons and leather armor and Keir was once again the fierce, well-armed warrior of the Plains. A pity really. He'd looked wonderful in those trous. Maybe I could convince him to wear them to bed? I felt my lips curl into a smile at the idea. Keir, lying on our bed, wearing naught but . . .

As if he caught my thought, Keir's lips brushed my ear. "That is an interesting look, Warprize." He nuzzled my neck. "What are you thinking of?"

I gave him a sideways glance, and decided to be honest. "You. Those trous. Our bed."

Keir cleared his throat and shifted on his stool.

I lowered my voice. "Our own private celebration." I put my hand on his thigh, and scratched my fingers over the leather.

He put his hand over mine, capturing it. "It would be rude to leave before seeing Atira's pattern danced."

I sighed. "Truth. But then, you are a Warlord of the Plains. Bold. Demanding." I wiggled my fingers in his grasp. "Rude, upon occasion."

"None of that now." Marcus spoke behind me. He was cloaked, and staying behind us.

"Mar-cus," I whined.

"War-prize," he mimicked. "Time enough for that after the patterns are danced. Woven especially for this celebration."

"Yes." Keir squeezed my fingers, looking smug. "Behave, Warprize."

I looked at him in astonishment.

Marcus snorted. "Like you aren't a stallion ready for his mare."

I straightened at that, flushing up like a girl. "Marcus!"

"Hush, the both of you," Marcus scolded. "I've a tent set up, down by the water, far from any others, where you can be as private as the Warprize desires."

"Warded?" Keir growled.

"Yes," Marcus answered firmly. "Close enough to guard, but far enough for privacy. I'll be close as well, with all your gear." He glared at me. "Including your satchel."

"Well, in that case," I said, smiling at Keir. "I'll wait long enough to see a pattern or two danced."

Marcus handed us both mugs of kavage, and nudged us to draw our attention to the area in front of us. I looked, and laughed out loud. Atira had woven a pattern dance based on a chess game. The pieces were all there, and two players stood at either end of the 'board'.

Only this game involved actual combat between the pieces. As each piece moved, it fought the others. It was a fascinating weaving of game and dance, and we all cried out our approval when the 'king' was finally checkmated.

At the end, Keir rose and swept me up in his arms. Laughter and calls came from all sides as he strode from the circle, following Marcus. I could hear the grasses pull at his trous as he walked. In the distance, along the shore, I could see a tent, as private as I could wish it to be. Behind us, Simus rose and summoned the others to follow behind us. Keir and I would be safe for this night.

I wrapped my arms about Keir's neck. "So, how shall we celebrate, my Warlord?" I asked playfully as he walked. "Perhaps you'd like to play a game of chess? Or I could read to you from the 'Epic of Xyson'."

Keir growled low in his throat. "I have something else in mind, Lara."

"Really? What might that be?" I asked, nuzzling his neck.

He turned his head and whispered in my ear. I flushed, my face hot. "Walk faster, Keir."

"As you command, Warprize."

Keir dismissed Marcus and carried me into the tent. I was pleased to see the lamp that Keekai had given us, its light sputtering happily.

Chuckling deep in his chest, Keir pinned me to the bed in one smooth movement and kissed me. I hummed in quiet pleasure, as he coaxed my lips open then explored my mouth, plundering deep then pulling back to nibble on the edge of my bottom lip.

As he continued to explore, I felt his hands travel over the fabric of my dress to cup my breast. I reached out then, to explore his back, but felt only the hard leather of his armor. I pulled back. "Keir, I want to feel you."

He rose then, one knee on the bed, and started to unstrap his weapons and the leather armor. I sighed, as he removed his clothing, one piece at a time. His eyes never left mine. "If you keep looking at me like that," he said, "this celebration will be over before it starts."

I smiled at him. "Oh, I think you are warrior enough for this battle." I reached up, intending to pull the ribbons from my hair.

Keir drew in a swift breath. "No, Lara. Let me do that." Still in his trous, he stretched out next to me, and tugged at the ribbons. My hair spilled out in a wave over his hand. Keir lifted a handful to his nose, and drew a deep breath. "I missed this. More than I thought possible."

"My hair?" I asked playfully.

"The sight of you." He studied me in all seriousness. "Your scent. Your presence in my tent. In my bed." He leaned down and planted kisses all over my face, soft warm touches to my skin. I closed my eyes as he moved to my jaw, nibbling along the edge. Keir sighed when I tilted my head back, granting him access. His warm breath caressed my damp skin. Finally, he moved back to claim my lips, and kissed me gently, until I was left breathless, tingling all over.

But he broke the kiss, an odd look of pain in his eyes.

"Keir," I asked softly, reaching up to cup his face, "what is it?"

"Skies, I thought I'd sent you to your death." His eyes were filled with pain.

"Stop." I rolled to my side, and started stroking his chest. I could feel him take a breath, and relax into my touch. "I'm here, alive and well."

Keir buried his face in my hair, nuzzling my neck with a soft murmur of enjoyment. He reached out and pulled me closer so that our bodies touched. His hand moved down my back, to rest his fingers at the base of my spine, and toyed with the lacings.

I wiggled a bit, at the faint teasing touch of his fingers as they eased through the lacings to caress my skin. "Keir, don't tease."

"Tease?" His breath was warm on my neck. "And where are your underthings, my proper Xyian woman?"

"They might have been seen." I moved my hips, trying to escape his teasing. "A proper Xyian woman does not expose her underthings to the world."

"Mmm," Keir mused. "So my very proper Xyian woman is open and waiting for me, under this dress." His hand stilled.

"Oh, yes." I smiled slowly, and spread my hands out over his chest, to tease the sparse hairs. I made sure to run the tips of my fingers over his nipples. "Unlace me, and you will see how open. How willing."

His fingers pulled at the knot. "It may take some

time to work my way through this tangle. I must have a care." Keir leaned in and brushed his lips over mine. "Marcus will have a fit if I harm this dress."

I squirmed again, as he started to pull the laces through. "Keir. That will take forever."

"I can think of a way to pass the time." His blue eyes gleamed, and he kissed me.

They were long, slow kisses that left me moaning. Try as I might, I couldn't get him to hurry. I shifted my legs within the confines of the dress and the soft fabric slipped over my skin. "Keir," I begged.

His fingers tugged at the next bit of lacings as his fingertips caressed the skin below. "So when I reach the end, and slowly pull your dress down, your breasts will be taut, and eager for my touch." Keir licked just below my ear, and I shuddered. "And when my hand slips under your dress, I will find you warm and ready." There was such satisfaction in his rough tone, a certain arrogance. I blinked at him, dazed with passion. His eyes were blazing, bright blue in his bronzed face. "Thus do I claim my Warprize."

I moaned again, and closed my eyes, surrendering to the pleasure of his touch. But just before I lost myself, I remembered.

Thank you, Goddess . . . Lady of the Moon and Stars, thank you.

I awoke in the morning, feeling wonderful. Warm and safe, spooned against Keir, his arm over my waist. There were faint sounds from outside. Horses perhaps. The distant sound of someone working around a fire. That had to be Marcus, seeing to our meal. I lifted my head, and took a deep breath. Marcus was making bread tarts.

My stomach rumbled.

Carefully, I eased out of Keir's arms and reached for

his cloak. I'd wrap up just long enough to get something from Marcus, and crawl back into bed with Keir. As I tied it at the neck, I smiled to see him sprawled over the bed, sleeping. Seems I'd worn my Warlord out the night before. I smiled even wider to see those white trous cling to his skin. Perhaps I could persuade him to take them off for me.

After I got some food.

I stepped out onto the flattened grass, and looked about. We were along the shore, a fair distance from the Heart. I couldn't see any movement in that direction. To my right, I could see a far smaller tent set up by the shore. That had to be Marcus's. There were horses there as well, grazing. One of them, a brown one, lifted his head and neighed a welcome. It was sure to be Greatheart.

I started walking in that direction, clutching the cloak to me, and watching where I put my feet. There was a path of flattened grass that I followed, between the tufts of taller grasses. It wouldn't do to cut my feet on anything. I'd never hear the end of that from Marcus. Or Keir, for that matter.

Marcus emerged from his small tent, and saw me coming. He waved in recognition, but started to work on some pans at the fire pit. I quickened my step, lured by the promise of warm bread tarts. The air was crisp, and the sun had not yet warmed the earth. I really should have put on my slippers, but the grass was soft enough.

Marcus straightened as I approached, a pleased look on his face as I walked up to his fire. "Kavage, Warprize?" His voice was low. "The bread tarts will be done in a moment."

I nodded. "And gurt, if you have some." I moved to stand in the area that had been cleared between the fire and the tall grasses. "Keir's still asleep."

"No harm there," Marcus noted. He moved about the fire, and reached for the kavage pot. "Hisself could use the—"

The grass behind him rustled with movement.

With no other warning, Iften leapt out, armored, with a dagger in his hand, soaking wet, and covered in dirt and grass. Before I could even react, he lunged at Marcus from his blindspot.

Frozen, I watched in horror as Iften plunged his dagger into Marcus's side. For one long horrible moment we stood, silent and stock-still. Iften jerked his blade free, and time flowed once again.

Marcus clutched at his side. He staggered back from the fire, managing a harsh whisper before he collapsed. "Run!"

I ran, screaming Keir's name.

Iften lunged for me, his hand reaching out for the hem of the cloak. He caught it and jerked. I stumbled back, jerking the cloth from his hand. But he was now between me and the tent where Keir lay. Iften's teeth gleamed as he snarled in satisfaction, his lips stained with brown spittle.

I darted off, straight away from the shore. The cloak flared out, the ties pressing into my throat. I risked a backward glance to see Iften's fingers just miss the hem. I used what spare breath I had for another scream, a warning to Keir. But the only response came from behind, an answering cry from one of the horses.

Iften hit me then, and bore me down to the ground. I rolled, coming up with my face to the sky, with Iften trying to pin me to the ground. He sat on my hips, and pinned my right arm under his knee, pressing it into the dirt. The cloak had fallen open. I was naked and that made his touch seem even more revolting.

My breath fled as his full weight came to bear on me. I had one hand free, but Iften grabbed it with his crippled one. There was still strength in that hand. I struggled to pull free as he waved the dagger before me, still dripping with Marcus's blood.

"So now, Xyian," he hissed, his eyes the merest pinpricks. "I save the Plains and my people." Iften raised the dagger to strike, aiming for my chest.

Something thundered up from behind him. Iften hesitated for but an instant, but it was long enough—

Long enough for Greatheart to appear, and bite deep into Iften's shoulder.

Iften screamed in rage, his dagger falling from his fingers.

My horse, my sleepy old brown horse, almost seemed to growl, and then wrenched Iften off me with a jerk of his head. Iften was dragged back, far enough that I was freed. I fumbled for the dagger and scrambled to my feet to see Greatheart swing Iften off in a half circle, so that the horse ended up between me and my attacker.

Greatheart released his hold and danced back, snorting and tossing his head. Iften's face was a grimace as he came to his feet. Cursing, he reached, and pulled out a sword. He took a few steps in my direction, but Greatheart snapped at him, then neighed in defiance.

There was an answering roar from the direction of our tent as Keir emerged, running at full speed.

Iften's attention shifted then. Cursing, he unstrapped a shield from his back, and jammed his crippled arm into the straps. Keir raced over the grass, swords in both hands, clothed in naught but white trous.

In horror I watched, clutching my cloak around me as I realized that Iften was armored, and that Keir had none. But Keir never paused in his charge. He closed in, swiping at Iften with first one blade then another.

Iften dodged, using the shield to fend off the second attack. He grinned, and there was madness in his eyes.

Keir stood there, eyes cold, swords poised before him. His chest heaved, the bruise on his shoulder still evident. Iften's muscles twitched, his teeth bared, glaring at Keir. For an endless moment, they circled one another in silence, graceful and deadly.

Keir attacked.

Iften parried the blows with his shield, giving some ground before lunging forward with his own blade. Keir evaded it and once again they faced each other, each waiting for the other to make a move.

I gripped the dagger in my hand underneath the cloak, but I knew better than to try to interfere. Marcus had taught me to stay out of the—

Marcus. I looked back toward his tent, but I could see no sign of him. The clang of swords drew my eyes back to the fight. Greatheart still danced between me and the warriors, almost as if he was trying to herd me away.

Iften raged like fire; Keir was cold as ice. I caught my breath when I saw Keir's eyes, intent on his opponent. There'd be no mercy here, no talk. This would only end with Iften's death, even if Keir died with him. I swallowed any protest, any warning. There was no point.

Keir's jaw was clenched as his swords moved in front of him, almost daring Iften to charge him. Iften was cagy, advancing with his shield held high, trying to get close enough to jab.

Greatheart neighed a warning. The big horse charged past me, behind me—

I turned, to see two warrior-priests, a man and a woman, emerging from the waters of the lake, scrambling onto the shore.

I froze, terrified. Time seemed to slow.

They moved fast, their matted braids swaying as they ran toward me. Dressed only in their tattoos and leather trous, the water poured off them and the blades of the daggers they held.

Greatheart was past me and headed for them, bellowing his challenge.

They split, darting each to a side. Greatheart followed the man.

The woman headed for me.

Air rushed into my lungs, but I stood frozen, my cloak gaping open in the front. Her teeth flashed, for I was alone and naked, an easy kill for a warrior. She trotted toward me, her blade ready, her eyes gleaming out from the tattoos that covered her face. Eyes filled with confidence and victory.

In that instant, rage flooded through me.

I heard Keir screaming behind me as he realized my danger, heard a wet 'thunk' as Greatheart reared up and kicked his foe in the head. But my focus was on my attacker, and the anger that filled me.

She was going to kill my baby.

She took a few steps closer to me, then paused, almost as if she bore good news. "You meet your death well, Xyian," she laughed. "I grant you—

I brought Iften's dagger out from under my cloak, and rammed the blade into her throat.

She was startled, too surprised to use the last moments of her life to attack me.

Dancing back out of reach, I pulled the blade with me.

She gasped, dropping her knife and falling to her knees. I took a few more steps back and watched calmly as she put her hands to her throat to try to stop the blood. My healer's knowledge told me it wouldn't aid her.

Nothing could.

As she crumpled to the grass, I turned to see that Greatheart had the man down and under his hooves. My old sleepy warhorse was making sure of that threat by trampling the body to a pulp.

I moved further away from the dying warrior-priestess and focused on Keir.

He'd tried to come to my aid, but Iften had blocked his move. They both realized that I was safe in the same moment, and Iften howled out in anger and frustration. Keir snarled, and the battle between them was rejoined. But now there was a new desperation in Iften's eyes as they clashed.

Even as I wondered how long this could go on, Iften charged Keir, trying to ram him with the shield. Keir dodged out of the way, but as Iften turned to face him again, Keir struck his shield, his sword biting deep. The blade caught in the wood.

Iften whooped in triumph, bringing his sword to bear. Keir blocked with his free sword and then twisted the other.

Twisting Iften's arm.

The bone broke, a clear snap. The shield dropped to his side and Iften's howl became one of pain as he staggered back. Keir let go the trapped sword, and swung the free one up. There was a spray of blood as it caught Iften's neck; his eyes bulged. He dropped his sword and lifted his hand to his neck, as if to stop the flow.

Keir plunged his sword deep into Iften's chest, and withdrew it in one swift move. A few staggered steps, and Iften collapsed at Keir's feet.

"Keir!" I ran a few steps toward him, but Keir shook his head. I stopped, waiting, trying to catch my breath. Keir stood over Iften, breathing hard, his sword steady. A thin stream of red ran down the blade, falling on Iften's body.

Iften was face up, his eyes open.

I held my hands to my chest, feeling my heart pounding within. "Is he?"

Keir waited a moment longer. Slowly, carefully he knelt next to Iften. Warily, with the other sword poised for an attack, Keir pressed his hand down hard on Iften's chest.

I held my breath.

"Dead." Keir's voice held a note of satisfaction as he rose. I threw myself forward, running into arms he opened wide. Our mouths met, and we kissed, desperate for each other's touch.

Seconds later, we broke it off and I stared at him in horror. "Marcus!"

I turned and ran back toward the tent, where Marcus had fallen. Keir was just behind me. But there was no body. Just a bloody smear in the grass and a path of blood—

Headed for his tent.

I looked at Keir, almost afraid to move. His face was just as grim. He reached out and took my hand. We moved quickly, following the bloody trail. Through the grass. Through the tent flap.

Marcus was on the floor, curled on his side next to his pallet. My satchel was there, open, its contents scattered on the floor.

Keir knelt, eased Marcus over and pulled him into his arms. I dropped my dagger and threw myself down next to the little man, my hands reaching for the wound.

"W-Warprize." Marcus's one eye opened as he stuttered my name. He stared at me, wide-eyed, clearly in shock. His hand was pressed under his tunic, blood all around the area. His tunic was filthy, covered in dirt and grass.

"Marcus." I reached down to peel back his hand, terrified at what I would find.

Only to stare dumbly at the crumbled mass of bloodmoss there, pressed against his side.

"I-I remembered. What you told Gils," Marcus panted, as he moved the plant away from the site.

Horrified, I looked at the skin, a thin red scar healed tight. Bloodmoss can't be used like that, it only seals the skin, not the organs underneath. If the dagger cut the bowel, or . . .

With a trembling hand, I smeared some of the blood from his skin onto my fingertips and held it up to my nose.

It smelled clean. No taint of feces or poison. No gut wound.

With a cry of joy, I threw myself into Marcus's arms, and started weeping.

Epilogue

It was the Longest Night; the night the People of the Plains gather to mourn the Dead. Wrapped in furs, I reached out for Keir's hand and let him lead me out into the deep snows.

Back in Xy, it was the night of the Grand Wedding of the God and Goddess, the Lord of the Sun and Lady of the Moon and Stars. There, it would be feasting, and dancing, and laughter.

Not so on the Plains.

The cold took my breath away as we left the winter lodge and walked out into the dark night. The snow crunched as our boots broke the crust. Keir reached out his hand to steady me as we walked, and gestured for Rafe and Prest to lead the way. An honor to be sure, but they also broke a path through the snow. I looked over at Keir, who looked back with his eyes twinkling. He'd dressed me in warm furs, so that the cold air only touched my cheeks. Keir had tugged the hood over my hair, and made sure I was snug before he'd let me set foot outside.

A month had passed since I'd been confirmed as Warprize. The season of the great cold is not as harsh on the Plains as it is in Xy, but harsh enough. The Heart of the Plains was gone. All that was left was the great Council circle of stone. The lake had frozen over, and the people and the herds of the Plains had traveled to their winter lands.

Only Keir and I, and those who had chosen to winter with us, remained. There were a few tents still up, used as shelters during the day for those that tended the herd of horses and gurtles. But at night almost all retreated into the winter lodges: long low shelters half buried in the earth, more caves than buildings. Apparently, west of here, there were a few lodges with hot springs, that allow some to remain close to the Heart year round. It sounded like the hot springs of Xy, the baths below the castle, and I was curious to see them.

But Keir intended that we would ride south, where the Tribe of the Cat traditionally wintered. Many of his people had elected to continue to serve him, despite the Council. We'd use the winter to consider our options.

Keir could fight to reclaim his status. Simus would certainly enter the challenges. The Warlord Liam had approached Keir to discuss offering his aid and assistance. If Liam survived the spring challenges, he'd be in a position to aid Keir. That would prevent another warlord from raiding into Xy.

Liam's help would allow Keir to forgo the spring challenges. That meant we could return to Xy as soon as the snows would allow. There was so much to do if we were to make this work.

Of course, Liam had made it clear that his help came at a price beyond the benefit to his people. Keir and I had exchanged looks at that, but we nodded our understanding. I suspected that Marcus would find himself under siege in the spring.

Nothing was certain. But then, nothing is ever certain in this life. Keir and I knew that the path ahead would be hard and uneven, whether it ran through the Plains or through the mountains of Xy.

Still, we'd walk it together.

Everyone spilled out of the lodge behind us, into the snow. They were silent for the most part, although there were no few gasps at the beauty. Heads tilted up to look in awe at the moonless sky, filled with stars. I felt like I could reach up, and gather a handful. I'd never seen so many tiny points of light, stretching out over the land.

Our mood was a somber one as we walked, even Simus was subdued. We carried torches, but none were lit yet. Instead, we all walked in darkness as Joden headed for the stone circle. The wind kept it clear of snow, and he'd decided it would be the perfect place for this ceremony.

Joden was still not a full Singer, having decided to delay asking for that status. He'd wait until his heart was truly healed. But Keir had asked him to lead the ceremony for this night, and he'd agreed.

For this was the Longest Night and all over the Plains, in the scattered tribes, people emerged from their winter lodges to participate in this ceremony.

Keir looked back, to make sure that I was managing. I gave him a wide smile, and he returned it. Marcus was behind us as well, as was every man, woman, and child.

An odd sense of peace filled me this night. I could almost find it in my heart to forgive Xymund, for all his madness, and his desire to see me dead. But for his decision to sacrifice me, who knows where I'd be now?

Certainly not at the side of my Warlord, among his people.

The snow was crisp beneath our feet, and in the light of our torches, I could see my breath. I'd never seen a night so clear, a sky that glittered so. I looked straight up, and all around, and there were more stars than I'd ever known existed. They lit the heavens and the snow with a soft glow.

We reached the stone circle, and the others gathered around us, all of us facing Joden. Everyone grew silent as he raised his hands to the sky.

"We wait for the dead," Joden said, his voice raising the hairs on the back of my neck. "Those who have died in this last season, who have ridden with us all this time. We wait to release them, and our fears, our regrets, our pain."

I couldn't help it, my eyes filled with tears, which trickled down my cold cheeks.

Keir squeezed my hand, and I looked into his eyes. Blue eyes that reflected the stars in their depths, and even as I wept, I smiled at him.

Marcus was beside me, well concealed in furs. Nothing of his body showed, for he would not offend the elements in any way.

"Welcome the dead," Joden whispered in the silence.

Everyone turned to look at the rises that overlooked the Plains. I turned as well, puzzled. What were we looking for?

I stood, as my eyes adjusted, and held my breath. All of the Plains seemed frozen and still, as if waiting.

"They come." Joden pointed off into the distance.

I heard it then, the thundering of hooves, and I gasped to see a huge herd of ghost horses appear over a distant ridge, galloping straight for us. I staggered, but Keir steadied me from behind.

It never occurred to me that horses die, too.

They were coming, wild and free, running over the snow with no effort, manes and tails streaming out, leaving a faint trail of silver light. As they grew closer, my eyes grew wide, and wider still.

They had riders.

With a swirl, the horses surrounded us, galloping in a wide circle around us. I could make out details now. The faces of the riders grew clear as they rode past, pale and white as clouds. But there was no sorrow there, only joy and peace. People about me started to call out names, hailing friends and loved ones. Keir called out too, names I didn't know. So many names.

Four times they circled us, and then they turned and rode right through our midst.

I could see them, riding and smiling, dressed as they had been in life. Isdra with her long braid, Epor with his beard and armor, their faces wreathed in smiles. I called their names as they moved past me, and Epor flashed me a grin.

"Keekai!" Keir called out, and she was before us, laughing. She reached out and I could have sworn she ruffled Keir's hair in farewell.

The crowd about me shouted their greetings to their loved ones as they galloped past, and I cried out as well, bidding my friends good bye. I looked around, seeking out . . .

Gils.

His horse paused before me, and there he was, his face alight, his curls dancing in the breeze.

"I'm so proud of you, Gils," I whispered, telling him then what I hadn't told him while he was alive.

His eyes lit up, and his smile widened as he urged the horse on. As he swept past, Gils leaned down and cold fingers brushed my cheek. I shivered, blinking as the entire herd thundered past.

They headed back to the ridge they'd come over, but

they didn't disappear. Instead, they rode up, and up, and right up into the sky, and into the stars themselves. They flowed up, as if with wings, up into the velvet night until their shadowy forms were lost to sight.

They were gone.

I wept openly, as did others around me. Tears flowed freely, to have our loved ones gone. I sniffed a bit and then my stomach cramped. Goddess, not now. I fumbled in my satchel for some dried peppermint leaves, and tucked them in my mouth to suck on. When we returned to the tents, I'd drink some tea, but this would do for now.

A flint struck a stone by Joden, and a flame flared up from a torch. "They have gone, beyond the snows and into the stars. So it is. So it will ever be."

For the dead, perhaps. But not for the living. I squeezed Keir's hand and he gave me a solemn look. He shifted his stance, and raised our hands so that they were palm to palm, fingers intertwined. I looked into his eyes, and nodded. He and I would bring change to both the Plains and Xy. With our love, we could change the world.

My stomach cramped again, and I shoved my free hand deep within my furs and pressed on my belly. Not now, little one. Later, I will be as sick as you please, but not right now.

The flame was passing through the crowd as the torches were lit. Marcus held one to the flame of another, and so the light passed around us.

"We dance, in thanks to the elements." Joden's words called us to order, and everyone started to join hands. Keir had explained the movements and I'd practiced the steps in the lodge with his help. We'd all join hands, and pace out the pattern in a twisting line.

All but Marcus. He stepped to the side, holding his torch high.

Keir took my hand, and Prest appeared to take the other. Rafe, Ander, and Yveni followed suit. Simus was holding the hands of two lovely ladies, and flirting with them. Atira and Heath joined in as well, although Heath had to fight to hold her hand. They were a source of much amusement within the lodge, what with Heath's pursuit and Atira's resistance.

A drumbeat started, and we all took the first steps of this long slow dance.

We'd return to Xy at the first sign of spring while I could travel. We'd arrive just as the first snowdrops appeared in the castle gardens. For my son would be born in the Castle of Water's Fall at the summer solstice, if all the theas who had pressed their hands to my belly could be believed.

Those who traveled with us were all known to Keir, and trusted. They supported us in our efforts, and welcomed my new knowledge.

Wild Winds had asked to winter with us. His position had not changed, but he indicated that he would welcome the chance to talk. I'd welcomed the opportunity.

Keir had rejected it completely, and no argument would sway him.

The drumbeat drew me back, and I minded my steps. We all melted into the pattern, holding hands and chanting, pacing out our sorrows in the snow. When we were done, when the rituals were complete, we'd return to the warm tents and lit braziers and Marcus would serve us warm kavage and the bitter gurt that I now craved. In the morning, we'd break camp, and ride south to winter in the milder lands.

But first food, and warmth, and my Keir in my arms.

Those of the Plains present a newborn babe to the elements, and listen for the sound of the child's name. But as I'd told Reness, I'd repeated to Keir in no uncertain terms that this babe would stay in my arms and be named and raised in my tradition, and he'd agreed.

I rather liked "Xykeirson." Keirson of the Tribe of Xy.

I could hardly wait to see Anna's reaction when my child was born and stained with the tribal tattoos.

The dance continued, our steps slow and even. Joden's voice rose in the night, singing of forgiveness, for the dead, and for us.

I looked over and squeezed Keir's hand. He returned the look, his blue eyes sparkling with pride, love, and hope. And a promise for this night.

For the future.

Forever.

Dearest Readers,

Well that's it then. My magic spell is cast and well done, as far as I can tell. Lara and Keir's tale is over, at least for now. The snows are starting, blurring my vision of the Plains.

My workroom is a mess. There are cold cups of kavage scattered around. I have notes and papers piled to the ceiling and all over the floor. I don't think I've seen daylight for about seventy-two hours. The fridge is full of moldy food and the cats are playing with gurtle fur and dust bunnies as large as they are.

Oh dear. No help for it then. Time to clean. Open the window, get out the broom and the dust cloth. Unfortunately the magic that I wield doesn't lend itself to sweeping.

I'll have to work on that.

So, to start, I think I'll shift these notes over . . . what's this? Under all these papers?

A pair of worn red leather gloves.

Oh, I remember her. A mercenary, with a sword for a heart. Bold and sassy that one, who faced destiny on her own terms. And what was his name? I can't seem to remember . . . a wounded soul, that I'm certain. Oh my, now that I think about it, they . . .

Cleaning is overrated. Let me turn the computer back on, and get some more kavage.

For I have another story to tell.

Elizabeth

ELIZABETH VAUGHAN
is a writer and a lawyer.
She lives in Ohio.

Lara of Xy and her Warlord, Keir of the Cat, have been through much together. Lara abandoned her land and people for love of him. She adopted his ways and learned of his tribe. Together they have faced plague and insurgency —and despite these struggles, they have known happiness and joy.

Now they face their most arduous task: Keir must take Lara into the Heart of the Plains, and introduce her as the Warprize to the warrior-priests. She must be tested—questioned, examined, watched—and must find favor with the warrior-priests and the tribe's elders before they will confirm her as a true Warprize.

But in Lara's heart there are doubts—for what if she is found wanting? Will Keir give up everything he knows to be with his Warprize?

($8.99 CAN)

Tom Doherty Associates, LLC
www.tor.com
Printed in the USA